SODIUM
HAZE

SODIUM HAZE

JONATHAN PAXTON

Library of Congress Control Number:		2023913932
ISBN:	Hardcover	978-1-6698-9022-5
	Softcover	978-1-6698-9021-8
	eBook	978-1-6698-9023-2

Print information available on the last page.

Rev. date: 07/31/2023

To order additional copies of this book, contact:
Xlibris
UK TFN: 0800 0148620 (Toll Free inside the UK)
UK Local: (02) 0369 56328 (+44 20 3695 6328 from outside the UK)
www.Xlibrispublishing.co.uk
Orders@Xlibrispublishing.co.uk
854311

Contents

......The only thing necessary for the triumph of evil is for good men to do nothing......

Edmund Burke:

.....Every exit is an entry to somewhere else....

Tom Stoppard:

CHAPTER 1

SS Headquarters, Berlin, 1700 hrs Jan 14, 1941

The soft brown leather briefcase was slowly raised for all to see and gently placed onto the end of the long, dark mahogany table. The case looked old and worn, with an unswept and faded demeanour. Beige, coarse strands of stitching bulged from each of the distorted and tattered corners. It seemed unsuitable in consideration of the occasion and the prize it held within. There was an air of anticipation in the moments of silence that followed. Five men were sat around the table. Two on each of the vast aspects and one isolated at the far end. It was he who broke the silence as his hand gently grasped the case and pulled it towards him. Dressed in full military splendour for the occasion, Colonel Heinz Reichzig, carefully and with assumed pride, flipped open the two metallic buckles that provided minimal security for the consignment within. He briefly perused the contents with a warm, but anxious smile. The anxiety was the produce of hope. He hoped that this select audience would receive and entrust the contents with the same confidence he showed having first been informed of the developments. He removed the case contents and placed the empty leather sheath down beside his feet.

'Gentlemen.....This is the solution', he held aloft a bound manuscript.

The report was around thirty pages of standard administrative paper in total and housed within a scarlet red cover. The cover was stamped in the header and footer with bold black lettering, **'STRENG GEHEIM',** providing the enclosed material with the classification of Top Secret.

Reichzig continued,

'This is the key to our inevitable success in making first Europe and then the rest of the world bow down before our beliefs.....the submission that the Fatherland has the power and resources to govern all walks of life is here...in this document...', the leaves of paper shook under his words.

'This document details a major scientific breakthrough that will assist with all our goals.....In my eyes this..' he shook the document once more aloft,

'...is far more valuable than acquiring more advanced aeroplanes, tanks and artillery directives...this will strengthen the very foundations that our war efforts rely upon.'

Reichzig had spent the best part of two days and a long evening perfecting the speech, which he could see, was successful in obtaining the desired effect of both excitement and transience on the faces of his congregation.

Klaus Berthold, dressed in a long black leather coat familiar with the Gestapo was more restless than most. His beliefs, he figured, were stronger than those of anyone he had come into contact with, barring Der Fuhrer of course, who he had met twice, both on social occasions and both times only a few gratuitous words passed His lips. They were enough though to embody enormous respect and loyalty into His beliefs. So strong a presence that Berthold had remembered the feeling of his first meeting. The stern look, power over all those around him including his highly decorated entourage. Berthold could smell the power as He moved passed him. A strange sickly-sweet odour that he could taste in his throat mixed amongst the smell of leather and body odour. He could only describe it closely as similar to that of death. A smell he would encounter often and become very fond of.

He remembered for that split second when their eyes met, it was like looking into the eyes of a loved one, wanting, longing for a touch, but at the same time feeling exposed and frightened like a cornered deer in the crosshairs of its hunter. He became aroused and uncomfortable and felt as though nature had deserted him. He stared down in hope that his arousal wasn't visible and tried his hardest to remove the urge ...but could not.

Berthold came from a very strict upbringing. His family attended the church at every spare opportunity. As a child he wasn't allowed games or even to socialise with other children in case they led him astray. Whilst other children skipped, howled, and screamed in the joys of youth, Berthold was forced to read chapters from the Bible, sing Psalms and learn manners and etiquette. His childhood was a reclusive one spent mostly behind closed doors. He was not naturally intelligent and found most school subjects difficult to grasp, apart from religious studies in which he, for obvious reasons, excelled at. His father had little patience with his inability in the other core subjects. He would stare over Berthold's shoulder and rasp his knuckles with a metal rule at the slightest grammatical mistake in written language or incorrect solution to a mathematical problem. He was a very sad and forlorn child. His mother would occasionally show him her love whenever she was out of the watchful eye of his father, who believed public affection was unnecessary and depraved. Those moments alone were the one's which he cherished. He was drilled with the morally correct and the rights and wrongs within the world. Feelings for a person of the opposite sex were allowed upon marriage, however, feelings for a person of the same sex was strictly prohibited, even if it were due to strong friendship. His father certainly would not approve of the feelings he felt at that time, but his father's wishes had long since depleted since he reached adolescence. The only feelings he had on the subject were one's of complete hatred for the man that helped bring him into the world.

Although in his later years he had rebelled against his early education, he never recalled feelings of a homosexual nature. The whole issue puzzled him and later that night he would remove his frustration on his personal maid. He was convinced that would quell the confusion that spread through him.

He was a huge frame of a man with typically blonde rugged looks. His hair was close cropped with the emphasis on neatness rather than style. His skin had hardened and tanned through exposure to the varying climatic changes. His most redeeming facial features were his squarely defined jawbone and his deep blue eyes. Mysterious, sifting cerulean eyes. The only personal attribute that he himself considered an advantage, was that of physical and mental violence. An attribute that he had mastered very quickly. All those who had come across him had absolutely no doubts as to his masculinity, if they had, they had not lived to regret it. It was the first time he had encountered a situation such as this and he had felt weak and submissive. He had been confused and frightened. He had decided to get drunk and seek his true sexuality.

His maid awoke the following morning with a face that barely resembled the youthful innocent one the night before. She was only 19. Berthold had spotted her whilst serving in Leipzig almost three years ago. She was a volunteer for a local orphanage. A task she had welcomely carried out having resided in the orphanage herself since the age of 10 after her parents were tragically killed in a road accident. She was extremely loyal to Berthold, although she didn't really have much choice in the matter. She dreaded the ever more frequent occasions when the Master would return intoxicated. As she grew older she noticed him staring at her developing figure. It was a figure to be proud of but one which she desperately tried to hide.

She lay painfully void of all emotion. Several large contusions scattered her jawline, and her nose was contorted at an obscene angle. The rewards for resisting and disobeying her keepers wishes. She had suffered internal bleeding as Berthold bludgeoned her with his sizeable fists as he reached his climax. The maid was left discarded in severe pain. She could barely raise herself from her bed to perform her morning's chores. After the third of such encounters in as many evenings she was found naked in her blood-soaked bed with her wrists slashed. The dried open wounds crudely exposed as she had been evenings before. A relieved smile adorned her face. Her living hell was over. Berthold was to begin his.

'What exactly is this all about Colonel?' Berthold could deny his impatience no longer.

'All in good time, Klaus'

Reichzig remained calm and ordered a couple of bottles of his finest chateau rouge. He prided himself on his collection of wine, which he had accumulated over several sorties into France. In his eyes when all of this was over France as a nation would have the sole purpose of providing the Fatherland with their exemplary cuisine and exquisite variety of 'the grape'. He was a mild-mannered man who in the past had been accused of being too easy going and not ruthless enough but making the rank of colonel and being appointed head of counter espionage proved that his methods had impressed someone at the top. In particular it was his contacts within the scientific and engineering world that probably landed him the job. It would have been all too easy to have appointed one of his cold-blooded, acutely psychopathic compatriots, there were after all plenty on offer, but they didn't have the education and intellect that Reichzig possessed. The choice was the obvious and correct one. Many parties didn't see it that way though, including a few of those assembled before him and he knew that a single mistake would enable any one of the others to demand his position. Now though, he knew he had the answer to all questions and made them sweat a little. Enjoying his uncharacteristic arrogance in making them wait.

Five glasses were placed on the table and each in turn was half filled with the blood red liquid. Reichzig commented on the body, bouquet and other similar vintage terms and proceeded to monotonously swirl the wine around his glass. He seemed transfixed by the way the liquid smoothly slid around the body of the glass, gracefully like a speed skater, energetically but elegantly carving out his territory on the ice. Having taken a moment that seemed like decades to the ensemble, Reichzig tipped the glass and the liquid disappeared through his lips. His audience followed his example and then to much appreciation his mood changed from a rather poor wine connoisseur into an established SS Officer. He stood up and with fists clenched firmly down on the table began the deliverance of Operation Unsichtbar.

'Some seven months ago I appointed a team of our top biochemists to research the possibility of manufacturing a strength inducing, energy restoring drug that could be administered quickly and efficiently on the front line....', Reichzig smiled.

'Preliminary tests were very rewarding....they concocted a compound out of readily available elements and an unusual ingredient which one of the scientists stumbled across in South Africa some years earlier...', he paused in the silence.

'This ingredient, a coarse herb, was used by a particular tribe...I won't bore you with the trivialities of their history...but in short it was renowned for its revitalising qualities....'

'..We managed to import enough of this herb for our means and tested various compounds on domestic mice.....'

Berthold laughed.

'Mice?...', he shook his head.

'I don't see what the problem with our men is....those that serve under me certainly have no energy or strength problems..' he smiled.

'That may be the case Klaus...but in other fronts we have had reports of severe fatigue and illness...it is costing us ground..', Reichzig explained to the agreement of the rest of the congregation.

Berthold snorted down his nostrils like an angered bull and tried to appear uninterested by the issue.

'I'm sure if you hear me out, Klaus, you will see the findings to be advantageous to our cause...' Reichzig calmed.

Berthold stared widely into the eyes of Reichzig.

As far as he was concerned too much scientific talk was costing them ground. All the time wasted in pointless discussions like this cost them the time they could be out killing.

'We put the mice through a vigorous routine..to the point of collapse.', Reichzig continued.

'...and then administered various compounds at various levels into a select few...the mice which were administered compound B recovered at a rate ..', he paused.

'FIVE times quicker than those administered with compounds A and C...and...NINE times quicker than those administered nothing...', he smiled.

'Upon recovery the compound B mice worked the exercise wheel faster and with less difficulty than they had previously....they also seemed more alert and looked at varying the routine....', Reichzig leaned back in his chair.

Berthold smiled cynically.

'That's all very impressive Colonel but mice don't fight battles.... has the drug been tested on men?', Berthold sniped.

Reichzig stared around the faces that waited for an answer to the inevitable question. He chose not to look at Berthold.

'Funny you should say that Klaus ....', he paused.

'Yes it has...', he smiled warmly.

Reichzig poured himself another glass of wine and revelled in the curiosity that swept the room.

'With almost exactly the same results...', he took a large gulp of the wine.

'We ran a man ragged around a running track until he almost passed out....we then administered the drug through a form of watered solution....and after twenty minutes recovery time the man was sprinting around the track faster and for longer than he had originally...'.

The room fell silent.

'Admittedly we had to increase the dosage, but the tests proved successful which was the aim...', he added.

'Now I'm sure you'll agree, if implemented, this will have dramatic affects in all areas of our war efforts...pilots will be less tired...they will be able to fly for longer periods without losing concentration or efficiency due to fatigue...the Army will be stronger on the ground and will sustain battle for increased periods of time....it will have benefits throughout all divisions of our forces...', Reichzig smiled

'Like I said…the very foundations will be strengthened…making us even more potent as an attacking and defensive force than we already are…all the high-tech machinery in the world is useless without a fresh and motivated force to operate them…'.

'So why haven't we been issued this wonder drug?', Berthold questioned with appeal.

'That is the problem…we had completed most tests…manufactured enough of the substance to trial a unit…when the allies made a direct hit on the laboratory in Hamburg…'.

Gasps echoed around the room.

'So why bring us here to tell us that?', Berthold sighed.

'Not all the research was damaged….we managed to salvage one out of the five containers of the drug and the manufacturing instructions and production reports….it will mean delaying the supply, but I have organised another team to produce the drug at another site….that is where you come into it Klaus..', Reichzig encouraged.

Berthold raised his eyebrows in anticipation.

'To prevent this happening again we have selected a suitable site in Stuttgart….it has the facilities for the production and is currently unknown to the allies…however our intelligence suggests that an ever increasing number of Allied Agents are managing to infiltrate our ranks and either steal or seriously hamper our operations…so just how long this new site remains a secret is anybody's guess…but the emphasis is on getting enough of the drug produced and distributed before the new site is discovered…the Allies have caught wind of our developments and will be frantically pursuing the demise of the drug….At present they probably think they have succeeded with intelligence reports of the lab destruction in Hamburg…so we have gained an advantage in time…', Reichzig stressed.

'What do you want me to do?', Berthold enquired.

'I have organised a train to convey the papers and the remaining drug to Stuttgart…I want you to guard it for the duration of the journey…I will supply you with a guard…several men…'.

Berthold nodded.

'OK…no problem…'.

'Now I have split the container into almost half....placing the liquid drug into two tubes...one tube will be required by the scientists in Stuttgart...the other I want you to administer equally between yourself and your guard...it will revitalise them and make them more alert to the task in hand...', Reichzig spoke clearly and slowly.

Berthold nodded.

'This is the last record we have of the drug...the mission must not fail...', Reichzig muttered sheepishly unable to hold eye-contact with Berthold. He could feel the heat from his glare.

'So, there you have it gentlemen...as soon as the plans are in Stuttgart we should be able to resume producing the drug immediately and then I shall see that quantities are issued to each concerned front...', Reichzig smiled.

'I am told that the new team waiting in Stuttgart are highly competent....the original team that invented the drug were all killed in the explosion...however, I am reliably informed that the production plans are adequately sequenced to enable continued production as long as they have the liquid prototype for comparison...the project shouldn't fall far behind the original production deadline', Reichzig sighed.

He could still feel Berthold's stare penetrating him. He knew he shouldn't have mentioned failure and Berthold's name in the same breath but planned it would stir him up...Which it did. Which was when Klaus Berthold was at his very best.

Main gatepost, SS Headquarters 2245 hrs, Jan 14, 1941.

The shouts were deafening in the still of the night. Franz Mulder had heard them since the wagon halted some minutes earlier. He had just removed his boots, lay back in his chair and intended on a peaceful evening listening to a vinyl his brother had sent him from Nurnberg. It was Mozart's Klarinetten A. Having poured himself a large cognac and blissfully appreciating the opening bars of his favourite woodwind carving the air with a warm elegance, he drifted away in a melodious heaven, only to be rudely returned to reality. It would be an understatement to say he was not best pleased. Having realised the commotion outside would not be alleviated without his intervention, he reluctantly prised his boots back on and, emptying the contents of his glass with fervent haste, made for the door.

As Mulder burst through the door onto the courtyard he could see one of his guards arguing furiously with the driver in the headlights of the wagon that still stood purring oblivious to the fracas that it highlighted.

"SEID STILL!!", it wasn't often Mulder had to raise his voice but on this occasion it most certainly was warranted.

"Was machst hier?"

The guard explained that Colonel Reichzig had given him an exact order to expect 12 troops who would be arriving here from Dresden and that he was to send them to their quarters in block 7A. They were to parade on the courtyard at 0600Hrs in the morning. This seemed a simple enough task. However, although the consignment had originated in Dresden and all papers were in order, there were in fact 13 men, not 12 as the colonel had stated. The guard apparently told the driver that they were not allowed into the camp until authorised by the duty officer, a statement which horrified him as he had been at the wheel since the early hours and so followed the unruly disturbance.

Mulder sighed.

He could not tolerate such trivialities. Having checked the papers himself and briefly glimpsing into the rear of the wagon to be faced by a coterie of equally bemused tired faces. He sighed again and told the driver to go through. Needing no second instructions the driver gave a quick look of disgust at the gate-guard and then revved up his engine and proceeded into the camp. The guard attempted to elaborate on the very specific orders he was given but was stopped mid-sentence by Mulder's raised outstretched hand.

'Do not....Do not disturb me again'

The guard understood that his proclamations were fruitless and resigned himself back to his post. Mulder gave his third sigh a far more drawn out one, one that could only be interpreted as one of disbelief and he retired back to his Mozart. Fastidious people often annoyed him especially over such mundane matters. He laughed quietly to himself and shouted back to the guard "Don't worry, the Colonel isn't superstitious!" and laughed louder, a laugh the guard could hear until the door finally decided to close the issue.

The guard demoralised and alone muttered his aggrievances and in his mind suggested that maybe the Colonel should have been superstitious.

Not for the first time tonight he would have been right.

The wagon screeched to a halt outside 7A. They were positioned at the far end of the camp, and 7A was a Nissan hut which stood apart from all other buildings. It was condemned and not the type of accommodation one would expect for such an important guard. It could only be that the hierarchy had wanted their identities to remain anonymous for security reasons. The guards stepped off the rear of the wagon including Karl Sammer the extra man the gate guard had so intently puzzled over. He had joined the party late but had already been accepted as a member of the team. The first hurdle in this obscene mission, but at least it had got him away from watchful eyes in France. Karl Sammer, aka. Thomas Procter, loved to work on his own, making his own decisions, playing it his way. He got a real kick out of the adrenaline rush and fighting it to stay calm enhanced the feeling even more. He knew this operation would be adrenaline all the way.....he was right so far.

The drizzle had subsided and was being replaced by small flakes of snow, twisting and spinning down manically to their death. Inside the hut each man got a bed and one musty, ragged blanket which could only realistically protect half of the body from the bitter wintry conditions developing outside. Procter sat on his bed and gazed around him. Most of the guards had already passed out and were breathing deeply in sleep. The others wandered around in a daze preparing a hot brew before retiring. These men were clearly heavily fatigued. It had been so easy to tag along with them onto the wagon. He had caught a few raised eyebrows, but he really didn't think they would have cared if he had have been wearing a huge sign bearing "Ich bin Englander" across his chest. They seemed oblivious to their surroundings; this was all just routine to them. They had switched off a long time ago. Procter stretched out on the bed and closed his eyes drawing a veil on his thoughts of tomorrow. In minutes few, Thomas Procter was also breathing deeply with the rest of them, it was strange that two nations who oppose each other vociferously in battle could sleep so soundly together in the same room.

Block 7A, SS Headquarters 0600 hrs, Jan 15, 1941.

They had been assembled, stood silently to attention, for at least 10 minutes, staring vacantly to their fronts. Luckily for Procter they had only formed a single file, two or three files and it would have probably been him stood out on his own un-uniformly from the rest. He was stood second from the right, he would have been the end man had not one of the guards forgotten his belt and had to race back into the hut. He was so terrified of being seen late that he just joined the parade at the nearest point. They all stood and waited. Procter began to feel impatient, his legs felt numb with the cold, he was just itching to move even if it was to shuffle his feet slightly just to bring back some feeling to his toes. He glanced out of the corner of both eyes scanning both prospective points of entry for the awaited guest of honour. It seemed deathly quiet, no sounds of vehicles, no birds, nothing. All that could be heard was the faintest sound of breathing witnessed by the exhalation of small clouds of breath. Then something could be heard almost like a tap dripping quite slowly at first then quicker. The drips were getting louder and louder until they no longer sounded like drips but were quite distinctly the sound of a pair of military boots clipping the cobbled roads and then he appeared round the corner into Procter's glance. He advanced towards them.

He stopped at the end man, stared him up and down and glared at the man's midriff. After a few seconds pause the visitor unleashed a ferocious blow with his right hand to the side of the man's face.

The sound of bone on flesh echoed piercingly in the silence. It wasn't long before a thin trace of blood crept down the nostril and weaved a path to the corner of the man's mouth. The host then grabbed the man's belt and jerked it around until it was square to his view and then nonchalantly moved down the line.

Procter's eyes met the pale blue stare of Klaus Berthold. They were of similar height and build. Procter averted his view almost immediately but long enough for Berthold to have captured his return stare. Berthold pushed his face close up to Procter and stared deep into his eyes. Procter felt a fire burning its way in, roasting the ends of the nerves, sending a pain signal to Procter's brain and then the pain relented and Berthold had already moved on. Procter felt the beads of sweat trickling down his back. He was unsettled. For a moment there he nearly lost it. He said to himself it was not Berthold that unsettled him but the fear of his cover being blown. He almost convinced himself that was the case.

Berthold completed his lengthy initiation and stepped out to the front. He gave a quick glance over his ensemble and laughed,

'They really have scraped the barrel this time haven't they.'

His accent was strong and Procter had a little difficulty in deciphering it. Berthold rested one hand on the stock of his Walther P38 pistol, which hung just inside his coat. For a moment Procter had this premonition that Berthold was going to provide his own private execution and he tightened his grip on the MP43, the assault rifle, which stood erect to his right side.

The MP43 was the first assault rifle ever made and could lay down effective fully automatic or single-shot fire with a 38, 7.92mm, round magazine. A marked improvement on the five-round 98K bolt-operated Mauser he had originally become familiar with. He felt if the situation turned ugly he could at least throw down a large amount of fire and take a reasonable body-count to the grave with him.

The eerie silence dissolved and Berthold spoke again,

'OK you are all probably intrigued as to why you have gathered here'.

He paused as if waiting for a response but of course nobody spoke or stirred, not through discipline, but through sheer fear. Berthold had an amazing presence. A presence that one associated with power.

He continued,

'Our mission is to convoy a package by rail to our chemical laboratories in Stuttgart, a trouble-free and simple task you may think. However, the consignment is a prototype rescued from the destruction of a lab in Hamburg. Which means it is one of a kind...... it is imperative that the consignment reaches its destination....that is our job. The journey will take approximately two days. So, what I demand from each of you is extreme vigilance. There must not be any mistakes.......The Fatherland depends on it. After two days of baby-sitting the consignment you will all be rewarded......The transport will leave from the main gate at 0800 hours... anyone of you who thinks he is not capable of embarking on this mission are welcome to visit me in my quarters...'.

A wry smile emanated from Berthold lips. He stared down the length of his guard pausing briefly at Procter, where their gaze met for the second time. Berthold smiled. It was a smile that stated he knew. Procter felt Berthold probe within his skull. Tearing away at the information he required. Procter felt dizziness ensue. Was his cover so transparent? Berthold sucked the cold morning air through his teeth and nodded knowingly and then turned and left in the fashion that he had arrived. If he did know why had he not done anything to confirm the fact?

Once he was out of sight the men breathed deeply and returned to the hut. Procter stood still for a moment. He now felt fear. Full blown fear bordering on panic. *He couldn't have guessed.....How could he?....Don't be stupid man....*

Procter pondered the thought anxiously until one of the men patted him on the shoulder and suggested that a hot coffee would calm his nerves.

Chapter 2

Berlin Military Rail Station, 0830 Hrs, Jan 15, 1941

The journey from the camp to the station had been a quite one. The men had been loaded onto the wagon silently and had reached the station quickly. There awaited a locomotive which appeared similar to any other vehicle that would convey prospective passengers to their destination, however, to the trained eye this one was only two carriages long and instantly emanated an air of suspicion as it stood motionless at the platform. Surrounded by an abundance of military support the guard entered the vehicle followed closely by Berthold, who seemed especially content and proud. He had a tattered brown briefcase gripped firmly in his left hand and a square larger silver case in his right hand. The silver case was particularly alluring and even in the low levels of light it seemed to shine from within. Neither of the cases were particularly heavy as Berthold moved with ease.

The crowd on the platform acted as though the war was over, cheering and saluting in a riotous joy. Procter stood emotionless at a window bemused by the reaction, so much for covert planning. He had quickly got over his bout of paranoia at the parade and convinced himself that it was just nerves that had clouded his judgement. He doubted if Berthold could be that clever. He concentrated on his objective. *What was in these cases?* He knew it was of extreme importance because intelligence had been so secretive about the operation. They sent him in blind hoping that he would figure it out for himself. All Procter was told was that he was to destroy the shipment and that it had been under close surveillance for months. So, he figured this 'shipment' was not just a flash in the pan, as so many of his successful missions had been prior, but this was the real McCoy. A mission that would gain him the recognition that he craved since the war began. A mission that would preserve the splendour of his nation. A nation and values that he would only too readily sacrifice his existence for.

The train crept slowly away from the platform. Berthold's mood changed to one of a more serious nature. The troops were gathered in one of the two carriages. The carriage was decorated in dark blue and looked as if it had been reconditioned for the journey. There were six thin plank tables spaced evenly along the carriage, adjacent to the carriage walls, and wooden benches with a cushioned seat along either side of the tables. The troops were stood crammed together in the aisle. Berthold delicately placed the silver case on a table and keeping his hand firmly gripped to it sat down behind it. He glanced at the troops and bellowed at them to be seated. Like the good animals they were they all responded effortlessly and found a seat. Berthold stared at each man in turn. An agonising stare as though he was scrutinising each man's strengths and weaknesses. When he found the suitable traits in the man's make up he was delegated for a particular task. The first four men were selected to be front and rear guards of the train, two at each end. A task Procter was relieved he had not been given, not only did in mean spending the whole journey outside the body of the train in near arctic conditions, but more importantly he would have been separated from the shipment. The next four were placed at the junction of the two carriages their tasks included guarding the sides of the train from possible dangers and also ensuring nobody passed through the entrances. In other words, Berthold had ensured that once he had positioned these men they basically were not to move. He then pointed over in Procter's direction and said that he was to be the roof guard, a job that meant lying on the roof for the whole duration of the trip. Procter's shoulders dropped noticeably. Berthold laughed openly and suggested that the guard should wrap up because 'it's a little bit chilly out there'. Procter stood up slowly and started to the door.

'Where are you going?', Berthold spoke in amazement.

Procter continued not quite interpreting the German version of the universal language.

'HEY!............', Berthold's tone increased an octave.

Procter stopped and turned.

'Not you......sit down..........YOU!', the guard next to Procter met the stare of Berthold and instantly sprung to his feet and brushing past Procter like a scolded dog with his tail between his leg's, made a sharp exit. Procter sat down again part relieved, but the way Berthold spoke implied that maybe an even worse a fate awaited him. Paranoia returned. He sensed a form of mistrust. Procter felt confused. If Berthold did mistrust or suspect him he certainly didn't seem to care either way.

Berthold then stood up and walked down the aisle selecting two guards to follow him into the rear carriage. Once inside the carriage the guards were faced with a plain white decor. The carriage had no windows, in the advent of darkness two oil lamps hung loosely on the cage that demanded half the area of the compartment. Inside stood a lead-iron safe attached securely to the rear of the cage. Its door was ajar and for the moment it was empty. Berthold entered the cage and placed both cases inside the safe. The outer walls of the safe were tightly hugging the cases firmly in position as Berthold closed the door. The lock made a firm thud as he pushed down on the handle. He then opened the top button of his tunic and reached his hand beneath it. His hand surfaced with a chain, which obviously hung around his neck, and at the end of the chain was a large iron key. He pushed the key into the lock and turned it once. He then grasped the handle and tried to budge it. His knuckles stood out proudly as the skin tightened around them. His cheeks flushed into a deep crimson with the effort that he used. The handle remained firm, oblivious to his relentless pressure. He exhaled a long, sharp breath that encompassed the safe in a swirling mist.

He stared at the safe for a few seconds until he convinced himself that the shipment was safe. He then stood up, stepped back and ushered the guards into the cage.' They were the privileged ones. They had the responsibility of being the direct protectors of the Nations future. Standing guard over a lead-iron box that held all the answers......', Berthold had mastered the techniques of installing fear in men. He knew there are many strings to fears bow. He did not issue violence, threaten with death, or speak coldly and viciously. He used the fear of letting down one's nation. The fear of failure. A much larger form of fear than all the others combined. The guards, burdened with thoughts of letting down their families, friends and the nation in general, stepped beside the safe. Berthold pulled shut the door of the cage. He pointed down at the key hanging on a hook by the door.

'Lock it..', he stated to the two men.

After a short pause one of the guards, the bravest under the circumstances, leapt forward and unhooked the key and turned it in the lock.

'Keep that in your tunic until we reach our destination...', Berthold pointed at the motionless guard. The guard nodded and retreated back beside the safe. Berthold rattled the cage door until he was convinced that the encasement was secure. The Guard seemed more alert now...refreshed and keen to fulfil the task. Berthold moved away, back to the front carriage.

On entering the compartment, Procter instantly recognised the cases missing. Berthold sat down, sighed, and stared at the two remaining guards. Procter averted his gaze immediately this time. Berthold told the other guard to make coffee using the gas stove at the far end of the carriage...enough coffee for everyone. It was going to be a long night and didn't everyone know it.

Procter stared out of the window watching the snow laden hills on the horizon slowly creep further away. He grasped the mug of coffee that had been delivered to him by the other guard, cupping his hands around it, feeling its warmth soak into his palms. He turned and observed Berthold who had reached into his breast pocket and produced a hipflask, the contents of which he used to warm his brew further. Having topped his mug he thought about replacing the cap but decided that a couple of long, neat swigs were first required before he returned the flask to its original position. He grimaced as the liquid began its journey to his stomach. He almost choked. Procter presumed it must be cognac, although, he noticed a small bead of blue liquid trickle from the corner of his mouth. Berthold aware of the spillage lapped at the stray liquid with his tongue. His tongue was also a discoloured blue. If it had been Cognac it was certainly a strange brand.

Procter never regarded himself as having a nervous disposition, however, he found himself gently shaking. The train was cold although not enough to produce the trembling which rippled through him. He tried to focus hard on the task in hand but found himself drifting away with the rhythmic sway of the carriage. He thought of home. It seemed so distant. He thought of his family. He was from a working-class background although they were far from poor. The whole family worked hard. They were winners and proud with it. His father was highly regarded at his trade and was respected within the local community. Procter felt so proud to bear the family name. He was the only son. He had a younger sister who had been nine when he left home to join the Army, she would be almost 12 now. He wondered how she would look. Three years can make an incredible difference at that age. He longed to give his little sister a hug. He recalled the day he left home. His mother cooked the whole family a hearty breakfast. Sausage, bacon, eggs, tomatoes, and bread all adorned the plate. He hadn't felt like eating, his appetite had been suppressed by nerves, but he forced every scrap down into his stomach. He kissed his sister on the doorstep and waved to her and his aunt from the back of a cab that his father had booked for this special occasion. The journey to the train station had been short, although it was almost ten miles. He recalled his father's face as his train approached the platform. A proud face. So very proud. His father had reached out and grasped his hand firmly and shook it. At that moment for the first time in Procter's life, he had felt like a man. His mother dived onto him and wept as she kissed and hugged her precious son. Procter had found it hard to resist the tears, but he did. He stared into his father's eyes and as he stepped onto the train he noticed the tear. He had never witnessed his father cry before. It alarmed him at first but then he soon realised it was not a tear of sorrow but a tear of pride. The tear, only small, but still a tear, slowly crept from the corner of one eye. They had waved the train down the track until the train drifted out of sight. It was at that moment that Procter had felt frightened and alone. The feelings he felt at this moment.

He shuddered at the recollection of the memories. He knew he had to return home alive. He had to witness his father's face again when it was all over. He breathed deeply as though spurned on by his thoughts and concentrated hard on the mission. He knew he didn't have much time.

The more time that passed the more anxious he became as to what plan he could design and whether it was good enough to succeed. In the hour they had spent on the train already, he had dismissed two possibilities. He realised Berthold was no imbecile and knew the plan had to be watertight. As he ran various decisions through his mind he sensed Berthold watching him. Procter slowly turned his head enough to glance out of the corner of his eye. As he did so, Berthold smiled and nodded his head slowly. Procter sharply swung his gaze back out of the window. He gulped noticeably. *He knows...He knows.. but How?* He knew he had to act quickly. He sensed the longer he sat there and did nothing the more suspicious Berthold would become. He also sensed Berthold would say or do something soon. *Why was he waiting?...Did he enjoy these mind games?*

The light was dimming when Procter finally decided on how he was going to play his hand and it had to be this evening.

Darkness had descended rather rapidly and the carriages held only faint lights. Shadows danced eerily around the carriage. Berthold had polished off the contents of his flask and in Procter's gaze he seemed a little heavy eyed. Procter stood up and Berthold stirred and stared at him.

'Noch ein Kaffee, Capitain', Procter gestured with his mug as to his intentions.

Berthold slowly nodded his head still glaring deep into his eyes, 'Ja'.

Procter collected the mugs and made his way down the carriage still feeling Berthold's stare burning through him. Once at the end of the carriage he placed the kettle on the stove and made through the doors.

The guard, startled by the intrusion, alerted themselves, but upon seeing Procter they relaxed again. They were in complete darkness and seemed weary because of it. The carriage door windows were open and piles of snow had collected inside. The wind whistled around the small space they guarded, and they were noticeably frozen, which Procter mused would slow their reactions if anything went wrong with his plan. He told the guards he had been sent by Berthold to check the guards in the other compartment. They murmured in unison and Procter stepped into the second carriage. Upon entering he saw the two guards stood either side of the safe contorted in shape from the glow from the lamps. Procter smiled at them as he stepped up to the cage. They too looked tired. He looked around the cage and saw the two empty mugs in the far corner and pointed at them asking the guards if they would like a refill.

One of the men sighed loudly in gratitude and turned and made for the mugs. The other guard produced a key and unlocked the cage door so that the mugs could be retrieved. It was a split second between the cage door opening wide and the other guard bending over to reach for the mugs, but a moment that produced an instinctive reaction. As the cage door swung open Procter had raised the butt of his rifle and caught the guard in the doorway with a massive upwards blow beneath the nose, the bone piercing up into his brain killing him almost instantly. The cage door rocked on its hinges noisily. The other guard turned and gasped in sheer disbelief at what Procter had done and before he could raise the alarm, Procter had dived into the cage and administered the same blow. But it was not as square on as the first had been and although the guard went down in agony, blood gushing from his splintered facial wounds, he had not been killed. The guard's mouth contorted gruesomely wide in an attempted scream, but no sound was heard as Procter slammed a second then third blow to the temple and watched the life drain out him. It wasn't a pleasant sight but was one that Procter had to come to terms with.

Realising that both guards were now dead, Procter quickly examined the safe, gave a tug on the handle to no avail. He frisked the two dead guards in search of the key but in hindsight wished he hadn't wasted the time. He knew Berthold would hold the key. He quickly stood up, rubbed the blood off the butt of his rifle on one of the guards' uniform, collected the two empty mugs and made his way back to the other carriage. He had taken longer than planned and must seem calm when he returned back into Berthold's gaze.

As he walked through into the carriage Berthold was walking towards him. Procter froze for a moment. Upon seeing Procter, Berthold stopped glared at him and returned back to his seat. He was coming to check on Procter's whereabouts, obviously not as intoxicated as Procter first thought. The kettle was just beginning to steam and with his hands still shaking Procter refilled five mugs. He beckoned the other guard over to him and asked him if he minded taking a mug to the roof guard. He obliged under the watchful eye of Berthold and made his way to the front of the carriage. Procter watched him through the front door and picked up a mug himself and started towards Berthold.

As Procter placed the mug in front of Berthold, he firmly reached out and grasped Procter's wrist, spilling a little of the coffee onto his exposed hand and causing his rifle to drop off his shoulder and onto the floor. Procter tried to grab it on its journey to the floor but failed somewhat distracted by the burning of his wrist and hand where the coffee had spilled.

'What took you so long?'. Procter felt dizzy.

Adrenaline pumped through his body and a bead of sweat dripped off his nose onto Berthold's hand. As their eyes met Procter saw the realisation in Berthold's eyes as he released his grip on Procter's wrist and made for his pistol. Procter raised the mug and with a quick thrust sprayed the boiling liquid into Berthold's eyes. He screamed a loud and piercing scream.

His hand now fumbling for his pistol, Procter clenched his fist and repeatedly smashed Berthold's face. Berthold retaliated blindly with a left blow just above Procter's right eye. Pain soared through his body and he took two steps back. It had been some blow. The fiercest blow Procter had ever received. Almost superhuman strength. Berthold's hand had grasped the grip of his pistol and the weapon, as though in slow motion, revealed itself from its holster. The muzzle slowly arced around towards Procter but just moments before he was in its line Procter sidestepped and sliced through Berthold's windpipe with the blade he had managed to produce from his belt. Berthold dropped his pistol and collapsed back into his chair holding his throat. A terrible gurgling sound echoed through the carriage as Berthold began to drown in his own blood. Procter stepped back still holding the blade tightly, ready to thrust again, but the sight in front of him was too ghastly to comprehend. Bright red blood pumped from Berthold's neck, splashing over his tunic and the table a foot away. Procter felt his stomach coming up to his mouth and he was violently sick. Berthold collapsed across the seat, his eyes seemingly bulging from their sockets, face pale and drained of blood, but the thick gore kept oozing out, the flow getting slower as the heart tired.

Berthold was dead. Procter gathered himself realising he had little time and picked up the Walther pistol that lay devoid in a pool of blood. He moved to the front door and waited. It was only seconds when the door opened, and the other guard returned. He froze motionless in the doorway mesmerised by the sight that awaited him. Procter raised the Walther and slammed it down on the back of the guard's head knocking him out cold.

The carriage was filled with the smell of death and Procter breathing irrationally was the only sound that could be heard. His heart pounding, skipping several beats. Procter raced over to Berthold's motionless body. The chain was hanging loosely in view over the blood-soaked tunic. He pulled at it and eventually the key presented itself. He ripped it off the chain almost removing Berthold's already severed head and placed it in his pocket. Running his fingers through his hair and composing himself Procter, picked up his rifle, pushed the Walther into his breaches under his tunic, and returned to the stove. Picking up two mugs of coffee he opened the door quickly and dragged it shut, concealing the carnage he had left behind him. He motioned to the guards that their coffees would be here shortly and moved into the other compartment. Procter was quite amazed that the guards hadn't heard Berthold scream, but the sound of the wheels bumping over the track and the now howling wind obviously filtered out any external noise that the guard's ears had not become accustomed to.

Procter stared at the two bodies slumped inside the cage. Their faces seemed relieved in a strange kind of way. The faces were already congealed in blood, but it was the eyes that seemed content on their release from the world. They showed no pain or torture, although their deaths must have been painful. Both sets of eyes watched him move to the safe. He turned the key in the lock and pushed on the handle and with a creak and a groan the safe opened. The two cases sat waiting to be collected. Procter picked them up and stepping over the bodies of his previous prey headed for the rear door. He placed the cases down by the side of it within reaching distance and cocked his rifle quietly. Raising the gun parallel to the ground he turned the handle on the door and taking one step back kicked the door open. The two guards startled by the rude outburst turned face-on into the spray of bullets. One of the men was catapulted back over the rear railing. The other took several shots to the chest, his finger jamming on the trigger of his rifle and several shots reported out from his limp weapon. One stray ricochet caught Procter in the thigh. He didn't feel it immediately only when he picked up the cases and lifted his leg to clear the railing and jump off the train. Then the pain hit him, but he was already over and had landed awkwardly in the drifts at the side of the track. The cold bit at him instantly, like it had a hunger that made it manic. Eating relentlessly into each and every area it came into contact with. The silver case slipped from his grasp and landed on the track. He rolled several times over, momentum pushing him through the snow until he slid gently to a stop. He looked back up over the track, saw the missing case and headed towards it.

As he clambered gingerly back up onto the track to retrieve it several more shots rang out, obviously from the roof guard. Having a case in both hands he tried to run down the bank but as he reached the side of the track a shot caught him in the left shoulder blade and knocked him off balance. He somersaulted down into the snow, but this time made sure the cases didn't slip from his grasp. Then he came to a standstill. The train still trudging off into the distance, but it would be halted soon surely. He had to get away. His body ached. His wounds screamed in agony. The shot to the shoulder had gone clean through, ripping sinew as it went, but was not too much of a problem to him. The bullet in his thigh was lodged firmly and he was losing a lot of blood fast. He made about five hundred yards into a dense forest when he realised he couldn't go any further.

So cold. His body shook. His vision becoming more and more impaired. He blinked furiously trying to clear the temporary blindness. The deep snow was impossible to get through in his state. He sat against a large fir tree and assessed his wounds. His trousers were darkened in blood. His leg, and body for that matter, seemed numb and only a coursing tingle made its way through the limb from hip to knee. He felt himself slipping in and out of consciousness. He had so nearly pulled it off. He wanted to lie down and close his eyes. Maybe dream a happy ending to what had become his nightmare. He felt remorse. Visions of his family back home in England began to haunt him, voices echoed around his head,

> *I will be deemed a hero, or will I? Maybe they'll cover this up and no one will ever know what I've done. Maybe it'll be another of those state secrets. I almost did it Mum.. You would have been proud, and Dad did you see me!*

He pictured the station again. His father's face. The tear. He realised at that second in time that he had never once told his father he loved him, or not since he could remember. He had said it to his mother on several occasions but never his father. It hadn't been the manly thing to do. He wanted to tell him. So badly. But he instinctively knew it was too late. That hurt almost as much as the pain from the wounds, if not more. He pictured his sister as he remembered her. That innocent young face. He wondered how she looked today at this moment. What would they all be doing as he lay dying deep in snow? He heard their voices, clear and warm. He told his father he loved him as he grimaced under the pain.

Shit..it hurts. What is in these cases? What was this for?

Procter cleared the voices from his head and pulled the leather briefcase towards him. He flipped the catch and pulled out the contents. There were several sheets of documented paper binded in a red file headed as TOP SECRET. Littered across the papers were several references to a compound mixture....named Testrilich.. or something like that..the writing was difficult to decypher. Various chemical symbols and detailed sketches stood prominently throughout the contents. Obviously, this was the object of the mission, to prevent a document on some discipline in biochemistry from reaching its destination. He laughed until it hurt, and he felt himself slipping away again. Blinking furiously again to prevent the darkness from edging its way further into his vision.

On one of the papers were the lab reports and the tests carried out together with dosage instructions. He reached into his pocket and pulled out a cigarette lighter. Collecting the papers together on top of the briefcase. He lit the corners and watched as Germany's future, their great hope, became engulfed in flames. The smell of burning paper was so distinct. It circulated into his nostrils. He could taste the musky odour. It reminded him briefly of summer campfires. He was just a child then, sat around singing songs, eating sausage and tinned baked beans. A smile found his lips. Then reality returned again in the form of a sharp searing pain. He pulled the silver case over to him; the pain was getting too much.

Inside was a sealed tube wrapped in foam, which contained a clear blue liquid. Procter held it up and laughed again. Anger briefly removing the pain,

'You stupid bastards' ... He took the cork out of the end of the tube and sniffed around the top. It had no odour. He thought about tipping it out onto the ground, then a wry smile adorned his face.

'Let's make a toast....' To Germany's future!!.'.....', Procter raised the tube and swallowed the liquid in three gulps. It tasted foul. He almost regurgitated it immediately. It had the palette of a bitter painkiller mixed with the bite of a cheap whisky, he choked on it for a while then leant back against the tree, letting the tube drop by his side. It landed upside down and any remaining droplets escaped into the snow leaving a slight stain. He didn't recall the liquid probably being the same Berthold had consumed on the train hours earlier. The thought never even entered his mind.

He felt himself swaying. The pain was going. He smiled. Everything was becoming hazy. The trees seemed to slip down on top of him. Darkness ensued, along with the voices again. He chatted along with his family, slipping slowly away. Getting darker and more peaceful with every moment that past, too late to go back this time, fell in far too deep. The voices grew fainter and began to echo unintelligibly. He seemed to be free falling through a sodium haze like a feather drifting slowly through the air. A blue sodium haze. Procter felt wonderful. He heard his own voice echoing quietly in the distance as though it had been separated from his body in some way. He heard himself say, "Please...", although he couldn't remember saying it. The word was repeated over and over and the more repeated it became, the softer and more frightened the voice sounded. It was as if the voice begged for admittance. It was all over. Less than a minute later Procter was unconscious. He never regained consciousness and within half an hour Thomas Procter was dead.

Out of life comes death,
and out of death, life,
Out of the young, the old,
and out of the old, the young,
Out of the waking, sleep,
and out of sleep, waking,
The stream of creation and dissolution
never stops.......

Heraclitus:

The only thing to fear is fear itself.....

Franklin D Roosevelt:

Chapter 3

"I will get you!!" the voice screamed. Bloodshot eyes bulging at him. Contorted pain-soaked face, flailing arms extended in front, the gruesome black figure stumbled after him. He frantically tried to run but kept losing his footing and the figure grew nearer. He could hear its breathless gasps and every time he picked himself up, within yards, he would have slipped onto his knees again. His heart pounded; his lungs grasped for pockets of air. He felt the tears well in his eyes. He turned to see the figure almost close. Those eyes....he tried to scream but nothing was heard. The more he tried to scream the more breathless he became but still no sound emanated from his mouth. His legs ached, the muscles burned and as they became numb he slipped again. This time though not on his knees but a crashing fall, one that left him prostrate on the ground. He tried to get up but could not, he felt as though he was being held by an excessive magnetic force, pinning him tight to the ground. He turned his head and saw the figure loom over him. He saw its face and the mis-shaped grin, it raised a hand, and the weapon came into view. A long-pointed dagger was raised above its head and the figure muttered "Got you!!!" and with that the blade began its descent down towards his chest.......

Billy Adams sat bolt upright in bed. Sweat dripping off his face and his sheets were moist from the nightmare he had just awoken from. He placed his hands over his face and wiped away the sweat, then reached for his bedside table lamp. He felt safer in the light. He glanced all around his room, checking to see if anything was out of place or if the room held any uninvited guests. Once satisfied he sighed a huge breath of relief. Billy was 16 years old and had suffered the same nightmare for as long as he could remember. It was always the same grisly figure chasing him and always the same conclusion. The scenery was sometimes different. For example, one time he was being chased through a forest, with brambles and branches clawing and resisting his escape, another time he was in sand. Sodden and heavy sand that gripped him to the knees. In fact, on reflection, he had probably had his nightmare chasing him through all types of climate and terrain. The one constant though was that it was always at night and he always eventually got caught. Sometimes the chase would last for hours other times only minutes, but one thing was for sure, Billy had suffered with this secret torture for longer than was necessary to leave him severely mentally scarred.

He flung back the sodden covers and swung his legs over the side of the bed. He still found himself shaking. It was something Billy just couldn't understand, I mean everyone at sometime or another had nightmares, but his seemed so vivid and so real. The older he got the more vivid and detailed the nightmare became. His mother had told him that even as a baby he would lie fast asleep twitching and murmuring and then suddenly awake screaming. Ellen Adams was a tremendously strong-willed woman. She was 26 when she gave birth to Billy and in those days that was considered odd to be bearing a first child at such a late age. At first she thought it was cute and would console Billy with a big hug and words of reassurance that everything was fine. But as it became a more regular occurrence she became more worried about her son. She spoke to her husband about it, after all he was a well-respected GP. He had said he witnessed reports like this every single day in his profession. It is perfectly understandable for a mother to be overprotective of their children and they are bound to have their safety and welfare at heart, however, life is full of nightmares and they engulf anyone of any age or size. They are not particular at all. His final remark had been,' He'll be fine Elly....trust me I'm a doctor...' he had smiled as he went out the door. She recalled that he said those very words far too often for her to trust them now. He had said in that smarmy mocking tone,' Trust me I'm a doctor', just minutes before Billy was conceived. She hadn't planned on having children at all. 'I'm not bringing a child into this filth and war. It wouldn't be fair.' She used to throw that statement into the faces of those who questioned why she wasn't yet a mother. The truth is she was terrified at the thought. He had also muttered those reassuring words when her mother lay dying in her bed. He had given her some painkillers and said that she would be fine now and free from pain. In the middle of that night her mother had lay screaming in agony for around two hours before she finally passed away. So now Ellen treated those words with caution, knowing sub-consciously that something awful was about to happen and all he could do was smile at her. That always seemed to annoy her as well. Then, when he re-entered the room and gave her the following lecture, which she remembered word for word, Ellen had to bite her tongue to prevent an outburst.

'A baby is very frightened and intimidated by the world and its surroundings, it's new to him. If he suddenly wakes up in a darkened room and you are not there for him, then of course he's going to be frightened and scream the house down. Don't do the over-protective mother routine on me please, get a hold of yourself, I really don't need this...'

She had stared at him in disbelief after his sermon and decided it was fruitless to pursue the matter further. As Billy got older he still had the dreams and became terrified of the dark. Again another 'normal occurrence in the rearing of a child', 'All kids dislike the dark'. Ellen found it strange how Billy wouldn't mix with other children and preferred to play on his own. In his first days of school, he instantly became bullied by the taller children, for in his early years his frame was very slight. His teachers expressed their concern that Billy was unusually quiet and failed to join in with the games of other children. He became a loner. However, it was apparent that Billy was a very bright child. He could read and write at the age of three and was extremely logical in his thoughts. His teachers felt very sorry for him and however hard they tried to encourage him to participate with the other children, the more reserved he seemed to become. The more reserved he became the more of an outcast he was made to feel.

He grew up with the same children, and by the age of eight, he was already streaks ahead of everyone academically. So much so he would switch off in his lessons because he found the work frustratingly easy and just sit and stare vacantly into space. The other children all laughed at him, and one in particular, James 'Jim' Boyce took exception to Billy's ways and constantly thrashed him whenever the opportunity presented itself. Boyce would spot Billy in the hall, stood alone, and walk up to him and repeatedly punch him in the face for no reason and then would empty the contents of Billy's satchel over the floor and proceed to stamp up and down on them. Then he would leave Billy in tears as he stomped away from the scene tracked by his entourage of 'hangers-on', who followed him everywhere as though they were his shadows. Although Boyce always hurt Billy with his blows, Boyce meant nothing compared to the figure that haunted Billy's mind most evenings when he was asleep. The figure in Billy's head began to take shape and he could see so much more of it. He felt very frightened and very alone.

As Billy grew older he became bigger and developed a more defined physique. His intelligence grew at an alarming rate too. By the age of thirteen he no longer had everyone poking fun at him. Most of the children now respected his intelligence and were keen to develop a friendship with him, although Billy just wasn't interested. He became the most sought-after prize within the female population of the school. They were all attracted to his mysterious attitude and wanted to share in his thoughts. Everywhere he went, he could sense everyone looking at him. Some eyes were that of admiration others were of jealousy. All the boys who had mocked and added to his misery were now very wary of him. Smiling and opening doors for him only to be met by Billy's icy stare. Boyce was a notable exception. He was still the school bully, but just glared at Billy whenever their paths met, with pure hatred in his eyes. He was so jealous of what Billy had become. Boyce now concentrated on bullying the younger children for sweets or money. He had lost most of his entourage and operated with three others who were probably too frightened not to stick with him. Boyce desperately wanted to take Billy back down a few pegs, he really did miss the fun he had bullying him, but there was something he felt that just held him back. The feeling was one he couldn't really relate to; it was one of fear.

Boyce would overcome this fear but wished he hadn't bothered. They were all in an art class. Billy had spent much care and dedication to his landscape painting. Everyone was amazed at just how good it was. He was three years away from his final exams, but this piece would have quite easy given him an A grade if it was submitted. Billy was silent, concentrating hard on his strokes, finishing off the horizon with meticulous care. Boyce was two rows in front, ribbing another boy about why he was painting a scarecrow in the middle of his paper. The boy explained that in fact it wasn't a scarecrow but a tree. To this statement Boyce and his three friends burst into laughter. The boy obviously embarrassed retorted with,

'Well, yours isn't much better!!'. Boyce instantly stopped laughing.

He threw himself up out of his chair and marched over to the now trembling boy, aware of what he had just said.

'You What!!'

'Sorry Jim, I didn't mean it'

'YOU WHAT!!', Boyce grabbed the boy by his lapels lifting him out of his chair.

'You know what I'm going to do with you..'

'Sorry...don't hit me', the boy was shaking, and tears filled his eyes.

'Ooh look at the big cry baby'

'Why are you bullying me.. I didn't mean it..You always used to bully him..' the boy turned and pointed at Billy as he sobbed.

'Now you are too frightened of him and it's my turn..I've done nothing to you!', the boy now wept uncontrollably. Everyone had heard the outburst including Billy, but he still kept his eyes on his work.

'Who said I'm frightened of him?..', Boyce looked around as though waiting for an answer. There fell a deathly silence on the class. Boyce looked at Billy still seemingly oblivious to the atmosphere, continuing his work.

'Hey..Adams..Do you think I'm frightened of you?'

Billy didn't answer.

'ADAMS!!..'

Billy still didn't answer. Boyce looked around the class, the pressure was immense. Everyone expected there to be trouble now. He couldn't just sit down and forget it. He would lose face and it would show that the statement would be true. Boyce walked up to the edge of Billy's table.

'Do you think I'm frightened of you?', Boyce's voice quivered slightly.

Billy looked up and met Boyce's eyes.

'I really don't care if you are frightened of me or not. It's unimportant and irrelevant...as are you!'

Billy looked back to his work. Boyce was amazed by the answer, a simple yes or no was what he anticipated. He looked around and people were smiling by Billy's clever reply. Boyce felt as though he was the one everyone was laughing at. He outstretched his arm and with a gentle sweeping movement knocked over Billy's water jar, flooding a pool of discoloured water all over the painting.

'I'm not frightened of you, Adams..remember that!!'

Boyce shakily turned to walk away as though sensing retaliation. Billy stared down at his now ruined painting. He breathed deeply and loudly before reaching out and grabbing at Boyce's arm, squeezing it tight and pulling him back before he unleashed his right fist square on Boyce's nose.

A loud slap filled the air and Boyce stumbled back over a chair before crashing face down onto the floor. As he looked up blood was already dripping from his nose. Boyce had never been hit before. He heard everyone cheering and coaxing Billy to hit him again.

Boyce put his hand to his nose and saw the blood. He immediately started snivelling and got to his feet and ran out the door. Billy cocked his head and stared down at his painting. The colours had all run together into a blurred effigy. He tipped off the pools of liquid and dabbed at the paper with a paper towel. To anyone else the picture would have been ruined. Upon drying the paper slightly, it soon became apparent that with the quick application of further colours the painting could in fact be saved. It was not as he planned but at least he knew that the events would keep Boyce well away from him in the future, which could only be a bonus.

From that day on, Billy had no further trouble. He had the everyday scenario of girls throwing themselves at him and the boys wanting him to join in with their fun and frolics, but Billy wasn't really interested. They seemed so immature and below him. He found that he had nothing in common with any of them, with the exception of perhaps one girl, Patricia Stevens. She was very intelligent also, and had never approached him like the others, in fact she seemed very shy. She wasn't as developed as the other girls still not wearing a bra and bore the tag of 'the boff', probably because she looked the intellectual type with glasses and all. Billy found himself occasionally staring at her and when she saw him looking she bowed her head sheepishly and turned a dark shade of red. It was a rare moment when Billy found his lips curling up and a smile adorned his face. She was one of the few people who he actually felt comfortable being around and for the time he was close to her he forgot the demons in his head that haunted him.

Finally, it was a Thursday morning in late January when she finally summoned enough courage to speak to him. They found themselves together alone in the library at a communal reading table. Their eyes meeting over the tops of the books they scanned far too slowly to actually be taking any of the information in.

Billy found this very erotic. He noticed how uncomfortable he was becoming and itched to move himself into a comfier position.

However, it did feel incredible. The throbs were so strong that Billy imagined her to hear them. He became flushed and sweat trickled down the back of his neck. The eye games continued for around twenty minutes until it was Patricia who lowered her book more than usual so that Billy could see her smiling at him. Billy blushed trying to hide his embarrassment back into his book. When he looked again the smile was still there but seemed more curious now and looked even more sensual. He really wanted to kiss those lips.

He felt a smile slowly drawing onto his face. They both sighed and continued to smile at each other for a few minutes. Billy felt like he had to do something. He had stood up and awkwardly made his way around the table to where Patricia was sat. As he got closer he could smell her. It wasn't a rich perfume smell like his mother occasionally wore, but a warm, musky smell that had washed over him every time he was close to her. Only this time it was much stronger the closer he got. He sat down next to her. She seemed to be shaking. He looked down onto the table where her slender fingers toyed with the edge of her book. Billy noticed it was Jane Eyre as it seemed to be magnified into his stare as the dizziness hit him and he opened his mouth and said,

'Would you consider..', He swallowed hard as the dizziness peaked and his mouth became very dry, '...going out with me..?', the words seemed to tail off at the end, but she knew what he had said.

Her heart missed a beat and she immediately replied, 'Yes...' It proved to be the start of a whole new experience for both of them. They were inseparable and did absolutely everything together. Billy also shared with her his nightmares. She was unknowingly honoured to be the first person that Billy had actually discussed the subject with. He had trust for her like he had never known before.

Billy threw cold water over his face. He always seemed to find it difficult to clear his head from his dreams. His head throbbed and was filled with a certain dark cloud. His eyes momentarily lost their focus and ached as though signalling the onset of a migraine. His mouth was distinctly parched of saliva and he found it difficult to swallow. He lived with these symptoms almost each and every day of his life. He threw on a plain white T-shirt and his well-worn pair of Wranglers and quietly tiptoed passed his parents bedroom door and made for downstairs. On entering the kitchen, he was surprised to find his mother standing over the stove still wearing her dressing gown. She was boiling up some milk and turned when she felt his presence.

'Thought you might need some milky coffee', she said.

Billy didn't answer still partly shocked at finding her there.

'You still having those dreams of yours Billy?'

Billy realised that he must have cried out loud enough to have woken her.

'Sorry Mum', he offered his apologies.

'I'm worried about you Billy...you would tell me if there is something wrong or something that might have upset you.... something I've done, or your fathers done...something...'

'MUM!...I'm fine..you are great, and dad can be great sometimes too..' Billy cut her short of the long list that probably ensued. She laughed with an air of sarcasm in her voice.

'Look mum it's just sometimes I have this nightmare..and it's very sick and it is just one of those things..I'll get over it...I'm almost getting used to it', he almost convinced himself.

Ellen thought Billy's answer was wonderful and reminded her so much of his dad. All that was missing from the end of it were the dreaded words his father used far too often. She was sick of being patronised. She knew Billy wasn't well. However, without his support, or the support of her husband, she knew that there was not the slightest thing she could do about it. She poured the frothing hot milk into the mugs and watched as the coffee swamped into the pure white liquid turning it a light brown colour. She put two sugars into Billy's mug but took her own neat. She needed the rich caffeine. She placed the mugs onto the table and offered a chair to Billy. He held up a hand and smiled and said,

'No, it's OK Mum I'm going to take it to my room. I've got some work to be getting on with.' He lifted his mug and made a sharp exit. Ellen sighed and then shouted after him,

'Are you seeing Patricia today?'

Billy stopped halfway up the stairs. He leant down peeping through the banister.

'Yes. It's Saturday. You know I always walk her dog with her around the park this morning.' Billy snapped.

'Oh yes..sorry I forgot..', Ellen smiled, quietly amused. She liked Patricia and she admired her for bringing Billy out of his shell. Although, she had only met her on a few occasions, the first time was after they had been together for almost two months, when Ellen persuaded Billy to invite her around to the house for Sunday lunch. They were both especially shy and secretive about their relationship and the dinner had been an awkward and unsuccessful affair, which by the end of it, Ellen was no nearer to establishing just how serious the friendship was. Patricia had hardly spoken apart from showing impeccable manners at the dining table and Billy had sat in obvious discomfort being unusually quiet and more retiring than usual. Ellen attempted to make conversation with leading questions but the pair of them returned with frustratingly monosyllabic answers. Her husband didn't help matters by appearing uninterested, which would have been a correct statement. It must have felt like an interrogation. But she obviously made Billy happy, he seemed vibrant and contented since the relationship began, which pleased her. Although, she was still curious to know what the attraction with her was. She wasn't the type of girl she would have imagined Billy to become involved with. Patricia was a very slim build bordering on almost anorexic proportions, with long straight dark hair. Her face was very pretty however, she had an intelligent aura about her. Her eyes hid behind deep spectacled lenses but were equally acute and innocent. She had worn a roomy floral dress that hid the slightness of her figure. Her command of the English language was faultless whenever she chose to use it. It was plainly apparent that she was, like Billy, an introvert and severely lacking in self-confidence as far as her appearance was concerned. But, as long as she continued to make Billy happy, Ellen was happy not to meddle in their affairs. However, she had hoped that she could have held a conversation with Patricia. Her husband

and Billy were neither very talkative and this frustrated her womanly persona. She quickly realised she would not be holding in-depth female discussions with Patricia either.

Billy stood on the crest of the grassy knoll. The park looked so beautiful from up there and he could get an early glimpse of Patricia. She was slowly strolling, so elegantly, along the riverside. Her reflection shimmering in the still waters as she moved along. Her hands were toying with her hair and occasionally she'd look down at herself to make sure she looked OK. He looked at his watch, 0933, ...three minutes late... but he chuckled as he thought to himself that it was a woman's prerogative to be late and started to run down the side of the knoll. At the bottom sat a bench. It was perfectly positioned. It was surrounded by a small copse of trees and sat above the bend of the river as it moved over the weir. Billy sat down. Patricia came around the corner and beamed at him. He stood up and walked towards her. He closed up to her, wrapped his arms around her and kissed her, like he'd waited a year for the moment. They both sat down. Billy held her hand. He looked at her and said,

'Had another nightmare last night......so bad it woke mum..'

'Oh no...what did she say?' Patricia said.

'She knows about them...well...a little...she gave me the' if ever you've got a problem you know you can talk to me 'lecture', Billy sarcastically mocked his mother's voice.

'Oh no!...what else did she say?', Patricia said.

'She didn't get the chance...I told her I was seeing you, to take your dog for its Saturday morning walk!' Billy laughed out loud.

'Oh no!...what else did she say?', Patricia said.

'Oh no!...what else did she say?', Billy mocked her and then leant over and gave her a huge hug. They kissed again. He looked into the depths of her clear blue eyes and found himself swimming. He was overcome by emotion and was almost in tears as he stroked Patricia's hair and said, 'I really do love you.....'.

Patricia was very shocked. He had told her before of course. But this time it sounded evermore convincing. She felt warm and a tingle tripped its way down her spine.

'I really do love you too..' she replied also close to tears.

They hugged even tighter and broke into a long passionate kiss. Billy explored her mouth with an eagerness that was unsurpassed. Patricia responded breathlessly. She felt his hand cupping her tiny breast. Squeezing harder as he kissed deeper. She became very aroused, like never before. Her body ached for him. Then she panicked and became conscious of the fact that they were in a public place, and that somebody might be watching, and pushed him back slightly. She smiled again and looked more seriously at him.

'Well....Billy Adams ..where is it?'

Billy smiled. He knew exactly what she was referring to.

'Where's my pressie?', Patricia sulked jokingly.

Billy found it difficult to move. Her beauty affixed him. Then he reached into his jacket pocket and pulled out a small square case. It was crimson red and had small gold clips hiding the contents. The box alone seemed magnificent to Patricia. She gasped as Billy placed the box into her hand. She looked at it for a while not knowing really what to do. Then she flipped up the clips and slowly lifted the lid. Inside, her eyes were met with the glow of a solid gold locket. Billy had noticed the item in the local pawnshop. Although it was second hand he had it polished and made it look good as new. It had cost him almost all of his savings. Inscribed on the front, etched above each other, were the letters P and B. She felt the tears well in her eyes. She opened the locket and read the inscription on the inside. It read, 'I will ALWAYS love you..' and on the other side, in the case, was a picture of Billy, the one he knew she liked best. She closed it and lifted it from the box. She sniffled as tears tickled her nose and dripped from her chin. She opened the chain and turned her back slightly to Billy and gestured for him to put it around her neck. He gently lifted her hair placed the chain around her slender neck and fastened it. She turned back and lifted the locket high enough to drop it below her dress. She dived for Billy and buried herself into his chest and sobbed,

'I love you so much...it really hurts sometimes Billy'.

He hugged her tight and replied, 'I know...'.

They were silent for a while just feeling the contours and the warmth from each other's bodies. The birds sang so sweetly, and the warm sun heated the gentle breeze that lapped around them. It was incredible. Pure bliss. Billy thought of the times they had ahead, they both agreed on marriage at eighteen when their parents couldn't persuade them differently, and that now Patricia was sixteen they would be able to fulfil what they both wanted so badly. She had said to him that she didn't feel it was right until she was sixteen. And that would he mind waiting, although, at times she found it very difficult to wait. Billy had been very honourable and in the 18 months they had been together he had done nothing but kiss her apart from the occasional petting which followed the final kiss of the night.

Patricia looked up at Billy and said, 'I've waited for this day for so long now. I want it to be really special.'

Billy agreed. It would be. They stood up and Billy offered to walk her home.

As they approached Patricia's house they broke hands and Billy said, 'Don't forget 9 o'clock tonight at the knoll.'

Patricia turned and smiled. She held a finger to her lips ushering Billy to keep his voice down and trotted up to her door. Taking a last look and a smile she waved to him and disappeared behind the door. Billy turned, sighed, and began his walk home, but it took no time as his mind was on other things. Once home, Billy ran the bath and got his clothes all laid out neatly prepared on his bed. He wanted to look his best as well.

CHAPTER 4

Billy soaked in the bath for almost an hour. He sank right down until his chin just rested on the surface of the water. His ears were tickled by the occasional wave of movement. He thought about the evening ahead. How he would approach the subject and how he would go about the act. He wasn't concerned with performance or strategically running through what he would do and wouldn't do in any particular order. He was more concerned about the scene being right. The feeling between them being right. That it was truly the right and exact moment. He knew Patricia wouldn't mind if the moment lasted for two minutes or ten, just as long as the depth of feeling and love was reciprocated. Billy convinced himself that it would only happen if both parties, even at this late stage in planning, felt the moment was unequivocally correct. He smiled and ducked his face under the water. He felt truly alive and that the ghosts from the past had withdrawn gracefully in defeat.

Billy watched the clock for almost five hours. Then it was time. He checked his appearance for the fifth time in a matter of minutes in the steel framed mirror that hung above his work-desk and smiled to his reflection. He crept downstairs and carefully, without a sound, opened and shut his front door. He was in the street. Taking a quick look behind to see if he had been spotted, he then turned and ran to the park. He knew he would be slightly early, but he didn't mind waiting. He got there 10 minutes early. In fact, Patricia was just leaving her house. She looked incredible. She didn't look sixteen, she looked older, but she still retained an aura of innocence. Billy had his hand in his pocket running his fingers over the plastic wrappings of two condoms he had acquired from his father's sock drawer. He took two in case one ripped or had a hole. He had stolen one from his father's drawer a month earlier to try on for size and to ensure he had the experience. He recalled nervously taking it out of the wrapping and giggling over the strange smell and shape of it. He remembered how awkward it was peeling the rubber back over him and how creased it had got. After an age of tinkering, he was satisfied the garment was fitted correctly and looking down at himself he felt like a man. Now the time had arrived for real he felt very nervous.

Patricia walked along Gresveney Road. It was quite a small road with a meandering and uneven footpath. She found it difficult to keep her feet in her mother's heels, which she wore. She knew the road so well and yet it seemed so different in the falling dusk. The road was lined with small maple trees that cast shadows along the footpath and prevented the fullness of the remaining light from reaching the concrete. Patricia found herself stepping over the dark fingers that the branches through onto the path. Thick and thin crooked fingers that seemed to claw at her in the developing evening breeze. She felt a little frightened. Her stomach felt tight. Whether it was the eerie surroundings, or where she was going and what for, that frightened her. She took solace in the fact that she would be at her destination, in the arms of Billy, in five minutes. The light was fading at an alarming rate. The few streetlamps that were scattered randomly along the road came into life and illuminated the spectral images further. She found herself staring over her shoulder after every two or three paces. Paces that had increased in tempo. Although, the faster she tried to walk the harder it was to keep her balance. She could see the lights of the entrance to the park shining like beacons in the darkening night. She felt relieved to witness their presence. Then suddenly, as she stared over her shoulder behind her, she noticed two bright lights slowly engulf her. The headlamps of a car. The car travelled unusually slowly and deliberately towards her.

Patricia grew alarmed,' *Oh no! They are slowing up beside me.....* *They've seen me....It must be Dad!'.*

As the car drew up along side her she saw it was not her father's car, in fact it was a small van. The window lowered and a young man leaned his head out.

'Excuse me, I seem to be lost. Could you point me in the direction of Slough?'

He was quite broad with short-cropped hair and she noted that his accent was certainly not English. But he smiled and seemed polite, so she told him the directions, but all the time she felt his eyes piercing her. He made her feel uncomfortably uneasy. When she had finished, he still seemed vague but smiled again and said, 'thank you' and drove off. She watched the red rear lights move away and then watched as the lights arced around a left turn.

Right at the junction ...not left

She muttered to herself. A left turn would take him back into town. She laughed and thought to herself that the man obviously hadn't been paying enough attention to her directions. She felt partly unnerved and partly to blame for maybe not being clear enough.

He was creepy though!

She shuddered and felt her stomach churn repeatedly faster. She moved closer to the park and passed under a large oak tree that blocked almost all light and made it positively lethal to walk under. As she moved under it she saw something move to her left. She wasn't sure what it was, but it seemed to be a shadow or a small animal. Her heart pounded. As she moved to the side of the pavement before crossing the road she looked to her left and saw it. It was the van parked up at the side of the road. It was motionless and had no lights on.

She wondered if he had crashed, the way it was parked, but felt far too frightened to step near it. She kept one eye on the van and one eye on the road as she crossed it.

Then from seemingly nowhere the young man stepped out of a shadow and almost bumped into Patricia. His eyes seemed vacant. Fear spread like a virus over Patricia's face. He apologised and said sorry, but still stood motionless blocking her path. She gave a terrified smile and stepped out onto the road to move around him.

As she moved past his shoulders he turned and grabbed her, one hand over her mouth and the other round her waist, dragging her in the direction of his van. She tried to scream but his grip was so tight. Like a vice biting a steel block into place. Relentless pressure.

His fingernails dug deep into her cheeks. She felt her skin tear and a burning sensation ensued as the surface capillaries were gauged open. She tried to kick and fight but couldn't, even though he was reasonably young, he was too big and too strong for her slender frame. She was helpless. She sobbed and reluctantly was thrown into the back of his van. She crashed with a sickening thud onto the metal floor and the vehicle rocked with the force with which he had thrown her

She screamed loud but it was a solitary scream. He followed her into the back and closed the door and all was suddenly silent.

Billy thought he heard a scream, but listening he heard no more. He checked his watch. She was 10 minutes late.

It would be a further hour and a half before Billy decided to go home. The moon cast a silvery glow over the river. Billy watched its reflection shimmering in the cool waters. The park was silent and still, apart from the odd scurrying of the nocturnal wildlife which called it home. It was the first time Patricia had ever let him down. He thought that she must have been caught sneaking from the house by her father who was renowned for his strictness. Although, to the back of his mind he pondered whether it had been a step too far too soon that had prevented her leaving the house. Whether she was just too frightened to go ahead with such a commitment. Whatever the case, he felt dejected and partly worried for her. He thought about going around to her house but noted that it was probably better to wait until the morning. He convinced himself that there would be a perfectly feasible excuse as to why she hadn't met him. Nevertheless, the journey home had been a depressing and sombre one.

When he got home he was startled to find Patricia's fathers car parked in his drive. *What's going on?* As he turned his key in the door he was faced with his father looking very irate along with an equally irate Mr Stevens.

'Where have you been?', his father shouted.

'And where is Patricia?', Mr Stevens added.

Billy looked bemused at the second question.

'Well, you should know, you must have kept her at home', Billy said puzzlingly.

'Her mother took a cup of tea to her room almost two hours ago and found that she wasn't there.', Mr Stevens snapped.

Billy was perplexed by the statement.

'Are you sure she wasn't anywhere else in the house', Billy looked concerned.

'Of course!!, Where is she?, Has she been with you?', Mr Stevens' patience was wearing thin.

'I came straight around here when I found her missing. It's not safe for a girl of her age to be out at this time of night. What have you been doing? I know she's been with you her room stinks of her mother's perfume!, so I know she wasn't seeing one of her girl friends'.

Billy looked confused and tried to comprehend what was being said to him.

'I was supposed to meet her at 9, but she never turned up.', Billy grew frightened.

'What do you mean?' Mr Stevens voice raised an octave.

'I waited for over an hour. I assumed she couldn't get out', Billy said. He began to shake. Where was his beloved Patricia?

'Well, she got out alright!, where were you supposed to meet?', Mr Stevens calmed slightly.

'At the park', Billy mumbled. His head was full of visions he didn't care for.

Then without a word of warning he turned and ran out of the door. He was going back to the park and from there retrace her steps back to her house. Maybe she had fallen over and knocked her head or twisted an ankle. She would need help. Billy ran all the way. His heart pounding deep in the back of his ears. He searched everywhere. He covered every inch of the park. He visited the knoll and searched all around the hedges and borders of the river. He searched the riverside path that she skipped along so many times. He wandered up and down Gresveney Road. He could hear his father and Mr Stevens calling out her name in the distance, but Billy remained silent. He was dumbstruck. Sweat dripped from him as though he had contracted a tropical fever although he felt cold. Ice cold. His body ached and he shivered through the chill. Upon rounding every bend in the road, he prayed he would see her walking towards him. He would run up to her and wrap her in his arms. But he knew it wasn't going to happen. He could sense she was in danger. That she was hurt and that she was not close-by at all but was being taken from him. The only bright light in an otherwise haunted lifetime was being torn from him. He could feel her pain and fear.

Close to midnight Billy slumped down onto the curb outside the park, only yards from where Patricia had been so innocently snatched hours earlier, and he sobbed. He sobbed uncontrollably. He shouted out her name hoping she would peer round the corner with her smile. She didn't. Billy was terrified. For that moment he was probably as terrified as the nightmares made him- if not worse.

<hr />

Three weeks had past and Patricia had never been seen again. Billy had long since gone into deep shock and hadn't muttered a single word since the second day of the investigation. He sat staring out of his bedroom window. He looked gaunt and frail. His hands shook uncontrollably. He would let out a murmur once in a while, but it was too quiet and distorted to be recognised as words. He wouldn't eat or sleep. He just sat in the same chair looking out the same window at the same corner of the street. As though expecting Patricia to come strolling around it. All the fingers had been pointing at him. His mother fell ill with worry. She collapsed when it was first suggested that Billy could have been responsible for Patricia's disappearance. She knew how they were together. How special the relationship was? They were far too engrossed with each other to even spare a single moment with thoughts of causing harm to each other. Now she watched with sorrow over the fragments that remained of her son. The real Billy wasn't in there. He'd gone. She knew she'd lost him. For that she could never forgive herself.

DS Goddard who was directly in charge of finding Patricia, had quizzed Billy for hours. Shouting awful things at him. Trying to put words into Billy's mouth. He painted a scenario of what he thought had happened. Billy felt sick. Nausea raced within him like a clockwork mouse. He knew exactly what Goddard was trying to do but all Billy's efforts and explanations to persuade him different were in vain.

Billy stressed with every cell of his heart just how much he loved Patricia and that he could never, ever, do anything to hurt her. He sobbed uncontrollably and loud. He banged his fists on the table. The table shook violently, and a cup of water flipped and showered down onto the tiled floor.

Goddard had stood up and his temper frayed. He began to raise his voice over Billy's sobbing and Billy gradually quietened. Goddard had shouted a question at Billy. He repeated it, 'Did you ever go to an acting academy Billy'. Goddard hadn't believed a word Billy had said or been taken in by his emotional display.

'You've got her, or have you already killed her Billy?'

'What was it...?....Wouldn't she let you get into her knickers ..?.. So you thought you'd take her anyway....only you were so forceful..... that maybe you held her too tightly round the throat...?..Or maybe she screamed so loud that you had to hit her...?..Is that what happened Billy?' Goddard anxiously paused.

The Scream. Of course. Billy thought for a moment and remembered that he thought he heard a scream on that evening. His stomach fell. It was a scream. It was Patricia's scream. He could hear the shrill cry echoing, again and again, inside his head. He immediately realised that it had happened just metres from him. He could have saved her. It was his entire fault.

Billy began to shake.

Goddard stared at him still waiting for a reply. Billy's eyes looked vacant. They were swollen and blood red from all his spilt emotions but deep inside they were sole less. Goddard's tone lowered and he grew concerned.

'Billy?.....Billy?..'

He grabbed Billy by the shirt and shook him. Billy continued his stare. Billy's thoughts were swimming with clouds of dark green mist. Everything seemed so distant. Just out of arms reach. He grabbed at objects as they hurtled passed him. He was being sucked into a deep abyss. A huge black round abyss. He could see the entrance calling for him to enter.

Hypnotic.

Magnetic.

A figure stood huddled over the edge. Billy rushed closer. The figure seemed deformed in some way. Even from afar it felt a powerful force.

Slipping.

Spiralling like a spider being sucked down into a plug hole. The green mist gripped him like the water would. Under both arms. Escorting him towards the chasm.

As he got closer he saw the figure. It turned out of the darkness. It was human, just, but its head seemed almost detached from its body. As he got closer the macabre picture painted itself. A collection of taut tendons and a thick ridge of skin and tissue were holding the head onto the body. Its neck was open, and it seemed like a pink and blue flower tried to sprout from within. A rotting, diseased flesh flower complete with the fragrance of death. The figure was smiling.

White teeth.

Brilliant white.

Separated by thin strips of black. The black widened as Billy rushed closer. The figure lifted up one arm. Billy noticed it had a silver case attached to its left wrist. Then Billy could hear what it was saying. In a contemptuous strangled harmony.

'Time to go Billy.......Time to go...'

'Time to go Billy...Time to go'.....

The speech became distorted as Billy reached the edge where his hasty travels abruptly paused. He was alongside the figure. It stared at him with dark deep Stygian eyes. A grunt led cackle came from its lips.

'Boy you have changed...'

'You never had a chance did you little man...?'..

It lifted the case higher. Billy stared at it, vaguely recalling the object but the longer he thought the longer he dismissed that he had seen it before. How could he? He certainly didn't own such a case and his fathers work case was black leather, not silver metal. All this considered, Billy still found himself drawn to the case, like a moth to a flickering candle. He faintly recalled the case being related to death. He pictured the clasps being opened and lid ajar. Billy suddenly felt extremely cold. He felt as though he was sat in deep drifts of snow. Pain ached throughout his body. Almost numbness but an underlying throb beat against it. He could taste the bitterness over his tongue. A vile, narcotic taste.

The figure shuffled its feet and lowered the case, nonchalantly raising its other arm and offering an open palm pointing in the direction of the darkness.

'Time to go now....'

'Gotta catch a train...'...It laughed deafeningly.

Billy could feel the rhythmic bump of the train. The smell of death. That cold death train on that freezing January evening. Billy began to understand. Only be it much too late.

'Good job I sampled the goods before we got on the last one together.....', laughs..,' otherwise I certainly wouldn't be here now',. Its laugh reverberating around Billy's head.

Although it felt as though Billy's head was separate from his body. He found himself looking down on himself. His body stood looking limp and extremely fragile.

Terror.

A void.

The distance between him and his body grew greater, almost ten feet. He became alarmed.

His body was intact, complete with head and all. It looked different than usual. Less strong. But it was definitely himself. So, who was he? How can he look at himself if his eyes belong to the body beneath him?

Five metres separated them.

The figure stood next to his body and looked back at him. Smiling again. It placed an arm around his body and squeezed Billy into its side. But he never felt a thing. He was separate from his body.

No feeling.

No smell.

No Taste.

He wanted to scream but couldn't. He tried but the option wasn't available.

He scrambled hard against the force that drew him away from his body, but it was relentless.

Ten metres.

Darkness was surrounding him. He saw the figure still smiling now looking down at him. It started to sing.

'*We'll meet again......don't know where...*'

It turned and began to walk away.

'*don't know when....but I know we'll meet again ...some suuunnny dayyyee.*',

The final words still echoed seconds after it had sung.

Then complete darkness ensued.

Silence.

Three whole weeks of mindless torture, sat in the chair and Billy Adams, sixteen and a half years old, gave up. He took a last look at the street corner and then passed away silently. His heart gave up the chase. Less than a month ago it was so strong and complete. Today it was broken and empty. His mother found him. She noticed he was dead as soon as she laid her eyes upon his ashen, blood-starved face. She dropped the bowl of soup, which she had brought for him, and had raced over to his motionless and cold body. He was still sat in the same position. Still staring at the same place. With what seemed to be a smile on his face. She hugged Billy's body tightly in her arms, pulling him deep into her chest. She kissed his mop of hair and rocked with him. She had lost her baby. She began to wail. A terrible heart broken wail, which echoed around the room and terrorised the ears of those that heard it. She stared at his vacant face and the smile. A relieved and painless smile. The nightmares for Billy Adams were over.

But somewhere, for someone, they would start again.

Man is what he believes......

Anton Chekhov:

Those who cannot remember the past are
condemned to repeat it..........

George Santayana:

CHAPTER 5

Bristol, England, 2130 Hrs, 4 July 1996

Frank Christie was sat perched on a barstool. The bartender, Chico, apparent due to the large rectangular nametag hanging above his right nipple with the name Park View Hotel dotted underneath it, delivered Frank's order. He knocked back his fourth straight Jack Daniels and continued his surveillance of the room. He knew there was an American convention staying in the hotel for this week and knew that they would all be out partying this evening. With it being Independence Day of course. He also assumed that there would be an abundance of intoxicated women to take advantage of. His last assumption was incorrect. As he eagerly surveyed the room, it seemed most, if not all, of them were paired off or in large groups. He tried to establish eye contact but was truly unsuccessful. In fact, his gaze and sickly smile were returned with looks of disgust and repulsion.

Frank was not a pretty face. He had a bad receding hairline, which he blatantly attempted to cover up by brushing his hair forward. This gave his head a very spherical look. He had broken his nose countless times and it seemed to jut out to the left, which didn't help his cause. He also had severe pox marks, the scars of very bad acne as a teenager. He tried to disguise it by wearing stubble, but the whiskers didn't grow in the scarred areas and the white lines in the beard were more so pronounced than if he'd remained clean-shaven. But he did try. He tried so hard. He knew that tonight wasn't like every other night. Tonight, if he could just buy a woman a drink he knew that she was going to be his. That she would want him with a passion and eagerness like she had never wanted a man before.

He had already booked a room. Room 212 on the second floor. A large double room with drinks cabinet and of course the king-size bed. Not that he thought that drinks would be necessary at that stage, but he thought he may actually need one if he managed to pull this off. He had been so thoughtful and sentimental. Everything was planned to his precision. The final piece to the jigsaw, however, was for the moment eluding him. Not to mention the fact that the powder felt as though it was burning a hole in his pocket.

He had witnessed the strength of the drug himself. He had been present in the room when Marco or 'The German' as he was known to be called in the underworld scene, had displayed the wondrous drug in action to Mr. Kimasatu, a Japanese associate. As usual the exhibition had gone to plan and those present were suitably impressed and astounded. Marco had made a cool $1, 000, 000 in half an hour's work. Frank had packed the 2-kilo bag into Mr. Kimasatu's luggage case and passed it to one of his heavies. Kimasatu oozed respect as for that matter did Marco. Marco however was brasher. He held all the cards. Kimasatu knew it and secretly detested the fact. If the drug hadn't been such a success he would have had Marco taken out, that was for sure. But it had thrived. The demand was trebling each day. A shipment like this would make him a 400% profit. After all money is power and all his clients were powerful men.

Frank was amazed at the effectiveness of the drug. He, of all people, could see that the market for it was huge. He had been with Marco for almost two years. It was good money. He occasionally had to get blood on his hands but then that was the business he was in. Part and parcel of the trade. It was different in the olden days. Frank had been in the business since he left school. Working off his gambling debts and funding for his heroin addiction. That was when Jimmy Dent had ruled the roost. Things were harder then. He didn't have complete control. There were various factions splitting from Jimmy and setting up on their own when Marco came onto the scene. He quickly quelled the probable rebellion and stamped his authority by 'concrete booting' Jimmy and throwing him into the Severn estuary. He made his feelings felt and everyone worked for him instead of with him. Mostly, through sheer terror. Since Marco had perfected what he called his 'Beneficiary', the money was pouring in. Frank treated himself to a 5 series BMW convertible. It was a dark blue model and slid through the city like a silent blue shadow. But it hadn't helped his cause. He needed a woman. He had never picked up a woman himself, not a good-looking woman anyway. He had been through all the local 'bikes' that would drop their knickers for anyone who bought them a pint of Guinness. Most of them didn't wear any though. That wasn't difficult. He wanted someone stunning. Pert breasts, firm body, long manicured fingers, long flowing soft hair. All the attributes that he had never sampled before. The 'bikes' had been the complete opposite.

Now he had the chance of a lifetime. Last night he had delivered a shipment to Filton airport. The shipment was not a large one, just a sample package, a 'taster', albeit an expensive taster at that, broken up into 10 small 2-gram bags. Frank resisted for nearly the whole half-hour long journey to the airport but on entering the car park slipped one of the bags into his pocket.

They wouldn't notice. It's only a sample. They wouldn't know how much gear was in a sample would they? Besides this client was a first-time buyer, he wouldn't know exactly how much he was getting as a sample surely....

A couple in the car park, one male one female, had met him as planned. Both of the couriers wore smart business suits and were very well spoken. Frank had been somewhat surprised. He was used to dealing with sixteen stone skinheads or Italians. He watched the couple climb into a metallic green Mercedes convertible and spin away at speed from the car park. Frank smiled. He surmised that the couple were probably pretentious Yuppies, maybe from London, that required the drug for a typically Yuppie party, where something new and obscure was always regarded as one-in-the-eye for other pretentious associates. He pictured them passing the drug around at their party. He laughed wishing he could witness the aftereffects not only for his amusement but also because the woman in the suit was particularly stunning. He would have loved to see her in action. Having met the couple, he was glad he had summoned enough courage to slip a pouch of the drug into his pocket. He was convinced they wouldn't miss it. They hadn't even checked the package in the car park. He could say the shipment was intact on exchange if, later, they complained of being shorted. Frank was on a high and almost couldn't wait to dispense with the evidence. But it was late and the type of woman he was looking for would not be readily available at that hour.

Frank pressed against his pocket feeling the slight bulge under his touch. He then scanned the bar again.

Nothing.

Not even a smile.

Frank ordered another JD. Chico responded with a smile and turned towards the optics. Frank pulled out a twenty from a wad of what must have been close to £300 and threw it onto the bar. As the twenty settled, lying up against the drip tray, the door to Frank's right opened. The sudden gust of wind fluttered around the edges of the twenty making it seem to shiver. Frank turned on his stool. There were two of them. One blonde, one brunette. Both exactly what he was looking for. The blonde had party streamers wrapped around her neck and tangled in her hair. Weaves of red, white, and blue. They staggered up to the bar. Tripping into it. Laughing. That terribly girlish laugh. The brunette seemed more sober and apologised in a strong Virginian accent as the blonde almost knocked Frank off his stool. They were American too.

'That's OK'

'It was my pleasure!', Frank laughed sheepishly.

He pleaded with himself not to become shy. This was the opportunity he had been desperately waiting for. They seemed to be together with no boyfriend or husbands in tow.

Be careful Frank. Don't blow it!

The JD arrived on the bar.

'Wow JD!...that's my drink', the blonde leaned right over into Frank's face then stepped back when her eyes focused on his skin.

She proceeded to stare at him as though he was some sort of circus freak.

'Can I get you one?', Frank opted for the pincer movement.

'Sure ..Thank you', the blonde replied.

She swayed to and fro as though being rocked aboard a boat and still tried her hardest to focus on Frank's face.

'Marylou....Don't you think you've had enough?', the brunette posed the question.

They looked seriously at each other for a split second and Frank's heart missed a beat.

'Naaarrhh!!!', they both sang in unison.

'What can I get you?', Frank eagerly interrupted their fit of giggles.

'Do they do cocktails?' the blonde retorted, then they both exploded into a fit of giggles again.

Chico handed Frank a cocktail list and winked at him. He knew Frank was in with a chance and to some degree that solitary expression from Chico eased Frank's nerves.

'A Harvey Wallbanger for Jo and I'll have a long slow comfortable screw...', again they laughed.

People began to notice them at the bar. Frank had to be quick. Having paid Chico, he reached into his side jacket pocket and with his left hand prised open the top of the polythene bag. He was prepared for the moment when his chance would come.

The cocktails arrived complete with umbrella and the statutory fill of ice. They both lunged at the straws, and both took long gulps of the liquid.

'I need to pee...', Marylou whispered just loud enough for Frank to hear.

'You be OK on your own for a minute?', she nodded at Jo seeking permission. She got the customary nod and Marylou headed off to powder her nose.

Jo seemed less forward. She obviously hadn't drunk as much.

'You got a smoke?..', she asked Frank.

He gestured by slapping his pockets that he hadn't, then realised he shouldn't have and hoped he hadn't spilt the powder into his pocket lining.

'There's a machine just out in the lobby by the men's toilets?', Frank saw his opportunity was close.

'Thanks...', she turned and walked to the door.

Frank quickly put his hand in his pocket and into the bag. He felt the powder collect in his hand.

'Save our drinks for us...', she turned back and almost gave Frank a heart attack. Chico was restocking his shelves and it was the ideal situation for Frank to spike the drinks.

Frank smiled and with his other hand dragged the glasses closer to him.

'Don't worry they are safe with me', Frank realised that he had put on an American accent and that by the reaction on her face it was perceived as extremely corny. He felt himself blush. He saw her exit into the lobby. He checked around the room to ensure he wasn't being watched. Checked Chico. Then lifted his clenched hand and first sprinkled the powder into the Harvey Wallbanger then into the Screw. He watched as the powder fizzed for a second then blended into the hue of the liquid. *Hope that was enough.* He placed his hand into his pocket for a second reassuring measure when Chico stood up and faced him again. He relaxed his hand letting the powder fall out of his grip. He slowly pulled his hand out of his pocket and immediately rubbed off any tell-tale residue from his fingers with his other hand.

Frank felt a bead of sweat trickle down his nose. He was sweating profusely. Now he had to wait. Jo returned with a packet of red Marlboro. She tapped out the first one and offered it to Frank. He declined. She lit it with a match from the house boxes that littered hotel rooms these days. She took a long drag then exhaled a large cloud of blue grey smoke.

She then took the straw into her mouth and took a mouthful of her drink.

No instant reaction.

It had taken about ten minutes when Frank had witnessed it. He checked the time.

'Where's Marylou?...Better go find her', Jo walked off in the direction of the ladies room.

She was gone for almost seven minutes before they both reappeared and headed back towards him. Marylou looked a little ill. Her face was pale and the effervescent nature to which she had entered the bar had all but disappeared. She took a large mouthful of her cocktail without using the straw. She retched as she drank the liquid, but it was obviously a more pleasant taste than the bitter sickly one before it. Jo also removed the straw from her glass and took two large gulps of the cocktail. Marylou followed suit; the colour still not completely returned to her cheeks. Jo swilled the remainder of her cocktail around the glass. The ice tinkled and toppled into the liquid. She then lifted the glass and finished the lot. Frank was pleased to witness the fact. She stared at the quickly depleting Marylou. She was bleary eyed and swayed against the bar. Her face seemed to hold a light shade of green as though she was again close to vomiting.

'I'm going to have to take her up to her room..', Jo said.

Frank's heart sank.

Ten minutes were up.

Nothing...

'Do you want me to give you a hand?', Frank played his final card.

Jo looked different. Her eyes seemed glazed, and her cheeks suddenly flushed.

'Errrm...OK...'.

She fidgeted uncomfortably.

It was working, Frank recognised the signs.

Frank got up. Swigged the last of his JD and helped her with Marylou.

They used the lift.

He noticed Jo looking at him. She licked at her lips, trying to moisten them. She was noticeably shaking.

'Second floor', Frank noticed.

'My room on this level as well.... fancy a night-cap', Frank dived straight in.

'Yes...', she replied breathlessly.

Frank felt nervous. This had been what he had dreamt about and now it was really going to happen.

He looked at her. She looked incredible. She stared at him. He noticed her breasts, now visible, through her white blouse. They were not hugely large but were ample and extremely pert.

Frank saw Marylou slump to the floor of the lift. Her knees rose to her chest and apart. He noticed her left hand working its way under the white fabric of her knickers. Her eyes were closed. Her head leaned back and her back arched as she pushed her fingers deeper into the visible white triangle. She started to moan. Everything was happening a little too quickly for Franks liking. He was desperate to get them into his room and out of the public's eye.

The lift announced they had arrived at the chosen floor with a soft chime and the doors slid apart.

Frank grabbed Marylou by the arm and lifted her to her feet.

She removed her hand and started to move her fingers along Frank's body. Over his biceps and down his stomach to his trousers. He wrapped one arm around her and gestured with his other for Jo to come with him.

They reached the door.

212.

Franks searched his trouser pockets. Where was the keycard?

Finding the plastic. Fumbling. Sliding the card up and down in the electronic lock to no avail. He spun the card around the other way and slid the plastic down the slot once more. The red LED quickly changed to green, and the door was flung open. Frank sighed.

They stumbled inside. He led Marylou to the bed and pushed her onto it.

Jo followed and sat on the edge.

She was panting and holding her right hand up against her chest as though in unusual pain. Subconsciously her body tried to fight the effects of the drug but failed with miserable results.

Frank watched for a second, he felt more at ease now they were in the privacy of his hotel room. He smiled and began to get incredibly aroused. He felt as though he was going to explode.

Marylou's hand had again disappeared under her skirt. She writhed on the bed.

Jo watched her wide eyed and longingly.

Frank started to unbutton his shirt.

Jo lay back alongside Marylou and began to fondle her own breasts.

Squeezing them together gently and then squeezing her nipples with her thumb and forefingers.

Frank couldn't believe this was happening to him. He felt in a haze.

There he was stepping out of his trousers watching two beautiful young ladies playing with their bodies.

Marylou removed her hand from under her skirt and turned on her side and leaned over to Jo, kissing her full on the mouth.

Jo responded breathlessly.

Marylou's hand raced down Jo's body over her now swollen nipples and down to her navy-blue wrap skirt. She tugged at it opening it wide.

Frank watched in amazement as Marylou grabbed at the thin black lace knickers that protected Jo's crotch. Forcing them down to her ankles eagerly assisted by Jo.

The drug was strong. Both girls lost all their inhibitions. Whether they had been in a situation like this before Frank did not know but they certainly felt at complete ease with each other's bodies.

Jo removed her blouse almost tearing the buttons with the desperation to expose herself.

Marylou followed suit and as Frank removed his shorts Jo was completely naked and Marylou just had her white knickers still half attached to her.

She was bent over with her head bobbing and swaying between Jo's legs.

Frank approached the bed.

Marylou's backside wiggled invitingly at him.

He pressed himself up against Marylou's rear. He could feel the warmth emanating through the cotton.

He reached down and touched her.

She pushed herself back into him.

Moaning.

Jo's moans were getting louder as Marylou's tongue toyed and teased her.

Frank felt incredible he knew he wouldn't last long.

Already he could feel an orgasm rushing upon him.

He grabbed Marylou's panties and lowered them down over her curves.

He guided himself to the warmth.

Ecstasy.

Frank's deep moans reverberated around the room as the warmth slid all the way up to his stomach. No resistance and so incredibly soft.

Frank moved really slowly at first, resisting the urges of what his body craved.

He slid in deep.

Feeling her encompass him. Wrap around him.

Softness.

He pushed deeper, throwing his head back.

He couldn't resist much longer.

Jo's moans grew louder and more irregular.

Frank wanted her. Badly.

He ushered Marylou further along the bed.

Frank looked down at Jo.

Her body open and welcoming.

He guided himself into her and pushed deep and hard.

She gasped and he felt her tighten.

Harder and faster.

Her body writhed.

Her moans muffled as Marylou pressed down harder on her mouth.

Frank felt the sudden rush of his orgasm approaching.

He lifted her legs to go even deeper. His head swimming. He felt his lower abdomen tighten.

The moans grew so loud none of them heard the door open.

Frank orgasmed long and deep shortly afterwards. It was only then that he sensed someone stood behind him.

He turned quickly to be met by Standt and Nielsen.

Standt was smiling, his eyes covered by round mirrored glasses, but his facial expression said it all.

Frank was speechless.

He panicked and also felt a little shy at being so exposed.

Standt unbuttoned his long black trench coat.

'Marco's not happy with you Frankie boy'

Nielsen moved around to the side of the bed getting a better view of the spectacle before him.

'Very nice...Very nice', he muttered his approvals.

The women oblivious to the situation continued regardless.

Frank began to sweat profusely in the uneasy silence that followed.

'I can exppplaain', Frank stuttered.

He moved away from the bed back towards his clothes, which he had flung against the far wall.

'Can you Frankie...can you really?', Standt reached into his trenchcoat.

The muzzle of his micro-Uzi appeared closely followed by the rest of the weapon.

'There can be no explanations Frankie...save your breath....it will be your last..'

Standt raised the muzzle and he let off a short burst into Frank's chest, throwing him back into the drink's cabinet.

Frank tried to move but the life was slowly seeping from him just as the orgasm reached Jo.

Bright red blood pumped out of his fatal chest wounds for almost ten seconds. The fountain of thick gore gradually abating to a seeping bubble. Then it stopped, as Frank's body lay dormant. He lay crumpled against the cabinet. His arms twitching uncontrollably as his bowels emptied onto the thick pile carpet.

Nielsen still unmoved watched the women closely.

He grabbed Jo's right nipple and squeezed so hard she screamed with ecstasy as she orgasmed again.

He laughed as he reached into his bomber jacket and pulled out his deer footed Bowie knife.

With two swift movements of the wrist both girls' carotid arteries were ripped open.

They had released their final gasps of pleasure and died almost instantly.

Standt searched Frank's clothes. He found and removed the half-emptied bag from Frank's jacket pocket.

Standt and Nielsen nonchalantly turned and left silently as they had entered.

CHAPTER 6

There were no complaints from other sleeping customers that night. No one disgusted by the moans and squeals of pleasure. No one stirred by the reporting of the Uzi. No one spotted the unwelcome visitors to room 212. All seemed perfectly still and normal.

The maid had arrived at around 10 a.m., doing her normal daily routine. Unlocking the doors. Wheeling her trolley with all the condiments necessary for the next guests or fresh ones for present customers. Small sachets of soap, shampoo, conditioner, after-shave balm, complimentary perfumes and various other bathroom accompaniments all lined her trolley in regimental fashion. A large black bin liner hung loosely to the side of her trolley for the often tarnished and stained sheets and towels.

She opened the door to 212 and immediately sensed that all didn't seem right. She could smell the cordite still hanging pungently in the air. Within seconds she had been confronted with the horror that littered the room. She acted bravely though. Within two whole minutes she had quietly alerted the front desk. No screams. No panic. No racing through the lobby shrieking 'Murder!'. Although by the time the police had arrived she had lapsed into a state of shock and had to be immediately sedated.

The whole floor had been taped off and evacuated as DI Jack Mitchell entered the scene. He was 39, around six-foot tall, stocky with the height, with short cropped black hair. His face bore scars of pain and anguish. He looked drained. He flashed his badge at the officer on guard at the floor entrance, ducked under the tape and strode along the corridor. He had been with CID now for almost 6 years and in that time had witnessed some horrific sights. What met him in room 212 was no different and he remained unmoved by the carnage. A woman PC sat outside the room with a colleague. She shakily held a cup of hot tea. She was deathly white obviously disturbed by witnessing the aftermath.

Inside the room was full of uniform, photographers and even forensics had beaten him there. He spotted the Super across the room.

Craven was giving orders to one of the uniforms. The Sergeant nodded his head and proceeded to remove all the surplus officers out of the room.

Craven loosened his tie as he saw Jack approach him.

'Nice of you to make it Mitch!!', Craven spoke in a sarcastic manner.

'Sorry boss had a rough night', Jack replied.

'You aren't the only one', Craven moved aside and looked in the direction of the cold bodies that lay exposed on the bed.

'What have we got?', Jack tried to become enthusiastic.

Craven sighed..

'Two women. American over here on a convention. Both with their throats slashed. No signs of force or resistance. The sad creature over there is Frank Christie. Several shots to the chest. Close range. He's got form as long as your arm. In and out of Wandsworth and Dartmoor. Possession, ABH, GBH, theft and most interesting dealing.' Craven paused for a moment whilst scanning the room.

He then straightened himself up. Pushing his tie back into the opening of his collar and fastened his jacket buttons.

'I've got to go and try and contact the Yanks and explain what's happened here. I'll let you wrap this up. Dr. Helen Thompson is IC. of the paths. Liaise with her and I'll send Briggsy over when I get to the station'.

With a pat on his back Craven left telling the photographer to get snaps of everything.

As he put it, 'I want to be able to recreate this scene like we were part of it. So, get on with it.'

Craven had the knack of leaving everyone confused. He bellowed his encrypted orders and disappeared back to his safe office as usual.

Jack was used to it. He had worked with Craven for almost three years and had grown used to his methods and ways. Most couldn't.

Jack saw the doctor stood over Christie's body. He made towards her. She was dressed in the familiar white noddy suits of the pathology department.

Her hood was down, and Jack could see she had a long silken mane of black hair. Although it was tied up with what looked like three or maybe four hair clips, the way it stood out from the rest of her head it was quite apparent as to the length of it.

As she looked up and saw Jack walking over to her, he noticed how her dark red lips stood out warmly from her pale complexion. Her eyes were big and seemed like huge pools of sapphires catching the light and giving off their sparkle.

Jack lifted his badge up into the glow and introduced himself.

Helen looked him up and down and instead of introducing herself began,

'He was killed first...', she pointed at Frank Christie's dormant body.

'Probably around midnight..

No sign of a fight which suggests that either he knew the killer or that he was startled by him..

Five bullet wounds to the chest and one to the side..

Very clean entry and exit wounds which suggest high calibre probably automatic or semi-automatic due to the grouping...

All shots were fired while he was still standing...

We have a good bullet that we pulled from the wall that has been bagged and can be sent to ballistics...', she paused.

Jack stared at her. He certainly couldn't doubt her professionalism. A face void of all emotion. Jack stared at her lips beckoning them to curl slightly at the corners and produce a smile. They didn't. Straight and only slightly trembled when she spoke.

'Anything else?', Jack asked.

Jack noticed the slight tinge of red appear to her cheeks and she spoke..

'Yes....erm....it looks like traces of semen or vaginal fluid around his penis and pubic area which in my opinion suggests that he was interrupted either shortly after or during sexual intercourse.'

Jack wanted desperately to smile aware of how uneasy her last statement had made her. She had explained it so articulately whereas Jack would have probably adopted a cruder explanation. He bit his lip and just replied, 'OK...that would explain the lack of clothes on all the bodies then..'

'What about the women?', Jack continued.

'Well....', she stood up. Jack noticed that she was quite small to his frame. Only 5'4"...5'5" max. He then found his eyes on her breasts. He watched hypnotically as they gently juggled underneath her suit as she walked to the bed. Considering the suit was quite baggy, he assumed her breasts were quite large, which puzzled him for a moment as just to how large they actually were. When Jack looked up her eyes burned a hole into him. A look of anger on her face. Her brow was furrowed. It was apparent that she had noticed Jack's stare. She spoke immediately and quickly as though wanting to get this over as quickly as possible.

'Both suffered deep lacerations to the neck.

The blonde seems to have the deeper wound and would have died within a minute.

Lost a lot of blood, quickly. Almost certainly a severing of the carotid artery.

The brunettes cut was not as clean, and she may have lasted for maybe five minutes due to the spread of blood within close proximity of her body. Maybe only nicked the artery but enough to immobilise her and cause her to bleed to death.

The brunette has traces of dried semen around her vagina the blonde at this point doesn't....but we will know more when we get back to the lab.', she seemed less embarrassed the second time.

Jack looked quizzically over the women's bodies, 'Time of death?'

'Around the same time as him', she replied.

Jack nodded.

'Thanks....When can I expect a report?'

She looked at him in disgust.

'Tomorrow...hopefully...looks straight forward but then I'm very thorough', she retorted.

'Ok..thanks.

She turned and headed for the door.

Jack looked around the room trying to picture the scene moments before the disturbance occurred.

He stood in the spot where the gunman must have stood to have slain Frank and then looked around him. He stared down at his feet and then around the surrounding area, trying desperately to visualise the picture. He let out a long deep sigh. The motive was obvious at first glance. Frank's track record had obviously reappeared and had got him into someone's bad books. Jack had witnessed several gangland drugs related murders and this one appeared no different although, the brutal slaying of the two women perplexed him. It was not unusual to find a wife or lover, or even prostitute, murdered along with the gang rival, but not usually innocent citizens. Although, drugs related, and territorial crimes followed no necessary chains of logic. From the professionalism and manner of death of the victims Jack could sense that this was the work of a major player. This wasn't small-time. This was big. It wasn't brought on by someone pimping or pushing in a designated area, a harsh beating was usually the prescription for that. This was the work of someone with power. The judge, jury, and executioner with power over life and death. Jack knew he was dealing with a big fish here and he knew he would have to tread on toes to find the answers.

Marco leant back into his leather chair. He raised his glass and took a large gulp of his finest cognac of which he received from one of his French associates. Standt and Nielsen stood before him. Silent.

Marco placed the glass down and raised his eyes to his disciples and spoke.

'I'm glad you solved our little problem so efficiently...', he smiled.

'It does pain me to think that my employees and associates are so easily lured away from my loyalty.....I do hope the message will be clear now....If it is not make it so..', he sighed lethargically.

'I have no patience for anyone who so much as even contemplates ripping me off...they shall all suffer the same terminal fate!', he added to strengthen his plea.

'Now...news!', he spoke more brightly, sitting forward in the chair. His eyes flickered over his two main men.

'I have been in contact with an associate of mine. It seems a certain DI Jack Mitchell has been assigned to the case of finding the killers of Frank Christie'.

Standt smiled.

Marco continued, 'It is inevitable that he is going to be snooping around the clubs and snouts.... Make sure the dealers are well briefed.... This man is special.'

Standt's smile dropped, he recalled the name.

'Remember the name..Jack Mitchell...he will try to hound you out...', he paused.

'He will be coming...you can bank on that!', Marco's smile widened.

Standt and Nielsen both looked puzzled.

'We're ready for him!', Neilsen laughed.

The smile dropped from Marco's lips.

'No....', he paused.

'No, you're not....not yet'.

Neilsen frowned and turned to see the reaction of Standt. Standt stared vacantly into space, emotionless.

'This man is different from the rest...', Marco added noticing the confusion painted across Neilsen's face.

'In what way?', Neilsen puzzled.

'He will have no fear of destruction...', Marco replied hastily.

'Fear of harm or death is the telling factor in a man's armoury...It causes mistakes to be made....It causes apprehension...failure to rely on gut instincts...it will stop you dead at that crucial moment...and dead will be the operative word...', he smiled.

Neilsen was still confused. The whole discussion had developed into something of an abstract riddle to him.

'I know that you are good boys, loyal and think you have no fear of dying. But at that moment when you realise you have an even chance of dying, believe me fear will burn a hole right through you and you will panic and try to hang on. Jack Mitchell has no fear whatsoever!..He would let his body slip away from him..', Marco clicked his fingers, 'just like that... and not even give a shit'.

'He has a tortured soul...', he added.

Standt stood open mouthed, and Neilsen gulped noticeably.

'Do not underestimate him.....'

There was a long pause.

Neilsen spoke quietly.

'How do you know him? You make him sound superhuman. He's only a fuckin pig!!'

Marco breathed deep through his nose. His nostrils flared in correspondence to Neilsen's ignorance..

'I've known of him for a very long time. All I am saying Mr Neilsen is to tread very carefully. You have been faithful to me and I respect that, but I fear for your lives. He is not only 'a fuckin pig' as you so eloquently put it.'

Standt looked worried. He was privy to slightly more information than Neilsen and he began to understand just who DI Jack Mitchell was.

Neilsen looked perplexed but did feel the stirrings of fear causing effervescence in his stomach.

'What do you want us to do?..Kill him?'

'NO!!!....don't even try...leave him to me...just put the word around and go about your business as usual. I will tell you when to act...but not yet...I want him closer to me...', Marco seemed to thrill at this thought.

'We have a score to settle.....', Marco nodded at Standt.

An uneasy silence followed.

Then Marco seemed to come to his senses and got back to business.

'This afternoon...push this to Tommy at the Pravada club', he threw them a bag with the powder in it.

'I'll contact you when I need you to visit me again'.

Marco picked up his glass and spun his chair around, the hint for Standt and Nielsen to leave, which they did without another word.

———•◆•———

Briggsy stared at the bodies. The colour drained slowly out of his cheeks and his legs noticeably buckled. Jack caught him with a chair just in time. Briggsy lowered his head down above his knees. His cheeks puffed out and he tried hard to control the retching in the back of his throat. Jack patted him on the back and said,

'Welcome to CID Briggsy.....I'll meet you in the car. Just going to talk to the maid.', Jack turned and left with a smile on his face. As he reached the door he heard Briggsy empty his breakfast over the floor, followed by the screams of displeasure from those around him.

Jack's grin broadened.

Briggsy was a nice enough lad. The coffee-boy of the team. He only looked about 23..24.. a flyer. He had not been in city uniform like Jack. His route of entry was through University, endless boring lectures, and legislations in a warm safe lecture theatre. It didn't prepare him for the cold harsh dangerous reality that he now found himself in. Of course, he had served his probationary two years walking the beat in a small well established town centre, where he would have had to deal with drunks and marital disturbances, maybe even the occasional week-end knife-attack. But bullet fatalities and severed heads were not, till now, part of his experiences.

He had been with the team for about 3 months but had not been a great success. Jack felt a little sorry for him. He was at the butt of many mindless jokes about his weight problem and also his neat side parting. Jokes he didn't appear to take too well. He hadn't mastered the art of the counterattack and for that reason would always remain an easy target. He certainly had the stereotype Superintendent look about him. He was slightly overweight, and his head was very neatly organised into various segments of hair but none of those things worried Jack. It was his inability to stand up for himself and from that his competency and confidence in the job appeared to suffer as nobody really took anything he said or did seriously. Jack knew what it was like to be picked on. He was bullied as a child. He was a loner and a highly intelligent loner at that. He figured that was the main reason why he was set upon. Jack was never interested in befriending his classmates, he considered them beneath him. They were immature and highly irritating. He realised at an early age that he had a gift. A gift which brought nightmares and downfalls with it. But ultimately it was a gift that in the fullness of time he had learnt to live with. He could see the intellect present within Briggsy. He could also spot the downfall signposts in his make-up. Briggsy didn't have the strong physique, which Jack possessed. That in itself frightened off would-by bullies and hecklers. Jack was naturally fit and had superior muscle definition that an athlete would be proud of. Briggsy was roundly overweight. His physique did not install fear into the on looking eyes. One guaranteed way of frightening off the bullies was to lash out at them. Something he couldn't honestly picture Briggsy doing.

Briggsy looked a little better when Jack got in the car. He was sipping from a plastic carton that smelled like stewed tea.

He had both windows down on the car although it wasn't the best of July mornings. The sky was covered in large puffs of white and grey cloud and the wind was strong enough to push a white Tesco's bag all the way along the street.

Jack looked at Briggsy.

'You OK?'

Briggsy looked embarrassed.

'Sorry about that..Sir.', his words tailed off as he recalled the earlier horrors.

'Its OK Briggsy....Bit of fresh air will do you the world of good... start the car and take a left at the lights.', Jack pointed along the road and fastened his belt.

Briggsy disposed of his cup neatly in the bin beside the car and then drove off in no particular hurry.

Jack sighed.

It took almost 10 minutes to cover the 2-mile distance across the city. Jack would normally take just over 5 on a good day, 7 at a maximum. As they turned into Slocombe Street, Jack told Briggsy to pull over to the right side of the road and switch off his engine. Jack peered through the windscreen. Briggsy looked bemused as Jack sat in complete silence just staring at the house on the corner.

It was a dirty looking terraced house. Its discoloured cream curtains drew a veil over the front window. The small plot of garden to the front hoarded a collection of common weeds and the grass was so long that it was beginning to bend over backwards on itself. Briggsy noticed especially the red door. It wasn't a nice scarlet or a deep crimson red. More of an industrial red. A bland metal-like colour. He noticed that it seemed to stick out from the rest of the house, as though it was fairly new and had replaced with an urgency rather than budget. Although in places the paint was beginning to flake.

Jack broke the silence.

'What time do you make it?'

Briggsy looked at his watch.

'One O'clock', Briggsy replied.

'Rovers are at home today aren't they Briggsy?'

'Don't know Sir...more of a rugby man myself..', Briggsy proudly stated.

Jack sighed.

'Wait a minute...There we go regular as clockwork...Stay here Briggsy..', Jack leapt out of the car.

Briggsy noticed the man exiting the house with the red door. He was fairly tall, stocky with an intentional severe lack of hair. He wore a blue and white football shirt and torn jeans. His right hand was covered in solid rings around his fingers. His left hand clutched to a cigarette. He took a deep draw and then exhaled quickly as he saw Jack coming across the road at him. He turned as if not noticing Jack and increased the tempo of his walk to a slight jog. He would jog a few steps then walk. Then he turned and disappeared down the alleyway between the two houses at the end of the street. Jack followed after him.

Briggsy felt uncomfortable. He wasn't sure whether to go after him or wait in the car as he had been told. He chose the latter. Jack Mitchell had a fearful reputation as one you shouldn't cross.

In the alleyway Jack had caught up with Den. Den waited arms waving anxiously at his side. The cigarette spiralling a red glow in the darkened surroundings. Den whispered angrily.

'What you doing here man?..I've told you don't come round here... Page me I'll get back to you straight away...I'm fuckin dead if anyone sees me with you...'. He obviously felt frightened of who might be watching or monitoring his visitors.

Jack apologised sincerely. Den had been his snout for almost 2 years now. He knew him well and knew that he dabbled in lots of things but was harmless enough. It was the company that he kept at the Rovers games that interested Jack. After the match after a good win and several pints of ale, idle talk would begin to flow and Den usually remembered most of it. It was usually fairly reliable information too. For his reward he would get slipped the odd twenty here and there and Jack's promise that his house wouldn't be raided. Which probably swung it for Den.

'Sorry Den couldn't be helped. There was a shooting over in the Park View last night. Needed to catch you before you went to the game.'

'I heard it on the news just before I came out', Den acknowledged.

Jack sighed. The press seemed to get faster and faster these days with discovering crimes. Nothing could be kept in secret for too long. Jack knew from experience that the next two days would be difficult with the added press pressures. After a couple of days, the story would become old-hat and, as the cliché goes, wrapping for fish-and-chips.

'Keep an ear out for me?..let me know if you hear anything..', Jack reached into his back pocket and pulled out his wallet. He withdrew a crisp twenty and slipped it into Den's Jeans pocket.

Den nodded then brushed past Jack and ran out of the alley and on down the road.

Briggsy saw him racing away and panicked. He started to get out of the car and just contemplated giving chase when he saw Jack re-appear no worse for wear.

Briggsy eased considerably. He had worked himself to a frenzy sat there for almost 5 minutes.

'Do I go after him?...Do I stay here?'

The same two questions reverberated around his head the whole time.

Jack got back into the car. Briggsy stared feeling slightly annoyed. Jack looked back at him.

'You alright Briggsy?'.

Briggsy never replied and just started the car.

Jack smiled. He was enjoying the company. It was beginning to amuse him.

The smile disappeared when he realised Briggsy missed the turn into the station.

'You've just missed our turn?', Jack spoke in amazement.

Briggsy smiled and looked very smug as he said,

'Sorry didn't I say?...Control called in while you were out and said that Dr Thompson had requested to see you..', Briggsy stayed quiet.

'AND?....', Jack's voice raised an octave.

'And...that the report will take a little longer...there have been developments...that may take some time..', Briggsy finished.

Jack sighed, his longest and most drawn-out sigh of the day so far.

'Great...This is going to be a long day'.

CHAPTER 7

Standt and Nielsen strolled into the Pravada club around 3pm. They acknowledged Erik the rather large head bouncer. Standt and Neilsen were both solidly built around the six-foot mark, but Erik towered over them. He had the long flowing blonde locks and a twisted face that could so easily have belonged to his ancestors when the got into their long boats many centuries before. Erik held a dual role at the Pravada, in addition to being head of security, he also shared the role of bar manager with Tommy Ward, the owner. Erik was indebted for the additional responsibilities and trusts Tommy showed in him and repaid that trust with unbridled loyalty. Tommy had given him the chance that others hadn't. In truth, Erik actually controlled the day-to-day running of the club and, although his pay was at a respectable rate for a barman/ bouncer, it didn't reflect his truth worth to the business. Tommy preferred to pick up the bills, handle the promotions and ensure his guests and members were well looked after in his own special gregarious manner. Ordering and receiving stocks, staffing matters and the finite minor details that contribute to the successful running of a club, bored him. Erik proved more than capable in handling these tiresome, mundane matters. Tommy sank all his energy and exuberance into ensuring the club was full of the right '*kind*' of people and that these people '*spend big and party big*' within his establishment. A slogan perhaps that should have taken pride of place above the entrance door because

The Pravada's members certainly adhered to it in an unhealthily extravagant fashion.

Tommy was sat in the reception lounge, a wide dais, positioned in the centre of the club. Original plans had put the reception lounge into a dark recess at the side of the main lounge. The club architects had envisaged an area where special guests would be untroubled by the watchful and curious eyes of other revellers. Tommy had the plans redrawn to accommodate his vision. An area where his special guests, and himself included, would proudly be displayed, and promoted at the centre of everyone's attention. The lounge was minimalist in nature, with a large, oval metallic table commandeering most of the area. Tommy chose metal for its reflective qualities. The table acted as an effective reflector for the variety of strobe lighting around the walls and ceiling of the club and also had a clean, mirrored appearance to reflect the vanity of those sat around it. A luxurious padded white leather sofa surrounded the table in an arch formation. Tommy loved the smell and feel of leather. He was convinced the texture and virginal colour had an aphrodisiac effect on those that sat on it. He raised his glass in acknowledgement when he spotted Standt and Nielsen approach the lounge.

They climbed the two steps up to the dais and slumped down into the sofa beside Tommy. With a nonchalant swing of the hand, Standt tossed a small Cellophane bag, containing a whitish coloured powder, into the middle of the table. Tommy almost choked on his malt, and quickly grasping the bag, he stuffed it into the inside pocket of his jacket. He glared over in the direction of Erik, who fortunately hadn't witnessed, to his knowledge, the blatant exposure of the drug.

Tommy stood up. He was a small fat man. Overweight through over-indulgence and over-spending. His head shone in the lights. He had just two patches of red hair above his ears but with a large bushy moustache to compensate for the lack of coverage on top.

He stumbled down the steps and disappeared behind the bar into his back room. Nobody was allowed into his back room. Not even Erik. Erik had control over another room that fed off from the bar down to the cellar and a small office where he could keep up to date with his stock keeping duties and accounts. Equally this was Erik's safe haven and Tommy didn't often venture into this area, not that he wanted to anyway. Tommy's back room was the place where he kept his valuables and all his dirty money. Tommy resided within the club, which was deemed slightly unusual for a man with his reputation and money. He could afford to purchase an external property that would cater for all his needs and more, but chose not to. Tommy lived and died for the club. It was not his only business venture but was the one which he ploughed most of his inherited fortune into, and was the one which he held closest to his heart. His back room was his living quarters. He used the downstairs room as an office and had a bedroom upstairs. He used the club's kitchen to prepare all of his meals, when he decided to cook, which wasn't often. Generally, he would get his kitchen staff to prepare him a little something or he would, more often than not, eat-out or receive take-away food from the nearby Chinese or Indian restaurants. His little room was the hub of the club. His own private temple. Most of his life was hidden behind that door and all of his secrets with it.

Tommy reappeared minutes later with a plastic bag concealed under his right arm. As he reached the table he placed it down in front of Nielsen.

'It's all there....tell Marco..that if it is OK with him ..I'll take the same amount again in a fortnight', Tommy spoke with a cockney accent.

Standt stared coolly at Tommy.

'Aren't you going to try the Heaven?', Standt referred to the powder which had adopted the name amongst those honoured to receive it.

Tommy laughed.

'I trust Marco…besides…..... I've seen what it does to men...I made that mistake the last time..cost me £2,000 to repair the damage and have just got the regulars coming back after that fracas….'.

Tommy continued, 'I'm not the macho type.....I've got a party over here tonight....I've got two well known actresses coming over and a few other female celebrities that I intend on getting to know a lot better...', Tommy laughed louder.

'I'll distribute it a little more wisely this evening..', he winked in Neilsen's direction.

He shook excitedly and a bead of sweat trickled down from the crown of his head onto the bridge of his nose.

Standt shook his head and smiled. He picked up the bag and just managed with some coaxing to stuff it into his long trench coat pocket. The bag was half full of fifty-pound notes and the weight of it made Standt's coat sit askew across his shoulders. Neilsen stared in disgust at the sight before him. He detested Tommy. He detested the way he abused his body. He detested his lifestyle. But, probably most importantly to Neilsen, he just hated his face. Tommy held an annoying smile in response to Neilsen's stare. Nielsen leant over the table and grabbed Tommy's glass with his right hand. Tommy was startled and watched in amazement as Neilsen slowly raised the glass to his lips and downed the malt in one sharp, swift motion, then slammed the glass firmly back down onto the table. He returned the earlier wink then turned and walked away from the table.

Standt smiled.

Tommy looked amazed and alarmed.

'What is his problem?'

Standt stood up and just shrugged his shoulders and followed Nielsen out.

Tommy sat and examined his empty glass then dropped it back on the table.

He then smiled and rubbed his hands together at the thought of that evening.

He just knew that the midnight punch he was going to be offering would have a certain aphrodisiac quality to it. He smiled and skipped off behind the bar to make a few more invitations for the party. He often held private parties for members and select guests. The demand for these parties was huge and the few tickets that were available for non-guests and non-members usually sold at an extortionate price and were snapped up within hours. He had a reputation for lavish and wild entertainments and all those that attended left thoroughly contented.

———•———

Jack and Briggsy entered the Pathology labs and almost instantly came across Helen Thompson's office on the left. Helen was sat behind her desk. She was at her PC terminal. Her long slender fingers bashed at the keys in a rhythmic manner. Her eyes focused directly on the screen. She wore horn-rimmed glasses and the image from her VDU was mirrored across the lenses of them. She felt the presence of someone at the door and turned aside to see them.

Jack stood and offered a solitary word,

'Hi...'.

Helen removed her glasses and stood up. Her lips still bore no resemblance to a smile. She wore a white blouse. It was quite thin because Jack noticed the lace frills of bra cup etching itself into the fabric. She wore a knee length navy skirt. It wasn't too tight or too loose but with enough style to show off her curves.

She walked over to the men.

'Bad news I'm afraid...', she said apologetically.

'There have been a few complications...'., she threw on her clean white lab coat.

'What kind of complications?', Jacked interrupted.

She walked past them and continued down the corridor. The men followed.

She continued.

'We've found something we haven't been able to recognise yet..'

She opened a solid grey door that she had to put all her weight behind to budge. Jack and Briggsy followed her inside. The room was noticeably colder and had a distinct air of disinfectant. Jack turned to Briggsy and suggested that maybe he should wait outside after this morning's episode. Briggsy looked hurt and proudly stated that he was perfectly fine and would go with him.

The room was quite sizeable. It was exceptionally clean and very white in colour, almost blinding to the eye. There was the steel slab in the middle of the white tiled floor and a collection of metal and plastic instruments hung neatly on a stand in the corner. Briggsy noticed the electric saw, the large knives usually associated with a butcher, the pliers and grips, the rubber mallet and the metal tray housing the scalpels and other dentist like precision instruments. He felt his stomach turn again then looked away quickly.

Helen had walked over to the large workspace area. Jack was beside her.

'We found a form of narcotic in their blood streams and still in the lining of their stomachs..'

'Cocaine?', Jack enquired.

'No...that's the thing..', she seemed perplexed.

'We've tested it against all other known narcotics on our database and it just doesn't match to anything.'

'Maybe you need a bigger database...', Jack mused.

'We are networked to a 250 Giga byte system', Helen proudly stated.

'I can assure you that this drug does not match anything..', she looked perplexed again.

'So, what are you trying to say?', Jack still couldn't come to terms with the scenario.

'I'm saying..', she said obviously frustrated by Jack's inability to grasp the situation,

'.... that this is not Heroin, not Cocaine, not LSD, not Angel Dust, not PCP, not Ecstasy, not any strains of those previously mentioned or any slang name or other explicit terminologies you may have come across in your line of work...', she paused breathlessly,

'This is a completely new drug...', her words hung silently in the air.

'A new drug?...', Briggsy smiled.

'That can't be....', he added.

Helen stared at him. The smile dropped from his lips upon realisation that he had spoken without engaging his brain first. It was apparent he had questioned her judgement in a terrible manner without consciously meaning to.

'So, is it likely to be a commercially available medication, such as Prozac, Viagra or Rohyphenol, which has been abused for social misuse?', Jack frowned.

Helen shook her head already in anticipation of the question.

'No, our database holds the structures in fine details of all known medications and most research projects passed by the Medical board…this drug doesn't match any of them'.

'We are making further discreet enquiries at this point into recently proposed research projects but as yet have drawn a blank…I would say, considering the environment and conditions in which the drug was discovered, that this is a non-approved venture..', Helen sighed.

'Black Market..', Jack stated.

Helen nodded.

'A new and more powerful drug for the Millennium, probably with a devastating human response..if past experiences are anything to go by..', She mused.

Jack looked shocked. Neither spoke for a while. Then Jack posed a question in a suddenly far more sober tone.

'Well what symptoms does it give?'.

Helen reached up onto a shelf and pulled down a Petri dish.

'We don't know yet…We'll have to do tests…'

'The funny thing is that no traces of the drug were found in Frank Christie's body…just the two women…'.

Jack nodded knowingly. He was beginning to get the picture.

'So, it must have been something that he gave them to make them horny', he said crudely.

Helen stared at him.

'Frank isn't an oil painting. I thought it looked suspicious', Jack smiled.

Helen looked unamused.

She placed the dish in front of Jack and removed the lid.

'We did find grains of the drug in Frank Christie's jacket pocket though..and they match with that found in the bodies.', she sighed.

Jack stared down into the dish.

The tiny grains looked just like a discolouring of the plastic surround of the dish. Almost white in hue but with a tiny hint of blue in there as well.

Jack was tempted to wet his finger and taste it to convince himself it wasn't coke or dust.

Helen must have spotted the glint in his eye and quickly whisked the dish away.

'We have to do extensive tests..', she said.

'I can't put a time figure on it ...it is just something that we just have to wait and see on..', she looked waiting for response from Jack.

Jack puffed out his cheeks.

Briggsy looked more perplexed than anyone.

Jack thought for a while.

'Anything else to report?'.

Helen shook her head.

'No that is all for now.... we are in the middle of a few tests and I'll let you know when there are new developments....', she almost smiled.

Jack nodded and expressed his gratitude before turning and leaving, closely followed by Briggsy.

Jack was deep in thought.

Having finally accepted the fact that this was a new drug, he tried to think of who would be able to get their hands on it, especially as it obviously had marketable qualities.

The conclusion he drew from his thoughts were not favourable.

It was as he thought ....something and someone big. The manufacturing costs alone of a drug of this nature must be huge. The people behind this must have money. Large amounts of money, which inevitably is directly linked to power.

He and Briggsy had been thrown in the deep end here. Jack thought the killings were especially merciless and brutal but this latest addition to the scenario made the case even more serious than he first imagined. He had to report this dilemma back to Craven.

A report that Craven wouldn't wish to hear either.

So much for the quiet life.

It had been a hell of a day.

It still had 7 hours left to run and Jack knew he would witness all of them.

They got back to the car and returned to brief Craven.

———◆———

Nielsen thumped the machine firmly on its side several times and then gave it a kick before he took a stool at the bar and sat down behind his pint. He drank cider in the summer but only the especially strong variety. If it was less than 6% proof he just wouldn't entertain it. He sat and stared back at the fruit machine. The three yellow bell fruits winked at him invitingly. He could never understand how these machines knew that you had no change left. He toyed with the idea of changing a note to teach the bastard a lesson. The satisfaction of seeing the flashing, cocky, jubilant display transform into overdrive and empty its guts into the tray below. The lights flashed inviting him to take a chance. Nielsen just wanting to kick the shit out of it. He only had fifties left in his wallet and thought that changing that into some coins might draw undue attention to himself.

Not that everyone wasn't glancing at him from the corner of their eyes anyway.

He let out a deep breath through his nose then turned to see Standt replacing the receiver on the payphone in the bay at the corner of the bar.

Standt came over to the bar and sat down beside Nielsen.

He lit a cigarette.

Then spoke.

'We are out tonight...'

Nielsen knew exactly what that meant.

Standt's voice lowered to a whisper.

'I'm over at Tommy's ...... Marco doesn't like the way that he is abusing his gifts..', he paused while the bartender approached and went by.

Then continued,

'Apparently, his parties are the talk of the town...getting too public....I've got to keep an eye on things...', he spoke seriously.

'You've got something else on tonight...I'll tell you about it in the car.', Standt closed the subject at that juncture.

Nielsen smiled. He loved his work.

He raised his glass and finished the final dregs of his pint. It was as his glass was to his lips he noticed the machine begin its flashing routine.

He lowered the glass staring wildly at the sheer insolence of it.

In a swift action, as he stood up, he hurled the empty glass straight into the face of it. It shattered on impact spraying fragments across the carpeted floor and the table beside it. But still the lights flashed. The bartender ran out into the bar. He looked in astonishment. Nielsen stared at him and the bartender stopped still in his tracks slipping slightly on the carpet.

Nielsen turned and swaggered calmly to the door only to slam it open testing the hinges.

The bartender stood agog as the door rattled back into place and he stared around at the other three equally bemused customers. The bar was silent. The only movement from an otherwise still picture was the shimmering kaleidoscope of lights darting through its demonstration routine.

———•———

Craven couldn't come to terms with the scenario either. He had to personally check with Dr. Thompson himself as to the validity of what he had been told.

He seemed stunned when he got off the phone.

'Ok Jack I'll get you some support on this...I'll clear it with the Chief...', he paused and scratched his head.

'If this is as serious as I think it could be...we could have major problems here.....I shall obviously have to inform Vice and the DLO on this..

I want you to shake down all the known dealers, pushers and users and see what they know...anything at all..... I'll get you some extra men...'.

Jack left Craven's office and ushered Briggsy over to the coffee machine.

'I want you to compile me a list...', Jack spoke slowly to ensure Briggsy understood the seriousness of his orders.

'I want all the names, addresses, hangouts, etc., of all the heavy-duty pushers and users on record in the area. Especially related to class A ....as quick as you can Briggsy it is urgent...I've got a few people I can see so I'll leave you to it..ok..', Jack issued an anxious tone.

'No problem Sir..'.

'Oh, and Briggsy....Keep it under your hat ...Ok.?.', Jack took the car-keys from Briggsy's desk and left Briggsy to it. He didn't envy him. Jack hated the research part. Typing endless searches into a terminal. Not his idea of policing. He preferred to work from gut instinct. His instincts told him that something was going to happen and soon.

Briggsy however enjoyed being sat over a keyboard and actually compiled the list within three hours. A feat that would certainly have impressed Jack.

———•———

Jack felt refreshed a little. He had returned home briefly for a shower and a change of clothes and the pungent smell of dried sweat and death had been removed from his body.

He got to the Blue Lagoon at around 8 pm.

He pushed open the door and entered the dark smoke-filled room.

The bar was almost open space. It smelt very musty, and dampness hung in the air.

The place was almost empty. Not surprisingly. Jack couldn't understand why anyone in their right minds would choose this bar for a social occasion.

However, he knew Charlie would be here.

He was sat up in the darkest corner oblivious to his surrounding. His face lit up as he drew on his reefer.

Jack sat down opposite him. It was then that Charlie realised who he was.

'Jack!...you aren't here to bust me are you?...there's hardly anything in this man...here try it.', he pointed the joint at Jack.

'Charlie...I want some info...', Jack waited for a response.

Not getting one he continued.

'There is some new gear on the market....a powder...know anything about it?', Jack posed the question.

Charlie took another draw on his fag.

'I've heard something about that...yeah...supposed to be wicked gear...', his voiced croaked as he retained the smoke in his lungs for as long as possible.

'Heard it does incredible things....not that I'll get any of it at that price....ridiculous money...only the fat yuppie business geeks can get a piece of that action...', Charlie took another draw.

'Who pushes it?', Jack grew impatient.

Charlie laughed aloud then quietened his voice.

'I don't know...', he toyed with the ash around the sides of the ashtray nervously.

'Who told you about it?', Jack remained calm.

'Hey man...I don't remember...what's with all the questions...It's doing my head in..', Charlie grew agitated obviously uneased by Jack's line of questioning.

Jack felt his patience break and stretched across the table and grasped Charlie round the throat pushing him back against the stone wall behind him.

Charlie squeaked like a trapped mouse. Flailing wildly to loosen Jack's grip but to no avail.

He held his hands up.

'Ok....OK!!', Charlie managed to speak.

Jack loosened his grip and returned to his seat.

He sat and glared intently at Charlie.

Charlie rubbed his neck tenderly with his nicotine-stained fingers and laid his cards on the table.

'A friend of mine heard on the vine that Tommy Ward was having a little party tonight at his club....£250 a ticket...this gear,...Heaven.. they call it, ..was going to be involved....He's known Tommy for a while and asked me if I was interested in going..', Charlie laughed.

'How he thought I could get hold of 250 quid is beyond me..'.

Jack thought, trying to recollect the name.

Then it came to him.

'Tommy Ward....runs the Pravada club..?'.

Charlie nodded.

'But you didn't hear it from me....apparently Tommy says it will be the party of the century!!', he laughed again then had an unhealthy coughing fit in which his lungs seemed to be gasping for clean air.

Jack left unnoticed by Charlie as the tears streamed down his cheeks from his coughing spasm.

The fresh clean air was an instant relief to Jack. He returned to his car. It was fast approaching dusk but at least he had now found something to work on.

As he sat and reviewed this new information his radio burst into life breaking the silence and startling Jack momentarily.

It was Briggsy. Apparently Den had called in almost an hour ago and said that he had a name for Jack. He wouldn't discuss the matter with Briggsy and requested that Jack met him at the usual place at 830pm.

Jack's eyed sparkled at the news. He turned the ignition and screeched away in the direction of the old mill.

Briggsy asked if Jack needed him, to which the reply was negative much to Briggsy's disappointment.

Jack glanced at his watch. 835pm. *Be there Den..Wait for me..*

Jack shifted through the gears, darting around traffic, having countless close shaves to which he received shaking fists and numerous horns.

He got onto the old bypass and headed towards the black silhouette of the old mill in the distance.

He turned off the road and entered the winding gravel driveway up to the building. As he approached the side of the building, he killed his lights.

The place looked silent and quiet.

He sat in the car and stared for a while. It didn't seem right. Normal practise was for Den to appear from the darkness and dive into his car.

He waited.

Surely Den hadn't left already. He checked his watch. 8:42 pm.

He waited, staring anxiously at the building.

He felt the flutter in his stomach. Something wasn't right.

He reached over into his glove compartment and drew his 9mm Browning from its holster then stepped quietly out of the car.

The door to the mill was slightly ajar. He slowly and gently pushed it open which to his amazement made no sound. Considering the mill hadn't been used for probably almost half a century, and that the only reason it hadn't been reverted back to rubble was because of its age, Jack expected a slow and drawn-out groan as he pushed it.

He stepped inside.

He paused waiting for his eyes to become adjusted to the darkness then moved further inside.

The place seemed not dissimilar to the bar he had been in previously although it had more of an earthy smell.

He stopped silent.

Listening.

He thought he heard something.

Waiting.

He walked further inside, almost into the centre of the room. He heard a creak. His hand grasped his pistol tightly. He could smell a distinctly familiar smell. It was the odour of blood. Fresh, pungent blood.

He heard something groan. His eyes peered through the darkness trying desperately to focus on the contents of the room. He heard the groan again.

He felt a presence to his left side and turned instantly raising his gun towards the noise.

In the light that shone through the door he could just make out a body suspended in the air. As he walked closer to it he recognised Den's twisted and contorted face.

He was attached to a beam by a rope around his neck. The rope groaned under the weight that it endured. His body hung loosely below. The rope groaned again slightly as it gently swirled around under the weight.

Den swung round to face him, and Jack noticed that his chest had been slashed open.

Blood covered the whole of his upper torso. His top half was naked but for the blood which seemed to clothe the front half of him.

Jack slowly lowered his weapon and felt immediate guilt.

Den obviously asked too many questions. Listened to the wrong conversations.

Whichever name he had obtained, had certainly ensured that he would keep it to himself.

Jack took one last look at the grotesque feature in front of him.

He returned to his car and called in.

CHAPTER 8

Standt had arrived at the Pravada at around 730 pm. Erik had been surprised to see him and although he wasn't on the guest list, he let him in anyway. The party had already started. Tommy was sat in his recess entertaining and was far too busy to notice Standt's entrance. He was laughing and leering and joking much to the discomfort of his guests, but Tommy knew that would change later. He had a redhead to his left sipping champagne from a tall flute glass. A blonde with what seemed like her partner to his right.

He ogled blatantly down the cleavage of her low-cut dress, much to the disgust and annoyance of her partner.

A blonde and a brunette then appeared from the ladies and joined the table.

Standt took a position by the fire exit at the far side of the club.

He leant back into the shadows and watched and monitored Tommy's behaviour.

The club was beginning to fill out.

Everyone seemed well attired. Marco had told Standt to dress up but even so with his slacks and tweed jacket Standt still felt underdressed in comparison with the Armani, Lagerfeld and Gucci that flaunted themselves around him.

Standt noticed another famous face approach Tommy's table. This was one Standt new. He probably watched her on television 3 or 4 times a week. One thing that Standt loved was soap operas. Even if he was out on a job he would make sure that his video was programmed to tape them for him. He knew it was her immediately from a distance but as she got closer she seemed different to on TV. More tartily dressed. She wore a thin long black figure-hugging dress that had two slits weaving up her thighs exposing white flesh above her stockings. It was also very apparent that she was bra-less. The dress obviously wasn't very supportive as her breasts bounced and wiggled as she made her way around the table shaking hands.

Standt was very disappointed. He liked her in the soap for her prudish naive behaviour. That really appealed to Standt. He liked the virgins and probably had one a week. With the help of Heaven of course. He fantasised about her a lot.

He felt cheated but curbed his disgust and anger and continued to watch.

The mill was now engulfed in a silver-yellow mix from portable lighting, which had been put in place, and the headlights from a number of police cars that now occupied the scene. A green tarpaulin shield was mounted up to prevent those on the road catching a glimpse of the activities inside.

Helen had arrived very promptly to the call. She examined Den's torso on the ground. His body had been relieved from its tourniquet, albeit far far too late. Den's face looked blue in the lights. No hint of colour in his cheeks. His lips were swollen and cerulean. His eyes bulged from their sockets. The look of sheer pain spread graphically across his bloodied face.

Helen puzzled over his torso looking very closely at the wounds. She produced a fluid from her bag and sprayed it onto Den's chest. Taking a cloth, she very gently and slowly started to remove the excess blood from his chest.

The longer she rubbed at the blood the clearer the picture became as to the nature of the slashes.

She stopped and dropping the cloth to her side stood up and turned towards Jack. Her eyes ushered him over to her.

Jack saw her eyes overt her gaze to the torso of Den's body at her feet.

He followed her gaze and for a moment couldn't quite make out the symbol viciously etched into his chest. Then it hit him like a medicine ball to the ribs. Folds of sliced skin and tissue carved a swastika proudly across him, stretching from his kidneys to his shoulders.

Jack felt himself stumble; his legs were like lead. All the thoughts racing through his head were ones he had never seen before. Explicit recollections of wartime Germany.

He pictured the uniforms.

Remembering the smell. A smell so foreign it was difficult to describe. I suppose it was *a foreign smell*. Certainly not one expected with the British.

He felt the bump as the truck caught a pothole in the road and then threw him forward as it ground to a halt very rapidly.

He could smell the brake fluid, smell the dirty exhaust fumes rising under the canvas at the rear.

He heard the shouting. The driver and another. All in German.

He understood it.

He looked down at himself and realised he was wearing the uniform too.

Helen grabbed Jack's shoulder,

'You OK?.....DI Mitchell', she shook him gently.

Jack suddenly regained a clear head. He didn't like the visions he had just witnessed. They were getting so clear and explicit these days. He was concerned for his sanity and thought that maybe the symptoms were that of pressures of work, although, work had never bothered him before. He certainly was not the flappable, oppressive type.

'Yes I'm fine', he eventually stated.

He removed his eyes from the swastika but still found the image burning into his pupils.

He felt a fear. A very deep and violent fear.

The party was being to swing. The band had finished its terrible session and the trustful DJ was now belting out the tunes.

'I'm too sexy for my shirt' was being screamed out of the speakers.

Energetic females and the macho men began strutting around the dancefloors. The men occasionally squeezing their packets as if to say, *'Come and get this baby!!!'* and flexing their muscles. The women pushing out their breasts running their hands down their bodies seductively and giving teasing stares and winks to the men, thinking to themselves, *'Just look at what you can't have!....but I'm going to tease you with it anyway!!'*.

Standt felt amused but continued to watch to see if it developed.

The song finished and was faded into 'Relax' a promiscuous classic from Frankie goes to Hollywood. Standt smiled. Tommy was certainly trying to get everyone in the mood.

The dancing and writhing on the dance floor continued but still remained innocent.

Standt looked around the rest of the party. Tommy was leaning over the soap star whispering in her ear. To which she began to laugh uncontrollably and pushed Tommy away.

Tommy lit one of his large Cuban cigars, his trademark, and gestured with his hand to a passing waitress for another bottle of champagne. He was loving every minute of it. The band had returned in a change of clothing and looking freshly showered after their very poor renditions of all girl bands classics. 'Eternal Flame' was particularly shrill and flat.

Tommy noticed them immediately. He leaned across and gave all four of them an appreciative hug and poured them a glass of champagne.

Standt stared at his watch. 10:20 pm. He thought Tommy must make his move soon.

Just as the thoughts had left his head, Tommy beckoned over a waitress and spoke in her ear. She headed off immediately towards Erik, who received the instructions and nodded back in Tommy's direction.

Erik raised his arm and caught the eye of one of his boys over by the games room adjacent to where Standt was sitting. He was suddenly engulfed in lights as the room was illuminated. Standt quickly stood up and headed out of the spotlights and into the crowd around the bar.

The games room was usually occupied by two pool tables and a couple of fruit machines but not tonight. The pool tables had been pushed one at each side of the room and a white cloth thrown over each of them.

On the table to the left of the room was a large punchbowl full of orange liquid and floating pieces of fruit. Surrounding the bowl were neatly laid tumblers, all in straight rows and columns.

To the right of the room, the table had the same articles except the punch was a light blue in colour but with seemingly more pieces of fruit.

Standt smiled.

Of course!

The DJ faded out Madonna's,'Like A Virgin' and made the announcement.

'Ladies and Gentlemen, ...If I could just have your attention for one moment please...', his mic gave off a piercing cry from feedback as he lifted it from its holder and made out with it from behind his system to the empty side of the stage.

'Firstly, I'd personally like to thank you all for making it a thoroughly enjoyable evening for me, but I know that your host.... Mr Tommy Ward...would also like to show his appreciation'.

Tommy, by this time, was already at the stage and stepped up to receive the mike His arms stretched out in the hope of silencing the clapping and cheering audience.

He waited, smiling broadly.

'Thank you....glad you are enjoying it....Well...', the clapping stopped.

'Thank you all for coming...by way of appreciation I have laid on free punch over in the games room....', Tommy pointed at it.

'...but before you party animals all dive in there and down the lot.....', riotous laughter ensued.

Tommy outstretched his arms again.

'The chef tells me they taste like the fruits of a Caribbean island but with a kick that'll knock yer pants off...', Tommy broke into laughter. If only they knew the truth in the statement.

'The Orange punch....which the chef fittingly calls Pour Homme...is for the men.....The blue one is a fruity more palatable taste for the ladies which he fittingly calls...Blue Silk......', Tommy raised his arms again.

'Now you don't have to move anywhere..... our waitresses will be bringing a glass around to you'.

The waitresses had already filled trays with glasses of the punch and were distributing them by colour to the respective sexes.

Standt watched closely.

He saw one blonde almost down her glass in one and take another.

Tommy continued.

'Once the punch has all gone...I'm going to go mad and call a free bar!!!', Tommy shouted above the cheers.

The waitresses were rushed off their feet. Tommy returned to his seat where the girl band, a selection of bimbo's and the soap star sat surrounded by the glasses of blue silk. They all sipped it appreciatively.

Tommy raised his glass of Pour Homme...a posh name for a Brandy and Rum fruit mix. Which he gulped frantically. The music started again.

'Roll with it' by Oasis pounding out from the speakers.

Standt moved back to his seat when the lights went out in the games room. It was going to happen soon. Standt became more alert and prepared himself.

Jack sat in his car, the door open and a refreshing cold wind rushed over him. He was trying to regain the senses, which he had momentarily lost. He couldn't understand or appreciate the images that had flashed before him. Every time he thought about it, the pictures, sounds, and smell washed over him. It was so explicit and detailed. He likened it to the nightmares that he had from a very early age. Terrifying visions. Visions he couldn't comprehend then and not dissimilar to the one's he had just witnessed.

He felt weak and could smell his perspiration beginning to encapsulate the interior of the car. He got to his feet and got away from the nauseating aroma just as Helen approached him.

'What happened in there?....you OK?', she seemed concerned.

Jack gave a nonconvincing nod of the head and replied,

'Yeah...Just seen far too much death lately.....I suppose it can even get to a seasoned pro like myself...', he tried to laugh but couldn't.

Helen sensed that Jack was keeping it to himself.

'Have you seen something like this before?...Do you know who did it?', she enquired further.

Jack looked confused by her questions.

'You don't want to know what I think...', he paused,

'I'm not sure what I know or who I know anymore...', Jack walked away more confused than ever now.

Helen stared after him mystified.

Jack found a spot yards away from the noise and commotion and sat down. The ground was wet, but he didn't even notice or care for that matter. He spotted a discarded can of Special Brew sat upright about twenty feet away. He picked up some loose stones around him and proceeded to throw them one after the other at the can. The third hit and sent it somersaulting down the bank and it disappeared hidden amongst the long blades of grass. Jack began to rub at his temples. His head pounded. He had to get a hold of himself. Get back on track. Find Den's killer.

'You OK Sir?,' Briggsy was stood behind him.

Jack turned and saw beyond Briggsy, Helen staring down at them with an anxious look on her face.

'I'm fine Briggsy....This just doesn't make sense that's all', Jack felt a smile creep onto his face.

He stood up and let out a long deep sigh.

'Well back to the drawing board', he patted Briggsy on the shoulder as he moved past him.

Jack was far from fine. But until he could work it out for himself he certainly didn't need the psychoanalysis he was beginning to feel.

He smiled at Helen as he walked past her, and she gave a very nervous smile back. Something that Jack didn't finally realise till much later. It was the first time he had seen her smile.

Briggsy caught up with Jack at his car.

'I'm going to go home get some food and a shower. You do the same Briggsy we are going out for the evening. Dress smartly. We've got a party to go to!', Jack got in the car.

Briggsy looked confused.

Jack felt too tired to explain now.

'Just meet me round my place in about an hour...I'll explain on the way', Jack said.

Briggsy nodded his acceptance and just as Jack started the engine Briggsy tapped on the window. Jack wound it down impatiently.

'That list you wanted Sir...Do you want me to bring it over for you?...Problem is there is over 30 names on it, so I don't know how useful it will be', Briggsy crouched down to Jack's level.

'Oh yes...thanks Briggsy', Jack gave an appreciate smile.

He wound back up the window and longed for a much-needed shower. His smell wasn't helping his nausea.

As he drove away he happened to glance into his rear-view mirror and noticed Helen stood with her arms folded staring after him. He saw the look in her eyes. She knew he was hiding something.

———◆———

Standt noticed the first happenings about 15 minutes after the DJ had introduced Tommy. It was the blonde who had downed the first glass. She wore a skimpy cream dress, which was cut into her breast, revealing ample cleavage, and a length just below her bikini line.

She sat a few metres from Standt, but his view was unobstructed.

She was sat with one middle aged man, probably 48 or 49, but who looked fit enough to be passed as younger, and a youthful looking boy who must have been barely eighteen. Standt guessed they were father and son and that the blonde, who could only have been in her late-twenties herself, was his father's fancy-piece.

The man leant over and said something to the blonde. To which she lifted her glass and finished what looked like G&T. He grabbed the empty, and his empty pint glass, and stood up and headed off for refills.

Standt turned his attention back to the blonde and seconds later he saw the drug taking effect.

Her hands were first to react, they slowly and secretively lowered themselves under the table. Standt had a perfect view of what followed.

She started toying with her knee. Slowly circling her fingers around it. She shuffled in her seat.

Her dress rose higher with the shuffling revealing her tanned and shapely inner thighs. She looked around quickly to see if she was being watched. The paranoia made it even more intense for her.

Her hand started to slowly creep along the inside of her thigh. She continued to look around and Standt had to overt his eyes momentarily as she glanced in his direction.

Her legs parted slightly. Standt noticed she wore no knickers and also that she was not a natural blonde.

Her hand reached under her dress and Standt witnessed the sheer pleasure beginning to appear on her face. Her cheeks blushed with urgency.

Her body began to rock very slightly, and she no longer seemed to care who was watching.

Her rocking caught the attention of the boy who was eyeing up a middle-aged lady sat opposite who kept winking at him.

He stared at her. Smiled. Not knowing what was going on. She smiled back. An uncontrolled smile full of passion. Standt saw by her expression that she had let out a stifled moan.

The boy stopped smiling and, noticing her now more rhythmic arm motion, looked puzzlingly under the table.

By now her legs were much wider and her hand was moving faster all the time.

The boy seeing this sat bolt upright.

He looked pale. Shocked.

He looked around for his father but noticed him stood at the bar chatting to another woman. It was only a quick glance otherwise he would have noticed the woman's hand inside the zip of his father's trousers.

The boy turned back to the blonde. He felt confused then watched as one of her hands came up from beneath the table and began to squeeze her right breast.

Standt grew restless.

This was getting all out of hand.

Standt saw the middle-aged woman stand up and walk over to the boy. She stood behind him and began to stroke his shoulders gently rubbing his head with her breast. The boy didn't know what to do. Then she came around to his side and hitching up her dress straddled him. With one quick tug she lowered her strapless dress and pushed her breasts into the boy's face. The blonde watched and lifted one leg up over the arm of her chair. A small stocky guy strolled over to her from the bar and exchanging few words she lowered his head beneath the table.

Standt watched as the effect of the drug spread through the club like a disease.

He looked for Tommy. He wasn't in his seats.

Standt panicked. He stood up and scoured his sights around the club.

He spotted one of the bimbo's who was at his table but the guy who had her bent over it certainly didn't resemble Tommy.

He saw the door to Tommy's back room slightly ajar and decided to take a look. He made for the hatch at the near side of the bar and had just put a foot through it when a very well-built redhead grabbed at his jacket and landed her lips fiercely onto his. Standt felt himself go for his switchblade in his trouser pocket but thought better of it.

He took hold of her flowing red locks and pushed her back through the hatch with such a force she went spiralling to the ground.

Standt headed for the door. It seemed the bar staff had taken the night off or had found better offers elsewhere. All the security must have been guarding the front and rear entrances because Standt went through Tommy's door unopposed. He put on a pair of black gloves to hide his prints.

Inside was like an office. A large table with invoices and paperwork littered across the top of it. Standt heard the giggling and noticed a small set of stairs too his left. As he climbed them the giggling grew clearer, and the moans grew louder.

The upstairs was open plan and Standt could see Tommy before he reached the top step. Tommy lay naked on a huge king-size bed. He had the brunette from the girl band sat over his face and Standt's treasured soap star riding him. She was naked and her perfect body bounced and jiggled on him. She giggled as the brunette reached over and grabbed at her nipples and she returned the favour. Standt felt sickened.

He could hear Tommy's muffled moans under the relentless gallop that the soap star gave him. The other three members of the band formed a lover's triangle, all frantically exploring each other, and were equally oblivious to Standt's entrance.

He stood pondering for a second not knowing what to do.

His mind told him to kill them all, but his instincts got the vote. He marched over to the bed and pushed the brunette off Tommy. His face was deep purple and sweat and saliva gave it a shining finish.

He looked shocked to see Standt.

'We have to talk now, Tommy!!', Standt said it calmly but loud enough to be read as a command.

Tommy laughed nervously.

'I'm a little bit busy at the moment ..can't it wait?'.

Standt shook his head and grasped Tommy's shoulder trying to get him up.

The soap star shouted something at Standt. Something Standt didn't hear or chose not to hear as he felt sick just being this close to her.

She shouted again.

'Hey!!...Fuck off you!!'.

Standt snarled and in a swivel of his hips he delivered a crashing blow to her nose. She fell back off Tommy clutching it. Blood beginning to seep through her fingers.

Standt snarled again.

'Explain that to your bosses on Tuesday'.

He pulled Tommy to his feet and dragged him to the stairs.

Again, at the top, his instincts took charge and Standt raised his foot and rammed it firmly into the base of Tommy's spine hurtling him headfirst down the stairs.

Tommy crashed off every other step and lay crumpled on the floor at the bottom.

Standt watched for movement as he slowly descended the stairs. There was none. Tommy lay face down motionless. Had he broken his neck or knocked himself unconscious? Standt stared a little longer over him. He noticed the veins gently bulging in Tommy's neck. He wasn't dead.

Standt reached down and grabbing Tommy by the forehead with his clasped hands and firmly pushing the back of his neck with his boots, pulled on his hands. A deafening crunch was heard and Standt released his grip and waited for a couple of minutes until it was definitely apparent Tommy was dead before he left. Standt wiped away a solitary bead of sweat from his left temple and admitted to himself that maybe he had gone too far. Maybe Tommy deserved a slap and nothing more. Maybe his instincts had deserted him. But Marco strictly wanted to keep the drug under wraps and here Tommy was serving it up to around 50 women as a punch. What if some of the women didn't drink and witnessed the sordid unexplainable behaviour of the other women. Maybe they would feel so disgusted that they would tell the police or go to the press or both. Maybe they could have been attacked or raped by men who thought all the women were after it. What would have happened if the police raided? These thoughts raced through Standt's mind trying to convince him he had made the right decision. Standt still felt guilty. Tommy looked so harmless and pathetic.

When Standt entered the bar again, everywhere he looked, it was the same picture, naked flesh being abused. Standt quickly headed for the exit. As he reached the passageway to the stairs up to the exit, he saw two men stood over a woman. She was taking it in turns sucking and kissing them. Switching from one to the other. As Standt got within feet of them she stopped sucking and started to use her hands. Standt noticed her face it was old and wrinkled. She must have been almost 60. Standt saw the expression of sheer pleasure on her face just as the men started to shake violently and gasp aloud.

Standt felt sick. What had he got caught up in?
This drug was too strong it was unnatural and spelled trouble.
At that point he realised he had done the right thing killing Tommy and had to brief Marco of the occurrences that evening.

***

Briggsy had arrived promptly at Jack's place. He wore reasonably smart jacket, tie and slacks but still had a square look about him. Jack on the other hand looked good in whatever he wore. It was his strong features and physique that paled the attention away from his attire.

They made good time getting to the club but found themselves having problems with parking.

Briggsy made the comment,

'Hope they aren't thinking of drinking and driving!', his humour was not of Jack's taste and he remained silent even though Briggsy laughed in an irritating squeaking manner.

Jack abandoned the car in a nearby street. To which Briggsy noted the double-yellow lines.

Jack walked briskly towards the club, Briggsy having to skip a few steps to keep up.

They reached the door and were met by Erik and four other bouncers.

They all stood straight and firm.

'Got tickets?', Erik firmly stated.

His arms folded exaggerating his huge biceps beneath his T-shirt.

'No...I'm a personal friend of Tommy's ....He told us to come along..', Jack lied.

Erik sighed.

'Got the list Joey?', he turned towards one of the other bouncers and received a piece of paper.

'Name?', Erik continued still with an abrupt tone.

Jack thought for a second contemplating his answer. Then suddenly, the door to the club opened and Jack noticed a figure push past one of the bouncers and move off to his right. The bouncer shouted after him, but he moved quickly. It was Standt. Jack just caught a glimpse of the side of his face as he turned to cross the road.

'Name??', Erik repeated slightly louder.

'We won't be on there...I only got back into town this evening and heard about it from a friend who can't come because he's got flu.....Tommy won't be happy if he finds out you turned us away... and he will if you don't let us in', Jack was almost convincing in the offensive role.

Erik sighed again and re-crossed his arms.

'No ticket....No name....NO ENTRY', Erik remained firm, and Jack noticed the annoyance beginning to simmer in Erik's face.

Briggsy had listened silently for long enough.

'Ok then...', Briggsy adopted a mimicking voice.

He reached inside his jacket pocket and produced his badge.

Holding it into Erik's face like he had seen so many of his heroes do on the TV.

'CID and we ARE going into this club!', Briggsy smiled.

Jack sighed and looked in complete bemusement at Briggsy.

Erik laughed.

'Got a warrant?'.

He laughed again when he received no reply.

'What are you two?...Escaped from a loony bin?..Get out of here before I cement the road with your brains..', Erik uncrossed his arms and took a step towards them, closely followed in synchronism by the other bouncers. Jack didn't want trouble not that he wouldn't fancy his chance but couldn't risk Briggsy. He grabbed Briggsy and whisked him back to the car.

'What the fuck..did you think you were doing?', Jack bellowed at Briggsy.

Briggsy stared at the floor.

'Don't you realise that you can't flash your badge and expect to get an olive branch...not in this country...maybe Kojak can do it Briggsy but not here...Jeez...Don't say another word to me...not now..', Jack lost his temper.

He slammed the car door shut and sat inside. Now that Briggsy had blown their cover, even if Tommy did hold the drug, you could rest assured that he would get rid of it rapidly, on learning of Briggsy's blatant actions.

Briggsy got into the car completely silent. Jack almost immediately felt sorry for him. He was still very green. It wasn't really his fault. He blamed the training establishments for their cavalier, gung-ho approach.

He apologised for losing his cool, but they still remained silent for the journey back to Jack's house.

CHAPTER 9

Jack didn't sleep much that night, which wasn't really unusual. He suffered nightmares from a very early age and as the years went by they got more detailed and explicit, but Jack could control them and learned to get used to them. However, this evening's spectacle provided Jack with a missing piece from his jigsaw. A jigsaw that he had been trying to finish since the nightmares began. He was left with just a few more pieces to find but Jack was beginning to recognise its features.

He stared at the clock on the table beside his bed. 06:20. Jack watched the sunlight slowly flooding into the room, unveiling the identity of the previously shadowed furnishings, before he got up and showered. The warm spray of water on his face felt good. Refreshing. He felt safe once more. The fresh smell of the soap that he rubbed all over his body cleansed him. The fragrance of his shampoo and the lathers, soft under his feet, added warmly to the refreshment. He could have stood there for hours. Then he heard something.

He turned off the shower and listened. He heard the impatient purring of his telephone.

Jack jumped out the shower and almost slipping on the tiled floor raced to get the phone.

It was Craven.

Tommy Ward had been found dead at his club at 6 this morning.

Jack replaced the receiver slowly in shock. It seemed every person he tried to approach was getting killed or dying suspiciously. He was always one step behind all the time. It seemed as though someone was baiting him. Jack felt annoyed and frustrated. The anger smouldered inside him with an extreme volatile nature. Jack had never been second best in his life at anything and he certainly wasn't going to start now. He had maybe lapsed into a frame of contention lately and this was what he needed to put him back on track. A challenge. Well Jack felt the force of the thrown gauntlet and as he stared at himself in the mirror and deep beyond the stare, he knew he had accepted it.

⬥

Jack arrived at the Pravada club at 7:05 a.m. He was led to Tommy's back room and instantly bumped into Helen. She gave him a knowing look and continued with her work. She was running her hands over Tommy's naked corpse squeezing for broken bones. Concentration etched across her face. She looked so beautiful. Jack stared at her features. Her hair was tied up back from her face and it shone under the lights. Her face was almost as white as her suit apart from a faint tinge of red in her cheeks. Her lips stood out in a dark red lipstick that had been applied with the precision of an artist, especially for this early in the morning. Her short nose and curved chin gave depth to her facial structure and her skin looked so soft and unblemished. Her eyes sparkled like polished sapphires. There was no doubt, Jack felt attracted to her.

She looked up to see Jack vacantly staring at her. Her eyes melted Jack's knees. They were hypnotic and Jack had to fight to overt his stare.

He looked down at Tommy and swallowed.

'Can you tell whether he fell or was he pushed?', Jack asked without meeting her stare again.

'That could be irrelevant at this stage...', Helen replied.

Jack waited for her to expand on her statement.

'I can tell you this....he wasn't killed from the fall down the stairs. The snapping of the spinal cord occurred here in the upper vertebrae'; she turned the head gently so Jack could see the back of Tommy's neck.

'The bruising surrounding the break is not consistent. He has no other bruises or lumps around the crown or his forehead. He would have had to hit that part of his head hard to have broken his neck in this scenario. But...nothing..', she inspected the head again for Jack to notice how thorough she had been.

'Nothing...but he has bruising on his elbows and knees and also has a dislocated jaw. Which suggested to me he went down the stairs headfirst...like this', she bent her arms in front of her and pointed them to the ground and went down on her knees and leant over slightly. She began to re-enact the fall by pretending to bump down the stairs.

'Bump....Bump....Bump... then..', she acted.

Jack smiled she did look in an uncompromising position.

Helen's dark red lips curled slightly in response and then she lifted her hand slowly up to her raised chin and clasped it with her palm.

'Bang....fractured chin', she leant back on her haunches and felt proud of her prognosis.

'And besides..', she continued.

'The bruising looks to have been made by a knee, shoe or some other smooth object'.

Jack agreed. It looked pretty much like murder to him. He could smell it.

He looked around the rest of the room. The decor was fairly reserved. Beige and cream painted walls with hanging lamps scattered freely around them. The desk sat snugly up against the wall adjacent to the door with neat piles of paperwork stacked in one corner. Jack quietly perused through them until he noticed the safe. It was partly hidden behind the door and could only be witnessed from this angle once the door was open. He motioned over to Briggsy.

'I want that opened....sort it will you...', he pointed at the small silver door with a black tumbler sat prominently in the centre. Briggsy nodded and walked away with his radio to his mouth requesting the services of a cracker.

Jack spoke to the officer at the door.

'Who found him?', Jack enquired.

The officer turned and pointed out across the bar towards Erik who sipped coffee at a table. He looked in shock and pale with it.

'What time?', Jack continued.

'He said he found him at around 5:50 this morning when he turned up for work', the officer replied.

'Bit early to start work isn't it after a late night?', Jack mused. Jack stared at Erik and then went back into the room. He noticed the stairs to the side and climbed them. At the top he saw a room in complete contrast to the one below. It was immaculate. It even smelled clean. The decor was far more flamboyant. Brightly coloured reds and blues. The huge bed was the main feature of the room. It sprawled across the centre of it. Jack noticed the bed neatly made with crisp white sheets and a navy-blue quilt thrown over it. Jack pulled back the quilt and stared at the sheets. They had no creases. No tell-tale blemishes or evidence that they had been slept in. Jack lowered his nose to the sheets. They smelled fresh and clean.

Jack looked around the rest of the room. Everything seemed polished even the chest of drawers smelled of forest pine. The brick red carpet looked freshly hoovered. In the far corner of the room stood a TV and underneath it a VCR. The TV was large, probably 28 inches screen, and the video was the studio sound type manufactured with editing and dubbing in mind. Jack checked the inside of the VCR, but it was empty. He briefly pictured Tommy sprawled across his king size bed watching his king size TV, probably eating at the same time, possibly crisps the large packet type or maybe a sausage or bacon sandwich dripping in fat. Jack felt immediately guilty at these thoughts, but Tommy was a man of luxury and exercise and health awareness were neither of his priorities. To the side of the TV was a cabinet, dark mahogany in colour. Jack clicked open the doors. Inside was a collection of spirits, whisky-malt, vodka, gin, and white rum. The whisky had been hit the hardest along with the vodka, both bottles two-thirds of the way down the label. Next to the spirits were two tumbler glasses, both clean and unused. To the other side of the cabinet Jack noticed several videotapes stacked neatly on the back shelf. Schwarzenegger and Stallone action movies, including the full Rocky collection, and by way of comedy three compilation tapes of Monty Python. Jack then noticed the blank four-hour tape that was sat in front of the others. It lay flat on its side, next to the two remote controls. The tab on the side read 'Em, East & St.'. Jack picked it up and went over to the VCR. He inserted the tape into the loading mechanism and switched on the TV. He took a second to select the correct channel and then the familiar music hit him. It was Coronation Street. Jack seemed perplexed. He wouldn't have thought Tommy was the soap type, but sure enough the whole four hours of the tape consisted of episodes of Coronation Street, Eastenders and Emmerdale. Jack felt very disappointed at his findings but also a little amused. His thoughts reverted back to Tommy lying sprawled across his bed keeping in touch with the latest developments of the Nations favourite soaps. Jack smiled and removed the tape and replaced it where he found it. Several pictures hung on the wall next to a two-foot vanity mirror, one neatly framed showing Tommy shaking hands with a young Bruce Willis, probably from his Moonlighting days. The others were people that Jack failed to recognise but for Tommy they commanded a position opposite his bed. Happy that he had seen enough, Jack descended back down the stairs.

Jack picked up two mugs of coffee from the bar and made over to Erik. Erik saw Jack approaching and immediately recognised him from the evening before. He lowered his eyes. Jack sat down and pushed a mug of coffee in front of him.

'What happened last night?', Jack said in a soft tone.

Erik looked up at him his eyes glazed still obviously in shock.

He couldn't reply.

Jack spoke again.

'Who killed Tommy, Erik?'.

Erik frowned as the words hit home.

'Killed?...What do you mean killed?', he stared at Jack.

Jack remained calm.

'Oh.. I think he was killed...the evidence points that way', he paused and watched for a reaction in Erik.

Erik's eyes seemed to wander as he mulled over his thoughts.

'Killed', he said again.

'No way', he laughed nervously.

Jack thought for a second in the following silence then started again,

'I can see how the average Joe Bloggs may come across a body.. lying face down at the bottom of a set of stairs and instantly think he tripped and fell ...maybe while half-asleep...maybe pissed......maybe just unlucky....', Jack monitored Erik's reaction intensely. His tone became sterner.

'However, we are trained in these matters and at this very moment there are several professionals in there telling me that he was murdered......and do you know what...', he paused and leaned forward slightly in his chair.

'I tend to take their advice rather than Joe Bloggs...but then maybe I'm wrong..', he leaned back again.

His voice returned to a gentler tone again.

'I hear you were the first to find Tommy dead?'.

Erik nodded.

'What time was this?', Jack asked.

Erik grew restless.

His eyes seemed to throb with anxiety.

'Around 6 this morning when I got in to clean up....from the party last night..'.

Jack listened.

'I switched on the lights.

Saw all the mess and rubbish about the place...it looked like a bomb had hit it...', Erik paused momentarily.

'Then I suddenly realised the alarm warning hadn't come on when I entered...I immediately found him shortly after that'.

'I knew I should have stayed on and secured the place myself, but Tommy insisted I left it to him....'.

Jack broke in,

'What time was this?'.

Erik thought for a moment then answered that it had been around 2 a.m.

'Was that the last time you saw him before you found him this morning?', Jack continued.

Erik nodded.

'Was he with anyone?...How did he seem?', Jack continued his line of questioning.

'No, he was on his own...he seemed fine ..that the party had been a success..a little merry..but fine', Erik looked down again and sighed.

Jack leant back and folded his arms and thought of the approach to his next question.

'You said the place looked like a bomb had hit it....What do you mean?'.

Erik looked up and answered,

'Well....We'd stacked the dirty glasses along the bar and put the chairs up on the table...but.. we didn't bother washing them and there was still paper, cigarette butts and stains on the floor.

So, it still looked a real mess,'.

Jack smiled and uncrossed his arms,

'So, when you found Tommy you called the police straight away?'.

Erik nodded.

'So, who cleaned up then Erik...?...The place was spotless when we got here.', Jack smiled.

Erik looked ruffled for a split second then composed himself.

'I did...It was embarrassingly untidy..'.

Jack laughed.

'So...you are saying you walked in.... found your boss lying dead at the bottom of his stairs ...then having phoned us ...you decided to get out your duster and polish the place....', Jack continued to laugh.

Erik looked solemn.

'It's what Tommy would have wanted...He loved this place to be spotless ...It meant everything to him..', Erik lowered his head and sighed again.

'Did you clean upstairs as well Erik?....I could still smell the forest pine..I use it myself', Jack pressed further.

'No!!...I didn't go up there...He didn't like anyone going into his room...I couldn't even tell you the colour of his quilt', Erik was quick to reply. Probably too quick.

Jack paused then replied.

'Quilt?...How did you know Tommy had a quilt..?..He could have had sheets and blankets..', Jack only posed the question to be obnoxious and try to make Erik crack from an almost flawless display of theatrics.

'Quilt..blankets...Does it matter...I've never been up there...Like I said Tommy was extremely tidy...I don't think I like what you are insinuating here Sergeant...', Erik began to stand his ground.

'Inspector!..', Jack corrected nonchalantly.

Jack sighed and began to stand.

'Oh...I'm not insinuating anything Erik....I don't think you killed him...but don't leave the area...you can bet I'll need to talk to you in greater lengths later...with a lot more questions..', Jack smiled, winked, and went back to Tommy's room. He knew Erik had lied in almost all of his accounts but the reasons why he lied, he couldn't yet understand.

Back in the room Jack spoke again with the officer who arrived at the scene first. He had first received the call at 6:02 this morning and had arrived at the scene shortly after twenty past.

Jack almost choked when he heard that it had taken almost twenty minutes to cover two miles from the station. He was then enlightened that the roster had just changed over and there was a delay due to a brief from the on-coming Chief reference the accumulating litter problems in the city centre.

Jack had laughed when he heard this.

It was completely typical.

Still, it only gave Erik twenty minutes to spring clean.

A feat that he could possibly have just achieved although the officer couldn't recall a wet floor or anything that would suggest the place had literally just recently been cleaned.

Jack puzzled around his thoughts.

Helen had packed up her equipment and was heading for the door. Jack called to her and met her just outside beside the bar.

Jack smiled.

'Any new news on Frank Christie or Den?'.

Helen sighed,

'Some..not a great deal..', she seemed tired.

'Do you want to come over later.....I need a coffee right now', she spoke with an especial longing for caffeine.

Jack thought, then suggested Sammy's Cafe along the street as he needed a drink too.

She looked surprised but then agreed.

Jack helped her with her things to her car, a metallic blue L reg.,VW Golf convertible. Jack was shocked.

It didn't seem the type of car that a straight routine sort of woman, whom Helen portrayed, would drive, more of your typical yuppie pretentious type of vehicle.

Jack smiled as she closed her boot and re-activated the alarm.

Helen caught his smile and felt inwardly content that she had obviously surprised him.

They walked off towards the cafe where Helen would bring Jack up to date with the latest information and also where they would begin to enjoy each other's company.

Jack returned to the Pravada at around 9. He had enjoyed the company of Helen and felt disappointed at having to return to the murder scene. Inside he saw Briggsy watching intently as the cracker went about his work at the safe. Tommy's body had been zipped up into a black bag and white chalk marked the spot where he had been found. The medics brushed passed him, scuffling with the dead weight. The photographer took several more snaps of the room. The flashes and whirring of his camera nauseated Jack. The room had a distinct smell of death and all the musky heat and sweat from the number of bodies in the room created a distinct lack of fresh air. Jack wandered over to the window and lifted it up. The fresh clean air was wonderful. Jack looked out across the street. He was just about to turn and go over to Briggsy when he noticed the car, a dark blue BMW with a single male driver driving very slowly along the street. The driver was too busy staring at Jack and almost veered into a parked car before correcting himself and driving off at speed. The acceleration of the engine and screech of the tyres echoed in the room. Jack found this odd. He couldn't get a look at the occupant and didn't have time to get a glimpse of the registration. Sub-consciously though he noted the dark blue BMW...probably a 5 series too.

Jack turned back to Briggsy just in time to hear the thud of the safe lock and see the door open. The cracker smiled and bragged to Briggsy that it was just a four-combination lock....very simple to crack.

Briggsy started to empty the safe onto the table.

Passport....

Cheque books....

Credit cards....

Documents....

Jewellery...including a diamond necklace...

A fresh clean pile of fifty-pound notes...probably around ten grands' worth.. and then Briggsy paused...

He lifted out five four-hour video cassettes.

Each was labelled with a name and date on them.

'Mmmm...interesting?'.

Jack took the tapes from Briggsy and ushered him back upstairs.

The first tape simply read 'Joanne and Sam, 24-6-94'.

Jack slipped the tape from its cover and slotted it into the video.

He hoped it wasn't going to be another of Tommy's favourite TV shows, but somehow he knew it wouldn't.

Briggsy was shocked at what he saw on the screen.

Joanne and Sam certainly left nothing to the imagination.

Jack stopped the tape almost immediately and selected the next.

It contained material along the same lines as the first.

Jack paused the tape and stared closely at the still picture.

He then turned his gaze over to Tommy's bed and surrounds.

Briggsy still looking shocked broke the silence,

'It's this room!', was all he could muster.

Jack moved over to the bed keeping a close eye on the TV picture.

He positioned himself at the point where he thought the camera was pointing and then turned to see his own reflection in the mirror on the wall.

Jack walked slowly over to the mirror and gently lifted the corner pressing his face to the wall to peer behind it.

He then lifted the mirror off its hook and stared directly into the endoscopic camera that sat secured behind it. An infra-red sensor was attached to the corner of the mirror which Jack failed to notice when it sat on the wall but was obvious from the two wires that stretched from it back into a hole in the wall next to the endoscope.

The mirror was a standard two-way type and it seemed Tommy was illegally filming his bedroom activities with his guests for the record, probably for later viewing pleasure. The endoscope was usually used in delicate medical operations or high security applications, but Tommy had resorted to an ulterior use.

Jack tapped the wall. It was false. The recorder or camcorder probably sat in the recess behind it.

Jack removed the picture of Tommy and Bruce and noticed two more wires- or more like cables. It soon became apparent to Jack that these cables fitted to the VCR.

He fumbled with them getting impatient and stretched them over to the VCR. Briggsy removed the tape from the VCR and the leads from the back. Jack affixed the leads in position.

Both Jack and Briggsy understood the importance of this operation.

Both hoped and prayed that Tommy had filmed the previous night's activities. It was safe to say that if Tommy concealed the camera from his guests then his would be killer would also be unaware of its presence.

The screen was blank. No snowy picture just a dead blank screen.

Briggsy broke the silence for a second time,

'We need to turn it on...Is there a remote?'.

Jack then remembered in the cabinet.

He jumped up like an excited schoolboy and removed the remotes.

The larger one had two large buttons on the top. One said TV the other VCR. It was obviously a dual- purpose model.

The other remote had simply play, record, forward, rewind and pause buttons.

Jack pressed the play button.

The picture remained blank for a second then lit up.

The first frames showed Tommy's close up face then as he moved away to the side two women came into focus.

Briggsy stared even closer at the pictures and muttered,

'I don't believe it!'.

Jack still staring at the pictures asked what the problem was.

'It's her ....isn't it?', Briggsy seemed dumb-struck then explained to Jack of her role in one of Tommy's favourite soaps.

Jack smiled.

Jack hit the forward button and the pictures danced across the screen in fast mode but with still enough clarity for Briggsy to mutter his disbelief's.

It took almost five minutes of fast forwarding before Standt entered the shot. Jack missed his entrance and had to rewind to capture his reappearance.

Standt had his back to the camera and Jack got ready with the pause button until he turned to reveal himself.

They witnessed Standt fist the woman off Tommy, but as she sank out of view Standt had turned back to Tommy. They saw him grab Tommy round the throat and lift him off the bed. As Tommy moved out of view the full-frontal picture of Standt was caught perfectly paused.

Jack smiled,........' Got you!!!'

Chapter 10

Marco was performing his usual early morning forty-length swim when Standt and Nielsen arrived. He saw them approach the side of the pool. It wasn't an Olympic sized pool, just short of 20 metres to be exact, but big enough to be spared the inconvenience of queuing and using the public facilities. Standt was with Marco when he had the extension to the house built, to encompass the pool. The pool could have been larger, but this would not have left enough room for the Jacuzzi and sauna, which also adorned the annex. The term 'house' may be construed to be incorrect. The 'house' was more likely to be referred to as an inner-city manor to those fortunate enough to view the entirety of the property. From the front, the house resembled others in the immediate area, two storeys high with the original quota of five reception rooms, five bedrooms and six acres of adjoining land. Upon purchasing the property Marco had extended each side of the house backwards to form a U-shape, each side possessing two further reception rooms and two large bedrooms. He used the top floor of the left aspect as the master's quarters and the top floor of the right aspect as the guest's quarters. Each of the quarters held a large en-suite bedroom and a smaller double room. He converted the original five bedrooms into four large rooms, a dining room, kitchen, lounge and sitting room. A long, wide corridor joined the two aspects together. The 9 ground floor reception rooms were converted into a study, library, gymnasium, sun lounge, conservatory, games room, office and the two remaining rooms were used for his business. The largest being for conferences and meetings, the other for his personal assistant. The annex was built only last year. It was only a single storey in height but ran parallel to the front of the house and joined both side aspects together completing the loop. Inside the loop was a large patioed area which he used for barbecue's and entertaining in the summer. The patio had complete privacy to outside eyes, although the annex held two large sliding doors of glass, the far aspect of the annex was constructed with re-enforced mirrored glass. This allowed his guests to have access to the pool, Jacuzzi, and sauna from the patio area, which added to the palatial feel of the property. Standt remembered its christening. A wild pool party thrown by Marco which redefined the term water sports and justified the need for thick mirrored glass to prevent outsiders witnessing the antics within.

The pool seemed so different now. All calm and quiet apart from the ripples and splashes and exhalations from Marco as he continued his workout. He still showed incredible strength and stamina for a man in his mid-fifties. Standt and Nielsen waited patiently.

The almost hypnotic sights and sounds of Marco gliding effortlessly through the water were rudely interrupted by the opening of the door to the far end of the annex.

Cath, Marco's latest flame for almost two years now, strolled out behind the door stark naked with a rolled-up towel in her left hand.

She made around four and a half steps before she noticed Standt and Nielsen staring at her in disbelief.

She quickly unravelled the towel and held it to her frame.

'You bastards could have told me you were here!..', she proclaimed.

Her faced blushed and she very carefully moved over to the door of the sauna trying not to expose any more of her body.

Not that she had anything to be ashamed of.

Although she was fast approaching forty she still had an incredible body.

Her face was just beginning to show signs of ageing. Telltale wrinkles and lines around her neck and eyes but her body was still pert and firm.

Standt noticed her breasts sagged slightly but not as much as one would expect from a forty year old.

He also noticed she dyed her hair dark brown and that her natural colour was ginger or maybe red.

Standt liked Cath.

He had taken her shopping when Marco was out of the country. On the bosses request of course.

She flirted with him almost all afternoon.

Purposely dragging him round all the lingerie sections in all the high street stores and making him wait while she tried on a series of sexy garments.

She would pick up the garment, place it across her clothed body and ask Standt's opinion, then she would disappear into a cubicle mentioning it was a pity he couldn't give her advice while she wore it beside her skin. For one split second Standt so desperately wanted to push open the door and join her inside.

But fear got the better of him although he probably wouldn't have admitted that.

Standt relived the four hours of torture and sheer pleasure in the time it took her to disappear into the sauna behind another closed door.

He felt uncomfortable.

Then he noticed that Marco had stopped swimming and had climbed out of the pool.

He approached them, briskly drying himself with a towel.

'I take it everything went smoothly...', he offered the statement rather than a question.

Nielsen smiled.

'No problem..'.

Standt paused then spoke

'Tommy's dead..'.

Marco threw the towel over his head and rubbed at his hair unmoved by Standt's reply.

He dropped the towel down to his face, rubbed his eyes and snorted,

'That bad was it?', Marco gazed at Standt.

Standt nodded,

'It was crazy....way way too far!!', Standt tried to express the seriousness of the situation without going into details.

Marco patted Standt on the back,

'Good work ...'.

'I want you both to disappear for a while....travel up to Hull and pay Pat McClere a visit',

Nielsen nodded.

'He's got something to give you....meet him on Wednesday... don't come back till Saturday...till things have settled a little..', Marco smiled.

The boys both understood.

Marco turned and walked over to the sauna room.

Standt watched as Marco slid out of his trunks and opened the door and entered the billowing clouds of steam.

Standt felt the first signs of jealousy.

Jack and Briggsy watched the tape repeatedly trying to gather more information from the scene where Standt entered to when he disappeared. The camera didn't pick up the actual scene where Standt killed Tommy, but it certainly proved that Tommy had received an unexpected guest. The lab could probably use their technology to establish the time of day the video was shot and compare that to the estimated time of death.

Jack continued the tape slightly further. The actress was seen to get up clutching her nose and looking bewildered around her. She moved passed the camera and disappeared out of view for probably 30 seconds. She then raced passed the camera again, to the bed. She looked pale and gaunt. Her body language showed signs of distress. She fumbled for her clothes, throwing her dress over her, pushing what looked like her underwear into her handbag. She danced back and forth around the room checking to see if she had forgotten anything. Her dress clung to her where she began to sweat. She reached into her handbag again and emerged with a tissue. She moved over straight up to the camera and wiped traces of blood from her nose. The picture looked grotesque as she pulled at her nostrils and examined their insides into the mirror. She then brushed at her sweat sodden hair with her fingers and raced out of sight again. She never returned.

Jack and Briggsy sat glued to the screen. This evidence made their job so much easier. If only all cases were captured on film like this. Jack and Briggsy waited. The girls from the band were still oblivious to the dead atmosphere, the four of them still writhed on the floor, seemingly very close to orgasm. Jack wanted to forward the tape on but resisted for fear of missing something important.

They watched the girls collapse around each other. Each of them breathing heavily, completely fatigued by their exertions. Then Jack saw exactly what he had expected to see, and a thin wry smile adorned his face.

It had been almost three minutes since the actress had left. Just enough time for her to go down the stairs, step over Tommy's dormant body, make through the bar, find someone on security and explain what had happened, then disappear into the night. Sure enough, Erik entered the room. He looked angered. He firmly ordered the women out of the room. They jumped up clawing at their discarded clothing and dashed in front of the screen. Erik, noticeably panicking, stood, and searched around the room with his eyes, trying to find a clue for what to do next. He held his hands to his head and began to sob. Then he disappeared out of shot.

Jack and Briggsy sat and watched the still screen for almost twenty minutes. What Erik did in those twenty minutes could only be known to him. The screen held no movement. The quilt still hung from the corner of the bed onto the floor. The two pillows lay at right angles to each other at the head of the bed. One of the pillows still dented by the pressure Tommy had exerted on it. The rest of the picture remained typical to that of which it would of any ordinary day.

Briggsy asked to forward the tape on but Jack stared at his watch timing the interval that Erik had left to when he would inevitably return.

19 minutes and 40 seconds to be exact.

Erik returned and looked far more composed this time.

He tore the sheets, quilt, and pillowcases from the bed. Capturing them in a bundle under his left arm, he took another look around the room searching for more washing. Finding nothing further he disappeared again.

He returned approximately 4 minutes later complete with a Hoover, and a tray that held visible cleaning implements.

Jack and Briggsy watched as Erik meticulously scrubbed and cleaned the room.

He polished and scoured every inch.

He was a man on a mission. That mission was to make the room pass a recruit's Sergeant-Major block inspection.

Having succeeded, Erik disappeared and returned with the ironed freshly washed bed linen. He just began replacing them when the tape finished. Jack and Briggsy stared at the blank screen for a second before Jack said,

'Wow!...What a movie!'.

Briggsy rubbed at his eyes, they watered from the previous two hours viewing with minimal blinking.

Jack asked Briggsy to make a copy of the tape which to Briggsy's relief wouldn't take too long as the VCR had a high-speed dubbing function, which meant the three-hour film could be copied in less than an hour.

Jack stood up and stretched.

Erik was about to receive further questioning.

The club had emptied and only one officer stood at the bar and two constables guarded the entrance. The place was so quiet. The officer was relieved to see Jack as he began to think he would be on his post all day. Jack asked him to make three mugs of coffee, one for Briggsy upstairs and to bring two over to him and Erik.

Erik sat in the same position. Staring blankly into the space in front of him. Shock had obviously consumed him. Jack sat down opposite.

'Was Tommy big into soap operas?', Jacks first question surprised Erik.

Erik stared suspiciously at Jack.

'I don't know...why?', Erik replied.

'So, you weren't aware that he recorded the weeks episodes onto one tape?', Jack continued.

Erik looked confused.

'No', he shook his head.

'Did he often invite soap stars to the club?', Jack fished.

Erik sighed.

'Well..yes..he had a lot of stars come here...some were from the soaps...he paid them appearance money....mainly to keep his members happy and to bring in invited guest punters.', Erik qualmed.

'Were there any here last night Erik?', Jack pressed.

Erik thought for a moment. He felt the heat. He began to sweat and felt the dizziness ensue.

'Possibly....yes I think so...', Erik's voice quivered noticeably.

Jack smiled.

'Oh...I think you know so Erik', Jack replied smugly.

Erik jumped to his defence.

'There was a lot of people here last night...Thinking about it Tommy was entertaining someone vaguely familiar...yes..I think she was from one of the soaps...yes..', Erik became restless.

'Entertaining!..', Jack laughed..' That's one way of putting it..'.

The agony was etched across Erik's face. His mask was beginning to crack.

Jack thought he would remove it entirely.

'What was your reaction then Erik when she came up to you last night and said that Tommy was dead!..', Jack thumped the statement home firmly.

Erik was speechless.

His face drained of all colour and his shoulders slumped.

He had no answer.

'I must say I am suitably impressed by the efficiency of your cleaning work though!...', Jack continued.

'I may even think of employing you myself....especially the way you scrubbed the carpet on your hands and knees...and the polishing was A1...', Jack remarked sarcastically.

'But then again...you probably will be past it by the time you get out of nick', Jack left his last statement hanging in the air.

Erik felt it stifling him.

He couldn't comprehend the accuracy at which Jack had recounted the events.

He tried to reply in innocence but the longer he delayed the guiltier he realised he looked.

Finally, Erik nodded...

'OK...I found him last night ...not this morning...but I've been in shock...', Erik admitted.

He sighed shakily.

'He was entertaining his guests in his room...the party was going a little wild as usual...then out of the blue she came up to me and said that Tommy was dead....', Erik paused uncomfortably recounting the events.

'I didn't believe her at first...then she said a man had come in... bashed her in the face and then somehow killed Tommy....she had a swollen nose, and I could see it had been bleeding....I panicked..', Erik continued.

'I went into his room...found him lying at the bottom of the stairs...his eyes glared at me lifelessly...', Erik choked back the bile in his throat.

'I got everyone out of the club and for some reason instinctively cleaned the place out...I somehow felt it was my fault he was dead...I was supposed to be his protector...', Erik's eyes welled with tears.

'I didn't do my job...', he stared down at the floor again.

Jack sighed.

'It was stupid of you to lie to us Erik...you can be done for conspiracy..even accessory to murder...', Jack calmly replied.

Erik jumped upright

'I didn't kill him!!', he shouted out startling the officer at the bar.

Jack motioned for Erik to sit down.

He slumped back into the seat.

Jack thought for a second then continued,

'Did anyone get in last night who wasn't on the guest-list?'.

Erik thought for a moment, rubbed his eyes, and ran his fingers through his hair,

'I don't think so...'.

Jack continued,

'You said the party was a little wild as usual...What do you mean?'.

Erik soughed.

'Well...Tommy always knew how to throw a party..but the last three or four times ...it has been just mental...', Erik replied.

Jack waited for him to continue.

'Sort of like a dream party...Everything would be pretty normal... Dancing...laughing...people having a good time...then when the club emptied just to members only and selected guests' things would start to go wild...', Erik shook his head still obviously quizzical.

'They would all start to get horny and start removing their clothes and the whole thing would develop into a mass orgy', Erik looked at Jack hoping he would believe him.

Jack nodded knowingly.

'Did it involve drugs?', Jack inquired.

Erik held his hands up.

'Yes...I think so...It always happened shortly after Tommy gave out the complimentary drinks...I presume he must have spiked them with something...', Erik showed a little comprehension of the situation.

'Did Tommy use a lot of drugs?', Jack asked quietly.

Erik shook his head.

'No...at least not that I know of...he just dabbled a little at times... usually as a pick-me-up to get him in the mood..'.

Jack stood up.

'I want you to come with me a second...there is someone I want you to see', Jack ushered Erik into Tommy's room. He told Erik to wait at the foot of the stairs.

Erik shuffled uncomfortably and stared at his feet. He was stood at the exact spot he had found Tommy hours earlier.

Jack ascended up to Briggsy.

He had almost finished copying the tape.

Jack told Briggsy to stop it there and rewind to the point where Standt appeared and to pause the picture at that point.

Briggsy soon found the point because he had cleverly electronically tagged it.

Jack called for Erik to come up the stairs.

Erik slowly climbed the fifteen steps.

Upon reaching the twelfth he saw the mirror propped up on the floor and the lens protruding from the wall where it once hung. He almost instantly realised just how Jack had recited the events so accurately.

He turned to the TV screen and saw Standt.

Erik looked angered.

'I knew it...the bastard!.', he proclaimed.

'Do you know this man?', Jack said.

Erik's face seethed before he nodded,

'He comes round to the club with his mate, a few days before Tommy has a party...Tommy gives them money they give him a package...he was here last night...', Erik spoke the words bitterly.

'What's his name?', Jack asked.

Erik shook his head,

'Don't know...I know he works for Marco Veart...he's a member here...wasn't here last night..rarely comes to the parties...', Erik continued.

'Marco Veart?...that name rings a bell', Jack stated.

Briggsy interrupted,' He's into security...runs a large firm in the city...big charity worker too...does consultancy and advises firms on security measures...gives lectures at the police college....very clever man...'.

Jack seemed shocked at Briggsy's knowledge.

'He's delivered a seminar in front of me before', Briggsy continued.

'Really', Jack interrupted mockingly.

'Anyway, finish copying the tape, get this place cordoned off, take Erik down to the station, get a full statement from him, then find out as much as you can about Mr. Marco Veart and his employees...', Jack instructed Briggsy.

'I'll have that tape...and I'll see you back at the station later', Jack said.

Briggsy sighed and handed the tape to Jack.

It would be another hour sat in front of the TV for Briggsy. Jack smiled.

Jack drove round to the labs and found Helen sat in her office eating a salad sandwich. Upon seeing Jack, she eagerly tried to finish her mouthful quickly whilst holding her hand up to her lips.

'I've got something for you..', she finally said.

She placed her sandwich down on the serviette at the corner of her desk and reached for a piece of paper in her tray.

'Ready for this...', she smiled.

Jack entered and sat in the chair opposite.

She swung sideways in her chair, crossed her legs, and leant back into the chair,

'Got the report back from the bio-lab....they did carbon 14 tests on the powder..', she swallowed again.

She lifted her glasses and slid them onto her nose.

Jack felt so comfortable in her company. So relaxed.

She made him smile.

'Ok...it's a complex compound as we expected....4 parts sodium nitrate....2 parts potassium chloride...5 parts methamphetamine....2 parts methadone.....2 parts magnesia...1 part palladium.....1 part calcium carbonate ....1-part good old sodium chloride...', Helen smiled.

Jack looked blankly.

She smiled again.

'Ok...the sodium nitrate and potassium chloride are mainly used in the manufacture of fertilisers...', Helen shrugged.

'The methamphetamine...commonly known as speed...and the methadone...an analgesic drug mainly used to relieve severe pain..a morphine or heroin substitute...which I'm sure you know already...', she continued.

Jack nodded.

'The magnesia....a carbonate used as an antacid or laxative...say no more...', she smiled.

'The palladium...occurs naturally in a lot of ores but is mainly used as a catalyst...to increase the effects......the calcium carbonate..or chalk..used to line the stomach.....and of course the finishing touches a little salt ...', Helen passed the paper to Jack.

He still was none the wiser really.

'Overall, Jack a lethal cocktail, such that it's not surprising that the brain gets mashed up and confused', she sighed.

Jack perused the paper for a second then said,

'Is it addictive?'.

Helen nodded ...' Very'.

'Can you explain the effects?', Jack asked coyly.

'Well, the narcotics probably make the user feel shall we say amorous....and the combination with the others we believe causes an imbalance in the body which may lead to various side-effects... one possibility could certainly be a craving for promiscuity...', Helen replied.

Jack frowned,

'Promiscuity..', Jack muttered mulling in thought.

'Frequent and diverse sexual relationships', Helen stated proudly.

'Pardon?', Jack puzzled just catching the end of her definition.

'Promiscuity..', Helen re-iterated.

'Oh yes...I know...sorry I was just thinking aloud..', Jack laughed.

Helen blushed.

Jack smiled.

'I've got something you may be interested in..', Jack reached into his jacket pocket and pulled out the video.

'Exclusive footage of the drug in action...', Jack continued.

'Have you got a VCR...?'.

Helen led Jack into the dark room. The room was small with photographic development facilities along one side and in the far corner behind a small side screen sat a TV and VCR. There was a chair directly in front of the TV, which Helen offered to Jack. She dragged another from the other corner and sat beside him. He placed the tape in the VCR and after rewinding it pressed play.

He enlightened Helen on the scenario of the spiked drinks and watched her response to the pictures.

She instantly recognised the main star as well. She shuffled uncomfortably at what she saw.

Jack noticed the blushes.

'It's very explicit isn't it', she commented.

'Errgh...good God..', she noticed the two girls together.

'Notice anything unusual about them?', Jack posed the question for want of an excuse to stare at Helen some more.

Helen leant closer to the screen.

'Well, the quality isn't brilliant, but this certainly isn't normal behaviour...well not what I would call normal anyway...', she blushed.

'And their eyes....can you see how vacant they appear...certainly drug related..', she laughed nervously.

'And for them all to have the same...well hunger...it is conclusive evidence of the effects of the drug isn't it'. She continued.

As she leant back in her chair her thigh brushed against Jack.

It felt so soft and sleek. She felt it also because she consciously closed her legs tight together uncomfortably to prevent it happening again. Jack felt himself wanting to open his legs wider so as they touched again, but as he summoned up the courage she stood up and turned off the VCR.

It was obvious that she felt uncomfortable and stifled by the situation. Jack felt like it was almost as though he was sat down watching a porno with his girlfriend. He wished it was.

Helen handed the tape back to Jack. Their fingers touched. Only for a second but long enough to catch each other's eye.

The final few minutes of their meeting was awkward and there was an uneasy silence. Neither really knew what else to say or do and they parted company with just a smile. Jack felt empty in his stomach but not through hunger...well not hunger for food anyway.

CHAPTER 11

Jack returned to the station around late afternoon. Briggsy had taken a full statement from Erik and on Craven's authorisation had released him.

He had scanned the best picture of Standt from the video tape and entered it into the database at HQ via the network system. The results of the search were disappointing. As far as the search was concerned, Standt had no criminal convictions, misdemeanours, or brushes with the law in the country, therefore, Briggsy was none the wiser as to Standt's identity or location.

The same results were found for Marco Veart.

Jack was equally frustrated by the news. Even more so, when Briggsy recounted that the soap star that had been entertaining Tommy, had left for two weeks in the Dominican Republic that morning. Her agent had said that she felt the pressures of work were getting on top of her and that her producers had granted her the last-minute break.

He told Briggsy to fax the picture of Standt to Scotland Yard and get them to check with Interpol for terrorists or wanted felons in their jurisdiction. He failed to believe that this man had committed a crime for the first time. The composed and calculated approach to the murder was too professional for that. He also told Briggsy to check with the registrar's office to obtain some background information on Marco Veart. He had to have some kind of portrayal of the man who he would ultimately be interviewing next. Date of birth, place of birth, family background, work history all the kinds of information that Jack would require to depict the character of Marco. The man everyone spoke so highly of, yet unknown to Jack. He felt he was playing catch-up again and wanted to remedy the situation immediately.

Briggsy got to work while Jack read through Erik's statement. Jack perused the littering of text in its usual loquacious form and attempted to gain something new he had originally failed to pick up on. Nothing new presented itself.

He filed the statement just as his phone rang.

It was Helen. She sounded pensive on the phone and asked if she could meet with him.

Jack agreed, suggesting 'The Dog and Duck', a quiet respectable country inn, outside the hustle and bustle of the inner-city congestion. Jack offered to meet her there, but she had insisted that she would pick him up from the station in around ten minutes.

Jack replaced the receiver quietly. He smiled for a second then deliberated over the uncertain tone to her voice. He was unsettled by it.

Jack stood up, told Briggsy he would be out for an hour or so, and that if any new developments came to light, including the information on Marco Veart that he was to page him immediately. Briggsy nodded, whilst still deep in concentration at his terminal. Jack noted at just how seriously Briggsy's commitment was to the research part of the job. He also sub-consciously noted that maybe this was the beginning of a blossoming partnership. Jack left the station leaving Briggsy engrossed in the pages that filled his VDU. He scrolled through them energetically only briefly looking up at the sound of the office door slamming shut in the breeze.

Jack stood waiting at the bottom of the stone steps that led up to the station. He stood just out of view from the large glass panelled doors and the inquisitive eye of the Desk Sergeant. The station was opposite the park. It wasn't an expansive park but large enough to have a calm sedative aura about it. The grass was emerald green and neatly manicured. A large silver birch towered above the scatterings of willows and boundary hedgerows. A stone path undulated over the landscape with a maze of routes available to select the most idyllic spot. In the distance a couple walked arm in arm with man's best friend trotting gracefully along side. The scenario enhanced the tranquillity of the situation. Jack realised he longed for peace. It was only when three louts on bicycles raced up behind the couple and forced them to step off the path and unlock their embrace that Jack realised that in this world one could never be in complete contentment. There would be times, of course, that one may be drawn into the illusion of total contentment, but in reality, there are always louts around the corner to disfigure it. Prevention or limitation of this was after all Jack's profession. He hardly received words of gratitude or appreciation, except from injured parties, he didn't expect it. He accepted the hostility and antipathy reflected from certain areas of humanity. It meant nothing to him. What affected him most of all though was the realisation that his quest for peace would be the death of him. But as long as the chance to succeed was there he would be damned if he rejected it. Jack felt remorseful. He wandered his eyes over the park, peaceful again, and dreamt of what could have been until the intervention of man's hatred and greed.

Jack was removed from his thoughts by the sound of a car horn. He turned to see Helen sat at the wheel of her VW. She smiled as Jack acknowledged her. Her eyes were covered with an expensive looking pair of shades. Jack noted to himself that there were certainly two sides to Helen Thompson, and he knew he was about to witness the other side today.

She drove carefully through the city. The top was down on the convertible and the wind whipped her long black tresses across her face. The deep bass of Portishead boomed from her stereo. Jack felt years younger. He smiled shocked by the transformation from the astute professional he had previously been in contact with. He found himself staring at her. Her lips pouted in concentration. Crimson red with cosmetics. Her white blouse flapped in the breeze offering Jack a sight of her cleavage through the three opened top buttons. Her navy wrap had fallen open, and Jack noticed her shapely thighs every time she changed gears. She wore no tights or stockings, she didn't need to, her legs were reasonably tanned to allow it. Jack felt comfortably transfixed by her beauty.

She turned to him and beamed a huge smile. Jack melted in his seat.

Jack wished the journey would have taken longer but they had already pulled into the carpark of the Dog and Duck.

The inn was covered in green vines, wrapping themselves tightly along the side of the building, pronounced from the white paint that decorated the outside. Inside, the inn was fitted with a blend of modern and antique furnishings. Helen retired to the seats in the far corner by the window whilst Jack approached the empty bar. He waited for a few seconds before the landlady appeared and poured him a pint of best bitter and a mineral water complete with ice and lemon.

Jack took the drinks over to Helen who had now removed her shades and intimidated Jack with her deep blue eyes as he uncomfortably progressed across the lounge trying not to spill the drinks. Being successful, he placed the drinks onto the table and then failed as he caught the table leg as he swung his knees under it, flipping the creamy top of his pint across the table face. Helen laughed and mopped up the head with a beer mat. Jack felt incredibly insecure and nervous. Vibes he was sure Helen had picked up on but one's she tried to ease by making a joke of the accident.

Jack looked around to notice the landlady had again disappeared. He spoke nervously,

'Had any other developments?'.

Helen smiled,

'No...nothing new...but that's not why I asked to meet you', she paused and lifted the glass to her lips and slowly let the water seep through them.

Jack's heart missed a beat.

Or several come to mention it, all at once.

The irregularity of his pulse made him feel dizzy. If he hadn't been sat down he was sure he would have fallen over.

She continued,

'There's something that has been bothering me....from the other night...', she paused again.

'When?', Jack became anxious.

'At the Old Mill...', she smiled trying to calm him.

Jack took a large gulp of his beer.

'What about it?..', Jack attempted to remain calm but inside he felt a burning.

'The way you reacted to the scars on Den's body....the swastika...', she spoke softly.

Jack took another gulp of the beer.

'He was a friend of mine...I was shocked by the way they had carved him up...', Jack tried to maintain eye contact but failed mid-sentence.

Helen smiled..., 'No..Jack...I saw your reactions when you witnessed the carnage at the hotel and the body at the club...you never batted an eyelid....it was the same at the mill until I wiped the blood off his body and you saw the swastika..besides can you honestly say he was a friend of yours Jack?.', her words trailed still in a soft tone.

Jack couldn't think of an answer.

He sat motionless like he was being ticked off by his mother for stealing apples from next doors orchard, head bowed.

'You were different then...vacant...Why?', she waited for an answer.

Jack didn't reply.

'I saw it in your eyes Jack...the terror...you were frightened.... weren't you?....why?', she begged for answers but got nothing in return.

'The way you acted afterwards...was just not like you...I mean I can't profess to know you really well but normally, in the time I have known you, you seem so strong and together .....but for the time when you wandered off...I could sense that something had affected you....What was it?...you can tell me Jack....What is it?', she pleaded sensitively for a reply. Jack knew she wanted to help. Her show of concern left an impression.

Jack looked deep into her eyes. She could see the glazed expression. Jack shrugged his shoulders and admitted he didn't know what it was. He felt as if he had known Helen for years. In the short time he had worked with her, he felt a bond growing between them. He hoped and prayed she felt the same.

Jack had an extreme case of deja-vu. He was just about to pour his heart out when it hit him that he was sure he had done this before. Although, as far as he was aware he hadn't spoken about his nightmares or situations that bring on a mental ordeal.

He paused.

Jack felt Helen's hand on his arm. Soft and tender to the touch. He looked at her again. He heard the words..' It's OK'...

Jack began...

'Since I can remember, even as a small child I can remember having nightmares....

They are the kind of nightmares that you wake up from in a sweat and they are so convincing that you believe you have actually lived them...', Jack spoke very quietly.

Helen listened.

'But the nightmares are almost always the same...with the same character...a grotesque figure chasing and haunting me....as I've got older I've learnt to cope with them...but still to this day I have them...although now I sometimes win and get away or kill it....but it always comes back....', Jack paused while he recounted the grisly half dismembered head.

'Then there are certain situations....as a child I couldn't watch war films...well not the films with the Germans in...they made me terrified...I don't know why...but I sensed the smell of battle, the intense fear of death...I could almost touch it...as though I'd witnessed it...but of course I was only a 12 year old boy...how could I....when I learnt about the war in history at school I had to take time off because the subject made me physically sick....the strangest thing of all though is I could speak fluent German after about the second lesson...it suddenly rushed upon me...and there I was speaking in a stronger accent than the teacher.....she always thought I was weird after that.....because of course my parents are both British...neither of them have even been to Germany let alone speak it....', Jack waited for a response from Helen.

She looked stunned but could see from her facial expression that she believed him.

'Then the swastika...I feel as though I had been surrounded by swastika's, men in uniform...being led onto a train...the distinct smell of German tunics....the smell of diesel...German voices...the pungent smell of death....a gaping blood pumping open wound...', Jack stopped. He felt the tears streaming down his face.

He wiped at them with his hand.

Helen watched on silently.

'You must think I am crazy...', Jack offered.

Helen shook her head.

'No...I must admit it sounds a little strange....', she paused trying to comprehend what she had heard.

'Maybe I've got a mental disorder...just forget what I have said...I'm just crazy!', Jack sweated realising he had probably said too much.

'And yes some people, who aren't broad-minded enough to accept it, may think you are crazy...but in my studies I have read about it...', she laughed.

Jack laughed with her relieving the tension in the air.

She told him about the American woman she had read about who took a vacation in France and when she heard the flow of the French language had lapsed into a state of mental unconsciousness... she pictured herself engulfed in flames....felt the searing pain of the flames eating into her flesh...smelt the acrid stench of burning meat... she actually re-lived in exact detail the symptoms and sensations one would get at being burned alive at a stake.

People passed her as mad, saying she thought she was Joan of Arc and was seeking attention. But the descriptions she gave held true both medically and psychologically as those one would expect at being burned alive. Whether she was Joan of Arc, or some other executed being, before in a previous life cannot be proven but the accurate events and symptoms were alarming. Helen was sceptical about reincarnation however she believed the mind was powerful enough to recount events passed in history. She believed it was passed through in the genes from previous ancestors or something similar and was stored in part of the brain that only certain people could access.

From what she had heard from Jack she believed he had the gift and told him so.

Jack felt relieved at her reassurance.

Maybe her ideas were correct.

But what Jack didn't tell her were that the visions were of course from World War 2 and that his father had been too young to be involved in WW2 and his grandfather had died of TB before the War.

But Jack thought he had said enough.

Helen hadn't run away screaming 'Madman' at the top of her voice.

She still sat there trying to comprehend what he had told her.

She thought for a while and said,

'So, when you saw the swastika on the body...you had the visions wash over you again...?'.

Jack just replied affirmatively.

'I see...', she replied puzzlingly.

'Who have you told about this?', she continued.

'You are the first...about any of it...', Jack proudly stated.

'I see...really...', Jack noticed her blush.

'I won't say a word to anyone about this...honestly', Helen confessed candidly.

'I know...', Jack smiled. He believed her. Jack reached out and wrapped his hand around hers.

He squeezed it gently. At first it felt as if she tried to pull her hand away but then Jack felt her squeeze him back. She still blushed as they looked into each other's eyes.

Jack wanted to kiss those deep red lips. He could almost feel the softness, taste the sweetness. He felt she wanted the same.

He stroked the back of her hand with his fingers. She smiled at him.

Just as he felt himself about to lean over the table and kiss her, his pager reverberated. The moment was lost.

Both slumped back in their seats saddened by the rude interruption of the beautiful moment.

Jack apologised unreservedly. They both smiled and Helen offered him a lift back to the station.

The journey back was quiet, but both knew that something had happened between them today. The impatient inner warmth crudely tried to explode from both of them, but they managed to curb it until they got back to the station.

Jack said his goodbye's and reluctantly stepped out of the car without embracing her. It was difficult. Very difficult. She felt the eagerness of the situation as well, but both still felt reserved enough to let it pass, just this once. The smiles were apparent though.

Jack walked backwards away from the car for a few steps, both still grinning broadly. Then Helen asked him to wait. Jack stopped dead in his tracks. She leant into the back of her car, her skirt opened wide, flashing her long slender thighs and white knickers. Jack wanted her there and then. She emerged with a pen and a card. She wrote on it and gave it to Jack. It was her home number.

'Call me!', she smiled.

Jack looked speechless but hesitantly replied...

'Definitely...I will!...'.

She smiled before driving away. Jack felt lost. He longed for her company. He would ring her tonight. He had to.

He placed the card into his jacket pocket and turned and went up the steps to the station.

Briggsy had come up trumps again. It was turning out to be a really productive day.

Their mystery man was very well known to Interpol. They were very keen to know his whereabouts.

Artur Standt....alias Luc Van Els....alias Dennis Smith....

Of South African origin....resident of Pretoria....

Wanted for the murder of five black families in Soweto in 1986...

A member of the Anti-Apartheid movement....

A man fitting his description is wanted by the Dutch authorities for his involvement in a hard drugs ring in Amsterdam....under the name Luc Van Els...

That was in 1988...

Interpol believe that he moved into the Republic of Ireland in 1989 under the alias Dennis Smith... apparently he disappeared into a terrorist organisation...IRA or PIRA...This is the first sighting of him since then.

Interpol requested that they should be kept informed as to the development of the investigation.

Jack was pleased at the results although he wondered if their man had already left the country with his Irish connections. They had sent his photo to the recognised ports and airports but the control of shipments across the Irish Sea was probably the most difficult to monitor. Jack decided against a press-release as it may encourage their man to disappear prematurely.

However, Jack felt he had enough derogatory information to present to Marco Veart. Which led him to the information on Marco.

Briggsy had obviously worked without breaking.

Marco Veart.

Born in 1942 in Eindhoven, Holland.

Mother was British. Father was Dutch.

They met during WW2. She was an aid worker; he was disabled in battle.

Marco went to finishing school in Geneva in 1957.

He graduated with a business and economics degree in 1963.

Set up his first business in Eindhoven in 1966.

A small electronics firm that specialised in the production of valves for transistor radios and early black and white TV sets.

Married in 1968.

In 1974, expanded the business into Amsterdam.

By 1980, he was pronounced a millionaire.

In 1988 he applied for, and obtained, British nationality when his mother died of ill health and then two weeks later his wife died in an unfortunate traffic accident.

In 1989 he set up an electronic security business that specialised in surveillance and alarm equipment.

By 1993, his assets are said to total around £36 million.

Jack read the impressive resume with care.

He asked Briggsy for a pen and circled a couple of areas on the page.

He then asked for the page on Standt and did the same.

Briggsy watched curiously.

Jack held the page on Standt in his left hand and the page on Marco in the right hand. He switched his attention from one page to the other several times. Then he smiled,

'What do you make of that Briggsy?....Coincidence?', he laughed and passed the papers to Briggsy.

Briggsy referred to the highlighted areas.

Jack had circled the fact that Standt had been wanted for the drugs ring in Amsterdam in 1988. He had circled the fact that Marco had left Amsterdam in the same year for residency in Britain.

Briggsy laughed.

'I think it is coincidence Sir....Amsterdam's a big place....you can't honestly think that Mr. Veart has anything to do with this Standt character do you?', Briggsy commented vehemently.

'I mean he is a pillar of the community...he lectures for the Force for God's sake..Sir.', Briggsy continued.

'Well, Briggsy...tell me this...Why did Erik put the two of them together?...Coincidence...I don't think so...', Jack shook his head and smiled.

'Let's go find out', Jack stood up, picked up the car keys from his desk and threw them into Briggsy's lap.

Briggsy looked concerned. Still muttering words of disbelief as he and Jack drove to Marco's.

Marco, as expected, lived in the equivalent of millionaires' row. The row consisted of three overly large houses each with winding tarmac driveways stretching from the front gates up alongside the front doors. The space the three properties covered would typically represent an area equivalent to that of fifteen or twenty terraced houses. Jack mocked at how the other half live. Briggsy drew up in front of the dark green wrought iron gates of the end house. Even though it was still light, the car was immediately filled with the glow from the halogen sensors that aimed directly in front of the gates. On the front of the gates, across the top, bore the sign 'Snowfields', written in fancy old style writing, and emulsioned in gold to stand out from the green.

Briggsy switched off the engine as requested and followed Jack out of the car.

Jack walked over to the gates.

He shook the gates, they hardly budged. They must have been almost fifteen feet in height with the tops of each bar fabricated into a serrated spike. The concrete walls to the side of the gates, and indeed encapsulating the boundary of the estate, were slightly taller in height but still presented the extra obstacle of the protruding spikes along the top of them. Jack was in awe at just how serious this man took security. But then again, as he was so reliably informed, security was his game.

Jack peered through the bars of the gates and along the twisting driveway up to the house.

The house was cream in colour in complete contrast to the black of the drive and the greens, purples, yellows, and blues of the tenderly nursed landscape gardens surrounding the building. Back down the drive just off to the left was a mini orchard with its branches still showing fruits. On the trunk of the nearest visible tree hung a white sign with black lettering.

Jack could just make out the inscription on it.

'BEWARE!!

'Guard Dogs'.

'No unauthorised entry permitted.'

Jack smiled.

The signs were a legality if one wished to attack would-be prowlers with the resident Rottweiler's or Alsatian's.

Jack turned away from the gate. Briggsy pointed at the camera up on the right wall, which panned down at them. The red LED flashing impatiently which meant they were being monitored.

Jack walked over to the wall and pressed the buzzer on the intercom.

The reply was immediate.

'Can I help you?'.

The words were just about legible through the speaker.

Jack pressed his mouth to the speaker,

'CID...We'd like to speak with Mr Marco Veart...', Jack spoke slowly and an octave higher than usual.

There was a pause.

Then the voice again.

'Can you show your warrant cards to the camera please...'.

Jack and Briggsy both selected their cards from their breast pockets and held them above their heads.

The camera made whirring sounds as it zoomed and focused on the identities.

After a few seconds pause the voice broke the silence again.

'Thank you...please drive up ..I'll meet you at the door..', the speaker fell silent, and the gates slowly began to open, slightly startling Briggsy. He dived back into the car and quickly started the engine.

Jack followed at a more sedate pace.

Briggsy slammed the car into first and screeched the tyres through the opening.

Jack looked at Briggsy in despair,

'Relax Briggsy, it's not like you've just got your ticket to get into a superstore car-park....The gates aren't suddenly going to slam shut because you haven't entered in the allotted five second period', Jack smiled.

Briggsy glared at him but said nothing.

Briggsy slowed up to the front of the house and pulled the car into the side bay, beside the Discovery and the BMW. Jack got out and took a long hard look at the BMW.

Midnight blue.

He noted the registration.

MV NO1.

Jack felt annoyed at not getting a glimpse of the plate back at Tommy's place. Such a distinguishable identity.

The door to the house opened and Marco Veart appeared.

He was around 5'10", 150 lbs fat-free with a short blonde crew cut. He wore the best tan that money could buy. Jack thought that he looked around his late forties, but he knew that he was actually much older. He wore an Argyle sweater with an open neck that revealed his tanned and muscular frame and slacks and Gucci shoes. The playboy image was complete. Now all Jack wished to see was the blonde dolly-bird draped over him.

Jack didn't have to wait long, although it was a brown-haired dolly bird.

Cath followed Marco out of the door, kissed him on the lips and headed around the side of the house.

Jack pondered over how she had managed to cram herself into such a tight dress.

Marco smiled.

'She's going shopping.....Women!...What would they do without shops...', Marco spoke with a slight accent. An accent that unsettled the lining of Jack's stomach.

He introduced himself and invited the officers inside.

Jack turned to see Cath speeding along the drive in the Discovery. As he turned back he caught the stare of Marco.

His eyes.

Piercing.

Probing.

Penetrating.

Numbing Jack to a standstill.

Then they became cooler.

More submissive.

Marco outstretched his hand and guided Jack inside with a smile.

He led them into his study, the first door on the left inside the open plan hallway.

The study was a large square room. An enormous pine bookcase covered the wall opposite to the doorway. Its shelves were littered mainly with factual material. To the right of the room sat a large teak desk. A black leather chair towered behind it. On the left corner of the desk stood a gold table lamp with a cylindrical head. On the right corner of the desk sat a telephone. Apart from that the desk was empty.

Behind the door was a large wooden globe, which was opened to display a selection of spirits.

Marco walked around his desk and sank into his chair.

He outstretched his hand and offered the two seats that sat in front of his desk to Jack and Briggsy.

Briggsy sat immediately.

Jack took a nonchalant look around the room before becoming seated.

He noticed the material on the bookshelves.

Large sections of history.

The great War in polished hard backed splendour.

Science.

Materials Science.

Business.

Economics.

Psychology.

Nature.

Biology.

Human Biology.

Human organs.

The list was endless.

Marco was truly a well-read man.

Marco stared at Briggsy.

'Don't I know you?', he smiled.

Briggsy blushed.

'Yes Sir!...you gave lectures at the college last year on security measures', Briggsy was quick to reply.

'Home security advice....latest technologies...security awareness...', Briggsy eagerly continued before Jack broke in,

'Well Mr Veart...I can only complement you on your awareness of the security of your place here...It's like a fortress..', Jack mused.

Marco dropped his smile for a second, then beamed,

'Yes..I suppose it is...My philosophy is practice what you preach...', he laughed.

Briggsy laughed in unison.

Jack sighed.

'Anyway..please call me Marco...', he remained polite to Jack.

His accent was beginning to make Jack nauseous, and he couldn't remain in eye contact with Marco for longer than was absolutely necessary.

The air was thin.

Jack felt incredibly odd.

He didn't feel in command of the situation and had to rectify the situation immediately.

'The reason we've troubled you Mr. Veart is we wish to locate one of your employees...', Jack paused.

'Who?', Marco replied.

'Artur Standt', Jack was quick to reply.

He waited for a reaction.

Marco shook his head.

'Never heard of him'.

Jack reached into his jacket pocket and placed the picture of Standt down in front of Marco.

Marco picked up the picture and puzzled over it intently.

'No...Never seen or heard of him before', came his reply seconds later.

Jack stared for a second into Marco's eyes until it became unbearable.

He averted his eyes to the photo.

'Maybe you know him as Dennis Smith...or maybe Luc Van Els', Jack probed.

Marco laughed.

'Dennis Smith...

Luc Van Els...

Artur Standt...', he laughed again.

'All the same man...I don't think you know me too well inspector... maybe you should speak with your Chief Super for a character reference ...I beat him at a round of golf only last week..he never mentioned any of this to me...', he strayed from the question much to Jack's annoyance.

'I perform extensive vetting on all my employees...I can assure you I would not employ a man with various aliases or personalities..', he laughed again.

'To the best of my knowledge this man doesn't work for me....but to be sure I'll check...one moment please...', he picked up the phone and pressed a button.

'Samantha...could you bring me a copy of the latest employee records...', he paused.

'Yes that's right..all the names of the employees on our payroll... include contractors as well please...

I'm in the study....thank you...quick as you like...', he replaced the receiver.

Marco smiled and offered Jack and Briggsy a drink. Both declined. Briggsy more politely than Jack.

Marco frowned,

'What has this man supposed to have done?', he enquired.

Jack felt Briggsy about to spill his guts and quickly butted in.

'Nothing....he might be able to help us with our enquiries..', Jack enforced.

Marco smiled,

'Yes of course!'.

Briggsy looked at Jack. Jack ignored the look.

Moments later there was a knock on the door and Marco's PA, Samantha entered the room. She handed Marco a file and smiled at Jack and Briggsy before leaving the room.

Jack felt he had seen her before or at least someone very similar to her.

He deliberated for a moment then dismissed it as Marco waved the file in front of his eyes.

'Still with us Inspector', Marco mused.

Jack flipped through the pages of the file.

'Can we take this away with us?', Jack asked.

Marco looked bemused,

'Is that absolutely necessary...That is confidential information'.

Briggsy broke in while Jack was caught in the stare of Marco again.

'It is a murder enquiry, Sir!'.

Jack broke the stare instantly and looked in complete amazement and shear disbelief at the words that had emanated from Briggsy's lips.

Marco tried to look shocked,

'Oh really...well in that case of course you can take them away with you inspector...but let me have them back as soon as you've read them...otherwise I won't know who to pay and we'll have several more murders on our hands...my wage clerks..', he laughed again at his sick quip.

It befitted Briggsy's humour and he followed suit.

Jack could take no more and stood up to leave.

He took back the photo and told Marco he would be in touch.

'No problem at all...If there is anything else I can help you with Inspector Mitchell..please don't hesitate...', he offered his hand to Jack.

Jack shook it. His last comment wasn't quite right. Something wasn't right. What was it?

It wasn't until Jack got through the gates and halfway back to the station that it hit him.

'How did he know my name?', Jack shouted out.

Briggsy stopped the car.

'Pardon Sir?', Briggsy proclaimed.

'How did Veart know my name?', Jack repeated.

'He said Inspector Mitchell...I never mentioned my name ...in fact come to think of it I never actually introduced myself....did you?', Jack enquired anxiously.

Briggsy thought.

'Well..no...I didn't'.

Jack looked pale.

Briggsy then suddenly realised,

'From the camera...he saw our warrant cards', Briggsy felt pleased at his first bit of detective work so far on this case.

Jack nodded.

'Yeah...maybe...', he still looked pale.

Jack thought about the meeting for the rest of the journey back. Certain other things didn't seem right. He just couldn't quite join the pieces together. But one thing was sure, he didn't like or trust Marco Veart. He put a chill up his spine. An experience Jack rarely encountered. Not while conscious anyway.

Jack told Briggsy to drive him home. His mind was unsettled. It was 835 P.M. He'd had enough for one day. He felt a vision just begging to embrace him. He had to fight it until Briggsy got him home. Briggsy felt uneased at Jack's silence for the journey home.

As they pulled up outside Jack's house he said,

'That rules Marco out then Sir...', he said it more as a statement than a question.

Jack snapped and grabbed tightly at the lapel of Briggsy's jacket,

'When he took you for those lectures Briggsy was he pumping you out back afterwards or what?.....If you want to carry on working with me then you are going to have to learn to be not so naive...it makes me want to vomit', Jack spoke viciously.

Briggsy cowered in his seat. He had witnessed the trait that all the other officers had warned him about.

Jack's temper.

A lethal weapon.

He was pretty angry.

He slammed the door and disappeared into his house.

Briggsy shook.

In fact, he shook all the way back to the station.

He had seen the look in Jack's eyes.

Naked and savage.

CHAPTER 12

Jack paced around his place for around an hour. Darkness had ensued and he found himself sat staring out at the eerie glow from the streetlamp across the road. The road was silent. For an hour he had reasoned with himself as to why Marco had rattled him so badly. Certain events he couldn't understand. Maybe Briggsy was right. Maybe Marco had seen the names on the warrant cards at the gate. But what Jack couldn't comprehend was that if Marco was such a busy businessman then why would he be sat watching as though waiting for someone to arrive at his gates. It had been only around a minute before the security camera had panned down to highlight them at the gate. Coincidence - possibly.

Also, Jack couldn't comprehend that in Marco's study, two chairs sat conveniently placed in front of the desk, as though expecting two visitors. Coincidence- possibly.

Jack also recalled Marco's PA, Samantha. He was convinced he knew her from somewhere or had seen her before. But where?

And finally, the amount of security his grounds encompassed, seemed a little extreme. Then again, the words 'Practise what you preach', sprang to mind.

All these points sustained Jack's suspicion.

Most of all though, Jack felt uncomfortable by the presence of the man. His eyes. The stare. His manner. Maybe Jack was biased through instant dislike of the man, but his instincts screamed at him. He took the opinion that Erik was telling the truth and that Marco was shying away or hiding the facts. But why and for what reason, could only be that he was involved. Jack purposely refrained from asking Marco if he was a member of the Pravada club until he had been to see Erik again and witnessed his name on the member lists. Otherwise, he was convinced he would have received another denial on that issue also.

Jack realised he needed to play his cards close to his chest and step gently around this one. Marco already had Briggsy, the Chief Super and by the sounds of it most of the force eating out of his hand. He knew he would quickly be told to back off if he didn't cover his accusations with hard evidence.

One thing was for certain, Jack knew he had his man. He was rarely wrong.

Jack switched on his table lamp and looked at his watch.

9:42 P.M.

He knew sleep wasn't really on the agenda this evening. He flicked through the pages of Marco's employees file for the third time in succession, still no trace of the man he was looking for. He flung the file onto his table in disgust. The file wasn't worth the paper it was printed on in his eyes. More lies.

He reached into his jacket pocket that hung on the back of his chair and took out his warrant card. He outstretched his arm in front of him and squinting his eyes tried to make out his name on it. It was barely readable from just two feet never mind twelve or more. Then again the zoom facilities on cameras today are resolute.

He sighed and noticed a card had dropped from his pocket onto the carpet below.

It was Helen's number.

Jack smiled and made over to his phone.

He picked up the receiver dialled three of the seven numbers then replaced it again.

He spent the next five minutes thinking of what to say before he finally heard her voice at the end of the line.

'Hello?'

'It's me...Jack Mitchell...'

'Hi Jack', her voice sounded so reassuring.

'You left it late...I was just about to go to bed...its 10 o'clock.'

Jack stuttered,

'Sorry, erm..I'll let you go then...I didn't realise'.

'No..It's OK..I was just bored...I wasn't going to sleep..probably just read for a while..I'm not tired..', she laughed at the end of the line.

Jack, to his amazement, found himself asking if he could come round for a chat, and was equally amazed when she accepted his offer.

Jack took a quick shower whilst waiting for the taxi to arrive. He was in her flat within twenty minutes later. She smiled as she opened the door to him. She obviously had recently showered too and wore simple flannel jogging bottoms and a loose white top. Her hair, still damp, was tied up in a bun at the back. She invited Jack to sit down on the sofa and offered him a cup of coffee.

Jack wished he had dressed more comfortably as well. He wore tight jeans and a denim shirt.

Her flat was small but typically feminine. The sofa was a small compact two-seater which was obviously second hand but comfy all the same. A TV and Hi-Fi occupied one corner of the room a multi-coloured beanbag in the other. A large coffee table sat in front of the sofa with a clear glass top. Telltale coffee cup rings littered the top right of it but apart from that the flat was extremely tidy. Jack licked his fingers and began to scrub at the marks on the table until he heard Helen come back into the room.

She brought the mugs of coffee in on a plastic tray complete with a bowl of sugar, two spoons and a jug of milk. She placed the tray onto the table and told Jack to help himself while she selected some music. Jack was not surprised when he heard Portishead gently throbbing through the speakers behind him. 'Mysterons', the first track on the album. Jack appreciated her musical tastes as well.

She went over to the beanbag and carried it to the other side of the table and fell bottom first into it. She shuffled in the small polystyrene beads until her position was comfortable. She smiled,

'These things are great aren't they...always handy when you need an extra seat when you've got guests.

Jack wished she had sat next to him.

Jack told her of the exploits at Marco's and asked her professional opinion on his suspicions. She was very accommodating and understanding which helped ease Jack considerably. He felt so relaxed and comfortable in her company.

He hadn't felt so calm for as long as he could remember.

As they sipped the second mug of coffee, the conversation switched to their childhoods. Helen described the area and family in which she grew up in and Jack did the same. Helen had a more flagrant upbringing. She adopted a cosmopolitan attitude and endured long breaks away travelling and sightseeing. She appreciated the various cultures and creeds. Jack on the other hand was fairly reclusive as a child. He was an individualist who was never quite sure just how much he trusted his peers. For that reason, he sustained only short-term acquaintances. Helen was amazed that he didn't actually have any real friends whom he remained in contact with.

The level of conversation was pleasing to both. They stimulated each other's minds with high degrees of knowledge, beliefs, and intellect.

They both sat for hours, chatting, laughing, and confessing. They both lay back. Jack on the sofa and Helen on the beanbag. They just chatted and chatted without even looking up. They both became relaxed in each other's company as though they'd been together for years. The music washed over them, and twenty strangers could have walked into the room and neither would have batted an eyelid. For Jack, this really was heaven.

By the third coffee, they had developed onto the subject of partners, without really noticing. It was just the natural progression of the conversation. Helen had been in a few messy relationships that had left her emotionally scarred and heedful of the opposite sex. Whereas Jack admitted to not being secure enough to have a serious relationship. He had several flings, but, in fact had not been with another woman for almost ten months. Helen had had about the same break too. They smiled at the uncanny similarities.

Later, after a few minutes silence, Helen sat up on the beanbag and noticed Jack had dropped off into a deep sleep. He still bore the smile on his lips. She laughed quietly. She spoke his name softly, but he didn't even stir.

It was late. 3 a.m. to be precise.

Helen quickly decided he could stay and that there was no need to wake Jack up. She quietly and gently removed his boots and lifted his legs up onto the sofa. She fetched a blanket from her cupboard and draped it over him. He slept so soundly.

She smiled before turning off the lights and making for her bed.

Helen had barely been asleep. Probably for just over an hour. She was startled awake by loud blood curdling screams,

'PATRICIA!!!!!............................PATRICIA........NO!!!!!!!!!!!'.

She dived out of bed without thinking of throwing on her gown. She only wore panties to bed. She raced out of her bedroom and quickly realised it was Jack screaming.

She switched on the lights to see Jack lying on his back his body flailing around wildly. The blanket had been kicked off him onto the table.

'NO...NO...PLEASE NO!!!!', Jack screamed still in his sleep.

Helen ran over to him. She shook him gently at first then harder. Jack reached out and grabbed hold of Helen around her shoulders and pulled her on top of him. He squeezed her so tightly she could hardly breathe. It was pointless to resist. He had a vice-like grip. Then he quietened and started to quietly sob in his sleep. She felt his grip loosen and in seconds he was back into deep sleep. Although, the occasional sob did breathe through his lips. She pushed herself up and stood over him for a while. She was very shocked by the sudden outburst. Jack stirred slightly. Helen quickly noticing that her breasts were exposed quickly darted back into the doorway. She watched Jack for a moment. She felt frightened and confused by what she had witnessed. Was this man really a gentle giant or was he an aggressive ogre? She went back into her room and locked her door.

Her clock read 5:47 a.m. Strangely though she didn't feel sleep tired. Fatigued, yes, but in no state to sleep.

Jack stirred on the sofa and opened his eyes. He slowly gazed around the room. Everything seemed strange. He looked at the sofa then sprang upright. He rubbed his eyes, as he became aware of where he was. His body was dripping in sweat and he smelled stale. His mouth was like the bottom of a birdcage. Arid and rough. He stood up in the dim light that filled the room. The birds were busy going about their noisy early morning routine. He wandered out of the room and into the kitchen. He put the kettle on to boil.

Helen heard him and threw on her jogging bottoms and T-shirt. She met him in the kitchen. She acted as normal as though nothing had happened. She took over the coffee duties and told Jack to go and sit down.

She explained that he had fallen asleep. She made a sarcastic comment that it was probably her boring conversation. Jack apologised profusely. She laughed.

Jack laughed.

Jack sensed that Helen seemed different though. More reserved. Maybe she wasn't a morning person, but Jack sensed something deeper.

The atmosphere seemed different.

Cloudy.

Less cordial.

Helen finished her coffee and stood up to leave the room.

It was then that she plucked up the courage.

'Whose Patricia?', she seemed concerned.

Jack stared at her blankly.

'Patricia?'.

Jack shook his head. He didn't recall the name but still felt the twist in his stomach.

'You woke up screaming her name this morning....surprised you didn't wake the neighbours actually.', she smiled.

'Patricia?..',Jack repeated.

He felt as if he should know the name but for the life of him couldn't put a face to it.

'I don't know?', Jack said anxiously.

Helen stared at him for a while not knowing whether to believe him or not.

She took her cup into the kitchen.

Jack ran the name through his mind.

'Patricia....Patricia...Patricia...'.

His stomach twisted at every word. He cringed under the pain.

Then the vision of a young girl hit him. She was beautiful. He witnessed her smiling face. His heartbeat galloped.

He pictured a grassy knoll. A gold locket with the letters P and B inscribed. A photo of a young boy inside.

The vision was hazy. Jack grew alarmed. He tried to dismiss the image in his head. It made him perilously uncomfortable. Tears streamed down his cheeks. He felt like he had just died.

When Helen came back into the room, Jack recounted his vision. She seemed to understand but Jack wasn't sure. How could anybody accept these ridiculous and seemingly farcical explanations at face value. They all appeared to be cryptic and far-fetched solutions to extremely simple questions. Jack felt ultimately embarrassed and would have quite understood if Helen hadn't believed him. He found it difficult to believe himself. His whole life appeared surreal. He questioned to himself if he really was alive and if his actual being was a reality. His latest feelings and discoverings were like something out of a Dean Koontz novel, possible but not probable. Defying logic and comprehension. She smiled at him and said,

'Will I see you today?..In a professional capacity that is?'.

Helen laughed.

Jack smiled.

'Probably!'.

Jack asked if he could order a taxi. Helen dismissed it and offered him a lift home. Jack was extremely grateful.

———— • ————

Neilsen had received the call from Marco at around 9 p.m. the previous evening. They had already delivered the money and picked up the goods from Pat McClere. McClere ran the trafficking side of the operation. The drug was manufactured in Holland and shipped to Hull where McClere would receive and fence the goods in a local garage until Marco sent someone up to collect it. Standt was a little disappointed when Neilsen told him that Marco wanted them back in the morning. He had planned to do a bit of clubbing and messing around and generally let his hair down. He still liked to keep with it even though he was only a few years away from 60. Their week's break or hiding, whichever way it was interpreted, had been dramatically cut short. They had hit the motorway at around 6 a.m. that morning. Neilsen was at the wheel. Standt lay back in the passenger seat wondering what dirty deed Marco had installed for them next. He was tired of the wrangle that he had been caught up in. For as long as he could remember he had been ducking and diving through dark alleys and seedy clubs. He'd been with Marco since they first met in Amsterdam in 1975. Standt had been heavily involved in the drug scene. It was where the money was. Marco had muscled in on the scene with plans for a new drug. It had taken a long time to perfect the drug and, in the time taken, many key players' toes had been trodden on. At one stage the situation had got very messy and dangerous with territorial wars and executions drawing unnecessary heat from law and investigative agencies. Standt had himself been ear-marked as a major player and was under scrutinous surveillance and investigation. In that time, it was Marco who was calling the shots, but he didn't even get a mention in police suspicions. Standt had to dive underground for a time while Marco brought the drug to manufactured perfection. It was then that the drug spread to Britain and Standt was allowed to return to the scene. Since then, he had lost count how many people he had killed or how much blood money had passed through his hands.

He longed to settle. He felt his age and realised that he was getting too old for all of this. He wanted somewhere to hang his hat, take off his boots and live a peaceful, trouble free existence. Maybe, spend most days fishing or just lazing around in a secluded and remote spot. He hated people. He hated their dog-eat-dog survival and greed. In his younger years he loved his job and the life he led. The power. The rush. The judgement over life and death. Now, he detested what he had become and mulled over his route of escape from it.

He watched as the suits with their mobile phones attached to their ears, raced in the fast lane. BMW's, Mercedes, Audi's. Those that hadn't quite made it in life but could smell it, almost touch it. The power.

Neilsen directed the car onto the M5, the trip around Birmingham hadn't been that bad.

Neilsen kept checking his speed, ensuring that he didn't edge above 70 and tried to keep out of the outside lane as much as possible. They didn't want to get caught speeding or draw attention to themselves considering the shipment that was in the case in the boot.

The service station was fast approaching. Standt suggested that they stop for a coffee and change over the driving. Neilsen agreed.

Neilsen pulled into the station and drove around into the Truck Park away from the main restaurant building as usual.

The park was almost empty. Just one German truck sat stationary. The driver had pulled curtains around his cab and obviously was catching up on some lost sleep during the busy period on the roads. Neilsen parked the car five spaces away from the toilet. A white square building neglected through the years that seriously needed a lick of paint. He turned off the engine and asked Standt what he wanted. Standt ordered a coffee and a burger or a sausage roll. Neilsen disappeared over to the shop about two hundred yards away beyond the small trees and bushes that sealed off the Truck Park from the rest of the station.

Standt stayed with the merchandise. He kept an eye on the truck checking to see if there was any sign of life. The curtains remained drawn, and the place was very quiet.

Neilsen returned ten minutes later. He wasn't happy. He had to queue. Standt ate his sausage roll and sipped his coffee, Neilsen scoffed his pork pie and scotch egg and slurped his can of cola in his usual disgusting manner. Standt finished his meal first and left the car to relieve himself before they started on the road again.

The toilet smelled stale. Dried urine stained the floor. The urinals were littered with cigarette butts and pubic hair. The smell almost made Standt wretch. He stood over the nearest urinal and read the graffiti on the wall. Toilet humour was very popular along with football teams. He became transfixed by the length and colour of a bogey that stretched across the tiled wall directly in front of him. Two maybe three inches at least. Crusty and well at home in the decor.

He was just shaking himself off when he felt the force tugging on his hair.

His head was snatched backwards, and he felt the cool blade against his throat. He heard the faint sound of his throat tearing and felt the gush of warm blood streaming down his neck. His mouth opened wide, and his hands clutched at his throat. He spun around stumbling against the wall. His fingers pressed tight trying to stem the bleeding. Bright red blood bubbled over his lips as he gasped for breath. He saw his attacker through his glazed eyes. It was Neilsen. He stood there still clutching his deer-footed weapon. Smiling. Standt tried to charge him but was weak and collapsed headfirst onto the floor. He lay watching the blood seep around him. Drowning in his own blood. He wanted to say 'Why?' and only asked the question to himself in his head. He was paralysed. Motionless. The pain had gone and Standt drifted away.

Neilsen cleaned his blade on Standt's jacket and lifted him by the feet. His boots were already wet with blood. He dragged him into the solitary cubicle and pushed the door shut.

He calmly went over to the sink turned on the hot tap with the sleeve of his shirt and washed the death from his hands. The red swirl around the basin was quickly replaced by clear water. Neilsen left the tap running and returned to the car.

He checked around the park to ensure no one was watching him or in view and opened the boot. He put on his black leather gloves and removed the case. He jumped into the car with the case. He opened the glove box and took out some cleaning fluid usually used to clean the windscreen and a cloth. He cleaned the outside of the case, removing all traces of prints.

He reached under the passenger seat and collected a black canvas bag. He transferred the contents of the case into the black bag and replaced it under Standt's seat. He cleaned the insides of the case and then reached into his trouser pocket. He pulled out a small plastic bag. It contained cocaine. He opened it and liberally sprinkled the powder over the inside of the case until the bag was empty. He wanted it to look like the case had contained a large amount of drugs and maybe one of the bags had been torn slightly in the rush of emptying it. It seemed convincing. The powder clung noticeably to the insides of the case. Neilsen made it look like a drug-war hit and the motive surrounding the death would be self explanatory and not suspicious.

He stepped out of the car and carried the case into the toilet. The place looked like a slaughterhouse. Blood pooled over the floor and had begun to trickle from under the cubicle door. Standt's dormant body prevented Neilsen from opening the cubicle door enough to get the case through the opening so he nonchalantly threw it over the top. The case made a slight thud as it landed on top of Standt's body. He then returned to the car and left taking just one last look at the truck. No witnesses.

Back in the car, he removed his gloves, turned on the stereo and whistled along to the sounds of the radio as he returned back onto the motorway. The remnants of Standt's Last Supper still decorated the dashboard. The empty sausage roll wrapper with a few flakes of pastry on the seat and the polystyrene cup with a centimetre of coffee shivering coldly under the throb of the engine. Neilsen finished off the remaining two bites of his Scotch egg.

Briggsy was in the office early. He had already prepared a coffee for the moment Jack arrived. It sat steaming at his desk as he sat down. Briggsy was purposely steering clear of him, after the previous evening, but at the same time was being his usual thoughtful self. Jack felt guilty at his outburst yesterday and quickly apologised. It had not been a good day for him. Briggsy cheered up at the apology and asked where they went from here. Jack shrugged.

The only lead he had was Marco, but nobody seemed to share in his suspicions. In fact, no sooner had he finished his coffee, the Super burst into his office and roasted him for insulting a respected member of the community. Marco. He had just got off the phone with the Chief Super and insisted to know why he was being questioned. Jack tried to play it down suggesting that he was just following up leads, but Craven knew Jack too well for that.

He warned him off Marco advising that the waters he had strayed into were deep. Very deep indeed.

Jack didn't need to be told that. He knew. He said all along it was a big fish and the biggest fish prowl the deepest oceans. Jack felt annoyed at the warning and the anger boiled inside him. He managed to curb it until he had received his ticking off. He had no plan. No evidence, apart from the word of a Norwegian head-bouncer and a notoriously elusive terrorist, Standt. It would be a waiting game. Jack would just wait until Standt turned up. Whether it be in the Bahamas or Rochdale, he would find him, and when he did he would harpoon Marco Veart. Jack smiled.

The waiting game didn't last too long. Three hours to be precise. Jack answered the call personally from the Mercia branch. He was jubilant to hear that they had found his man but quickly gutted to hear he was dead. A German truck driver had discovered the body. He had slept for most of the morning, waking around 10:30 and, deciding to freshen himself up with a wash and a shave, had stumbled in on the carnage.

Jack had slammed down the receiver making Briggsy flinch.

Neither said a word to each other on the way to the service station. Jack's appetite for conversation had deserted him. Briggsy didn't fancy the gamble.

It was midday by the time they arrived. The route into the Truck Park was blocked by two squad cars that reversed to let them in when Jack flashed his badge. The toilet was surrounded by squad cars, paramedics, and unmarked vehicles. The only alien site was the large Warsteiner truck parked alone fifty yards from the rest. A line of civilians stood under the trees behind the tape that prevented them from getting a clearer view of the morning's spectacle. Jack was met by the reporting officer. He escorted Jack and Briggsy inside the toilet. Jack saw the blood. Large pools sat over the floor still wet. The marks where the body had been dragged into the cubicle. The paramedics had been allowed to remove the body.

The officer confirmed to where they found him and the fatality of the wound. Jack walked into the cubicle stepping carefully around the pools of blood. What a place to die? He looked around the cubicle.

'Was the door locked when you found him', Jack enquired.

The officer shook his head,

'No just shut...the German trucker saw all the blood and immediately got someone else to call us.

Jack stood up against the toilet seat. He scanned the cubicle. No visible traces of anything else other than blood. He read the graffiti on the sidewalls of the cubicle. He sighed and looked at the door as he closed it.

He spoke from inside the cubicle,

'Did you check the back of the door?'.

There followed a short silence.

'Erm...No..I don't think so..', the officer replied.

Jack opened the door and walked out,

'You'd better get the photographer back in then', Jack walked out of the building.

Briggsy dived into the cubicle just before the officer and looked on the back of the door.

Written in blood just a few inches above the bottom of the door was the last thing on Standt's mind before he died. Written with his own blood, with his own trembling fingers.

M A R

Briggsy saw the letters. He knew immediately what was on Jack's mind. Was it to be Marco Veart? It could have been something completely different. He may have had a girlfriend called MARGARET or something else. It could be anything but Briggsy knew by the reaction of Jack of his one and only permutation. Briggsy sighed. He didn't for one minute believe Marco was involved in this, but the way things were progressing he couldn't help but agree with Jack that fingers were beginning to point at him. It then became apparent to Briggsy that Marco was being set-up and perhaps Erik was in on the plot, and he would deliver his theories to Jack. Coincidence was beginning to become less likely.

Jack was over with the paramedics. He had unzipped the body bag and recognised Standt from the video. He noticed the same neck wounds as the girls in the hotel. The wound lay crudely open. The officer and Briggsy quickly joined him. The officer spoke again.

'Another statistic for drugs killings!'

Jack turned to the officer confused.

'What do you mean?'.

'We found a case, obviously once full of cocaine, still traces of it in it...', he paused.

'Obviously came here to swap the drugs for money...but got shit out of luck ...had the drugs nicked and got killed to boot...never learn will they?'.

Jack stared at the officer still perplexed.

'Wait a minute ..What case?'.

The officer realised he had forgot to mention it,

'Oh sorry..yes a case was found thrown open on the body...they must have been in such a rush they ripped open one of the bags taking it out'.

The officer pointed over to the forensics car.

'That's it!'.

Jack turned and walked over to the case. It was quite large and bulky. As he got closer he noticed the case was silver in colour.

His stomach twisted. He winced under the pain.

He slowed. Briggsy reached the case first and stared inside it. He witnessed the powder stacked around the corners.

Jack never got that far.

He stopped yards away from it staring at the case.

He'd already witnessed the inside of it once before..

It was a test-tube.

Quite large.

Wrapped in foam.

Bunged at the end.

Containing a blue liquid.

He saw the hand reach inside and grasp the tube.

He saw another hand slowly prise the bung out of the end.

The tube was raised, and he felt the cool liquid slip down his throat.

It's bitter taste.

Jack was pale. Briggsy noticed.

'You OK Sir', he questioned.

Jack turned away and walked back to the car.

The journey back was as quiet as the journey there. Briggsy sensed all wasn't quite right but again couldn't take the gamble on speaking. He knew Jack's suspicion of Marco had increased and although he had his reservations, he decided not to mention his theory.

Jack knew the drug thing was a scam. An illusion. Standt was killed to protect Marco and for no other reason. All they had now was Erik and his story wasn't exactly watertight.

Jack felt he was right back at the beginning but the issue that worried him the most were the increasingly clear and vivid visions filling his mind.

The silver case had been present in his dreams or rather nightmares since he was a boy. He had seen several varieties of cases since then, black, brown, and silver. But none of the others had stirred up the emotion and feeling within the pit of his stomach as this particular one. It was in Jack's mind, THE case.

But how? Where?

He recalled the cool sensation, not only in his throat, but the more he thought about it, the whole of his body deep into his bones felt the chill. As though he was on ice.

He thought harder.

No, it was snow.

Deep snow.

He could smell it. Taste it. Feel it.

It was snow alright.

It happened. Slowly and distorted, but Jack knew exactly where and when.

It was already mid-afternoon when Jack and Briggsy got back to the office. Briggsy immediately went away to fetch two coffees while Jack unlocked the bottom drawer of his desk and took out the case file. It was beginning to become quite a thick affair. Sordid pictures of Frank Christie and his bullet riddled body, the American girls, naked and half decapitated, Den hanging from the old mill, the close-up of the carved swastika in his torso, Tommy lying blue and lifeless at the bottom of his stairs. Jack laid the pictures out on his desk side by side. He added to it the picture caught on camera of Standt. There would soon be a couple more pictures to add to the file once Mercia forwarded them on.

He knew Standt had killed Tommy, so he took the picture of Standt and laid it to the left of his desk along with that of Tommy. He scanned the others. Standt had been killed with a blade. So had the American girls and Den. He assumed then that Standt had probably killed Frank and laid the picture of Frank to his left as well. He stared at the remaining pictures. All knife wounds. This was the work of someone else. A professional with a blade.

The precise and accurate slashes were no work of an amateur. The carving on Den's torso was done by a controlled and expert hand. Someone who wasn't timorous or indeed phased by the graphic delineation onto a still warm human body the slits etched with a honed and carefully maintained edge.

Jack thumbed through the rest of the file. Lab reports, witnesses, statements.

Statements.

He found Erik's statement and quickly read through it till he found the part he was looking for.

Standt had arrived at the club days earlier with a friend of his.

A friend.

Jack mused at what a strong friendship they had. Laughing, drinking bottles of beer, messing around with women, confiding in their secrets, and of course slitting each other's throat with a 9-inch serrated blade.

Some friend.

Jack felt angered that he had completely overlooked this part of the statement. He was so intent in tracing Standt that he never clicked that he had an accomplice in the atrocities. He should have got a description from Erik. That was careless and a procedure straight out of the handbook.

He tore off two pieces of stick notes from the pad and stuck one label to the left of his desk, the other to the right. He wrote 'Standt' in black marker on the left label and 'A Friend' on the other.

Jack leant back on his chair and smiled as he stared at his layout.

Briggsy returned with the coffee and noticed the pictures laid out neatly on Jack's desk. He noticed the labels too.

'A friend?', Briggsy had a puzzled look on his face.

Jack smiled,

'Don't you see it Briggsy?'.

Jack stood up and threw on his jacket.

'Look at the pictures and then read the file.', Jack stated.

'Then pay close attention to Erik's statement...and see what answers you come up with', He patted Briggsy on the shoulder.

'While you are doing that I'm off to see a Norwegian on the way home...see you tomorrow Briggsy', Jack turned and walked out of the office.

He stopped in the door and shouted back at Briggsy,

'Oh and do us a favour...put everything back in the file when you've done, the keys still in the drawer', Jack smiled. Briggsy was some help.

Briggsy sat in Jack's chair and scanned the pictures. He searched for Erik's statement and tried to rescue the information that Jack had found. He puzzled over it for a few minutes.

Erik's flat was on Jack's way home. He called in at the paper shop first and picked up a Daily Mail and a packet of chewing gum. He needed the gum to curb his incredible urge to start smoking again. When the visions began to become clearer he would smoke 40 maybe 50 cigarettes a day. It didn't help his mental state or his lungs. He had given up almost 18 months ago and the stress of this case had re-instated the urge. He unwrapped two sticks of the gum and forced both into his mouth. He sat in his car for a second, just flicking through the paper for any national headlines on the case. The press still hadn't picked up on it yet, which was always a bonus.

He threw the paper down onto the passenger seat and headed off for Erik's place. The Pravada had closed down since Tommy's death and apparently Erik had resorted to a reclusive lifestyle until he felt capable of looking for work again.

Jack reached Layman Way thirty minutes after leaving the office. The city was a nightmare in rush hour. He parked the car and approached Erik's place. Number 11. Layman Way was a council estate. The houses were no bigger than rabbit hutches and the road was lined with rust-ridden vehicles, which was in line with the character of the area.

As Jack walked up the path he noticed that Erik's door was wide open. He knocked on it loudly and shouted inside. He heard nothing and slowly stepped into the hall.

The hallway was small and narrow. Two rooms led off to the left and one room led to the right. Jack peered around the first door. It was the kitchen. The sink was brimming over with pots and pans. Empty take-away boxes and cartons littered the side worktop. The bin was overflowing and some of its contents, beer cans and more take-away cartons, had spilled onto the floor. The place had a stench of stale food and rancid meat. Jack continued down the hall. He heard a noise. A bump. He paused. Listened. He raised his right fist ready to catch the person moving around in the room to the right. He edged forward to the doorway. Another bump and crash.

Jack slowly and inconspicuously peered around the door. Erik was on his hands and knees trying to lift himself to his feet. Empty beer cans surrounded him. They had made the noise as he placed his weight on them. He looked up when he felt Jack's presence in the doorway.

His face was a mess. Blood ran from his nose; his right eye was already closed up through intense swelling. The bruising beginning to appear around his jaw line. His lower lip had expanded to twice the original size and split open under the pressure.

Jack helped him to the chair.

He ran into the kitchen and picked up the cleanest tea towel he could find and emptied a tray of ice from the freezer into it. He wrapped the ice in the towel and handed it to Erik.

Erik was slumped in the chair. Jack thought of calling an ambulance, it looked as if Erik was about to pass out. Erik signalled with his hand that it was not what he wanted.

He applied the ice pack to his eye first then pressed it tenderly against his lip. He squirmed under the stinging pain.

'Who did it Erik?', Jack posed the question quietly.

Erik shook his head slowly whilst staring at Jack through his one good eye.

His breathing became erratic.

He started to sob and shake his head.

'It had to be someone strong and vicious to put you over.....Was there more than one?', Jack continued trying to get Erik to answer.

Erik continued sobbing and shaking his head.

Jack saw the pain in Erik's eye.

He read so much from the look.

His eyes were full of sorrow.

'It was him wasn't it?', Jack stated.

Erik stopped shaking and relented his sobbing.

His eyes still holding their watery focus on Jack.

'It was Standt's friend...wasn't it?', Jack knew.

Erik moaned aloud and began sobbing again.

'Who is he Erik?...Where can I find him?...What's he look like?...', Jack paused.

'I'll get him for you...he'll pay for this...he helped kill Tommy Erik... among others...he's got to be stopped...Who is it?', Jack urged Erik to reveal what he knew.

Erik shook his head and continued breathing erratically.

Then he spoke,

'I don't know who it was', Erik's eyes lied.

His lips could barely form the words under the swelling, and it caused him great pain to speak.

'You do Erik...', Jack insisted.

'I'll protect you...I'll put you into custody...in a safe-house ..anywhere where they can't get at you...just tell me what you know', Jack showed feeling in his tone.

Erik shook his head.

'NO...', he shouted agonisingly.

'I don't know him'.

Jack sighed.

'I suppose you don't remember who Standt's friend was or what he looked like either?'.

Erik shook his head.

It was enough for Jack. He understood the situation Erik had been forced into. The man sat in front of him feared for his life. That was obvious. He didn't blame Erik but nevertheless felt angered at the way things had developed.

Jack stood up.

'You're protecting Tommy's murderers Erik...I thought he meant something to you?....You know where I am if you change your mind...'.

Jack left Erik's house amidst the childlike sound of a grown man sobbing and moaning. He shut his door and drove home.

Jack felt it was over. He'd lost. Marco had won. That was it. The end. For the first time in his life Jack felt the full force of failure. He was swathed in self-pity. Anger boiled within him. He had nothing.

He needed a drink and decided to go out. He went to a local bar, The Golden Goose. It was reasonably upmarket. The beer was expensive but it also meant that the clientele would be less troublesome. Jack didn't need trouble tonight. The bar was half full of people in suits and dresses, obviously called in for a drink on the way home from work. Jack found himself a corner and retired there with a pint of bitter and double Scotch malt. He downed the malt almost immediately. The warmth filled his body and the bite made him quiver. It felt good. He gulped at the cool liquid of his beer. The alcohol was already beginning to affect him. He felt his body relax slightly. He stared into space and tried to empty his mind of the case.

He took his glasses back to the bar for the third time. He felt himself stagger. The suits had long since left and the bar was beginning to fill out with smartly dressed evening socialites. Jack returned to his seat with difficulty. His head felt heavy and ached. His legs seemed to wander in a direction away from where he commanded them to go. He finally reached his seat and slumped down relieved to find it. He looked around the bar hoping he hadn't made a spectacle of himself.

It was whilst looking around the bar that he noticed two women walk through the entrance and up to the bar. They perched themselves on a bar stool each and ordered their drinks.

Jack thought he recognised them. He adjusted his vision several times before it sunk in.

The blonde in the tight jeans and black T-shirt was Samantha, Marco's PA. The dark-haired girl with her Jack couldn't quite make out but he was sure he had seen her before too. They laughed and joked at the bar. They kept leaning towards each other, whispering in each other's ear, and then breaking out into fits of laughter.

Jack watched them for almost half an hour. They put five pounds into the fruit machine and drank three Vodka and lemonades each.

Jack's glass was again empty, and he made the treacherous trip to the bar. He completed the journey with increasing difficulty. Several tables and chairs were bumped and knocked but he arrived next to Samantha. He ordered a pint in a now slurred tone. Samantha turned and looked at Jack. Jack smiled.

'Hi...'.

'Hi..', the girls broke into fits of laughter.

'I know you don't I?',Jack enquired trying his best to sound sober but failing miserably.

Samantha turned back and looked at Jack again.

'I don't think so..is that the best chat up line you have?', they laughed again.

'Don't you work for Marco Veart?'

The girls stopped laughing.

'Well yes I do...How did you know?', Samantha seemed more serious.

'I met you the other day...only briefly...', Jack slurred.

Samantha thought for a second.

'Oh yeah...you were the police officer..', she realised, looking him up and down surprised by his drunken state.

'Jack', Jack introduced himself and shook her hand.

'I'm Samantha and this is my best friend Jo', she returned the greeting.

Jo smiled.

'Ooooh..Why aren't you in the kinky blue uniform then?', she quipped.

Both girls laughed aloud again.

'Tart', Samantha noted.

Jack smiled.

'How long have you worked for him?'.

'About 5 years...Why?'.

'Did you know an Artur Standt?'.

Samantha though for a second then shook her head.

'No...don't think so..'.

'Did you know Tommy Wright?', Jack continued.

Both girls looked sombre.

They nodded.

'We went to his club a few times....that's a tragedy isn't it...what happened to him'.

Jack nodded and agreed.

Jo downed the remaining half of her glass and stood up.

She apologised to Jack saying sorry they had to go and patted Samantha on the back. Samantha stared at Jo then understood they had to leave. She gave a parting smile and followed Jo out of the door. Jack couldn't persuade them to stay for another no matter how hard he tried. He noted it had been Jo more so than Samantha that had been uncomfortable with the mention of Tommy's name..

Jack turned and saw his seat in the corner had been taken. He sighed.

He noticed the payphone standing on the end of the bar. He reached into his jacket pocket and pulled out Helen's number. He flipped the card for a few times and stared at the number on it.

He edged along the bar and dialled the number.

She answered quickly and said she would be along for a drink shortly. Jack felt in a spin at the sound of her voice again.

Jack waited patiently for ten minutes. Helen pulled up outside the Golden Goose about three spaces from the dark blue BMW that had been sat in the same spot for almost two and a half hours. She walked inside the bar and was shocked to see the state that Jack was in. He met her with a huge grin. She laughed after getting over the shock of his obvious intoxication. She stayed for one mineral water then gave Jack a lift back to his house.

She helped him inside and made a pot of tea.

Jack told her of the day's occurrences.

It took some time in his state, but she listened, nevertheless.

She was shocked to hear of Standt's murder. It wasn't Jack's animated description of Standt's fatal wounding that shocked her but more the news of his untimely demise. Jack wasn't sure if it was the alcohol or the fact that he felt completely at ease in Helen's company, but he also confessed to his visions. Helen listened with a sympathetic ear. Jack began by recounting the German uniforms....the train....the snow...the silver case....the liquid he drank.

Then he reiterated the locket with the young boy's picture...the inscription..the girl Patricia...

It was a relief to be able to talk openly about these things, but he subconsciously realised that he must have sounded crazy. Subconsciously Helen found his confessions a little unnerving but at the same time fascinating. Stories of this nature had interested her from a very early age. It was a subject that intrigued her, and no amount of high-technology wizardry could prove or disprove theories of regression. She told him she had done a lot of research into deja-vu and reincarnation. She hadn't completely rejected the fact that it could be possible. The mind is an unknown entity in a lot of respects. She kept a very open stance on the subject and listened with interest, even if she felt aware of the growing surrealism to the story. Jack continued to relive his visions, albeit in a somewhat spasmodic and fragmented fashion. Then there was an uneasy silence. Jack sighed loud and deeply feeling the reliefs of revelation escape from within. He felt lifted. He stared at Helen waiting for a positive response or at least the slightest hint of understanding. She smiled back at him with that heart-dissolving smile.

Helen broke the silence and said that she would dig out her old University notes on the subject and see if she could help him in any way. She had studied Psychology for a period of time as part of her medical degree. It was by no stretch of the imagination an extensive study, but she felt it would be better for Jack if she appeared to be helping or indeed interested in his plight. If the truth were to be known, Helen was beginning to find Jack completely irresistible. She loved his company, his darkness, and complexities. She found herself aching for him when he wasn't with her. A feeling Helen hadn't experienced to this intensive level, it was a sensation that was strangely erotic. She felt honoured by his openness and understood that he wouldn't confess his troubles to just anyone. That made her feel special as though it was a two-way emotion. In truth, Jack too felt utterly besotted with Helen. He adored her frankness, her sensitivity and her arcanic mind-set. They had a balance of character and personality that fused in the centre but had sufficient individual differences to create a mystical intrigue around the outermost corners.

She joined him on the couch and gave him a hug.

She ran her slender fingers through Jack's hair. It felt so good. Jack felt incredible. He squeezed her tightly.

She released from his grip and planted a small peck on his cheek. Their eyes met. Jack sank deep into the pools of blue. He focused onto her bright red lips. He leant forward and gently kissed them. She leant back shocked at his response.

Then their eyes met again. The wanting plain to see in both.

She leant forward and kissed him.

Her lips felt so soft.

She pressed harder and their lips opened.

Her tongue felt warm and soft as it gently brushed against his.

Jack kissed breathlessly and more passionately.

His hands moved along her spine feeling the contours of her naked skin through her shirt. His fingers bumped over her bra strap and moved up to her neck.

He ran his fingers under her hair and felt the soft warm texture of her skin.

He massaged her neck gently as he kissed her.

She grabbed hold of his hair and pulled gently as the kiss got deeper.

His hands responded and moved down to her bottom. He squeezed her through her skirt. Feeling the soft flesh collect in the palms of his hand.

She moaned as his hands wandered around the front and along the outside of her thigh and under her skirt.

Her thighs felt like silk.

He lifted them and moved his hand round under her bottom again.

The kiss became more breathless as he squeezed her again through her white lace panties.

She ran her hands all over his body urgently and harshly.

Then, suddenly, she stopped. She jumped up and adjusted her dress and hair.

'Sorry...I'm not sure about this...', she was breathless.

Her cheeks flushed.

Jack was equally the same.

He stood up and wrapped her in his arms.

They kissed again deeply.

Helen felt Jack pressed against her stomach. He felt so firm. She wanted him. He grabbed her behind and pulled her towards him. She moaned as he gyrated slightly on her.

His hands moved down her sides then up and over her breasts. Jack could have melted.

Her nipples felt hard through the thin fabric of her shirt.

Jack longed to touch them and began to unbutton the shirt.

He had unbuttoned two of the buttons when she backed away again.

'No Jack...please...I'm not sure about this....please..'.

Jack sat down.

He held his left hand to his mouth and muttered through his fingers,

'I'm so sorry...Helen...I've had too much to drink...I'm so sorry', Jack felt deplored by his behaviour.

Helen smiled.

'It's OK...I really wanted too as well...but ..not like this...not yet...'.

'Look I'd better go..', she felt awkward by the situation that had unfolded.

Jack jumped to his feet.

'No..please stay...', Jack begged,

'I don't know what came over me....I'm really sorry Helen', Jack's sincerity filled the room.

She smiled.

'I do Jack..It came over me too...If I stay any longer I might not be able to control myself'.

'I'm going to go', she looked deep into Jack's eyes.

Then hesitantly she left.

Jack slouched back into his sofa. He knew he'd gone too far but the urge was too great to resist. He wondered if he had blown it but secretly inside he still felt confident that eventually they would be together. It just felt so right and meant to be. So much so that the pain ached and throbbed inside him.

Every action of our lives touches on some
chord that will vibrate in eternity.........

Edwin Hubbel Chapin

CHAPTER 13

Jack arrived at his office early the following morning. He felt disconsolate at the way he had fouled up the evening before. He tried to bury himself in his work to take the whole subject off his mind. He thumbed through the case file again trying to find further hidden information but to no avail. There were no further leads. It was now a waiting game. He knew something further would develop and had to make sure he was prepared this time. He couldn't understand how Marco was always one step ahead of him. Baiting him. It was as if all the death and occurrences in the case so far were a sign. A gentle reminder of Jack's hidden past. He was infuriatingly close to unlocking the secrets but still just out of arms reach. The office was quiet. The Desk Sergeant was going about his duties in the distance, seen through the window in Jack's office but no sound was heard. Jack thought back to the swastikas. He pictured himself on a truck. He could smell the mix of damp canvas and diesel. A deep musty smell. His nostrils flared to inhale the smell further. He felt the truck come to a halt and he and several other men dressed in German uniform left the rear of the vehicle and entered a hut. It was a dark and damp building. The only form of light were two oil lamps that hung at the rear. He could see the faces silhouetted in the eerie glow. Drained and ashen faces.

Jack shivered but remained composed to continue the vision.

He saw a figure removing his boots. Another dismantling and cleaning a rifle. Another stumbled at the far end of the building and lit a cigarette. He saw his face contorted in each draw of the smoke. Jack felt himself lie on a bed. The hard mattress beneath him. The moist stale blanket pulled up to his chin. He stared into the face of the man closest to him. He scrubbed and polished at his boots. His eyes closed drifting into slumber. Jack pictured his face closer. He still pictured the face in the cage. Lit up under the same eerie glow. He saw the distress and horror in his eyes. He felt himself exert a sharp blow and pictured the butt of his rifle lunging into that same sorry face. The blood spraying out. The face distorted and showing a silent scream. Jack flinched at the further two blows he felt himself issue to the face. The crunch of splintering bone and squelch of crushed flesh. He pictured the lead iron safe. The two bodies that lay either side of it, still twitching. He felt the cold of the iron as he tried to turn the handle. He felt his muscles burning as he tried to force the door open. It didn't move. Jack looked hard at the two men lying on the floor. They were now still. Eyes wide and face bloodied and cold.

Jack was startled by Craven, walking passed his office window and nodding a good morning gesture. Jack felt himself sweating profusely. His shirt was already soddened under his arms. His hair damp with moisture. He didn't want to return to the vision but felt he must. He thought long and hard again.

He pictured his hand reaching down and clasping a hot steaming mug of coffee. He was on a train. The carriage rocked gently. He looked out of the window. It was night but the landscape was bright with a layer of thick snow. He remembered walking slowly down the aisle of the carriage. The carriage was empty barring a single figure sat down on the left with his back to him. Jack walked towards the figure. As he approached him he placed the mug down on his table. He looked straight into the figure's eyes. Jack could feel the fear racing through him. Those eyes. Piercing. Evil.

Jack tried to escape from the vision but found himself transfixed in the stare. The stare of Klaus Berthold.

Jack screamed aloud. Craven burst into Jack's office and instantly released Jack from the vision.

'What the hell's the matter Mitch?', Craven sounded alarmed by Jack's outburst.

Briggsy followed in close behind Craven.

Jack realised that tears ran down his cheeks. His face was flushed red. His hair dripping with sweat. Craven looked startled by Jack's appearance.

'What the hell is it?', Craven said.

Jack stared at him through his glazed eyes and found he had no answer.

He stood up and brushed passed Craven and Briggsy and dived into the washroom.

Craven stared at Briggsy in dismay.

'Is he OK?', Craven said.

Briggsy shrugged.

'Keep an eye on him Briggsy and tell him when he's sorted himself out and calmed down a little to come and see me in my office', Craven's tones were still of disbelief. Jack was one of his best officers and to see him in this state concerned him deeply.

Briggsy nodded and stayed in Jack's office while Craven disappeared down the corridor into his own.

Jack stared at himself in the mirror. His eyes bulged and his face seemed colourless. He continually threw cold water over his face trying to rid himself of the images he had bore witness to. His breathing was erratic. His chest heaved with each breath. He unbuttoned his shirt and took two drenched paper towels and dabbed at his body. The refreshing chill of the towels cooled down his body and mind. He eased considerably. He sat down on the tiled floor and sighed deeply. He could still feel the relentless throb of his heartbeat, but his breathing returned to normal. He desperately tried to regain his composure. He told himself he had some vivid imagination muttering words of disbelief aloud like some madman. He tried to humour the situation and cackled nervously to himself. Deep inside though he knew the visions were real and that he had at some time lived every minute of them. He stood up and stared into the mirror again. His face had returned to a normal colour and the fear had ebbed from his eyes. He dried himself off. He finally had got it. For as long as he could remember he had fought with the visions and nightmares, fending them off, refusing to be taken in by them. All along if he had accepted them and embraced them then maybe he would have understood sooner what they urged to tell him. He always thought he was a freak of nature now he knew. But just maybe, he had the confidence now to discover why he had suffered. What it all meant and how it came about.

Jack felt frightened but somehow felt so much stronger. He felt like a huge burden had been lifted from his shoulders. He couldn't come to terms with the feelings that circled within him but then who could. He was convinced that he had relived occurrences from his past or previous lives. He shook his head and laughed aloud at the inability to except the logic behind it. Was it possible? Was it a gift or a nightmare? Jack soon realised that his secret must be kept to himself. Not even Helen must know. He knew that if he started to discuss it he would be institutionalised within the next breath. He laughed again. His eyes seemed to sparkle. That was it. All his pain and torture throughout the years had been released. The explanation was there, no matter how unscientific and impossible, Jack believed it. He now held the answer.

He rebuttoned his shirt and brushed his hair with his fingers. One thing bit into him though, the stare of Klaus Berthold, he had witnessed that stare recently. He quietly wondered if he was the only one to have the gift.

Jack left the restroom to be confronted by an impatient and unnerved Briggsy.

'You OK Sir?', he said.

Jack smiled.

'Never felt better Briggsy my boy!'.

Briggsy looked confused but equally relieved at Jack's response.

'Erm...the Super wants to see you', Briggsy muttered.

Jack beamed.

'Yeah...I though he might', Jack straightened his tie and set off down the corridor.

Jack knocked only once on Craven's door before stepping inside.

'Shut the door Mitch and sit down'.

Jack did as he was asked. He still had the faint smile on his lips.

'Would you mind telling me the reason behind your outburst earlier?', Craven said.

'Yeah..sorry about that Sir...this case has really got to me lately... it was just a release of emotion...I feel better for it.', Jack smiled.

Craven looked concerned.

'If this case is getting too much for you Jack I can re-assign it to someone else...as it is, Division wants me to pass it higher up...but I ensured them my best man was on it.', Craven said.

'No..honestly I'm fine...I've still got a few avenues to look into'.

'You sure, Briggsy tells me all your leads have dried up....What happened with the bouncer from the Pravada...Erik isn't it?', Craven enquired.

'I've still got to lean on him...someone beat me to it last time...', Jack replied.

Craven nodded.

'But I've still got something else to check out', Jack smiled.

Craven looked pensive.

'This wouldn't involve Marco Veart would it?'.

Jack smiled.

'Stay off him Jack...You've been warned....the Chief's giving me daily grief over the last meeting you had with him...He's not a suspect.'

'Don't worry Sir...I know ...', Jack lied.

Craven stretched in his chair.

'OK. Mitch ..get on it...Oh and you'll have to do without Briggsy this afternoon..'.

'Why?', Jack said.

'He's playing a round of fourball with us..'.

'Fourball?', Jack seemed perplexed.

'Yes..the Chief's invited myself and Briggsy along to play a round of golf with him and Mr. Veart...to show there is no ill feeling between us all'.

'Golf?', Jack exclaimed.

'Yes..he personally asked for Briggsy...good player you know.. plays off 6..makes my 11 look average...Still I think it will be a close match we get 4 strokes off the other two before we start.', Craven assured Jack excitedly.

Jack sighed and shook his head.

'Really...', he stood up and left Craven still thrilled by the thought of the afternoon's competition.

Marco had them all in his pocket. Jack felt alone in his quest for justice and understood that he would have to investigate this one privately with little or no external assistance.

Briggsy apologised liberally over his inclusion in the golf game insisting he had no choice in the matter. Jack understood. Briggsy's incapability to stand up for himself had shone through yet again. Jack assured Briggsy it was all right but told him to keep a close eye on the behaviour and appearance of Marco. Briggsy sighed at Jack's persistence on the matter but finally agreed, if only to keep the peace. Jack sat in his chair.

'Coffee would be lovely Briggsy', Jack smiled.

Briggsy sighed and trudged off to the kitchen area.

Jack breathed deeply and aloud.

'Right, you bastard...Time to play...', Jack spoke vehemently.

Marco stood in his personal office to the front of his property. He wore chequered slacks and a navy blue and white Pringle sweater. He was gently brushing and wiping his sand iron with a specialised cleaning brush. The brush had many attachments for a variety of functions. He used the metal spike to clean along the grooves of the blade of the club, ensuring no residue sand had collected within that may impair a future shot, not that he intended playing from sand today. Neilsen stood in front of him.

'What's the word?', Marco murmured calmly.

'Nothing much....Standt won't be missed and as for Tommy they still think it was an accident.' Neilsen said.

'Good..', Marco sighed.

He replaced the cleaned club back into the bag.

'Any more trouble with Mitchell?', Neilsen stated.

'No..He doesn't know where he is or what day it is at the moment.', Marco said.

'Don't you want me to deal with him then?', Neilsen smiled.

Marco shook his head.

'No..but I want you to meet me here on Thursday morning 10 a.m. ...I need you to drive me somewhere...'.

Neilsen nodded silently.

'I'll be taking the Merc so dress accordingly', Marco added.

Neilsen understood.

Marco leaned over his desk and picked up his phone.

He pressed the intercom button.

'Samantha...Can you come to my office please....'.

Neilsen headed for the door.

'See you tomorrow morning then boss'.

Marco shouted after him.

'Not tomorrow...Thursday morning....today's only Tuesday.'

Neilsen thought for a second then smiled in agreement. He could be excused for losing track of the days.

'Sorry Samantha...yes now...', Marco continued.

Samantha tapped on the door gently. She was always concerned when she was summonsed unexpectedly to the office. She entered and Marco smiled at her and told her to be seated.

He remained calm as he spoke.

'Did you go out last night?'.

Samantha looked puzzled.

'Yes..for a while...only down to the Golden Goose for a couple of drinks.

'I thought I saw you in there', Marco smiled.

Samantha frowned.

'Were you there?', she asked.

'No..I just drove past..', Marco replied.

'I saw you speaking to that Inspector who was here..', Marco pressed.

'What did he want?', Marco's tone became more serious.

Samantha shifted uncomfortably in her seat.

'He asked me how long I'd worked for you....If I knew a man I'd never heard of and if I knew Tommy Wright..', she looked down.

'And..what did you tell him..?', Marco quickly said.

'I don't know...he was very drunk..I said I'd been with the company for 5 years...I had no idea who the other man was and that yes...I knew Tommy Wright...but I didn't tell him how well I knew him..', she replied.

Marco nodded.

'We got out of there as quickly as we could', she finished.

'Good girl', Marco said

'I'm getting a little fed up with this constant harassment from this officer..', he added.

'If he tries to contact you again let me know will you?...I'm going to speak with his superiors this afternoon..', Marco smiled.

'OK Samantha .....that's all for now', Marco stood up and smiled, the cue for her to leave.

Marco took his driver from his bag and moved into the centre of his office. He took his stance and swished the club through the air. He commented on how the ball flew 300 yards down the fairway straight as a die and laughed aloud.

The office didn't quite feel the same without Briggsy's innocent chit-chat and endless supplies of caffeine, however, Jack enjoyed the quiet. They would have probably tee-ed off by now. Jack flicked through the file of Marco's personnel. While it was quiet he thought he would check out the employees on the database. He sat at Briggsy's PC. Jack wasn't exactly computer literate, but he did have a vague general competency. He scrolled down the list illuminated over the screen until he reached the criminal record heading. He selected it with the mouse and the screen changed accordingly. A further menu appeared under the heading. He scrolled down to the SEARCH sub-heading. On selecting this, a small window appeared centre screen with the message 'ENTER NAME' and a flashing cursor beside it.

Jack entered the first name on the list. Alan Mason. He selected enter and the window disappeared to be replaced by the words SEARCHING. Five dots counted the duration of the search until the message appeared, NO RECORDS FOUND. At the bottom of the screen was the instruction 'Press 'y' for a further search Press 'n' to return to menu. Jack mused at the simplicity of the program before selecting 'y'.

He continued throughout the entire list. It was a tedious and mundane process, which rewarded Jack with the occasional motoring offence- speeding, illegal parking, nothing major that could disprove Marco's vetting procedures. The best he could come up with was John McDuggan and William Holding. McDuggan served 6 months community service in 1983 for assault in a pub brawl. Holding was fined £1,000 for damages at a Greenpeace rally and possession of Cannabis back in 1982. Nothing major. If anything, Marco probably appreciated Holding's dedication to a cause and McDuggan's ability to stand up for himself.

Jack finished the list in just over an hour. It was an hour wasted.

Then it hit Jack. Where was Samantha on the list? Jack double-checked the names again. Nothing. No Samantha. Jack pondered the thought, well maybe if she was missing from the list then others may be too. He pictured her face again. He was sure he had seen her before. Jack thought of just phoning her and asking outright for her surname. He then thought better of it. Craven had verbally warned him off for the second time again this morning. Jack knew that Marco would be on his back if he thought for one minute that he was still investigating him.

He stared at the number on the file. He smiled then dialled it.

'Hello Secure Alliance', the voice was Samantha's.

Jack spoke in his best Italian accent,

'Hello...Can I speak with Marco Veart please.', Jack paused.

'I'm afraid he is not here at the moment ...Can I ask who is calling?'.

'It's Luigi's restaurant...I'm calling with reference to his booking for this evening..'.

'Oh right...Can I take a message?', she replied.

'Well..he wanted his favourite table for 8 p.m...Unfortunately it will not be vacated till 8:15 ....Do you a think that will be a problem?', Jack found the accent demanding.

There was a silence for a second.

'Erm...I don't think so no...I'm sure that will be fine...', she said hopefully.

'AAH..Good...Could I have your name please for confirmation of the booking...', Jack pressed.

'My name?', she seemed surprised.

'Yes..sorry we have to have a name for confirmation...It's a stupid rule I know but it's the managers policy', Jack said.

'Erm OK..It's Samantha Parkes...I'm his PA'.

'That's..P...A...R...K...S', Jack replied.

'No E...S..', She corrected.

'Thank you very much Miss Parkes', Jack hung up.

Samantha looked at the phone suspiciously for a moment then thought nothing more about it until Marco returned, when she would pass on the message.

Jack typed the name into the window.

The search seemed to last slightly longer than the rest and then the page lit up.

At the top left of the screen was a picture of Samantha. It was an old photo and barely resembled the person he had twice met previously. The record this time was far more rewarding. No wonder she had been left off the list.

The page read:

14 Jan 1987 Charged with prostitution in Sheffield.
22 Dec 1987 Charged drink-driving without licence
22 Jul 1989 Charged with prostitution in Leeds.
12 Dec 1990 Possession of Heroin
08 May 1991 Suspected of murder

Jack highlighted the first offence and clicked the mouse.

She had been just 15 years old when found soliciting in the renowned red-light district of Sheffield. The court gave her a verbal warning and fined her parent's £500.

He moved onto the next offence.

She was just 16 years old driving with a provisional licence unaccompanied whilst twice over the alcohol limit. Not that she was old enough to drink in the first place. The blood test also revealed traces of cannabis and amphetamine abuse. Her mother had left the area and her father was a registered Heroin addict. She was taken into care for a period of no less than 6 months.

At 18 she was found soliciting in Leeds. Having already received a verbal warning she was requested to pay a fine of £10,000 or face imprisonment. She served 4 months of the 10-month sentence in Holloway.

At 19 she was found with 5 grams of Heroin in her possession. She claimed it was for personal usage and was registered an addict and sent to a rehab clinic rather than be imprisoned again.

At 20 her drug-dealing boyfriend was found murdered at their flat. He had three gunshot wounds to his chest. Neighbours heard a man and woman shouting minutes before the shots. No forensic evidence was found at the scene. Samantha had said she was away at a friends in Nottingham at the time of the shooting. Her alibi stood firm and she was released through lack of evidence to prove otherwise. The murder is still unsolved and put down to another drugs war statistic.

Jack read through the pages with enthusiasm. So much for Marco's vetting system. Jack stared at the photo of Samantha Parkes again. It was taken in 1989. She looked so young and in such a mess. Jack stared at her features. He had seen her before somewhere. But where?

He got up and decided to make a coffee. It was as he stirred the dark brown liquid that it hit him like a bolt of forked lightning.

He ran back into his office, fumbled with the keys to open the bottom drawer of his desk. It slid open and Jack flicked through the contents. He found the videos. He turned the videos onto their sides revealing the white labels. There it was,

Joanne and Sam 24-6-94

Jack grasped the tape and headed off to the conference room. His legs were light, and he felt a tingling up inside his groin. Adrenaline pumped through him in gushes.

He walked into the room. It was fair sized with tables and chairs consuming most of the free space. The TV and video were at the back of the room next to the whiteboard.

Jack slipped the tape into the video and pressed play. He switched on the TV and immediately recognised Samantha or Sam as she obviously preferred to be called. Joanne was the Jo he had met briefly in the Golden Goose. It was apparent that they knew Tommy better than most. Intimately in fact, very intimately. She had changed dramatically in the last few years. In the video she had long peroxide blonde hair, her face was caked in make-up, bright red lipstick, she had a youthful look in her eyes. Today she wears a natural mousy-blonde bob and very little make-up with a subtle shade of lip colour. She seemed to have matured and refined since the shooting of the video. He couldn't believe the woman in the film was the same one he had met previously. Yes, she didn't portray herself as having an impeccable pedigree and didn't have that look about her. But what Jack witnessed in the film was quite disgusting and rather disturbing.

Jack stopped the tape and returned it back into his drawer under lock and key.

Maybe, this was his lever to prise information from Marco's loyal PA. Jack smiled.

He sat back at his desk. He picked up the phone and re-dialled the number.

'Hello Secure Alliance', the familiar tones echoed down the line.

'Sam...Hi...It's Jack Mitchell...DI Mitchell'.

There was a pause at the other end.

'Hello...yes', she said.

'I need to speak with you again', Jack replied.

'What about?', Sam questioned.

'Tommy Wright', Jack said.

'Look DI Mitchell...I've told you all I know...Mr. Veart is getting sick and tired of your harassment and is expressing so to your superiors today...and quite frankly so am I', Sam said angrily.

'Oh..this has nothing to do with Marco...it's more to do with you...', Jack paused.

The silence continued on the other end.

'I have a video in my possession of you and your friend Jo doing rather strange things with bananas and whipped cream...', Jack laughed.

'What?', Sam exclaimed.

'Yes and Tommy Wright makes a guest appearance in it too', Jack stated.

Still silence.

'Back in June 1994.', Jack explained.

'I know it was a while ago but I'm sure it will come to you...In Tommy's flat?', Jack posed.

Still silence.

'You still there?', Jack asked.

'Yes...', came the quiet reply.

'When can we meet....?', Jack asked.

Silence again.

'Sam?...'

'Erm..I finish at 6', she replied shakily.

'Shall we say 7 at the Golden Goose?', Jack propositioned.

'OK'.

'Oh, and Sam don't mention a word of this to Marco because I'm sure he wouldn't be too pleased at us meeting..', Jack insisted sarcastically.

The phone went dead.

Jack smiled and leant back in his chair.

———•———

'Oh, unlucky son!!', Marco commiserated.

Briggsy's four-foot putt just fell short of the hole.

'That's another half so that means we are still three up with five to play Jerry', Marco smiled at the Chief.

'I thought you had a decent handicap Briggs', Craven scowled.

'I could have sunk that with my eyes closed!'.

Briggsy shrugged

'Sorry Sir, you put the pressure on by taking three to get out of the bunker'.

Craven glared at Briggsy before stomping away to the fourteenth tee.

Marco smiled at Briggsy. The Chief laughed.

They appreciated his polite response and subtle transfer of the blame.

From the fourteenth Marco, Briggsy and the Chief all found the fairway, Craven hooked wildly into the rough on the left. His face boiled with anger and frustration.

'So, you've given Mitchell a dressing down then Alec?', the Chief reiterated in a single statement most of the morning's topical conversation.

'Yes Sir..He is well aware of your feelings on the matter..', Craven replied happy to take his mind of his game.

'I've expressed my deepest apologies to Mr. Veart but you know how it is Sir...an Officer is given some information and he has to check it out...'

'Yes Alec I agree...but a decent officer should also be able to interpret when information received is feasible or not....and relying on the word of a Norwegian bouncer has to be questioned...Doesn't it?', the Chief delved into Craven's theories.

'Well Sir...I can assure you the matter is now closed...DI Mitchell has finished his route of investigation and it has all checked out', Craven smiled at Marco.

Craven felt ashamed of the way the four of them had ridiculed and picked the bones out of Jack's policing methods for most of the morning. He was growing tired of it. Jack was an outstanding officer. He didn't much care for the way he was being constantly tarnished. At first Craven himself thought it was a bit of a joke, but now the joke was wearing thin. He was dismayed that Briggsy never once stuck up for Jack but he himself found the whole subject amusing also. Craven was annoyed with Briggsy for that reason and also because of the crucial putts he was missing. OK so Craven was having a particularly bad game but Briggsy shrugged off his incredible approach play and diabolical putting as though it didn't really matter. At that moment Craven wished he had partnered Jack this morning. Jack was a competitor. He didn't like losing or for that matter being slagged off. They certainly wouldn't talk about him like this to his face. Chief Super or not. Craven knew the Chief feared Jack and that is why he was always waiting for him to slip up. It all boiled down to pure jealousy.

Craven found his ball nestled in the coarse grass twenty yards from the fairway and eighty yards from the green. He selected a nine iron and with a ferocious back swing launched into the ball. The ball popped up out of the rough, whistled passed the heads of the other three stood admiring their perfect lies and landed on the edge of the green. The ball arced around the contours of the green to within five feet of the hole. Craven smiled a 'fuck you' smile. The other three stared in disbelief. It had been Craven's best shot of the day. Craven and Briggsy would eventually lose the match 2 and 1 but Craven had restored some of his self-esteem.

He didn't mind buying the customary losers first round of drinks but did object to the continuing topic of conversation which became more and more insulting and derogatory towards Jack the more drink was consumed. He left after just two pints and attempted to take Briggsy with him. Briggsy was forcefully encouraged to stay by Marco and the Chief, so he did. Craven drove home alone dreading to think the way the conversation was going to develop.

———•———

Jack checked his watch. 19:12. She was late. He nursed the remains of his first pint, swilling the dregs round and around in the glass. The Goose had the same clientele as the previous visit. Businessmen and women knocking back drinks eagerly and recklessly before rushing away into their fast cars and disappearing at speed into the distance. For a moment Jack was alone in the bar sat in his now familiar corner seat. He had already read every beer mat scattered liberally over the table, counted all the nicks and notches in the veneered top, and noticed the collection of burns in the carpet at his feet, provided by slothful individuals who found it too much effort to extinguish their cigarettes in the ashtrays provided.

As he looked up Sam was stood in the doorway. She was dressed in a long white outfit that clung to her figure and a navy-blue cardigan. She looked in sombre mood as she strolled over to him. She sat at the table.

'Can I get you a drink?', Jack asked politely.

'No thank you...Lets get this over with..'.

She reached into her handbag and produced a packet of Bensons and lit one. She dragged at the cigarette shakily.

'How well did you know Tommy Wright?', Jack started.

'I met him a few times...he invited us to a couple of his parties...'.

'Was that before or after you started working for Marco?', Jack continued.

'After', she drew a deep breath of dense blue smoke.

'So, you met Tommy through Marco then?'.

'Sort of...I started working for Marco...just cleaning around his house at first...Tommy was around there one day, and we got chatting...the next thing I know is I've been invited to a party at his club', Sam spoke quietly and hesitantly.

'Was that the time with the bananas and whipped cream?', Jack smiled.

'No that was the second time'.

She stubbed out her cigarette angrily.

'I can't believe he filmed it', she spoke in a disgusted manner.

'You didn't mind doing those things in front of him with your friend?...Were you drunk? Drugged?..or what?', Jack questioned.

Sam smiled.

'No, we didn't mind at all, Jo and I have been lovers for almost six years now...actually we got quite a kick out of it', she smiled.

Jack tried to keep the shock from his eyes.

'Did he pay you?', Jack stated.

Sam looked anxious.

'It's alright I know all about your past', Jack assured her.

'Look all that shit is way behind me now...I was young and naive... as you rightly put it it's my past', she jumped onto the defensive.

'I came down here to get away from all that...start afresh...I got a break with Marco, he gave me a job...trained me up on courses and now I have a very respectable position earning a decent hard-earned pay', she seemed bitter at having to re-live her past.

Jack nodded.

'Where did you meet Jo?', Jack continued.

'We were in the re-hab clinic together.....both with the same shitty problems...we cleaned up and got out together and have never looked back since...till you dredged it back into my head..', she stared bitterly at Jack.

'Sorry...that's not why I asked you to come here', Jack confessed.

'Does Marco know about it all?'.

'What is it with you and him?...I don't know why you hassle each other....he's a very generous man..', she insisted.

'He told me he has a very strict vetting policy...surely he would have checked you out too', Jack replied.

'I didn't tell him to begin with...but he found out...probably through his vetting policy...he knew everything and didn't let on for months....he gave me a chance...no one else was prepared to give me a fresh start...He just told me never to lie to him again and to be loyal to him...which I am..'.

'Until now', Jack smiled.

'No..I'll always be loyal to him no matter what you say or do..', she spoke adamantly.

She stood up ready to leave.

'What, even if the video found its way into the hands of the press', Jack whispered.

She sat down immediately.

'You can't do that'.

'Why not?...I don't need it anymore...I'm sure they will find it very interesting viewing...Top local businessman's PA performing pornographic lesbian acts together with a murdered club owner...I can see the headlines right now can't you?'.

'You bastard!', Sam turned white.

'I'm sorry Sam but my backs against the wall right now...I have no straws left to grasp...only you'.

Jack spoke freely,

'Look Sam...I'm not trying to persuade you to be disloyal or trying to frame Marco...He's just not co-operating on a couple of issues and it raises my suspicion towards him...I'm sure he is completely innocent, but I do need the answers...even if it's for my own piece of mind...you surely know how meticulous we can be..', Jack smiled.

She nodded.

Jack continued,

'I promise you that if you help me he will not find out...you will be helping him in the long run...then I'll get off his back and more importantly I'll get off your back...Isn't that what you want?', Jack spoke sympathetically.

She lit another cigarette.

'I'll have a vodka and lemonade', she said anxiously.

Jack fetched a pint and the short.

'What questions do you need to be answered?', she spoke uneasily.

Jack stared around the bar. The place was still relatively empty and those that were there had no direct interest in the conversations in the far corner.

He reached into his jacket pocket and pulled out a folded piece of paper. He opened it to reveal a laser scan of Standt's face taken from the video.

'Do you recognise him?...Ever see him round the house?', Jack questioned.

Sam stared at the photo.

'Who is he?', she asked.

'Do you know him?', Jack repeated.

'Did Marco say he knew him', she queried timidly drawing another long drag on the cigarette.

'Think of the headlines Sam', Jack replied calmly.

She sighed and nervously looked around the bar.

'I saw him at the house a few times...', she whispered.

'Did you speak to him?'.

'No, I was never introduced I saw him chatting with Marco in the drive a couple of times through my office window. I'm sure it was him', she shook nervously.

'Was he on his own?'.

'Sometimes..then other times he was with another man..'.

'What did the other man look like?', Jack continued.

'Tall, skinny, short cropped light hair....ugly looking...', she frowned trying to recollect the image.

'Did Marco ever mention them to you?', Jack took a large gulp of his pint.

'No never...', she shook her head.

'Do they work for him?', Jack persisted.

'I don't know..I work at the house I don't have many dealings with the workforce itself..', she replied.

'When was the last time they were at the house?', Jack posed the inevitable question.

She sighed.

'I hope I'm not going to get Marco in trouble?...I'm helping him right?', she asked.

'Of course,...It'll clear the whole thing up', Jack lied.

'The ugly one was there this morning on his own'.

Jack tried to remain calm.

'I saw him arrive...sometimes we get quiet periods and I find myself just staring out of the window for hours.'

'What time?', Jack asked.

She shook her head.

'I don't know around 10 ish'.

'Did he seem odd or different in any way?', Jack continued.

'He always looks odd...quite spooky really'.

Jack laughed.

'You didn't see Marco talking to him then?', Jack probed.

'No...I heard him leave when Marco asked me to come down to his office', she innocently revealed.

'You saw him then?'.

'No...I heard him leave...I was on the end of the phone line when they said their goodbye's', she grew impatient.

Jack pondered for a moment while she lit her third cigarette.

'He sent me down to warn me off about you', Sam glared at Jack.

Jack smiled.

'So, you heard him just say goodbye then?', Jack continued.

'Well not goodbye exactly...he said he would see him on Thursday or something then I heard the door shut', she quickly corrected Jack.

Jack smiled. He had gotten what he wanted. Something to work on.

'He saw me talking to you in here last time you know?', Sam said.

Jack's smile disappeared.

'What?'.

'Yeah..he said he happened to be driving passed and noticed me chatting to you...he wanted to know if you'd been harassing me and what you wanted from me', she said.

Jack grew alarmed. He scanned around the bar at first then peered out of the windows to the side. There were a few cars in the lay-by, but all seemed unoccupied. The Golden Goose wasn't in a part of the city that you would just happen to be driving passed. Maybe Sam was still more naive than she thought. Jack realised he must have been followed that evening and wondered if he had been followed tonight, if so, he may have put Sam's life in danger.

'What's the matter?', Sam anxiously asked.

She had noticed the change in Jack's behaviour.

'Nothing...look thanks for the chat...let's just keep it to ourselves OK', Jack insisted.

'Of course..', she added.

Jack stood up.

'What about the video?...Can I have it?', she asked.

'You have my word that I'll keep it locked in my desk till this is all over then I will personally destroy it....honestly Sam...you've been a great help', Jack smiled.

'Promise?', Sam worried.

'My word is my bond', Jack held his hand to his heart.

'OK', Sam gave in. She almost trusted him.

Jack walked out of the bar and left her finishing off her drink.

Jack eyed everyone outside on the street. He checked every parked vehicle until he was satisfied he wasn't being watched.

He got in his car and drove to the Chinese take-away on Valdour Road. He ordered two portions of egg fried rice, a beef chop suey, sweet and sour pork, and a crispy duck. He drove around to Helen's place with the peace supper in apology for his rude behaviour the evening before.

Chapter 14

Briggsy was especially quiet in the office the following morning. Whether it was from guilt at conspiring to rubbish Jack's name or just sufferance from the amount of alcohol consumed the previous evening. Either way he looked decidedly green and lethargic.

Jack looked extremely contented. He had not only received confirmation that Marco worked with Standt from Sam but also had a very pleasant evening with Helen. He definitely felt as though his luck was picking up.

It was 10 a.m. when Jack's phone rang.

'Hello..DI Mitchell', Jack answered politely.

'It's Erik...', Jack recognised the voice immediately.

The line wasn't particularly clear, and Jack could hear a tannoy in the background blasting out messages.

He couldn't quite make out what the messages said.

'I've only got one minute...so listen carefully...', Erik shouted.

'I've done a little checking around and the guy you are looking for is called Neilsen...he's an evil son of a bitch..so be careful...', Erik elaborated.

'He's the one who paid me a visit...', Erik referred to the battering he had received.

'What's he look like?', Jack interrupted.

'Tall, blonde, skin head ...vicious looking', Erik recounted.

'Listen...he told me Marco would finish me off if I ever spoke a word to anyone....but I want you to get these bastards...for Tommy's sake..', Erik's voice quivered.

'Where are you Erik?', Jack heard the tannoy again.

'I'm at the airport...I'm getting out of here...that why I'm telling you now..', Erik replied.

'Where are you going?', Jack asked.

Erik laughed.

'Only I know that...you can't stop me...I'm gone'.

'Listen...they knew you were coming around', Erik continued.

'What do you mean?', Jack asked.

'That day I got the visit from him...He said you'd be coming shortly and that I'd not to tell you anything...', Erik paused.

'How could they possibly know I was coming to see you?', Jack asked perplexed.

Erik laughed.

'That's what I can't make out...but I have my theories...He's got someone inside!', Erik said.

'What here?', Jack whispered.

He looked around the office.

'Must be...did you tell anyone else you were coming to see me?... It wasn't a precautionary measure he said you were on your way...', Erik shouted.

Jack felt shocked.

That would explain why Marco was always one step ahead of him.

'My money has run out...gotta go...get them for me...and for Tommy', Erik's final words tailed off and the line went dead.

Jack slowly replaced the receiver.

He knew it was too late to stop Erik. He would probably be boarding the plane at this very second.

Jack tried to recount just who he had told of his proposed meeting with Erik.

Briggsy knew of course.

Craven knew.

Two other detectives were in the room at the time, Steve, and Dave.

Craven probably enlightened the Chief.

Then of course there was Helen, he had phoned her just before he left the office.

Jack knew the Chief hated him and also knew that he had a close relationship with Marco. He was top of the list.

Jack realised that he had to keep this to himself and that he couldn't trust anyone anymore.

Not Helen surely.

Jack knew he could handle it being anyone else, even Briggsy, if it was just not Helen. That would hurt most of all. He decided he would have to pose a few leading questions in the direction of those suspected and monitor the response.

Briggsy was the first to greet him, offering a mug of his now traditional mid-morning brew.

'How did the golf go Briggsy?', Jack enquired.

'Lost miserably Sir...the Super was a little rusty..', Briggsy smiled.

'So, you didn't spend the afternoon discussing me and the case then?', Jack fished.

Briggsy looked embarrassed.

'You've spoken to the Super then?'.

'No not yet...should I have?', Jack was intrigued by Briggsy's reply.

Briggsy squirmed awkwardly.

'So, you did then', Jack stated.

'Well, the Chief did lay into you a little', Briggsy understated.

'The Chief?', Jack tried to sound surprised.

'Between me and you Sir...let's just say I don't think you are top of his Christmas card list'.

Jack laughed.

'I guessed as much!'.

Jack approached Craven's office and gently rapped on the door.

'Yes Mitch...feeling better today?', Craven asked with the nauseating concern in his voice.

He was half-heartedly scanning through the recent directive on curbing the increasing levels of graffiti in the city. Needless to say, it was a riveting read and he was glad to be released from it.

'Yes thanks Sir...must have been PMT or something',

Jack pondered his words for a moment.

'The case I'm working on...', Jack paused.

Craven nodded.

'Do you brief the Chief regularly on its progress?', Jack cut to the chase.

Craven frowned.

'Yes I do...its regulations...besides he is extremely interested in the developments since you paid a visit to his close golfing partner..', Craven smirked.

'Why?'.

'No reason...', Jack replied.

Craven leaned forward over his desk.

'So, you came in here just to ask me that?'

'Are you sure you are OK Jack?'

'Yes ...I just wanted to make sure you were keeping him abreast of all my hard work. its promotion board next month...', Jack grinned.

Craven laughed aloud until his face turned a faint shade of purple.

'You'll kill me one of these days Mitch!', he choked.

Jack stared at Craven the grin disappeared. Maybe there would be cause to exact his last statement. Jack hoped not. For all Craven's annoying habits, Jack still liked him and regarded him as a good copper.

Jack took an early lunch and decided to take a trip round to the lab. Helen was in her office. She looked so excited and pleased with herself. She jumped up frantically and started to speak quickly and sometimes incoherently,

'I've been looking at my old Uni notes and this morning I went to a seminar in the city....It was by a great pioneer in neurology, Professor Kreitzman..I've read a lot of his works....anyway the seminar was on electricity in the brain and more precisely his extensive tests on electroencephalogram machines...', she spoke without breath. Jack was lost already.

'Woah...wait a minute lets sit down for this shall we...and talk a little slower please...Biochemistry was never a strong subject of mine in high school', Jack protested.

Helen smiled.

'Sorry...OK..', she took a deep breath and began to speak slowly.

'Right, you are having visions...correct', she questioned.

Jack smiled.

'Correct'.

'Visions are normally caused by activity of the brain correct', she continued.

'Correct....look you don't have to go that basic...', Jack laughed.

The excitement spilled over into her cheeks.

'Right, I'll tell you something about the brain', she took another breath.

'The largest and most developed part of the brain is the Cerebrum. The two massive cerebral hemispheres account for more than 70% of the weight of the entire brain. Also at the back of the brain is the Cerebellum and the brain stem. The brain and the spinal cord together form the Central Nervous System...the control centre for the body.', She looked beautiful in full flow.

Jack listened intently.

'... It gathers information about the environment and the body from the peripheral nervous system and then initiates appropriate actions..so basically the nervous system transmits messages from one place to another. The nerve cells that do this job are called neurons. These neurons have several short branches coming off them called dendrites and a single long branch called an axon.', she spoke slower as the description became more technical.

Jack appreciated it and smiled.

'The dendrites allow communication with nearby neurons. The axon permits messages to be carried to distant neurons in other parts of the body. The neurons function by conducting electrical signals down the length of their axons....Now this is the crucial part', she took another breath.

'At their end, nerve axons usually branch into many small terminals that come into close contact with the dendrites of other neurons. The axon and the dendrite never actually touch. There is always a small gap called the synaptic cleft. When an electrical signal reaches a nerve terminal, it causes the nerve to release neurotransmitters. These transmitters jump the short distance to the nearby dendrites. The neuron releasing the transmitter is called the pre-synaptic neuron and the one receiving the signal is called the post-synaptic neuron. Now depending on the type of transmitter released, the post-synaptic neurons are either encouraged or discouraged from firing....You still with me?', Helen asked.

'Just', Jack replied trying not to break his concentration.

'OK like I said neurotransmitters are the messengers for nerve communication across synapses. However, there are many different types of chemicals that serve as neurotransmitters. So, you may be asking ...how do the receiving cells distinguish all these signals?... Well they do this by having very specific receptors. Each receptor is like a lock that can only be opened by a particular key, as in the correct transmitter. For example, one of the most important transmitters is acetylcholine or Ach, which is released by the neurons that stimulate the muscles. Receptors on the muscle fibres recognise ACh as the signal to contract.', Helen continued.

Jack sat silently, engrossed. He did wonder to himself what exactly all this fascinating information had to do with him.

'Opium and its derivative morphine have been used to relieve pain for more than 100 years. It wasn't until 1973, that scientists discovered the actual receptors in the brain that morphine binds to. You told me you pictured yourself drinking a liquid..like a drug of some kind?'.

Jack nodded.

'My guess is that the drug fired up a neuron and passed an electrical signal onto the end of its axon. It produced a transmitter that was eagerly searching for a receptor in another part of the brain. It couldn't find one..', Helen smiled.

'Bare that thought in mind for a moment', she insisted.

Jack nodded.

'OK my transmitter is looking for a receiver', Jack smiled.

'As I said I sat in on Professor Kreitzman's lecture...he is big into the brains activities whilst in sleep. He uses a machine called an electroencephalogram..which basically records the electrical signals produced by the brain. EEG recordings of people during sleep show two grossly different patterns. One pattern is produced during REM (Rapid eye movement) sleep, and the other during NREM(non-rapid eye movement) sleep. During REM sleep, the brain becomes extremely active electrically, producing an EEG pattern similar to that of an awake person. People awakened during REM sleep often report vivid dreams. Now then this is my theory..', she paused for breath and smiled at Jack.

Jack sighed and returned the smile.

'You drank the drug....It fired up a neuron in a part of your brain that is not normally used...it releases a neurotransmitter..... the transmitter is desperately searching for a receptor...to no avail yet....the drug is so commanding it shuts down the rest of the bodily functions and all the electrical energy is pumped along this one axon. The axon acts as a short circuit and at the end of it the transmitter channels every ounce of the bodies vast resources of energy.... hurriedly searching for a receptor...The energy is so great...not only can it jump the short distance across the synaptic cleft, but it can actually leave the body until it finds it's receptor...which it eventually does in another body....', she paused for breath.

Jack was dumb struck.

'So, what you are saying is that an electrical surge shoots out through the top of my head along with vital information from that bodies lifetime and finds itself another body to live in.' Jack laughed.

'I thought I was crazy'.

Helen seemed a little insulted by Jack's remark.

'Think of your stereo Jack...your tuned into Radio 1...your stereo will only receive the information transmitted on radio 1 frequencies... it won't allow radio 2, 3, 4 or 5 to interfere with it...unless of course you change the receptor...plus you don't see the electrical signals passing through your house and appearing on the end of your antenna...do you?', Helen defended her theory. 'The radio wave is modulated so that it can travel long distances...', she added.

Jack nodded.

'I suppose so...but when the body dies the transmitter will have died also...so you will no longer pick up the signal...', Jack pondered.

'But Jack...your receiving body has already received and stored the information before the transmitter died. If you like, you taped the best bits so you can always replay them again', Helen smiled.

Jack shook his head.

'This is weird...you've freaked me out now...', Jack smiled.

'I'm some sort of satellite dish then ...'.

She laughed.

'It's just my theory.', she said.

'Also, I believe the receptors are only available in a baby...as man develops past a certain age the body quickly realises that certain parts of the brain are unused and they are naturally closed off for access...In a baby all areas are open and the firing of the receptor leaves the gate open in the normally unused part of the brain for future reference as in your case.', Helen surmised.

'So, this is a form of reincarnation then?', Jack asked.

'In an electrical sense...yes I think so...How else can you explain your visions?...You believe they actually happened don't you?', Helen said.

Jack nodded.

'Yes I do...'.

'Have you expressed these theories to anyone else?', Jack asked.

Helen smiled.

'No, I haven't I'm too frightened they might send the straight jackets round'.

Jack laughed.

'But I do think it may be beneficial hooking you up to an EEG machine and maybe taking a lumbar puncture to examine your cerebrospinal fluid.', she suggested.

Jack smiled.

'Don't like the sound of that...sounds all too kinky for me...didn't know you were into S & M Helen..'.

She blushed.

'Jack!...I'm serious'.

'So, let's say your theories are correct how would you reverse the process?', Jack enquired.

'Well, you would have to devise the antibody that would prevent the neurotransmitter from firing...', she replied simply.

'Not that easy then...?'.

'No not really...the body has millions of nerve cells...this would be just one cell probably...finding it would be like finding a needle....

'In a haystack', they said in unison.

'Oh good', Jack spoke sarcastically.

'So, when I died the first time I took the drug..the second time I didn't', Jack frowned.

'The body will naturally produce the chemical just prior to death ...the identity of the endorphin will be transmitted along with the other information for future use at the point of death again and again. After all it was proven long ago that energy can never be consumed into nothing...it just transforms from one form into another..', Helen smiled.

Jack scratched his head. He was certainly enthralled by the debate but the logic behind it was certainly confusing and quietly unacceptable, but nevertheless, he agreed with Helen if only to keep her pride intact and as thanks for her concerned research into the subject.

Jack walked over to her and gave her a big hug.

'I think I am as crazy as you', she laughed.

Jack stroked her hair.

'Well let's just be crazy together....'.

She hugged him tighter.

The hug didn't last for too long. Jack's mind wandered over their discussion.

'So, what you are saying....', Jack scratched the back of his neck,

'Is that either I can remember accounts from my previous lives... which is far too screwy to even comprehend...or I'm a fruitcake...', Jack stared anxiously at Helen.

'Either way I'm a freak'.

'There is no way of proving it...there is no way I can realistically discuss it with anyone else...there is just...', Jack paused.

'No way....'.

Helen frowned and thought for a moment.

'Do you remember their names?...Where they lived?..What they did?...How they died?', She asked.

'Have you ever thought of checking up the information you see?', she continued.

Jack shook his head.

'Until now I really thought it was just an overactive imagination.... and a strange one at that', Jack laughed nervously.

'Well...?', Helen encouraged Jack to divulge some information.

Jack sighed and sat down.

He looked into the back of his mind.

'I remember the name Billy Adams...I can hear a teacher calling out the name during registration...he was only young...16...17 maybe...', Jack recalled.

'His girlfriend was Patricia....', Jack felt his stomach twist in pain.

'He loved her dearly...Something happened between them...I don't know what exactly', Jack whispered.

Helen sat up at hearing the name she had witnessed Jack calling out in his sleep.

'Where did they live?', Helen enquired.

'I don't know', Jack shrugged.

A thin line of sweat slowly trickled down his right temple. He was finding this extremely painful, not physical pain but a stronger more intense mental variety.

'They used to meet on a grassy corner by the bend of a river and sit together on a bench..', Jack's voice quivered as he spoke.

He stared at Helen with glazed eyes.

'That's all I can remember', Jack spoke in disappointment

Helen smiled. A consolidating smile.

'What about the Swastika's?', She changed track, she could see the memories of Billy Adams were too painful for Jack to recall.

Jack wiped his eyes and thought hard again.

'I remember being on the back of a wagon...dressed in German uniform...', Jack sniffed.

'I was surrounded by a group of other German soldiers...We stopped and got off the wagon and went into this dark and damp hut', Jack recalled faintly.

'It was strange ....I remember looking out of the hut in the morning and seeing the swastika's flapping in the breeze above the buildings in front of me'.

'I felt cold and frightened...', Jack shuddered.

'I remember the name Klaus Berthold...It wasn't me...but I remember him more vividly than anything else...', Jack gulped.

His mouth became dry.

'The stare...I have nightmares about that stare...', Jack shook.

'Billy had nightmares about that stare', he added.

'He was an SS Officer....brutal...vicious'.

'I remember looking into his eyes seconds before I slit his throat....', Jack admitted the murder.

Helen looked shocked but continued to listen in silence.

'I killed a lot of those German soldiers that evening...', Jack felt pained at having to recount the killings. He witnessed every painstaking blow and merciless slaying but decided to keep these visions to himself.

Helen could see the visions through Jack's eyes but didn't interrupt his chain of thoughts.

Jack continued.

'There were two cases....a silver metallic one and a brown leather satchel....', Jack pictured them vividly.

'The silver one contained the blue tubed liquid...the leather one a mass of paperwork...', Jack sweated profusely.

He could hear his voice echoing through the room. Somehow he felt detached from the office. The concentration throbbed inside his head.

'I was in incredible pain....I think I'd been shot ...I drank the liquid and burned the papers...I can smell the smoke drifting into my nostrils in the crisp clean air...I lay down in the snow beside the trunk of a large tree....', Jack paused.

'And drifted away into a blue sodium haze', he fell silent.

Helen noted that Jack's final words seemed almost poetic.

'Drifting away into a blue sodium haze'.

She was speechless. She could tell by the emotion on Jack's face, the sweat that dripped from him, the tears that paved a path over his cheeks, that he truly believed in what he had said. This was not the picture of a madman. This was real.

She felt fear grip her tightly.

She stared at Jack still not knowing quite what to say.

Jack returned the stare.

He smiled and wiped away the moist droplets from his face.

'The crazy thing is...', Jack paused.

'The silver case turned up with Standt's body...'.

Helen's mouth opened and she shook her head..still speechless.

'The reports that came back said that the case was manufactured in Germany in the late 1930's and that they were primarily used for crude courier services and that they went out of production in the early 1950's.', Jack smiled.

'What do you make of that?', he posed.

Helen stuttered.

'I...I..don't know'.

'It was the same case Helen...I felt it...inside here..', Jack patted his chest.

'But how?', She questioned.

Jack shrugged.

'You tell me?'.

Jack smiled.

'I wasn't the only one to drink that stuff', he paused watching the faint colour Helen had left in her cheeks drain away.

'He's here!', Jack proclaimed.

Helen suddenly felt ice cold.

She shivered and shook.

'Who?', she stammered, but knew the answer to her question.

'Klaus Berthold is here Helen...in Bristol..and he is looking to seek revenge...', Jack spoke coldly.

'NO', was all she could muster.

Jack nodded.

'That explains everything...', Jack spoke rapidly and freely.

'Why he's always been one step ahead of me....Why Tommy was killed...Why Den was killed...Why the silver case was left with Standt...He's laying a trail for me...Baiting me to find the answers and relive the past..', Jack spoke bitterly.

'Who is it?', Helen whispered.

'I don't know but I've already met him...I can feel him around me...', Jack felt anger.

Helen sighed.

She felt void of all emotions.

Her mind was an emptiness of all logical reason.

It was as though she too had lived Jack's nightmares with him.

She tried to understand it all but failed miserably. There was no way of understanding.

Finally, after the two of them had sat together silent for almost three whole minutes she spoke,

'Why don't you check up on Billy Adams?...See if he is registered in the database...maybe with the Births, Deaths and Marriage registrars', she tried to find reason.

'Don't be upset Jack but maybe it is a medical condition...', she spoke quietly and more hopeful.

Jack laughed.

'I knew you'd think I was crazy!', Jack raised his voice and stood up, pacing around the office.

'No Jack I don't...but it is worth checking ...if nothing else to prove the validity of your story not only for me but also for yourself.', she expressed concern.

Jack looked at her and realised that what she said made sense.

He sighed.

'Do you have access to the stations database?'.

'Yes I'm connected to the server, but my clearance won't allow me to access confidential records', she admitted regretfully.

'That's OK...just get me into the network and I'll do the rest', Jack walked round to her side by her console.

Helen used the modem link to obtain the network menus. Jack turned the monitor and pulled the keyboard towards him. The main menu was displayed over the screen. Helen only had access to the internal E-mail slots and various admin areas. Jack pulled down the connection info menu and highlighted the remote heading.

'You need a clearance code to use that!', Helen insisted. She had familiarised herself with the whole network and had tried all the headings to reveal just what she was allowed access to.

A box appeared centre screen with the title 'Remote Site'. Below the title was an empty box with the words 'Enter Authority Number' beside it.

'I know...', Jack replied.

He reached into his jacket pocket and pulled out his wallet.

'The system allows us to access the database from a remote site.. just in case we desperately need information quickly and are out of the office at the time', Jack smiled.

He opened his wallet and removed from the side leaf a folded slip of paper. He opened it.

'It just so happens I have the authority here', Jack smiled.

'Could you look away please..', Jack laughed.

He wasn't really serious, but Helen did so anyway.

He typed in the eight-figure authority code and the screen filled out with further information.

'Now it's just as though I'm sat in my own office', Jack joked.

Jack selected the access toolbar menu and selected Birth, Deaths and Marriages.

The screen went blank for a second with only the words 'Connecting' displayed in the bottom left corner.

Then Jack was in. He selected 'Deaths' and a further box appeared which asked for 'Name and Year'.

Jack thought for a second.

'I was born in 1957...So let's say he probably died in either 57 or 56', Jack commented

Helen agreed.

Jack typed 'Billy Adams- 1956' into the box.

The word 'SEARCHING' appeared on the screen.

After a few seconds the words' NO RECORDS FOUND', returned on the screen.

Jack's shoulders dropped.

'Try William Adams?', Helen excitedly intervened.

'It's unlikely you would have been christened Billy', she added.

Jack warmed at the way she had said 'You' in her last statement. He realised that she almost certainly believed in him.

Jack tried again.

The screen returned with a list of 8 records found.

The youngest of the dead William Adams in that year was a 24-year-old man from Glasgow. Jack knew that wasn't him. He was looking for a boy really around the age of 16 or 17 and definitely English.

He tried again with the year 1957. The screen returned with 5 names. He eliminated three immediately, all too old. Of the two remaining, one had been 19 when he died the other 16. Jack opened the file of the younger boy.

WILLIAM JAMES ADAMS
b. 12-2-41 d. 7-6-57

That made the boy 16 when he died. The registration was facilitated in Reading. Helen wished to look at the other file, but Jack knew instantly that this was him.

Helen agreed when she saw the tears fill into Jack's eyes.

She noted the name and dates onto a leaf of her notepad, and also noted the registration and the counter information of Mr G.W. Adams and Mrs E Adams, 15 Elm Road, Reading, Berkshire.

She tore off the slip of paper and proceeded to close down the files.

Jack returned to his seat and sat with his head in his hands.

Helen closed down the PC and said,

'Got anything planned for this afternoon?'.

Jack looked up.

'Not really?...more research...triple checking paperwork...?', Jack answered quizzically,

'Why?'.

'Fancy taking a trip?', she said smiling.

'Trip where?'.

She held up the slip of paper.

'Oh No!...Are you crazy?..What are you trying to do to me?', Jack said.

'It's the only way to help these nightmares...Confront them...If this Berthold character is around then it sounds to me like you need to prepare yourself for him...understand fully what is going on...', she smiled.

'You are crazy!', Jack laughed.

Inside he melted with the genuine support he was receiving from her.

'Well, if you go back you might get a clearer picture of what happened...sort of retrace the events if you like...It might be very painful, but it can only help...', she insisted energetically.

Jack sighed.

'Are you sure?', he wasn't convinced.

'Come on Jack...be strong', she encouraged.

Jack smiled.

'Pass me your phone'.

He told Briggsy he would be out for the rest of the day and to cover for him with Craven.

Briggsy tried to protest but Jack reminded Briggsy of his previous afternoons golfing excursion and Briggsy submitted. Jack told Briggsy to meet him early in the office the following morning.

Jack finished the conversation and watched as Helen walked past him and lifted a coat hanger from a peg to the side of the door. She asked Jack to turn away. She eagerly removed her blouse and hung it on the coat hanger and lifted a navy pullover from the other peg. She tossed it on and told Jack that she was ready to leave. Jack turned to witness the change of attire.

'More comfortable to travel in', she smiled.

She locked her office and produced her car-keys from her handbag.

'We'll take my car....Quicker!', she laughed.

Jack smiled.

Jack could see the fear and excitement in her eyes. They entwined erotically together giving a sparkle like polished sapphires.

Jack realised that if it wasn't for Helen, he probably wouldn't have been able to cope with the revelations that had ensued.

The journey would take almost two hours and although Jack felt fearful at what awaited him he was also content at the company he would share for the journey and he felt stronger for the support.

CHAPTER 15

They reached the junction turn off for Reading on the M4 in remarkable time. Helen hadn't lied when she said it would be quicker in her car. She had consistently broken the speed limit for most of the journey, travelling an average 80 mph. They hadn't spoken much. Jack found himself gripping the side handle of the passenger door, he was a terrible back seat driver, especially at those speeds.

Helen spotted a petrol station on the outskirts of the city and pulled in to refuel. She put twenty pounds worth of unleaded fuel in the car and disappeared into the shop. Jack sat alone for a while. He felt a nervous tingle in the pit of his stomach. They were close, not only did he anticipate it, but he could also feel it. The sun shone brightly and warmed the inside of the car. His face burned behind the windshield. He lowered the passenger window and felt the cool breeze immediately fan over him.

Helen returned. She had a small collection of objects with her. She pulled the car out and parked at the side of the station.

She tossed a packaged tuna salad sandwich into Jack's lap and inspected her own before ripping open the top and biting into one of the insufficiently filled triangles. She chewed quickly and turned to the index of the city's A-Z, which she had also purchased.

'Right ..OK..', she spoke still digesting the mouthful of food.

Jack looked at his packet and chose not to open it until he was really desperate. He placed it on the dashboard. Besides he really didn't feel hungry yet.

'Here it is!..', she blurted out.

'Elm Road...'.

Jack's stomach turned.

'It's to the west side of the city....so we carry on up this road... here....till we come to this crossroads....hang a right...then..', she flicked through several pages.

'Go up Priory Road and then...', she flicked a further page.

'We need to get onto Broad Avenue.....so take a right then left.... right again at the T-junction and it's around those roads there...', she showed the book to Jack.

'Can you follow that?', she asked.

Jack nodded scanning the pages she had folded over the corners to.

Helen quickly finished her sandwich and screeched out of the station.

She had an incredible memory. She found herself on Broad Avenue without even having to confirm her whereabouts to Jack.

'Right where now Jack?', she asked flicking her gaze from one side of the car to the other noting all the road names at the junctions to either side.

Jack saw Elm Road on the map. He found exactly where they were.

'Take the next right..', he said.

Helen smiled at Jack's participation. She was worried he had begun to have second thoughts about the visit.

The roads were quite wide and fast in this part of town. It was quite a suburban area. Very green and almost rural, for a city anyway.

Lines of trees marked the trail along Park Street. The traffic had thinned, and it was reasonably quiet. Just an odd selection of cars and vans passed in the other direction. They passed a football pitch and a play area for kids. A slide, swings and a small roundabout stood colourfully to their left. A small child was negotiating the top of the slide accompanied by a smiling mother waiting at the bottom to catch her child. Jack looked at the map again.

'Slow down the turn's around here somewhere', Jack said.

Jack noticed the small stream to his right. It meandered a path through the open fields and into the thickening trees and bushes out of sight.

His stomach ached. Helen drove slowly along the road. An impatient Fiesta roared at the back of them before slipping down a gear and hurtling passed them.

'Prick!', Helen commented.

Jack saw the two large pillars at the front of the park. His heart stopped.

His head pounded as though the insides were trying to break out from the confines of his skull.

'STOP THE CAR!!!!', he shouted.

Helen screeched to a halt.

Jack turned in his seat and looked back at the entrance to the park.

He paused for a second before jumping out of the car and running across the road to the gates almost getting caught by the speeding truck on the other side.

Jack stared at the gates.

Helen shouted after him, but Jack walked briskly through the gates and up the path into the park.

She fumbled with her seatbelt and parked the car and locked it before running off after Jack.

She ran up the path and came to a joining. She could go left or right. She couldn't see Jack. The right path led into the distance and there was no way Jack could have covered the distance in that short space of time. She took the left route.

She ran up to the bend and as she turned it she slowed.

Jack was sat on the side of the grassy bank opposite a bend in the river. He stared at the water in front of him. Helen approached him slowly and cautiously.

'What is it Jack?', she asked.

Jack turned to Helen. Tears welled in his eyes.

'This is the place I was telling you about...', Jack couldn't stop the tremor in his voice.

'This is where we came...', he added.

Helen looked around at the scene. She remembered the bend in the river Jack had referred to, and the large grassy hill that climbed behind them.

'There used to be a bench..just here...', Jack pointed beneath him, 'The place wasn't so open then...they have cut back the bushes and trees so it's not so private anymore....but this was our place.', Jack found it difficult to control himself.

He stood up and climbed the hill behind. Helen followed silently.

The breeze pushed out the tears in his eyes and made them fall down his cheeks. Jack had no desire to remove them. He stood and turned to his left and looked out over the path in the distance. In his mind he could picture Patricia strolling innocently along the side of the riverbank. Her pretty dress. Her long flowing hair and infectious smile. He couldn't hold the image and turned away. Tears streamed from him.

'Why is this happening to me?...I can't control myself...', He begged Helen for the answers.

She hugged him tightly as Jack poured out his emotions on her for almost a minute.

She ushered him back down the hill and back to the car.

They sat silently for a while. Helen held Jack's hand. His hand felt clammy and cold. She was worried that maybe the journey wasn't such a good idea after all. She didn't like to see Jack cut up like this. A strong, respectful man blubbing like a frightened child. It was then that she realised that she loved him. Real love. Not a passing thought that occasionally in certain situations presented itself but a real fire. A burning and painful love that ached through all her bones. She wanted to cry with him. Hold him tight and kiss the tears away, telling him she was there and that it would be OK.

Jack took a while to compose himself then finally he took a deep breath and turned to Helen and squeezed her hand tight.

'Sorry...', Jack offered.

Helen smiled and wiped at his tears with the back of her hand. Her hand felt so soft and gentle that Jack found himself closing his eyes and leaning into it. He kissed the salty moisture over her knuckles. She smiled a heart-warming smile.

'Come on...', she said lovingly.

'Let's go home...'.

'No..we've come this far let's carry on..', Jack stated.

'Are you sure?', Helen exclaimed.

'Yes...I know where we are now...just up here and take the next left then second right...then there should be a post box on the side of the road ....take the first left after it...', Jack sounded resilient again. He felt angry and bitter that he was having to be subjected to all of this and he was determined to get to the bottom of it. They trotted back to the car together. Jack felt like he was running on air. What he felt was indescribable. Helen felt nauseous, maybe the sandwich had not been a good idea.

Helen followed Jack's directions and was quietly astounded to find Elm Road just after the post box on the left as Jack had said.

Helen pulled up outside number 15.

Jack smiled.

'It's changed a bit...different colour....new windows...modernised... but...that's the place...'.

Jack peered up at the small left-hand window with the pink and yellow curtains.

He smiled.

'That was my room...'.

Helen looked at the window that was now, obviously, the room of a young child.

'Nice...', she smiled.

'Yes...', Jack grew more solemn. His pictured himself staring out of it onto the street all those years before. His eyes were swollen and empty. His heart gently throbbed. A tiring and painful throb.

'I died looking out of that window...'.

Helen's smile dropped.

'What?', she gasped.

Jack nodded.

'Yep...just there..', he held back impending emotions with difficulty.

A middle-aged woman strolled along the pavement with a small child. She looked anxiously into the car. She stared at Jack first then at Helen. Curiosity written all over her face. She continued to look back as she walked past the car and up the path to the door of number 15. She ushered the child inside the house and stared again at the car. Helen jumped out.

'Excuse me...Do you live there?', Helen stated the obvious.

'Yes...', the woman replied puzzled by their interest.

'Are you a relation to the Adams family?', Helen asked.

'What?...Are you trying to be funny?', her daughter watched the popular children's version of the sixties comedy show.

Helen realised what she had said and laughed.

'Sorry...No...the family...Adams used to live there....Are you a relation?', Helen's rewording was more appropriate.

The woman shook her head in thought.

'No...the Greens used to live here before us...and we've been here for almost ten years...', she proudly stated.

'Oh..OK...sorry to have troubled you', Helen returned back to the car.

The woman watched from the downstairs window as Helen drove away from the house.

Jack had remained silent for the whole of the questioning.

Then he spoke,

'There is one last place I need to see...', he said.

Helen pulled up outside Patricia's house. In comparison the house was almost exactly as Jack had remembered it. It looked distinctly out of place with the buildings around it. The paint was exactly the same colour. The windows were still metal lined. The house seemed oblivious to modern trends. The garden was still neatly manicured. An elderly gentleman toiled in the patch to the right of the lawn. He turned the earth around the fuchsia's removing any strands of potential weeds. The flowers shone brightly in reds, purples, and whites. He didn't even notice the car beside his front gate, but Jack doubted if he would have cared if he had. The garden was obviously his pride and joy. Clematis climbed the side of the house in full bloom. The surrounding hedge was trimmed flat as though performed with the aid of a spirit level. The lawn was well covered. It gave a fresh light green glow from the pruned blades of grass. The old man beavered away unmoved by the goings on around him. An elderly lady appeared at the door. She looked frail and wore a white lace pinafore. She lowered her head and struggled to focus on the car outside the gate. She said something to the old man. He looked up for a second and then continued to work on his garden uninterested by the disturbance.

Helen got out of the car again.

'Excuse me....Is this the Stevens house?', she asked politely.

The old woman answered back shakily,

'Yes...'.

Jack's eyes grew wide at her reply.

He stared at the frail old lady in the doorway. Had they really stayed at the same old house for all this time.

'Is Patricia your daughter?', Helen asked.

The old lady looked shocked at the question and used the doorframe for support. Her legs almost gave way. The old man dropped his trowel and turned to look at Helen. His face drained of all colour.

'Where is she?..Is she with you?..', the old lady tried to peer into the car.

Jack decided it was time to show himself and stepped out of the vehicle.

Helen didn't know how to reply to the question. She could see the blind hope in the eyes of the old lady. The momentary smile on her lips. The excitement of having heard her daughters name from the lips of a stranger. Patricia's name hadn't been mentioned to them for almost twenty-five years. Joe and her often spoke of their precious and that one-day she might return, but the neighbours had long since forgotten her memory. They had either died or moved away.

Jack spoke,

'No..I'm sorry Mrs Stevens...I wish she was' he spoke with difficulty.

'Oh...', the disappointment was evident.

'What do you want?', Mr Stevens spoke.

His voice wavered. His hopes had been momentarily lifted too.

Jack looked hard into the eyes of Mr Stevens. He could see the bitterness still etched inside as he had the day he had returned from his proposed meeting with Patricia on that tragic evening.

'Do you remember Billy Adams?', Jack asked gently.

Mr Stevens broke into a coughing spasm.

His lungs rattled and writhed under the intensity of the choking.

'Joe, be careful, go and get a tablet..', she ticked off her husband.

They hadn't heard that name mentioned for almost thirty-six years.

'We are friends of the family...', Helen said.

'Oh..How is Ellen?...She is OK isn't she?', Mrs Stevens hoped.

'Yes she's fine...', Jack interrupted without knowing if his statement was correct.

Mr Stevens turned and continued with his weeding.

'Would you like a cup of tea?', Mrs Stevens offered.

'Love one..thanks', Helen replied.

Jack followed Helen into the kitchen.

Mrs. Stevens reached out three cups and saucers and put on the gas to boil the kettle.

The kitchen was small and full of items, which in today's market would probably fetch a considerable amount of money.

Helen sat at the small square oak table on one of the two chairs. Jack stood by her side. Mrs Stevens filled the pot with hot water and delicately and shakily carried the pot over to the centre of the table and placed it on the cork matting.

She gingerly sat in the other chair.

'Milk...sugar..', she asked.

It had been along time since she'd had company.

After Patricia's disappearance the family had rallied around them offering words of condolence and giving them hope, but as the years went by they had grown fed up with topic of conversation. They grew uncomfortable with the way they kept the house in the same way that it had been when she disappeared. Her bedroom still held the same decor and bed linen as she had left it. Although, the family found it heart rendering they also found it sickly strange and after a while tried to convince the Stevens that she had gone for good, for ever. It was a harsh and cruel statement that plunged an inevitable rift between them and their family members. A rift that still to this day hadn't been bridged or healed.

'It was such a shame what happened to Billy..', Mrs Stevens began.

Jack listened.

'We didn't blame him you know....', she insisted.

Helen sipped at her tea.

'They were just like Romeo and Juliet...Shakespeare would have been proud...I can picture them now...', she smiled.

Jack's throat went dry.

'Laughing, joking, holding hands....inseparable they were..', she continued.

'It was true love...not like what youngsters today think of it...this was a romance...', she smiled.

Jack stared at the floor.

'Joe took it really badly...you know what fathers and daughters are like...'.

Helen nodded.

'He didn't mean to say all those things to them....he had to blame someone you see...he couldn't understand why his daughter had been taken from him...'.

Jack's face twitched. He was finding this unbearable.

'He felt so guilty of the things he had said when Billy died... Heart attack they said...but I think it was more of a broken heart that killed him...', she whispered over to Helen.

Helen looked over to Jack. He was still staring forlorn at the floor taking in every word. Feeling each sentence thrash him.

'They stayed around for a while after he died...but then had to move and start afresh..... the memories in the house were too much for them...we understood that....but we had to stay and wait for Patricia to come home...', she spoke happily.

'I used to make her evening meal for months after and sit it on the table waiting for her to come through the door...', she recalled.

'Now I just make sure we've got plenty of food in so that I can get her something when she comes back...'.

Helen felt incredible pity. This poor old woman still believed her daughter would still come bouncing through the door, bright eyed, youthful, and full of life as she remembered her. Helen thought that Patricia would be about 54 years old now.

'She loved beef stew you know..that was her favourite...with dumplings...and apple pie and custard for pudding...', her eyes began to water.

'Although on Friday's she was very partial to a nice slice of haddock...', her words trailed off into sobs.

Jack felt the tears stream down his face.

Helen too could control herself no longer. This was the saddest sight she had ever witnessed.

Her eyes filled and dripped.

The tears burning her cheeks as they rolled over them. Her eyes sore from the salt.

Jack walked over to Mrs Stevens.

He grabbed her hand.

'Your daughter was so special.....so loving...so intelligent...so very special...', Jack sobbed.

Mrs Stevens sobbed aloud with him.

'I'm so very very sorry...', Jack shook uncontrollably and lowered his head onto the hand of Mrs Stevens.

Jack stood up and ran out of the kitchen.

Helen asked her if she would be all right. She nodded.

'Look after yourself....OK?', Helen said.

'We will be with her again soon you know..', Mrs Stevens said.

'I know...', Helen replied.

She looked up and stared at Helen.

'Tell Billy that we forgive him....please', she pointed after Jack.

Helen looked aghast.

'Pardon?', she murmured.

Mrs. Stevens smiled.

'Billy..', she waved her hand in the direction of the doorway.

'Tell him we forgive him....you've got a good one there you know...', she sniffed.

'I will....', Helen replied. Her stomach raced up to her mouth and her legs felt like lead. The statement had stifled her with a blend of confusion and fear.

The old lady mopped away her tears with a white lace handkerchief.

Helen smiled and awkwardly left.

She walked past Mr Stevens who by now was staring straight at Jack as he sat in the car. He had a puzzled look on his face.

Although the pair of them were now bordering on senility, Helen knew that they saw it. She found it very frightening. She hadn't really bargained for any of this.

The journey back to Bristol was ultimately a strange one. The atmosphere was so thick it could have been sliced with a knife. Jack had learned a lot from the visit. His mind ticked over the day's events. He was beginning to appreciate the gift he had been given.

Helen on the other hand had been the composed one on the way down. Now it was she who was utterly bemused by it all. Her silence was one of confusion, bewilderment and ultimately fear.

It was no longer a theory or a game, now it was reality. Jack knew she had a lot to contend with. The picture was delicately painted over her unyielding facade.

Behind it he could sense the dazed ticking of her brain.

She drove home on autopilot. As the sun dipped over the horizon, Jack was already contemplating the morning, when he would stake-out Marco's house and wait for Neilsen to arrive.

Jack felt he had strengthened his hand and tomorrow he would up the bidding.

Marco had a relatively quiet day. He had his courier deliver the package to his office late-afternoon, which he immediately locked away out of sight in his safe. It wouldn't have been wise to leave quarter of a million pounds worth of merchandise just lying unguarded on his desk.

He had also received a phone call earlier in the morning warning him to keep his eye out for Jack. Apparently he had gone unexpectedly missing and that the caller suggested that maybe he was contemplating paying Marco another visit. Marco had employed all of his sophisticated security equipment to monitor his home. A camera even scanned the street. Not a sighting or sound was heard in relation to Jack Mitchell.

Marco returned the call late on in the evening and reported that Jack had not turned up. The caller became highly suspicious of Jack's whereabouts and what exactly he was up to.

Marco retired early to bed and having satisfied his girlfriend Cath in an hour's sex, he dropped off to sleep.

He was always excited the evening before an important meeting. A meeting that made him vast amounts of money. He slept with a long wiry smile on his face.

CHAPTER 16

That evening Jack had made two important phone calls. The first was to Briggsy, telling him to pick him up from his place at 6 a.m. The second was to Sam. He had called on his, as he put it, one last favour. She obliged somewhat reluctantly, but finally agreed. Helen had left Jack at around 9 p.m. The atmosphere had been uncomfortable. She couldn't come to terms with the day's events, and both were mentally and physically fatigued. Jack had noticed her just staring at him eerily. The stare wasn't pleasant, and Jack knew what was running through her mind.

He hoped that a night's rest, would allow her to weigh up those thoughts and that in the morning she would continue to offer the strength of support that she had up till now. Jack's sleep was animated, and he thrilled over the morning's agenda.

Briggsy arrived a minute before six. Jack gave him a confident smile and walked around to the driver's door.

'Morning Briggsy....move over ...my turn at the wheel today'.

Jack's politeness at such an early hour instantly raised Briggsy's suspicion. Briggsy crossed the centre console and fastened himself into the passenger seat. Jack looked at the perplexed and astonished visage of his co-pilot.

'Beautiful day isn't it?', he smiled.

Briggsy answered sceptically.

'Yes..I suppose it is..'.

Jack drove to the newsagent at the end of his street and disappeared inside.

Briggsy watched through the window as Jack collected a handful of newspapers, probably six different editions, and threw them onto the counter. He disappeared into the refrigerator section and collected a handful of sandwiches and other edible items and a selection of crisp snacks. He returned to the car with the goods in a bulging white plastic bag and the newspapers slung over his arm.

'There we go...that should do us..', Jack smiled.

He threw the newspapers and bag onto the back seat.

Briggsy looked even more confused.

'What are we doing Sir?', the curiosity got the better of him.

'You'll see Briggsy...patience my boy..', Jack drove towards Marco's place.

Briggsy sighed. He was beginning to wonder if Jack was going mad.

Jack pulled the car into the lay-by on Carter Street. He reached into his jacket pocket and pulled out his mobile phone. He rested it on the dashboard and made sure it was switched on. He then reclined his seat slightly and reached onto the back seat and selected a sandwich and a packet of crisps from the bag and picked up the 'Daily Mail' newspaper and turned to the sports section.

Briggsy watched his every move in gaping astonishment.

'Sir?...What's going on?', the tension rose in Briggsy's voice.

Jack bit into a sandwich.

'Patience!!', Jack raised his voice.

Briggsy shuffled around in his seat. His face turned a shade of crimson.

'I'm sorry Sir...but I can't just sit here eating ham salad sandwiches and salt and vinegar crisps reading yesterday's news without knowing EXACTLY what's going on..', the anger and frustration boiled over from him.

Jack smiled. It was the first time he had seen Briggsy angry. It was good to see.

'Besides...while you were away yesterday I spoke to the Super....', Briggsy continued.

Jack still smiled.

'I showed him the list that I compiled ages ago and he agreed with me that we should check out the names....or at least do something relevant to the case...', Briggsy almost broke into a shout.

Jack laughed.

'Briggsy ...calm down...OK...I suppose you should know...', he paused to remove a piece of ham from his back tooth.

'Going to have to get to the dentist...this tooth is a food trap!'.

Briggsy sighed aloud.

'OK...you know that Standt had a partner in crime', Jack stated.

Briggsy shrugged.

'Maybe...yes'.

Jack laughed.

'OK then...Standt did have a partner in crime...', Jack restated.

'I spoke to Erik about it...this partner's name is Neilsen...he paid Erik a visit just before he left the country..', Jack said.

'Erik's gone?', Briggsy interrupted.

'Yes...long gone...anyway he gave me a description of him...', Jack sucked his teeth.

Briggsy calmed and listened intently.

'I also spoke to Marco's PA...remember her...Samantha...Sam...', Jack continued.

'Sir..you were warned to stay clear of him..', Briggsy reiterated.

He shook his head disgustedly.

'Hear me out will you...', Jack insisted.

'Those videos we got from the Pravada....', Jack paused.

Briggsy nodded.

'Well Sam was the girl on the first tape we looked at...remember?'.

Briggsy looked shocked.

'Are you sure?'.

'Yep...I checked her out..she's got a record as long as your arm.... Prostitution...Drug abuse...', Jack said smugly.

Briggsy fell silent.

'Anyway...I thought that was odd for a man who claims to thoroughly vet his employees to allow someone with her record to work for him...especially so closely to him...', Jack noted.

'So, I chatted with her about it....', Jack smiled.

'She confirmed that Marco received visits from Standt and another man fitting the description of Neilsen...'.

Briggsy looked disappointed.

'I can't believe it.. Are you sure?', was all he could offer.

'Why would she lie?', Jack commented.

Briggsy puffed out his cheeks.

'And in answer to your original question Briggsy...the reason we are here is that Marco is meeting Neilsen today....Sam is going to let my mobile ring twice when he arrives and then twice again when he leaves...', Jack continued to consume the sandwich.

Briggsy stared at the mobile, now aware of its relevance in full view on the dashboard.

'Well?', Jack questioned.

Briggsy nodded.

'I did wonder why we were parked just along from Park Place..I thought we were going to pay Marco another visit...', he said.

Briggsy sat silent for a while as Jack calmly read through the football news.

Briggsy turned towards Jack again.

'So, what do you intend to do?...Wait till Neilsen leaves then follow him?', Briggsy questioned.

Jack smiled.

'See Briggsy...I'll make an inspector of you yet...'.

Briggsy sighed and picked up the copy of the Telegraph.

It was 9:55 when Neilsen drove passed them on Carter Street. Neilsen hadn't noticed the conspicuous vehicle parked in the lay-by hidden amongst several other vehicles. He wasn't aware of the curious shopkeepers who consciously inspected the vehicle at regular intervals. It was the topic of discussion for them for almost three hours. He just slid past them unnoticed too by Jack and Briggsy. He turned into Park Place, drove along the drive, and pulled up outside

Marco's house. Sam spotted the navy-blue BMW the instant it came into view along the drive. She monitored its progress and as it drew closer noticed Neilsen at the wheel.

She reached into her handbag and produced the slip of paper that she had jotted Jack's mobile number down onto. She hesitated for a second, listening to ensure no one was either approaching the office or was watching her.

She picked up her phone and dialled the number.

Briggsy jumped as the mobile purred twice on the dashboard. He gave a nervous glance at Jack. Jack smiled and threw the newspapers into the back seat. He returned his seat back into the upright position. Briggsy's hands were shaking. Jack was aware that this was probably the first stakeout that he had participated in, and the fact that they were about to tail a possible cold-blooded murderer didn't help his disposition.

'Sir..what happens if he goes the other way out of the house...up towards Mill Street..', Briggsy wavered.

'We'll wait till we know he's left from the second call...give him twenty seconds or so to pull out of that junction...', Jack pointed behind them,

'If he doesn't appear I'll spin the car around and get after him... Mill Street is a long straight road...we'll catch him...', Jack smiled. Jack marvelled at his precise and ingenious plan.

Sam sat at her desk watching Neilsen. He briefly glanced up at her window, she turned away before he caught her eyeing him. As she looked down again she saw Marco appear. He was dressed in a charcoal suit and carried a black briefcase. It seemed as if he was attired to attend a form of business meeting. Neilsen opened the right rear door and Marco sat inside. Neilsen glanced up again at the office window. It was as though he subconsciously knew he was being watched from that point. Sam averted her gaze.

As she looked up once more, the car was already speeding up the drive. She panicked and almost dropped the phone off her desk. She urgently typed in the digits and was relieved to hear the ringing tone. She let it ring twice as instructed and then replaced the receiver.

She told herself that this was the last time she would do something like this. She felt betrayal rushing through her veins. It made her nauseous.

Jack started the car's engine. He told Briggsy to count. The inside of the car suddenly felt like a furnace.

'9.....10..', Briggsy counted.

Jack peered through his rear-view mirror.

'Shit...Briggsy get down...', He pushed at Briggsy's head forcing him beneath the level of the dashboard. Jack lowered himself too.

He had seen Neilsen in Marco's BMW pull up to the junction behind them. It turned left out of the junction and sped passed them. Jack briefly noticed Marco sat in the back. Marco had stared in their general direction, but Jack hoped they had dived for cover just in time to preserve their identities. He released the grip on Briggsy's head and lifted himself up in the seat. The BMW was moving at a reasonable speed along Carter Street. Jack indicated and pulled out quickly, cutting up the number 44 bus which had to brake suddenly.

There were two cars between Jack and the BMW. He kept a distance of around 20 metres between them. He would have liked to have been further back, but in this traffic he could quite easily miss the favour of traffic lights and leave enough room for other drivers to infuriatingly pull into and delay them further.

The BMW took the route away from the city centre, which was of great relief to Jack. Unfortunately, the two cars separation had now increased to five cars as they got held up at the lights on Kings Road. The driver in front had kindly let out three other drivers in front of him. Jack cursed but dare not draw attention to himself. Briggsy tried leaning up against the side of the car to peer around and get a view of the BMW. Jack slapped his thigh and told him to sit still and keep facing his front. Fortunately, Neilsen hadn't been observing the traffic behind at that instant and hadn't witnessed Briggsy's amateur violation of surveillance techniques. Jack pondered as to whether it had been such a good idea to bring him along, but then he may need support if things turn ugly. The little support Briggsy could offer could make all the difference.

They turned into Filton. Jack hoped it wasn't the airport that they were headed for. The cars between had thinned to just two again. Then at the roundabout Jack noticed the two went straight on, whilst the BMW turned right. Suddenly he was confronted for the first time with the situation of being directly behind them. He slowed the car right down and left a gap of almost forty metres. The gap grew and Jack drove out of their immediate sight. So much so, that as they negotiated bends and corners in the road they were for long periods out of sight.

As Jack turned a sharp right-hand bend he noticed the T-junction in front. The BMW had already executed it. He sped to the junction and stopped, looking anxiously both ways. In both directions the road bent away after a short distance, the BMW was not in sight on either aspect.

'Shit!!', Jack exploded.

'Briggsy ...which way?'.

'Ermm...', Briggsy hesitated.

'QUICK!!', Jack insisted.

'Errm....right...', he finally appreciated the urgency of the situation. Jack turned left.

He accelerated through the gears and negotiated the bend at speed. The road continued to meander until it hit a long straight section. Far in the distance, appearing as almost a black dot, the BMW turned left into a fenced off area. To the left were several hangars and warehouses that were under reconstruction. Each entrance up to the hangars had building contractors names signed up on the fence in front of them. Jack drove slowly along the road. He noticed the BMW, now more clearly, pull into the fifth hangar along and disappear out of sight. Jack slowed up past where they had left the road and noticed the sign on the fence.

Marchants Builders was highlighted in large red letters.

Underneath in smaller black letters was the name ALLIANCE SECURITY.

Marco's company. Jack smiled and continued to drive up to the next entrance along.

He turned into the drive and slowly made his way up the uneven and potholed mud track until he reached the sixth hangar. He pulled the car to the right of the hangar out of view from the previous one, which Marco had disappeared into.

Jack looked around at the hangar. It was similar in size and structure to the others. It spanned probably 10 metres by 6 metres and was constructed with concrete to the front and back and had an arched corrugated iron roof. To the sides were large metal concertinaed sliding doors painted in an industrial blue colour. Each hangar had two large windows high up from view along the front and rear to allow a necessary amount of light inside. The hangar was marked with the number 15 to the front right side. In the distance Jack could make out the number 16 on the hangar which the BMW had disappeared inside. To the rear of the hangar was a large 12-foot wall which stretched along the perimeter and encompassed all the hangars. Stacked just away from the wall was a square of oil drums. Each hangar had its own stack in approximately the same place. Residue oil blackened the spot. Jack ushered Briggsy around the rear of the hangar and between the wall and the oil drums. They would act as perfect cover to approach the other hangar. Jack crept quietly and slowed along the man-made alleyway closely followed by Briggsy. Jack ran between the gaps in the oil drums. Finally, they were close to hangar 16. It was a carbon copy of 15 except the side door was open. Jack could smell the fumes of a running engine. From his position he could just hear the echo of the engine ticking over. He felt Briggsy at his shoulder peering behind the end of the drums. Jack thought of running across and behind the pile of wooden palettes that sat adjacent to the next stack of oil drums when another vehicle suddenly appeared and turned into the hangar. Jack and Briggsy both ducked for cover.

Now there were two cars suspiciously meeting in a derelict building. Odd? Jack tended to think so, and Briggsy was beginning to think that way also.

They heard a car door slam and a muffled sound of voices. They had to get closer. Jack ran for the palettes and dived behind them.

He turned to see Briggsy take his chance. Briggsy wasn't as light on his feet as Jack and his shoes made a distinct sound under his gallop. Jack sighed as Briggsy ducked next to him. Jack peered through the gaps in the palettes to see if they had been heard. No one appeared much to Jack's relief, the car engines had probably filtered out any external sound. Jack continued along the side of the wall ensuring the large black oil drums shielded him from the hangar. As he reached the side of the hangar and peered through the recess between drums he noticed a man appear from the side entrance. He walked out and leant against the side of the hangar facing the front. From his back Jack could tell he was of sizeable physique and had the obvious task of watching the road up to the hangar for unwelcome guests. The lookout reached into his pocket and produced a packet of cigarettes. He stuck one bent cigarette in his mouth and cradled his hand around a match and lit it. Large clouds of blue smoke rose above his head as he drew on the fag. Jack was glad that he had left the car out of sight at the adjacent hangar and that the guard didn't care to look behind him in search of the unwelcome guests concealed in the oil drums.

Jack motioned for Briggsy to be silent by placing his right index finger upright against his lips.

Briggsy nodded.

Jack stared at the hangar, he had to take a look inside.

What was happening in there that was so secretive?

He quietly moved along to the edge of the drums and keeping a steady eye on the guard slowly crept across the open courtyard to the side of the building. The guard didn't stir. Fortunately, his mind was on enjoying his cigarette rather than being aware of his rear.

Once Jack was alongside the hangar he could no longer see the guard, which was good because it meant that the guard couldn't see him also. Jack slowly crept along the outside of the hangar watching his every step and checking to the front and rear to make sure he hadn't been spotted.

Briggsy watched anxiously from his safe position. He watched Jack's movement and also kept a close eye on the guard.

A stray oil drum that stood alone up against the side of the hangar blocked Jack's path. He carefully negotiated his way around it and approached the far side of the hangar. He quickly looked back to check if the guard was still in position. He slowly crouched down onto his hands and knees and then lay flat on the floor. He crawled the remaining few yards on his stomach and gently eased his head around the bottom corner of the hangar. He found it difficult to breathe under the tension of the moment and the fact that his lungs felt crushed under his weight didn't help matters.

This side of the hangar wasn't guarded, and the doors were open. Jack could hear the voices a little clearer, but the sound of the engines still rendered them unintelligible.

He quietly slid around the corner and slowly peered inside.

He saw Marco and Neilsen stood together. There were another two men alongside them, both of which Jack didn't recognise.

They stood against one aspect of the hangar in front of a wooden table. Jack noticed two cases open on the table. From his position he couldn't make out what was inside them, but he was sure one would hold money in return for the contents of the other case. He was right of course.

Briggsy could only see Jack's feet from around the side of the hangar. His curiosity reached fever pitch. He left his position and, as Jack had done previously, slowly made his way across the forecourt. He too made it undetected by the guard. He noticed the oil drum against the wall. It was positioned directly underneath one of the windows. Briggsy paused for a moment then decided he had to see inside. He gently raised himself on top of the drum and stretched up to the window. The window was caked in grease and grime and was virtually impossible to look through. He stretched further onto tiptoe and peered through the only remotely clear patch in the pane. He looked directly at the backs of the four men stood huddled together.

Jack edged himself slightly closer.

He could just make out Marco's voice.

'Use it sparingly Dennis...it's the last that will be available for a while...'.

'Why's that?', Dennis questioned.

'I'm stopping trading for a couple of months...', Marco returned.

'A couple of months?', Dennis shouted.

Marco slid his case over to Dennis and closed the other before handing it to Neilsen.

'I'm expecting some heat...', Marco answered.

'Heat?'.

'I've got CID breathing all over me at the moment..', Marco spoke bitterly.

Dennis quickly closed the case on hearing this.

'OK then Marco..two months it is...but I'll order in advance...5 kilos..the day you start trading again..', Dennis smiled and reached and shook Marco's hand.

Neilsen turned away from them and walked back to the BMW. Jack ducked back behind the door. Neilsen spotted a movement out of the corner of his eye. It was up at the window.

'Boss!', he screamed hoarsely.

Briggsy sharply lowered himself from view. The speed at which he moved lifted the edge of the drum away from the wall. Briggsy tried to balance but in an instant he had been thrown down onto his back. The drum clattered loudly at being toppled and rolled away into the centre of the courtyard. Jack jumped up and looked around the hangar behind him. He saw Briggsy lying prostrate on his back, his mouth wide trying to inhale oxygen to his seized lungs from the force of the impact. Jack noticed the guard peer around the corner and then disappear. A car screeched away out of the far end of the hangar.

Jack ran around to the entrance just in time to see the BMW skid around the corner and disappear at speed out of the grounds. Jack dropped his shoulders and sighed.

He thought of chasing them, but by the time he had got back to his car they would have been long gone. Besides he couldn't really abandon Briggsy, although at this moment it was probably the most rewarding option available.

Jack returned back to Briggsy. He was picking himself up off the floor.

'Sorry Sir!', he still hadn't regained comfortable speech and spoke breathlessly.

His face was scarlet from the pain of the fall and the anguish of embarrassment.

Jack stared speechless.

'They gone?', Briggsy commented.

Jack laughed.

'No..they were all so frightened by the noise you made..that they thought they were under artillery fire and are all stood in there with their hands on their heads!', Jack's sarcasm stung.

'Really!', Briggsy smiled.

Jack sighed and rolled his eyes away from Briggsy.

Jack walked into the hangar and over to the table. Briggsy followed with his tail between his legs.

Jack checked the tabletop, underneath, and the surrounding area. Nothing.

Briggsy walked over to where the cars had been parked. The only visible evidence that the meeting had even been held there were the black tyre marks where the cars had evacuated at speed and with it the air of burnt rubber. Jack slammed his fist down firmly on the table.

'Sir!', Briggsy shouted across at him.

He bent down and picked something from the floor.

Jack turned and saw Briggsy holding the item from his hand. Jack moved towards him and as he got closer he noticed the item swivelling on its chain.

Round and around.

Jack steps shortened. His chest tightened.

The item caught the light and briefly sparkled in his eyes.

Jack held out his hand and Briggsy dropped the gold locket into his palm.

Jack stared at it.

He paused before flicking open the clasps.

He gasped as he witnessed the insides.

A picture of a young boy neatly filled the right segment of the locket. In the left was the inscription,

'I will ALWAYS love you'.

The picture was of Billy and Jack's mind instantly flashed back to the sight of Patricia's face when he had presented the locket to her on her sixteenth birthday. The warm glow. The animation. His heart sank.

He closed the locket and stared at the initials on the front.

'What is it Sir?', Briggsy asked innocently.

Jack gritted his teeth and looked up at Briggsy.

His eyes had filled, and he breathed deeply and heavily.

Briggsy stood back.

'The final straw Briggsy', he spat.

'The final fucking straw!', Jack grasped the locket tightly in his hand.

Jack brushed straight passed Briggsy. The fire boiled behind his eyes.

'Expecting some heat...', Jack recalled Marco's words in his head.

'I'm going to send you to the infernos of HELL, you fuck....'.

———◆———

Jack slid the car outside Marco's closed front gates. He leapt out of the door and scampered over to the intercom button. He hit the button firmly and impatiently several times until the speaker crackled.

'Yes', it was Marco's calm and collected voice.

'GET THESE FUCKING GATES OPEN!', Jack was far from calm and collected.

Briggsy shuddered still sat in the passenger seat. The journey back to the house had been a white-knuckle ride and Briggsy was visibly shaken by not only the journey but also by Jack's fury. He had never seen him like this before. Jack had been shouting expletives and muttering strange statements aloud like an estranged madman. Tears and spittle sprayed around the car with every jolt and sharp turn.

Briggsy hadn't dared look at Jack, he just held on tight and watched the car veer through a complicated path of congested traffic.

'Excuse me?...What's the problem Inspector?', Marco continued to express an innocent tone.

'Open the gates before I drive the car straight FUCKING through them', Jack spoke through gritted teeth.

His words sent the shiver down Briggsy's spine.

Jack waited for a moment then raced back to the car.

He revved up the engine and just as he was about to charge into the wrought iron barrier, they shivered and began to swing open.

Jack screeched inside them and jerked the car through the gears up to third until he slammed the brakes outside the door. The car slid sideways for almost five metres. Briggsy was thrown over the centre console and almost into Jack's lap. Jack jumped out of the car and sprinted up the steps to the door. Without slowing he raised his left foot and thrust it at the door. The door rocked in its hinges but still held firm. He kicked it again and again.

Marco opened the other side.

Jack saw the terror on his face as the door opened.

He dived inside and grasped Marco around the throat. Using all his weight and anger he pushed him back against the wall. His grip tightened. Marco choked. He tried to use his hands to release Jack's hold of his windpipe. His body flailed around. His eyes filled with water and bulged.

'Sir...SIR...you'll kill him!', Briggsy appeared startled in the doorway.

Jack released his grip slightly.

Jack leant up to Marco's face and whispered,

'What did you do with her?'.

Marco stared into Jack's eyes.

'With who?', he choked painfully.

Jack applied the firmer pressure again.

'WITH PATRICIA...', he screamed at him.

Marco's face turned a faint shade of blue. He choked and flailed against Jack's grasp.

'Sir...Sir!', Briggsy tried to pull Jack from Marco.

Jack used his left shoulder to push Briggsy away and then clenched his right fist and releasing his grip on Marco delivered the blow. Marco was thrown off his feet and landed curled in a ball on the hard floor. The blow had hit him square on the jaw and almost knocked him unconscious. Jack seemed to calm suddenly, rewarded at the discharge of over a lifetime's pent-up emotions. He strolled over to Marco and turned him over onto his front. Marco cowered as Jack stared at him. He anticipated another blow. None came.

Briggsy was ready to jump at Jack again.

He watched as Jack produced the gold locket from his pocket. He held it up in front of Marco's eyes.

'This Patricia!', he spoke softly.

Jack could have quite happily hit Marco again and again until he was a bloodied pulp on the floor, but he wanted answers.

Marco stared at the locket.

'I've never seen that before!', Marco spoke slowly.

Jack gritted his teeth and raised his right fist again.

Marco lifted his arms over his face trying to protect his features from the impending blow.

'We found this where you dropped it!...in your hangar!', Jack shouted.

'I've been here all morning..I don't know what you are talking about...', Marco's lies incensed Jack further.

'But you know we were there...we saw you...', Jack laughed. Marco's audacity and false innocence was almost comical.

'Anyway, that doesn't matter to me anymore...I don't care ...What I do care about is where you got this and what you did with her?...', Jack's voice quivered.

'I don't know what you are talking about...you are insane!', Marco replied.

Jack felt the anger boil inside and he delivered another forceful blow onto Marco's exposed cheek.

'SIR!...',Briggsy begged to intervene.

Marco looked up. His lips already swollen, and a trace of blood dripped from the broken tissue.

He spat and stared at Briggsy.

'Are you going to let him do this to me?', Marco issued astonishment in his tone.

Jack stood up. His legs were weak with the numbing effect of the adrenaline that pumped through them.

'I could quite easily squeeze every ounce of life out of you right now...', Jack said bitterly and with disgust.

'But then we both know that you'd come back and start all this over again...'.

Marco stared wide-eyed and smiled.

'But I am going to nail you .....for good...in a way so you'll never get back..', the rage and bitterness spilled from within him. It mixed with the pungent smell of fear encasing the hall.

'You're losing it Jack...you're insane!', Marco spat the blood from his mouth.

Jack stepped backwards and laughed sarcastically.

'Look at you!...you're not even half the man you were....I'm very disappointed in you Klaus...'.

'Klaus?...You're working with a maniac ...', Marco spoke to Briggsy.

'I'm sure the Chief Super will be very saddened when he hears about this!', Marco smiled with bloodied teeth.

Briggsy stared at Marco.

His eyes burned through him as he shook his head.

Briggsy turned and followed Jack out of the door.

Marco hadn't called the Chief Super as he had threatened. He had received a call around an hour after the visit. The caller had told him to be at a further meeting later. In fact, the meeting had been arranged at 5:30 a.m. the following morning. Marco had excitedly agreed. Marco contacted Neilsen and briefed him on his duties for that morning. Neilsen too was animated at the news. It was the part of his job that he loved.

Marco told Cath of his early morning business meeting and as usual they retired to bed. Cath was a very astute lady. She lay in bed watching Marco sleep. Her insides ached. She stared at the bruises on his jawline and the split lip. She hadn't believed his 'fell up the steps story'. As she stared at him, he seemed almost lifeless, like a wax doll. She sensed him dead. She ran her fingers over his body as though for the last time and sobbed herself to sleep.

CHAPTER 17

Briggsy dropped Jack off at home. Both were visibly shaken, and a rage pulsed uncontrollably through Jack's veins. Briggsy remained silent whilst Jack boiled beside him. Jack held the locket firmly in the palm of his hand, such that it felt as though it was embedding itself into his skin. He knew he had lost his composure. He had lost the edge. He desperately needed to regain himself. Whatever himself was? He didn't fancy going back to the station, as he knew Craven would be waiting for him. He realised as soon as the Chief got wind of his actions on Marco he would be suspended on the spot. It was far from professional behaviour.

He said nothing to Briggsy as he stepped out of the car. Briggsy drove away slowly watching Jack deftly climb the three steps up to his front door.

Jack's mind wandered to Patricia. Where was she? What had they done to her? He realised it was his entire fault. He was to blame. He should have stayed a loner. He thought of Helen. Had he placed her life in danger too?

He reached into his trouser pocket and produced a bunch of keys. As he offered his house key to the lock he thought he saw his curtains twitch. He froze staring at the drawn veils. He stared at the window for a couple of seconds. Was he seeing things now as well? Paranoia began to consume him. He moved back down the steps and stared at his house. He could sense a presence inside. He looked up to his bedroom window. They were no signs of forced entry from the front. His lock was intact as too were the front windows. He climbed the steps again and slowly turned his key in the lock. The door crept open. He could sense the person's presence even stronger once inside the darkness. He could almost hear them breathing. He reached inside his jacket and found the grip of the Browning, which he had holstered for the operation with Marco. He gently withdrew the weapon and rested the weight by his side. He stepped into his house and waited for a second until his eyes grew accustomed to the dark. He edged towards his lounge. His heart raced. His stomach turned with apprehension and fear. The presence grew stronger. He was close to it. He could smell it. His ears pounded in sympathy with his heartbeat making it so much more difficult to listen to any forms of disturbance. He peered around the doorway to the lounge. The presence was in this room. His fingers slid up the wall of the lounge in search of the light switch. He could hear the breathing and made out the dark figure sat in his lounge chair. The figure had long flowing hair but still remained motionless. He found the switch and pressed. As the room became engulfed in artificial lighting he raised his pistol in the direction of the dark figure.

'At last,...thought you were never coming home!', Erik smiled at the end of the pistol's barrel.

Jack sighed and the tension ebbed.

'How the hell did you get in here?', he firmly asked lowering the pistol back down to his side.

Erik smiled.

'You know for a copper I would have thought you would secure your house before you left it...the bathroom window was left open...', Erik commented proudly.

Jack shook his head and moved back to the front door, slamming it shut.

Upon entering the lounge again, he noticed how calm and collected Erik now seemed compared to the gibbering wreck he had witnessed days previously. Here he sat, uninvited, in Jack's house, crossed legged, smiling as though he hadn't a care in the world.

'I thought you had left the country?', Jack questioned.

'I almost did...got within metres of stepping on the plane...', Erik smiled.

'So, what made you stay?', Jack removed his jacket and sat down in the chair opposite placing the pistol down on the table beside him.

'I couldn't run away from it....I didn't know if I could trust you lot to catch the bastards!...besides I knew you needed my help...', Erik smiled.

Jack laughed.

'How can you help me?'.

'I've already done everything I can...', Erik replied smugly.

He rubbed at his right hand. Jack noticed the two grossly swollen knuckles.

'What have you done Erik?', Jack spoke in alarm.

'Gotten you some information..', Erik winced at the tenderness of his joints.

'Think I broke a knuckle in the process...'.

Jack sighed.

'Go on...', he snorted, beginning to lose his patience with the Norwegian's priggish attitude.

Erik smiled.

'I told you there was someone on the inside supplying all the information...', Erik stated.

'Yes..', Jack sighed.

'Well, that's definitely the case...', Erik replied.

'Who?', Jack enquired.

'I don't know ...couldn't get a name...but I know he loathes you... hatred with a passion..', Erik laughed.

Jack pondered in thought. *Must be the Chief.*

'From what I can make out this whole operation is a trap to get at you!', Erik frowned.

'Why they would go to such lengths I don't know...', he paused.

Jack sniggered to himself bitterly. He knew why.

'So, what exactly have you found out?', Jack probed.

'Well, I spoke to a few people I knew I could trust....they have good ears...most of them were only too happy to spill their guts....', he paused.

'Most of them all knew and liked Tommy, and they were disgusted to learn of his murder...'.

'They knew of Marco's involvement in the drug trade...one of them had actually been to one of his parties and was quite disgusted at what he witnessed....he said it was unnatural...', Erik laughed.

'Who was it?', Jack asked.

'You know I can't tell you that....I promised him he wouldn't get a mention..', Erik grinned.

Jack shrugged.

'But he did inform me of a courier..', Erik sniffed.

'A courier?', Jack frowned.

'He's the face that damaged my hand...', Erik held up his injured fist.

'It took a good beating to get him to talk but I managed to persuade him in the end..', Erik smiled.

Jack listened.

'He worked alongside Frank Christie....couriering the goods from one place to another...Christie thieved some of the goods and got wasted for his efforts...', Erik sighed.

Jack nodded in agreement.

'This courier used to get a call from Neilsen or Standt, never Marco himself, and he was told where and when to deliver the shipment...', Erik paused.

'This lowlife, who probably never had an honest job in his life, drove around in a fucking Audi A4...I mean can't you lot spot these people..they stick out like a sore thumb...', Erik smiled.

Jack sighed. It had been a long day and he wished that Erik just got to the point. His attitude was seriously beginning to annoy him.

'He dealt with a guy named Pat McClere...the goods were shipped from Holland to Hull...McClere was the fence who stored the shipment away until a courier came to collect...McClere works at the Hull docks...you should have no problem getting hold of him...', Erik sighed.

'Was McClere the only fence?', Jack asked.

'I believe so although they also used Filton airport as drop offs or to fly the goods to wider locations...', Erik replied.

'You certainly were quite thorough in your investigation then...', Jack spoke sarcastically.

'Like I said it took a while to get him to spill his guts but when he did it flowed out of him like shit from a sewer', Erik's analogy was not in best tastes.

'He also told me about your mate...', Erik smiled.

'My mate?', Jack puzzled.

'Den the snout...', Erik replied matter-of-factly.

'Den!', Jack muttered.

'He asked a lot of questions and found a lot of answers...too many answers...Neilsen sliced him up..', Erik swallowed hard.

Jack gave a nod soaked in guilt.

'I suppose I should be grateful he didn't slice me up...he's an evil bastard...he attacked me while my back was turned you know... otherwise I might have had him...', Erik paused recounting the beating.

'A merciless, vicious bastard..', he added.

Jack sighed.

'What about Tommy?'.

Erik shook his head.

'They wanted to keep the drug low key...only to those that could afford it...I suppose Tommy was making the drug too public for their liking...', he snorted.

'And Standt was removed because he was caught on camera..', Jack added to complete the killings.

He realised he was leaking confidential information but figured that Erik knew the facts already. He was smarter than Jack had first thought.

'I suppose so, although apparently it was common knowledge that Standt had a thing about Marco's girlfriend as well which couldn't have helped matters....', Erik added.

'Really!', Jack smiled.

'This courier does give out some useful information...where can I find him?', Jack continued to smile.

'Funny you should ask that..', Erik laughed.

'I've kept him tied up for you...literally....'.

'What!', Jack smiled.

'After I'd finished with him I tied him to his kitchen door with a bungee...he isn't going anywhere...and I used a pair of his smelliest socks to gag him...', Erik smiled proudly.

Jack laughed.

'Where is he?', Jack asked again.

'I'll take you there..', Erik suggested standing to his feet.

'Are you sure he doesn't know who the insider is?', Jack questioned.

'Well, you can try him if you like...but whoever it is holds one huge grudge against you...he's making sure Marco is kept informed as to what you are up to...they are trying to nail you...that's why I am here!..', Erik frowned.

'Why did I deserve your loyalty?', Jack asked.

'You were fair with me...I could tell you were straight and honest which is very unusual these days...just returning the favour...besides if you don't get the bastards who will....', Erik smiled.

Jack nodded and returned the smile.

'Is this place within walking distance?', Jack asked.

'No..it's over in the city centre..I hired a car at the airport we can take that..I parked it at the end of the street...',Erik noticed Jack had observed the lack of vehicles directly outside his house.

'Hire Car?', Jack laughed.

'Damn right!...didn't think I was going to get a taxi or walk back from the airport did you!...I got it for four days...I'm taking it back later this evening...I'm taking the 0830 flight back to Oslo tomorrow morning...', Erik frowned.

Jack stared at Erik and raised his eyebrows.

'For good this time...I'm going home to stay for a while..maybe two or three years...', Erik's tone was serious. It was a decision he had obviously spent some time contemplating.

Jack nodded in acceptance. He wasn't going to stop him.

———•◆•———

Pat McClere received the call at an unusual hour. Unusual being because he usually received at least 48 hours notice of a pick-up. He was told to package-up the remaining thirty kilos of shipment stored at the rear of his garage and have it ready for collection within two hours. He also thought it was unusual because it would leave the garage empty and another shipment from Rotterdam was not due until next month. But it was not his position to question the request, after all, he had made a fair packet since he became involved in the trafficking. He was amazed no one had questioned his lifestyle being a fisherman by trade. He had ferried the drugs into Hull for almost two years. He would sail his boat out to the boundaries of the Dutch waters and begin fishing as usual. There, he would be met by the Dutch trawler that would switch the shipment onto his boat. He had a steel enforced lower compartment in which he hid the drugs. He did a lot of his fishing at night and in the early hours of the morning, so it was a simple operation that had not drawn undue attention. His boat would always return with a healthy consignment of fish, as he was particularly skilful at his trade, and hence, not seem at all suspicious. Even if he was suspected he doubted as to whether customs would find the secret compartment anyway. Once docked he would open the hatch in his cabin and reach into the compartment. He would place the shipment into his large holdall, which he used for his flask, sandwiches and dry clothing and transport them in his van to the garage just one mile from the docks. The bag he removed from the boat would have appeared bulkier and heavier to the lightweight contents he took on to the boat should anyone have been monitoring him. As yet, nobody had, and he tried to conceal the weight of the bag by carrying it over his shoulder to support the weight better. If it was a particularly large consignment he would have to make two or three runs back to the boat. The garage was one that he still used for storage of unwanted household items amongst other things. He always placed the shipment at the back of the garage in a padlocked fish-container, which sat under a pile of old carpet. It was a very meagre surrounding for such priceless goods. The thought sometimes made McClere laugh. The million-dollar garage.

McClere was no criminal, as one would expect from a criminal. He was very plain and never really thought of what he did as wrong. It was all for money. Just another day's work. That is probably why he never seemed phased by an operation. He didn't get the telltale shakes or sweats. He had no real idea what he was involved in. All he knew was that it paid well, and it was a simple and straightforward task. People who dodged the taxman whilst having considerable funds to meet the costs and those that screwed the benefits office with no attempt to find employment were more criminal than him. In this day and age everyone moonlighted and received back-handers, and those that worked hard for a living at the same time were OK by him. People needed extra cash to get by and survive, especially when children were involved as in McClere's case. He had two young boys, 6 and 8. His wife had no idea where the extra money came from, but she didn't care. They struggled early on in their marriage trying to make ends meet. Their children were never neatly clothed or spoilt by way of presents. In the last two years they had bought a new house with a £20,000 down payment and had begun to live a comfortable life in which they had most things that they wanted. His wife probably suspected that the money was not solely coming from fishing, although her husband did work long hours, but she really didn't want to know. She accepted their new lifestyle opened armed, no questions asked.

McClere waited in his van at the garage for the courier to arrive. He was forewarned that it would be a different person today. He would be driving a red Rover and would answer to the name of Dave. McClere did not care who it was.

The courier was late. Dusk had fast approached and gone. McClere sat listening to his radio and smoking his fourth cigarette since he had parked the van. His cigarette lit up the inside of his van with each draw, casting his face in an eerie orange glow. He blew large gasps of smoke through the half-opened window. He tapped the steering wheel in beat with the tune on the radio. Life was great and he made sure he used every last second of it.

The set of garages belonged to the block of flats where he had previously resided. It was a rough part of the city and shouts and screams were heard through most of the night. McClere was used to it. It was an ideal spot for the shipment to be stored. Noone noticed his comings and goings and in truth, noone cared. One thing the people in this area believed in was 'Don't shit on your own doorstep'. If ever a vehicle, house or in this case, garage was safe from theft, it was this part of the city. All the local thieves resided here and so it was the safest place to be.

The Rover finally showed thirty-five minutes late. Dave stepped out of the vehicle and introduced himself. He had a large black holdall in his left hand. McClere invited him inside the garage. Dave seemed more edgy than the normal couriers and found it necessary to scan around the nearby flats to ensure they were not being watched. McClere laughed noting that behaving in that way was more likely to draw attention to yourself. Once inside the garage,

McClere pulled down the door and switched on the solitary light bulb that precariously hung in the centre of the garage, hanging by exposed wires. The garage smelled stale and with a serious imbalance of the necessary oxygen level. Dave gagged for a second. McClere lifted up the old carpet at the rear and, producing a single key, unlocked the box. Dave found himself holding his breath as he unzipped the holdall and began to load the bags of the drug into it as they were passed to him. The process only took two minutes, but Dave was desperate to get out into the clean air. He zipped up the loaded holdall and made his way to the door. He had to wait a further twenty seconds whilst McClere locked up the box and lifted up the door again. He exhaled deeply as his lungs took in the clean air. McClere laughed. Dave trotted back to his car, again staring up in the direction of the flats. McClere laughed slightly louder. These Southerner's amused him with their ways. He watched the Rover pull away from the area, headlights blaring. He shook his head as he turned to lock the garage door. He placed the key in the lock and then noticed the spot. The red spot that shone on the garage door. He stared at it for a second, then lifted his hand up to it. The spot now shone on his hand.

'What the...', were his last words.

As he turned towards the flats he saw the red light momentarily blind his left eye. It glistened and sparkled in the dark night. He didn't feel the bullet enter his forehead, nor did he hear the slight thud of the muffled rifle. He was seconds from death as his body flailed back into the garage door and made a loud bang as it thumped into the aluminium sheet. Far louder than the firing of the rifle. To those that didn't know, it would have sounded like somebody forcefully shutting their door. Certainly nothing to be alarmed about. Pat McClere slowly slid down the door leaving brain pulp behind as he slowly dropped into a heap. The assassin had monitored McClere's movements through his sights to the point of impact. He quickly slipped the rifle back into its carrying case and descended the steps at the far end of the flat's balcony, where Dave waited impatiently. The assassin dived into the car and within a minute of the solitary shot being fired, they were gone. The hole in McClere's forehead was clean and black. The rear of his skull was scattered on the door and wall behind him in a neat two-foot diameter. From a distance it looked like graffiti freshly sprayed into the shape of a comical red splat. His eyes were wide and clear of pain. The garage key still stood out, adjacent from his hand, between thumb and forefinger. He had used the last second of his life. Pat McClere's involvement in the trafficking of the drug had been callously removed without a single despairing thought for the wife and children he would leave behind.

Erik drove slowly and carefully through the centre of town. He was especially vigilant and methodical in his driving methods, taking full use of the car's mirrors and gears. The couriers name was Alex McClelland. He was a big burly Scotsman who had taken some putting down, but once Erik had bludgeoned him a few times, McClelland gave in to self-preservation. He lived in the scum part of the city, Northfields. The area had received a large government grant to tidy itself up and although the houses now seemed respectable from the outside Jack knew the rats still lived inside. Erik parked the car outside number 4. He switched off the engine and smiling broadly turned in his seat to face Jack.

'He's in that one!', he beamed.

Jack stared at the house. It was one of the small single bedroom type that stood towards the end of the avenue. The house was in complete darkness.

Jack stepped out of the car closely followed by Erik. He stopped for a second and stared down the avenue. It seemed too quiet. Suspiciously quiet and not quite right. Erik stared at Jack clearly puzzled by his apprehension.

Jack reached into his jacket and felt the cool steel of his pistol. He patted it for comfort and began to walk along the small path leading up to the front door. Erik followed at his heels. Jack stopped at the door. It was ajar. The house emitted a mysterious quality as though spectres and ghouls danced within.

'I shut that!', Erik whispered noting the door.

'It was unlocked but definitely shut...', Erik reiterated.

Jack licked his lips nervously.

'Wait by the car...', he quietly ordered Erik.

He placed his hand inside his jacket and slowly withdrew the pistol. Erik saw the weapon edge into view and stepped back shakily.

Jack stepped inside the door.

The room was dark and eerily silent.

His senses burned as they tried to scan for valuable information.

His nostrils twitched. He could smell it.

Erik stood by the side of the road.

Jack had slowly drifted out of sight into the dark abyss that represented the house.

Erik waited for almost two minutes. He sweated nervously. He felt vulnerable out on the street and would have preferred to stay with Jack and the pistol. Then suddenly a light beamed out of the front window of the house casting a yellow square onto the path before him. It was the ideal invitation Erik needed and he ran along the path and into the house, where he would feel safe. Upon discovering Jack in the front room, he would have wished he had stayed on the street.

The bungee that he had used to tie-up McClelland, hung limply from the lounge door. The socks were strewn a further metre away. Inside the lounge Jack knelt beside a body. Erik could only see the crumpled feet and legs from his position, jutting out stiffly from behind Jack's crouched frame. As he edged around he received the full picture. A body, barely resembling that of Alex McClelland, lay face-up and still. Erik tried to focus on the horror before him. At first his brain would not register. It knew there was something odd about the figure. As Erik drew closer and tilted his head slightly his brain engaged.

McClelland had two large flesh cavities where his eyes once sat. Tears of thick blood had run down both cheeks and temples. His mouth was grotesquely swollen and outstretched in a silent eternal scream. His neck had been sliced in similar fashion to the previous victims. Blood had soaked the carpet down to his waist where he had fallen. Erik noticed the splattered and smudged walls where McClelland had obviously thrashed against in an attempt to escape his merciless killer. This was obviously the work of Neilsen.

Erik shook. How close had Neilsen been to finding him in the house as well. He would have loved that. Two birds with one stone. He stepped back from his panoramic viewpoint and felt something squelch under his right boot. Jack turned in disgust. He had felt Erik's presence since he entered the room but could not force himself to look at him.

'I told you to wait by the car!', he shouted.

Erik lifted his boot and screamed at realising he had trodden on one of the eyeballs. It seemed to stare up at him in antipathy at the carelessness of his movements. Erik turned and ran out of the house. Jack soon followed.

He met Erik at the car. He sat revving the engine.

'I'VE GOT TO GET OUT OF HERE!!', Erik screamed.

Jack jumped in beside him.

'I DIDN'T DO THAT!!!', Erik sobbed.

Jack sighed.

'I know....but now they know you are back!', Jack replied.

'NOT FOR LONG!', Erik laughed manically.

He thrust the car into first and then second gear and raced out of the area.

'WHERE DO YOU WANT DROPPING?...THE STATION?', Erik still screamed. He checked his mirrors even more vigilantly although erratically.

'No..', Jack replied quietly.

'AREN'T YOU GOING TO REPORT THIS!!', Erik bellowed. Spittle dripped from his lips and chin like a rabid dog. Jack could smell the fear in Erik's sweat.

'No...', Jack remained calm.

'WHAT!!!', Erik screamed briefly taking his eyes of the road and leering at Jack.

Jack grasped hold of the wheel and steered the car around the oncoming vehicle in the other lane, which Erik would have ploughed into barring his calm intervention.

'I've got other things to do...', Jack muttered.

'...Let someone else find him!'.

Erik puffed out his cheeks and shook his head.

'Drop me off at this corner..', he issued to Erik.

Erik obliged eagerly.

'Listen...take care OK...', Erik appeared calmer.

'Yeah...and you...get on the plane this time...', Jack replied smiling.

'DON'T YOU WORRY ABOUT THAT!...I'M FUCKING OUT OF THIS CRAZY PLACE!', Erik screamed again patting Jack on the shoulder.

Jack watched Erik squeal away and round the corner. He had let an eyewitness disappear but didn't care. He knew he had to settle the score. Besides, he had already been informed that Erik's statement or evidence wouldn't hold water. Not against Mister clean Marco Veart and his bent buddies at Division. He decided he would deal with Marco first then get the Chief. The Chief would be easy it was Marco that he knew he would need all his energy and wits to overcome but he felt he was ready.

Jack walked the half a mile through the city to Helen's. He needed to protect her and maybe selfishly knew she would protect and help him through this nightmare.

CHAPTER 18

Helen was relieved to see him. She had phoned him several times that evening and almost thought about calling the police with worry. Jack had recounted all the evening's atrocities. He told her everything in gross ghastly detail. She took it well, but then in her line of work she was probably used to it.

Once Jack had finished his deliberations and explanations he produced the locket from his pocket and placed it into the palm of Helen's hand

Helen held up the locket and opened it.

'Its beautiful Jack', she admired the subtlety.

Jack smiled.

'Her face when I gave it to her will always remain etched in my mind...', Jack recalled fondly.

'It's as though I've had amnesia for all my life...or should I say... this life...', he pondered.

'And now I've got my memory back I realise that I am a completely different person..', Jack frowned.

'You are still the same person Jack...but you just remember what you were before...', Helen smiled.

'No...', Jack paused.

'No ...I AM different now...'.

She handed the locket back to Jack.

'So, it is Marco then?', she enquired.

Jack nodded.

'I don't know how I didn't kill him today...'.

Jack paused for a second then looked deep into Helen's blue eyes.

'I've got to stop him Helen...for good I mean...'.

She sighed.

'Kill him?', she swallowed.

She sat down on the sofa beside Jack.

She saw the pain in Jack's eyes as he nodded.

'I don't know if you should be telling me this Jack', she frowned.

Jack reached out and clasped her hand gently.

'Look I know that I'm asking you to help in murdering a human being...but..think about it...he's not a human being...he's evil Helen... he's a creation of hell...as am I', Jack spoke gently and quietly.

Helen stared into Jack's eyes.

'No...don't say that..'.

'I am Helen...I'm inhuman...all this needs to end...', Jack insisted.

'I got dragged into this unintentionally....doing my duty...and I've had to suffer the torture and heartache of losing everyone close to me...I've suffered for more years than anyone can comprehend...', he continued.

Helen began to cry.

'I really love you Helen...and I'm convinced he's going to take you away from me as well...', Jack spoke with sincerity.

Helen sobbed.

'Why don't we run away and sort something out together...We can emigrate...or..'.

Jack stopped her mid-sentence and squeezed her hand tighter.

'He'll find us...he's followed me here all the way from Germany.... he'll find us Helen!', Jack hugged her.

They hugged silently for a few minutes, gently rocking in each other's arms.

Then Jack broke the silence.

'Is there any way you can come up with an antidote to reverse the effects of the drug?'.

Helen shook her head.

'In my opinion, and an opinion is all it is, because it is only my theory don't forget....,it would be almost impossible....'.

She thought for a moment.

'The only way you might possibly stop it happening is to remove the part of the brain which produces the transmitter shortly before death.'.

'That way there would be no path for the energy to channel..an open circuit if you like..', she continued.

'But then again it would have to be a precise operation...you'd only get the one chance..but then maybe there are several parts of the brain that can accommodate the transmitter.'.

Jack thought of her comments.

He nodded.

'But Jack..I hardly think that he is going to let you tie him down and open up his skull without a fight do you...?', she laughed nervously.

Jack thought for a second then spoke,

'How about if I blew his brains out!.. Would it stop him coming back?'.

Helen's face contorted at the statement. She felt nauseous.

'You mean shoot him in the head?', the words turned her stomach. She pictured fragments of brain separating and exploding in congealed segments of matter.

Jack nodded.

'Well..', she swallowed the bile back into her stomach.

'It would have to be a clean shot and would have to obliterate the brain parts...even then you would have to be sure that you hit the correct spot...', she said.

'On impact the body would enact the death routine and the transmitter would be set-up...you would have to make sure you had separated this part of the brain from the other with the single shot... another shot would be too late...', she tried to keep the contents of her stomach below her throat.

Jack thought.

'A dum-dum bullet might work...', Jack suggested.

'Dum-dum...that's a crude method', Helen was familiar with the term.

'Well..it expands on impact and splits into tiny fragments tearing into any flesh, bone and matter that comes in its way..', Jack said.

'If I fired it into his brain it would rip open. Probably three-quarters if not more of his brain...that would increase the chances of taking out the relevant area wouldn't it?', Jack insisted.

Helen went pale.

'Yes..the chances would be increased...but it may still be possible you'd miss the area...'.

She wanted to get to her feet and race to the toilet.

'But the odds of hitting would be greater than the odds of missing though Helen...', Jack smiled.

Helen held her head in her hands. Nausea was encapsulating her. Her head spun. Her body convulsed.

'Look Jack..I'm not sure about this?', she begged.

Jack placed his arm gently around her.

'It's OK...I know what you are saying...just forget about the conversation now OK...I know what I've got to do..I don't want to involve you any further in the discussion...', Jack tenderly squeezed her shoulder.

'It's my choice Helen...I have to end it...'.

Helen knew Jack was adamant. It would be fruitless to try and persuade him differently.

Helen freshened herself up with a shower. Jack took the opportunity to carve cross-slits into two 9mm rounds from the magazine of his personal Browning pistol. It was not CID issue but a personal weapon he had acquired for the home. A protection weapon that usually lay untouched in his desk drawer in his bedroom. He used his Swiss Army penknife to carve the slits. It was more difficult than he imagined. The metal was tough, and it took a continued sawing action to make the necessary indents. His thumb and index finger were blood blistered by the time he had finished. He worked up quite a sweat performing the task in the short space of time he had whilst Helen was out of the room. He had involved her too much in all of this already. The last thing he wanted her to witness was him perfecting the utensils of the pending execution.

He hid the doctored rounds loose in his jacket pocket and replaced the magazine now with only 8 standard rounds back into the pistol. He hid the pistol in the other outer jacket pocket.

Helen returned to the room. Her hair was damp and tied back. She looked better for the shower. The colour had returned to her cheeks. She wore a navy jogging top and bottoms. Both garments were loose fitting. Jack marvelled at how beautiful she looked even in the simplest of attires. She asked if he would like to freshen up. Jack made a joke of her suggestion saying, *'Why do I stink or something?'*. She smiled at him. Jack agreed that possibly it would be a good idea.

Jack was quick in the shower. Although the fresh smell around him from Helen's previous shower was aromatically soothing, he felt stifled by the relentless spray of water to his face. Steam billowed up around him. He felt enclosed and caged. Alone, his mind had chance to wander off track. He had to remain focused. His body felt as though it was being cleansed of his choleric deliberations. Water, indeed, had many therapeutic qualities but at this stage Jack didn't need to be relaxed, calmed, or cleared in mind. It was too late and too dangerous to back out now. He stepped out of the shower and picked up the towel hanging over the side rail. It was still damp and had the fragrance from Helen's body. Jack held the towel to his face, inhaling those sweet smells. It smelled of home. Not a home he had witnessed before but a home where he longed to settle down. It was where his heart was.

He rubbed the steam and condensation from the wall mirror and stared long and hard at himself. Was he witnessing the stare of a killer? Jack didn't think so. He questioned that when it came down to it, would he be able to follow it through, and take a man's life in front of his own eyes. Would he be able to return here and live a normal life with Helen when it was all over? Would she want him? The shower had succeeded in placing the questionable doubt in his mind. Jack wrapped the towel around his midriff and sat down on the toilet. He placed his hands over his face. He closed his eyes and began to rock.

Help me Patricia....What do I do?.....What do I do?....Tell me?..

Jack looked upwards into the air. His eyes burned with tears again. This was the ultimate of nightmares. Confusion cascaded over him. He didn't have the answer.

He knew that fate would decide at that crucial moment. He dressed and left the bathroom in an uncomfortable state of indecision. It was painted across his features.

Helen was in the sitting room kneeling over the table. She poured brown tea into two mugs from the freshly made pot. She looked up and smiled as Jack stood in the doorway. Jack sat on the sofa. Helen placed a mug of tea in front of him and joined him on the sofa.

'Do you know what you are going to do?', she asked.

Jack looked at her and smiled.

He huffed,

'You know...sometimes I think this is all someone's childish game...and we are just the pawns in it....Is it really happening?', Jack laughed.

Helen laughed.

'The same thing has been on my mind!....', she replied.

Jack reached forward and picked up his mug.

He sipped at the hot liquid.

'I keep thinking that one morning I'm going to wake up and find that its all been a dream ...none of it ever existed and everyone has gone away...and I'm left alone living a normal life...working normal hours...in a normal job..', he paused.

'I'll get out of bed and make coffee and laugh aloud in my kitchen....saying to myself .'wow..what an incredible nightmare!'... and realise that it was all a macabre invention of my over-zealous imagination.', Jack smiled.

Helen looked down.

'Would you be happy then?', Helen asked.

Jack thought for a second then nodded.

'For most of it ..yes...', he paused and looked at her,

'But then..I wouldn't have met you would I...'.

Helen laughed.

'But Jack if you had the chance of a fresh start....a chance where you didn't have to suffer all the torturous emotions and situations you have been subjected to..as you say, 'live a normal life'...you'd take it wouldn't you?', she laughed.

Jack smiled and thought about her question.

'In all honesty... I don't think I would...', Jack paused.

'If someone would have asked me the same question maybe last month then I'd have probably bit the offer out of their hand but not now..', Jack sipped his tea.

Helen looked shocked and slightly unsure.

'Are you saying it's because of me that you would continue with all this pain and anguish?', she felt embarrassed at having to ask the question.

Jack looked at her and slowly nodded.

She stared deep into his eyes. Pools of emotion placed her into a hypnotic trance.

Jack grasped her hand. He slowly stroked and caressed it. She felt the warmth flowing into her. All the nerve endings throughout her entire body sat up begging to be touched and caressed in the same way.

'Nobody is worth that sacrifice Jack!....You really think that much of me?', she asked feeling the blood rushing to her cheeks.

Jack smiled.

'Much more than that!', he squeezed her hand tighter.

She couldn't stop herself flinging her arms around him. They embraced. A magnetic embrace.

'Will you stay with me tonight?', she asked quietly.

Jack smiled.

'I don't intend letting anyone harm you..', Jack could feel her shaking under him.

She stood up and walked to the door. Jack positioned the cushions on the sofa and prepared to make a comfy bed for himself.

She turned.

'Jack..Would you mind sharing my bed with me?', the difficulty of the statement was obvious in her tone.

Jack stood up and followed her into her bedroom.

She turned off all the lights. After his eyes had adjusted to the darkness he could just make out her silhouette slowly lifting her top. He saw the outline of her pointed breasts protruding out into the dark night. She bent and slipped off her bottoms before diving under the quilt. Jack felt her eyes watch him as he slipped out of his clothes.

The bed felt cool. He didn't know quite what to do. He lay on his back staring up at the ceiling. His head sank into the pillow.

He felt her arm at first reach over him. Then he felt the softness of her breast against him and the warmth of her stomach and thigh pressing against his side. Jack turned onto his side and faced her. He ran his fingers through her still damp hair. He slowly moved his hand down over her neck and arm. He leant forward in the blanket of darkness and found her lips. Soft, moist, warm.

Jack felt her smile with his fingers. His hand moved down over her hip and the thin fabric of her panties to her thigh. So soft and warm. She turned her back towards him and pushed herself back into his arms. They lay entwined. Jack felt her bottom press against his groin. She shook a stifled laugh in recognition of his arousal. She wiggled on him for a second and let out a contented moan. She grabbed his arms and pulled them tighter around her. Jack felt her shudder. This wasn't about sex. It was more than that. The thought hadn't even entered either of their minds. They just lay gently rocking each other. They slept huddled tightly together as though starting hibernation. The warm grip of love embraced them and if nothing else this moment would remain untarnished and precious for eternity.

The phone rang at around 5 a.m. Jack stirred first. He nudged Helen gently from her sleep. She awoke suddenly and jumped out of bed and raced out into the hall. She was oblivious to her nakedness. Jack watched smiling.

'Hello?', she said on answering the call.

She paused frowning.

'Yes..he is..', she pointed the phone towards Jack, quickly realising her naked breast and wrapping her free arm across them.

'It's Briggsy..', she said surprised.

Jack's smile disappeared. He too dived out of bed.

Jack stopped midway towards her and realised he was completely naked. She looked him up and down and smiled.

Jack felt himself blush. For a second they both stared at each other's bodies, now visible in the early morning light. Jack brushed passed her and took the phone. They both laughed nervously and excitedly.

Jack watched Helen dive back into bed. He covered himself as best he could with his free hand. She laughed aloud.

'Yes...Briggsy..How did you know I was...', Jack stopped mid-sentence and listened. The smile dropped from his face.

'What?'

'NO BRIGGSY...WAIT FOR ME...', Jack shouted.

'NO...NO..BRIGGSY WAIT FOR ME IT'S TOO DANGEROUS...'.

'I know ...I know..but wait for me...Briggsy?', Jack removed his hand and placed both on the receiver.

'Briggsy?...BRIGGSY?', Jack slammed down the receiver.

'Shit!', he raced back to the bed.

Helen looked concerned.

'What is it?', she said.

Jack threw on his clothes as quick as he could.

'It's Briggsy...he's been working all night and he says he's found out something about Marco...', Jack buttoned up his shirt.

'What?', Helen sat up.

'He wouldn't say..he said he's going to go round to his house and confront him with it..', Jack looked worried.

'He said he's sorry for not believing my instincts and that he was wrong about him...He's very angry..'.

'Be careful Jack...I want you back in one piece...', Helen almost sobbed.

'I know...', he kissed her.

'Briggsy has NO IDEA WHAT HE'S getting himself into here...', Jack screamed.

He slipped his shoes on and grabbed his jacket. He checked his pocket for the pistol. Helen noticed the bulge.

'Can I borrow your car?', Jack asked.

'It's quicker...', he smiled nervously.

'The keys are hanging up on the side by the door...', she said.

Jack leant over the bed and kissed her again.

'See you later...Lock the door after I'm gone ..OK', he stated.

He was just about to open the door when Helen shouted after him. 'Jack!...'.

He poked his head round the door and stared at her.

'I love you....', she said almost in tears.

Jack smiled.

'I love you too....the next time I see you this will all be over!'.

Jack reached Marco's drive in record time. The traffic proved little resistance at this early hour. He swung the car to the gates. They were open. Invitingly open. Jack reached into his pocket and cocked the pistol. He screeched the car along the drive. The house looked deserted. He leapt from the car and banged loudly on the door. He stepped back and tried to peer through the windows. The house was in darkness. He banged again, so hard his fist ached. A light came on upstairs. Jack waited. He grasped the pistol in his pocket but didn't yet want to produce it in view. The door slowly opened. It was Cath. She wore a long pink night robe and looked still dazed from sleep.

'Where's Marco?', Jack insisted.

Upon receiving a blank expression, Jack barged passed her into the hallway.

'HE'S NOT HERE!,' she shouted.

'Who the fuck are you?'.

'DI MITCHELL', Jack answered.

Cath gave a knowing nod.

'Well, he's out on business...what's the problem?', she anxiously asked.

Jack stared at her.

'OUT ON BUSINESS...WHERE?', Jack shouted.

Cath's ears banged under the increasing yells.

'I don't know...he left at 5...a business meeting at the usual place he said...wherever the usual place is..', she stated.

'WAS ANYONE WITH HIM WHEN HE LEFT?', Jack grabbed her shoulders.

She forcefully struggled from Jack's grasp.

'I don't know...I was asleep in case you couldn't tell....', she replied.

'What's he done...He is OK isn't he?', she insisted.

Jack thought to himself.

Usual place?..Usual place?

'Shit!', Jack leaped the steps back to the car.

'IS HE ALRIGHT?', Cath screamed after him.

She watched the VW scream along her drive and out through the gates.

She returned inside now fully awake and grabbed by fear.

Jack was breathless. He drove at an increasing speed out towards Filton. Thoughts racing through his head.

It must be the hangar...he knew I was coming...the usual place....the bastard...

he knew I was coming....Briggsy!...you stupid little...

Jack swung the car out of the city centre.

shit!.....you'd better not hurt him...your history...you're gone...dead...

Jack reached the T-junction and turned left. He rounded the bend and stared at the hangar in the distance.

Be there!...please...

Jack knew they would.

He swerved the car inside the fence and along the drive to the hangar. Jack noticed the light from inside. His heart raced. He slowed the car. A cold sweat ensued. Was he too late?

He slowed the car up yards from the entrance. He stepped out onto the track. He finally revealed the pistol. He flicked off the safety catch and slowly walked towards the side doors. He raised the gun in front of him and slowly stepped into the throw of light.

He saw Briggsy. He was sat on a chair in the centre of the hangar. His face was bloodied. His right eye closed under the swelling. Dark red blood seeped from his nose. Marco was stood behind him. He held a pistol to Briggsy's head.

'Hi Jack...Nice of you to join us...', he said smugly.

'You bastard!', Jack replied pointing the pistol straight at Marco. He stepped closer.

'Still as articulate as ever I see!', the priggish tone wound up Jack's insides.

'I TOLD YOU TO FUCKING WAIT BRIGGSY!', Jack shouted at the bloodied mess sat still on the chair. Briggsy sobbed.

Jack scanned around the rest of the hangar. He expected to be flanked by Neilsen at any moment.

Marco sensed Jack's concern.

'No, It's OK Jack...It's just us for the moment...I'm expecting some more guests any minute!', Marco smiled.

'What?...What do you mean?', Jack replied anxiously.

Jack could hear the screech of another car scrambling along the track outside.

'Oh, perfect timing!..', Marco laughed.

The BMW swung in at the far end. Its lights momentarily dazzling Jack. Jack saw Neilsen appear from the car. He dragged another body out beside him.

Jack's heart sank when he recognised it was Helen. She was dressed in the navy jogging suit from the evening before. A thin trace of blood slowly wound its way from her soft lips.

Jack exploded.

'YOU BASTARD...'.

Tears impaired his vision. He shook uncontrollably.

'JACK!..JACK!', Helen shouted in terror.

'Jack ...Jack..', Neilsen mocked placing the blade tight to her throat to silence her. The silencing effect was almost instantaneous. Helen whimpered into a quiet sob.

Jack pointed the pistol at Neilsen.

His heart was broken at the sight of the sheer horror plastered over Helen's delicate features.

'Now the party is complete!..', Marco moved away from Briggsy. Jack followed him with the barrel of the pistol.

'Please Jack...Do you have to point that thing at me...You're not going to use it...', Marco walked towards Helen.

'If you did of course, your precious Helen would lose the ability to speak and in fact live...', he laughed.

He walked up to Helen. Marco stared deep into her swollen blue eyes.

'MMM..have to admire your taste Jack', Marco raised his hand and firmly squeezed Helen's right breast. She flinched at his touch. She felt sickened and shut her eyes.

'Very nice..so firm and supple..and so big...I do like big tits!.', he smiled.

'You're gonna die...you're gonna fucking die!', Jack spat.

Marco turned and walked back to Briggsy.

'Have you figured it all out yet Jack?'.

Jack nodded.

'I figured you out years ago...', Jack spoke bitterly.

Marco laughed aloud. The laugh echoed around the hangar eerily. His confidence boiled over.

He continued to laugh.

'You know I really don't think you have!', he insisted.

Briggsy spat the blood from his mouth. Marco stared at him.

'You're not as clever as you think!', Jack tried to insult him.

Marco laughed aloud again.

'That's the most incredible statement yet..from the dumbest man I know...'.

Jack blinked the tears and sweat away from his eyes and continued to focus the gun on Marco. His hand shook uncontrollably. Neilsen laughed aloud along with Marco.

'For years Jack we have laid the path of clues for you to find....I heard so much about you...but I honestly can say that I am disappointed...very disappointed..', Marco continued.

His pistol waved around in the air like a baton conducting an orchestra. Jack felt his finger shaking on the trigger.

He was getting confused by Marco's talk. He looked at Helen. She was white as a sheet and looked close to passing out.

'All along Jack it was staring you in the face....right alongside you...', he laughed.

'How do you think I knew exactly where you were and exactly what your intentions were going to be?', he said.

'How do you think I knew Den was your snout?...', he paused.

Jack felt a bead of sweat tickling a path over his left eyebrow. His eyes ached but he dare not blink.

'He heard my name mentioned in conversation and like an amateur sleuth continued to press for answers...How much did you pay him Jack...10...20 pounds..', Marco smiled.

Jack bit his lip.

'I had to have Neilsen here take him out...', he pointed at the smiling and proud face of his henchman.

'Of course, it wasn't my idea to slice him up in that way...that was done for your benefit...', Marco smiled.

'Any ideas Jack?', he posed the question.

Jack remained silent.

Confused.

'OK then...How do you think I knew you had a tape of Standt killing Tommy....and that you were close to finding him?.... Coincidence?...Come on Jack!', he urged.

'Work it out!'.

Marco sighed.

'You nearly caught us out when you planned to visit Erik..but Neilsen just beat you to him and managed to persuade him to remain silent...He's good at that you know...', he laughed aloud again.

Jack grew more annoyed.

'Look..I know what happened...I killed you once Berthold..and I will kill you again..this time you'll never come back...', Jack spat out his words with venom.

'There you go again...', he laughed.

Jack saw Briggsy slowly lift himself from his chair. Jack begged with his eyes for Briggsy to sit back down. Briggsy crouched, slowly moving forward from the chair.

'You keep calling me Berthold...you still haven't worked it out...', he laughed, the pistol hung loosely at his side.

Jack frowned. His arms ached with the weight of the pistol stretched out in front of him. He watched from the corner of his eye. Briggsy was almost behind Marco.

Jack stared at Neilsen. Neilsen watched Briggsy's moves with curiosity. Jack frowned at how he didn't warn Marco or at least do something.

Jack lowered his pistol to the great relief of his arms.

It seemed everyone else in the hangar watched Briggsy whilst Marco was so engrossed in his discussion he was completely unaware of him.

'I'm not Klaus Berthold Jack...', Marco stretched out his arms.

'But...'.

Briggsy lunged out his hand swiftly and grasped the pistol. He twisted Marco's hand around and aimed the barrel at his chest. Alarm consumed Marco's wide eyes.

He stared at the barrel. He felt Briggsy's fingers squeeze his on the trigger. He closed his eyes as the pistol recoiled. The pistol dropped to the floor. Briggsy stumbled back from Marco. Marco clung at his chest. His hands already soaked in bright red blood. Jack raised his pistol again. He focused on a shocked and stunned Neilsen. He had released his grip slightly on Helen. He watched as Marco staggered around the hangar. He watched as he sank to his knees and outstretched a red hand towards Briggsy. His eyes asked many questions, but his tongue was pressed to the roof of his mouth. Glued in sheer agony. He fell onto his front and coiled up like a snake.

Jack stared at Helen then Neilsen. Helen turned away from the gruesome scene and caught Jack's eye. Jack flinched his head to the side. Helen understood. Jack aimed the pistol at Neilsen's head. Helen jerked her body to the left and just managed to slip the weakened grasp of Neilsen. He lunged after her, but it was too late. The moment she had moved a 9mm round had struck him above his right eyebrow. The lunge turned into a backwards fall. He slumped against the BMW. Blood pumped from the entry hole. Jack stared down the barrel of his pistol. His hand could now shake again. Smoke curled out from the discharge.

Jack ran over to Helen and hugged her tightly. She sobbed on him.

Jack slowly and quietly removed the magazine from his pistol and reached into his jacket pocket. His hands shook as he struggled to find the loose, doctored rounds. He found them and slipped them into the top of his magazine.

He whispered in her ear.

'Get in the car ..start the engine..keep your head down...if this doesn't work out ..drive out of here...drive fast and don't look back....', he said quietly and shakily.

She didn't want to release from his hold. Jack had to forcefully push her into the car. As she fell inside she did as she was told. She shut the door and started the engine. Jack re-cocked his pistol and turned towards Briggsy.

Briggsy stood over Marco's lifeless body. He had retrieved the pistol from the floor.

He looked up and stared at Jack as he moved towards him.

'Sorry it had to work out like this Jack!', Briggsy smiled.

Jack noticed the difference in Briggsy's eyes.

'I wanted to tell you myself...I wanted to see the look in your eyes...watch the shock and horror illuminate you...as you witnessed the final confession....', Briggsy turned towards Marco again.

'This piece of shit spoiled it all!', Briggsy kicked Marco's dormant body.

'Why?.....', Jack stammered.

'WHY!..', Briggsy shouted in disgust.

'You know exactly why Jack...don't play the naive now...that was my role in all of this...', Briggsy smiled.

'You played a very convincing part!', Jack replied.

'Yes..I did didn't I...it wasn't easy...', Briggsy paused.

Jack laughed.

'You fooled me...I really trusted you..'.

Briggsy laughed and spat,

'I didn't mean fooling you or getting you to trust me...that was easy...', he smiled.

Briggsy walked over to the chair and nonchalantly sat himself down.

'The hard part was finding you...tracking you down...', he sighed.

'Then all those boring fucking lectures at college...Law and order ..what a fucking joke!', he laughed.

'All the boring pounding of the beat...living on the other side of the law...that was difficult...having to make the pointless arrests...my own kind...that cut me and made me hate you even more...', he spoke with a bad taste in his mouth.

'I watched you develop your career...I begged for a place in CID...in your department... all the additional boring courses and seminars...', he sighed.

'Then finally meeting you and resisting from slitting YOUR fucking throat...', he raised his voice an octave.

Jack swallowed.

'I had to beg that prick Craven to be allowed onto a case with you....he kept on telling me that you were one of the best detectives he'd ever worked with... that he wasn't sure if I was worthy of working with such a great detective in such a short time in the department...I had to control myself from bursting into fits of laughter!', Briggsy choked.

'Great detective?...I could see you were good...but certainly not great...you'd agree with that now wouldn't you Jack?', he smiled.

'All that was the hard part...deceiving you was surprisingly easy...', he laughed.

Briggsy swivelled the pistol around his fingers.

There was an uneasy silence.

'You don't know how long I've waited for this moment Jack!', he revelled.

'I'm glad I followed my instincts before I got on that train....', he smiled.

'You do remember the train now don't you Jack!'.

Jack nodded. He had figured it all out.

'You took Patricia then?', Jack asked stepping a couple of steps closer.

Briggsy nodded.

'Well not me personally ...but I ordered it yes...', Briggsy confirmed.

'After you had so rudely cut me off in my prime on the train that night...I came back as Dieter Weiss...I organised a small syndicate of young men...we specialised mainly in protection ..but with a little drugs and robbery thrown in on the side...It was then that Standt asked to join the gang....we accepted him and he was an extremely good soldier...he became my lieutenant if you like...I was 17 and he was just a boy of 16 ...but even so he remained extremely loyal and showed a unique trust of my judgement......', Briggsy revealed the story.

Jack listened.

'He took Patricia...I had taken many trips over to England...I'd watched you...with her...I could see you were incredibly fond of her...', he laughed.

'I got him to snatch her and bring her back to Holland to me...'.

Jack felt the pain soar through him like a cold blade.

'I thought you would come after her...but then Billy was weak willed and pathetic wasn't he...', he laughed.

'She put up a hell of a fight...Standt was covered in bite marks....
then I heard you had passed away...pathetic Jack...why couldn't you
have faced up to it like a man...', Briggsy continued.

'So, you took her just to provoke a reaction from me?', Jack sniffed.
Briggsy nodded.

'Yep..basically...'.

'You see unlike you it didn't take me long to discover the side
effects of the drug ...it was manufactured for strength restoration
and energy rebuilding....they got that wrong.....I knew what was
happening...whereas I could tell by the pain and fear in your eyes that
you didn't have a clue...', he laughed.

'You see there were two tubes of the liquid drug back then...',
Briggsy smirked.

'I'm just so glad I devoured the first all to myself instead of
sharing it out amongst the troops as ordered...', he laughed.

'I could sense you had done the same with the other tube....I
subconsciously knew I was not alone on this time plane...and low
and behold I found you...none the wiser...', Briggsy's laugh echoed
around the hangar.

Jack shook his head.

'Well, I know now!'.

Briggsy smiled.

'Bit too late though isn't it...'.

'For all my early childhood, I read up on chemistry and biology
and the time came when I was adequately prepared to try and copy
the drug...I monitored levels of unusually high toxins in my body
and mixed them together... I tested the compound on Patricia. After
all I had no other use for her. ..and you know what happened Jack?',
Briggsy paused and laughed.

Jack struggled for breath.

'To my great and welcomed surprise...all she wanted to do was
fuck me!', he laughed.

'She was good Jack..really good...tight and untouched...', Briggsy
smiled as he remembered her eagerness.

Jack swallowed hard.

'After a while I got bored of her and passed her over for Standt's disposal...he loved virgins and young girls...he was in his element... three or four times a day...until she got so loose he lost interest in her...', Briggsy laughed.

'But at this stage I realised I had developed a stronger more marketable drug to make my fortune...what a discovery...', he laughed.

Jack raised the pistol through watered eyes.

'You bastard!'.

'Oh Jack...yes you can kill me now...but you know I'll find you again...and next time I'll play the game harder....and each and every time it will be more and more fun for me...', he smiled outstretching his arms in anticipation of a bullet to the chest.

'What happened to her?', Jack stuttered.

'Well, we'd finished with her...we passed her on to a local pimp in Amsterdam...she was not the Patricia you'd remember Jack..she was warped through all the tests...a junkie...she'd long forgotten you when we let her go...she just waited for another fix...', Briggsy continued to smile proudly.

Jack edged closer to Briggsy. His pistol still pointed at him.

'Fortunately for me..the second time I came back I returned to an English-speaking family...probably because I threw myself off a bridge in the Thames...about 7 years after Billy's death', he laughed.

'I had to keep within a reasonable age gap you see...I soon found Standt again..that wasn't difficult... I put the word around the underground...and found him within a couple of months....but he was working for Marco by then..... I scared the shit out of him when I revealed gang secrets from almost 20 years ago that he knew only Dieter Weiss would know about...It took some persuading, but he finally was partially convinced and equally disturbed...', Briggsy laughed.

'Persuading Marco was more difficult...he thought I was a fruitcake ...but he was interested in the drug I had developed....I had to bribe him with it...Once he had seen it working, he had to go along with what I said. It made him millions...', Briggsy smiled.

'He was so greedy!...It wasn't the money that interested me Jack it was the power...and of course the revenge...', Briggsy raised his pistol parallel to his body. Jack figured it pointed at his chest. Jack flinched. He didn't quite know what to do. He had to get closer to Briggsy. To do that he had to keep him talking, he realised that Briggsy was only too pleased to reveal his successful part in all of this.

'So that's why Marco was always one step ahead of me...because you were the mole...', Jack said.

Briggsy choked.

'Marco wasn't one step ahead of you!...I fucking was....I organised the whole lot...', Briggsy shouted insulted by Jack's statement.

'I especially enjoyed the reactions on your face when you saw the silver case and the locket again...It was so difficult not to laugh you know...', he laughed.

Jack felt sick and faint. He found himself swaying. He stepped forward a couple more paces to pump the blood around his legs again.

'I bought an identical silver case in an old junk shop...by chance really and stashed it away along with the locket...I knew it would stir up favourable memories in you...', he pierced Jack with his stare.

'I went back to the old bank years later with forged ID and signed out the contents ...and voila..I had my torture tools...', he laughed.

He stood up slowly from the chair now with a concerned look on his face.

Briggsy stared over Jack's shoulder at the car.

'What do we do now Jack?...just walk away?..or do we have a shoot out...?..', Briggsy kept peering at the car.

He stepped sideward to get a clearer view. Helen was still ducked down. She could hear the muffled voices under the throb of the engine.

Jack stepped across to place himself between Briggsy and the car.

'Leave her out of this Briggsy!', Jack warned.

'Love to Jack..but you know that just can't happen...', Briggsy continued to slant his walk around. He got closer.

'You either take me out or I have to take both of you out...', Briggsy smiled.

'Then I'd better blow you away!', Jack remarked.

Briggsy shrugged.

'Matters not to me Jack...I'll be back to visit you in around 16 or 17 years time...', he laughed.

'You know that!'.

'What's it like to be haunted Jack?', Briggsy's voice echoed inside Jack's head.

'You never know Jack you may even get to enjoy it!', Jack had never witnessed Briggsy's sick sense of humour before. But this wasn't the Briggsy that he had grown attached to over the past few weeks. That Briggsy had been a role in a macabre play, a character...a portrayal by an actor.

Briggsy waved his pistol in the air.

'Hell, I even put on extra pounds and made myself look unfit and geekish...all for you Jack!', Briggsy chuckled.

'Why did Marco beat you up?', Jack pondered staring at Briggsy's swollen face.

Briggsy laughed.

'That old fuck...beat me up?...I did this myself against the wall over there...I actually enjoyed it....It was for effect...I should have been in theatre!...the look on your face...it was certainly convincing... Marco always had a big mouth though and the effect in truth was wasted..but nevermind...it's over now...', he smiled.

'Anything else you'd like to know before we start?'.

Jack felt his grip tighten on the pistol.

'No...', Briggsy stared at Jack.

'OK..then...'.

Briggsy dived and leapt down onto the floor and released two shots in quick succession.

Jack thought he had been hit but in fact both bullets had missed him intentionally and Jack heard the distinct sound of piercing metal and glass. Briggsy had dived to get a clear view of the car. He shot one bullet through the windscreen smashing broken glass over Helen in the front. The second hit above the mudguard and buried itself in the centre console beside her head. She screamed aloud. Briggsy watched for her to show herself before releasing the third shot.

Jack reacted quickly. He let off a shot. His weakened arms couldn't control the recoil and threw him partially off balance. His head raced.

He heard Briggsy scream.

Jack cleared his eyes and saw Briggsy clutching his left leg. Jack had hit him just above the ankle. His foot hung on to the remainder of his leg by its tendons. Briggsy stared at Jack open mouthed. His pistol had slipped from his grasp under the pain he had been subjected to by the dum-dum.

He turned and slowly began to crawl towards his pistol. His left leg dragged limply behind him. His foot twisted at an obscene angle. Briggsy screamed with every slight movement. His face was pale. White, ashen.

Jack slowly walked over to him.

Briggsy stretched out his hand and felt the cold steel of the pistol on his fingertips. He tried desperately to haul the weapon towards him. The pistol reached his palm before Jack stamped his foot down hard on Briggsy's fingers. Briggsy hardly felt the pain. It was nothing compared to the pain that soared along his leg although it was numbing slightly.

Jack slid the pistol further away with his foot.

'Helen?...', Jack shouted staring back at the car.

'You OK?', he asked.

There was a pause before a quiet reply came back.

'Yes.....'.

Jack smiled.

'And you said Marco was the greedy one!...you had your chance to shoot me but all you were interested in was taking away another person special to me.....', Jack spat.

Briggsy laughed through the agonising spasms.

'Yes...I'm going to do it every time...take them away from you and make you remember and suffer!'.

'Well, you didn't succeed did you...', Jack smiled.

'Not this time...but there will be others Jack!', Briggsy smiled a grim smile.

Jack laughed.

'I don't think so!'.

'It's all over now...this is the end...the final chapter in your age long play..', Jack grabbed Briggsy by the shoulder and threw him over onto his stomach.

'The end...No Jack it's just the beginning...!', Briggsy choked.

'Now who is the stupid one Briggsy!...Didn't you for one minute consult with anyone as to exactly how the drug worked?', Jack asked.

Briggsy wrestled under Jack's pressure on his back.

'What do you mean?', he panicked.

Jack leant forward and tapped Briggsy on the back of the head.

'It's all done up here...'.

Briggsy shouted.

'YOU HAVE NO IDEA!!....'.

Jack grasped Briggsy around the neck and lifted him.

He placed the barrel of the pistol firmly into the lower back of his head.

He tilted the pistol slightly and pictured the angle of entry.

Jack gritted his teeth.

'Oh, I know exactly!!', he spat.

Jack slowly felt the pressure on his trigger finger.

The shot was muffled by the sound of tearing flesh and cracking skull. The instant Jack depressed the trigger he saw Briggsy's skull rip open. He felt the warm sticky matter splatter over his hands, neck, and face.

The smell was sickly sweet.

He felt the warmth of the matter soak gently into his skin. He stared down at the remains of Briggsy's head.

The hole was immense.

Jack was sure he had ended it.

He brushed the remnants of brain from his face. They left a thin sludge over his cheeks and lips. He tasted it in his mouth and quickly turned and vomited beside the body.

He removed his jacket and used it as a towel, wiping every scrap of the offending substance from him. He discarded the soiled jacket over the remains of Briggsy's head. He covered the eyes, which bulged unnaturally from the sockets. Those piercing and evil eyes.

He walked over to the car and opened the door.

Helen cowered curled in a ball beneath the steering wheel. She peered at Jack. He smiled at her.

'It's over!', he stated. He lost his legs and sank to his knees. Jack found himself sobbing uncontrollably.

Helen raised herself to the seat and peered through the open windshield.

She saw the remains of Briggsy lying prostrate on the ground. The jacket spread covering the fatal damage.

'Briggsy?', she asked breathlessly.

Jack nodded.

She climbed out of the car and embraced Jack in a tight hug.

Both sobbed uncontrollably.

The nightmare was over.

Or at least they both longed and hoped it was over.

The memories and the distinct smell of the final death, the calm quiet of the still morning, the cordite hanging densely in the air.... these features would stay with them forever.

But together they knew that they would cope.

Where there is love there is life......

Mahatma Gandhi:

I have spread my dreams under your feet. Tread softly because you tread on my dreams.......

William Butler Yeats:

CHAPTER 19

<u>Paris, France, Two months later</u>

The aftermath of the investigation had been tiresome and difficult for all concerned. Craven and especially the Chief Super had wanted answers. Jack was placed under immediate suspicion of murder. Fortunately for him he knew he had the support of Helen and surprisingly Cath, Marco's partner, came forward and confirmed that Marco had dealings with Standt and Neilsen. Most of the dealings, too, being illegal. Investigations into Marco's accounts found huge discrepancies with monies deposited into his many bank accounts. His house was searched thoroughly and inside his safe, a large bag of class A drugs was found along with a considerable amount of unbanked money. The drug was 'Heaven'. In lieu of Helen's excellent work, a now registered narcotic, albeit a secret one.

Jack had put Marco's prints on his Browning and lied to Craven that it was he who blew out Briggsy's brains. Jack concocted a tangible storyline and Helen had backed him up. Her support swung it for Jack. Jack and Helen both had to attend the funeral and convincingly mourn Briggsy's passing. Marco and Neilsen were posthumously charged with the deaths of Frank Christie, the American women, Den, Tommy, Standt and Briggsy. Erik read the news in Oslo and reappeared in the city to make a further statement. This further report proved Jack's statement and repelled any ambiguities in the case, or the police work sustained by Jack.

Erik refrained from mentioning their visit with the courier. He was indeed more intelligent than Jack had first thought. Jack received a sincere verbal apology from Craven and complete silence from the Chief Super, which was probably a compliment in itself.

Jack was commended with a medal of bravery from the Commissioner, as too was Briggsy albeit posthumously.

The case was closed.

Cath was cleared of any involvement in Marco's illegalities. She has now taken full charge of his legal security business. Sam still works as her trusted PA. The company lost a lot of its regular customers but still manages to keep its head above water.

Erik took over management of the Pravada...now re-named Tommy's Bar...business is thriving. Jack and Helen were invited to the opening night.

Mr and Mrs Stevens still waited for the return of their precious daughter. Neither Jack nor Helen had the heart to tell them of her fate. They decided to keep their memories intact for the short time they had left together.

Craven was still as confusing as ever and an empty chair sat hauntingly alone at the desk of DS Briggs. Jack had still felt his presence around the office.

Jack stared at the Eiffel tower. It was the first time he had seen it this time around, but he recognised it from his Army days.

He held Helen's hand.

She turned and issued that heart-breaking smile towards him. Jack leaned over and kissed her. He felt the sharp edges of the diamond ring on her finger. He lifted her hand and stared at the gem. He kissed it and smiled at her. This was their official engagement weekend. He had bought the ring, unbeknown to Helen, shortly after the inquests and procedural red tape was concluded. He presented the ring on their first night in Paris. Jack booked the Marriott for the special event. He produced the ring on one knee in front of a massed restaurant. Surprisingly, Helen wasn't embarrassed or disappointed in his old-fashioned method but instead, her face beamed. The smile could have lit up the darkest night. It would have warmed the bleakest Siberian winter. It vibrated around the restaurant turning everyone's head to her beauty. When she answered 'yes' to his proposal, the restaurant erupted in raucous applause. They didn't even finish their meals. They were no longer hungry. They weren't hungry, to be honest, to begin with. Jack guided Helen by the hand to the hotel room he had booked. He lowered her onto the king-size bed and they slowly and very deliberately made love all night. In fact, they made love all morning, all afternoon, and the following evening. It was only on this day that they decided to, at the very least, take in some of Paris' tourists' attractions. They planned to visit the Louvre, walk the Champs D'Ellyses and climb the Eiffel Tower. They both doubted they would manage all the sights; it was so difficult keeping their hands off each other. Even as they walked down the road they groped and squeezed each other's bodies and kept stopping to kiss each other in public view. They didn't care. She would make him so happy for the rest of this life. They agreed not to discuss the past but only the future.

Jack didn't want to return again. He hoped maybe in time that he wouldn't be able to regress.

Maybe this was his last time too. He wanted it to be. Desperately.

He pondered the thought of if he did return... would he be able to pull the trigger on himself? Would he have the bottle or nerve? He didn't think he could cope with going through the re-living of all his past lives and memories. One thing he did know is that he didn't want to love anyone else the way he loved Helen. This was special. His emotions had been stretched to the limit. There was no room for anyone else. She consumed every inch of him. He felt warm and secure.

He wanted these feelings to last for ever. Although, deep inside he knew that they just might.

Printed in Great Britain
by Amazon

26099655R00169